'Brilliantly well told and tremendously exciting'
Spectator

Reluctant Odyssey is the second in a trilogy of novels
about World War II, originally published in 1946 to
remarkable critical acclaim.

Each title carries the distinction – rare in any novels
of World War II or any other war – of being written
almost contemporaneously with the action. All
convey the immediacy of journalism as well as the
more profound qualities the reviews proclaim.

'The battle scenes are terrific . . . Miss Pargeter gets
fiercer and more intense with every book.'
Monica Dickens

Also by Edith Pargeter

The Eighth Champion of Christendom
She Goes to War
The Brothers of Gwynedd Quartet

And writing as Ellis Peters

The Chronicles of Brother Cadfael
Mourning Raga
Death to the Landlords
Piper on the Mountain
City of Gold and Shadows
Funeral for Figaro
Death Mask

Reluctant Odyssey

Edith Pargeter

HEADLINE

ISBN 0 7472 3336 5

Printed and bound in Great Britain by
Collins, Glasgow

HEADLINE BOOK PUBLISHING PLC
Headline House
79 Great Titchfield Street
London W1P 7FN

CONTENTS

PART ONE

LIBYA

"And the spear was a desert physician, who cured not a few of
ambition, and drave not a few to perdition."
FLECKER: *Saracen War Song.*

I

SEEN from the north-east, along the hard sand trail from the
coast road, Petrol Parva looked like nothing but another
irregular, shallow escarpment among the thousand or so
stretching out of sight on either hand, another sharp shadow
in the grey dappled waste of limestone; but seen at close
quarters it assumed a character of its own, and became, perhaps
an insignificant but certainly a purposeful, living organism. The
hard black shadow of the scarp was quite unlike the other black
shadows along the barren plateau, for in it refuged a decorous
row of light armoured cars and lorries, instead of pathetic little
migrant birds and an occasional unexpected man. The stretch
of hard sand beyond, whitish gold in the sun, was unique in
that it covered the second largest fuel-dump in all that stretch
of country. Petrol Magna, which fed it, was many miles away,
inland of rail-head at Matruh. There were a great many men
in and around Petrol Parva, but by day or night most of them
were invisible. There were plenty of shadows into which they
could disappear; and in every deposit of firm sand they had
made themselves dug-outs, cool in the heat of the day, warm
in the chill of the night. There was a buried storage-tank of
fresh water, periodically replenished by lorry from the coast;
and this was the most precious possession of this city of
troglodytes.

It was a queer world, this rough rolling waste of grey limestone, silent, vegetationless, sown with boulders, too far inland
for the traffic of the coast and the sight of the sea, too far north
for the expected monotony of sand or glamour of palms. When
first they had come there, early in November, fresh from the
shimmering blue of the Mediterranean and the white villas and
princely palms of the coast, it had seemed to Jim that they
were driving into the heart of a nightmare, a sterile world
bleached and turned to stone. He had seen trees which in all

I

seriousness had been turned to stone, petrified into a rock so hard that no knife could chip it, yet still retaining the veined markings of the living bark. He had seen mounds of hard-packed earth and sand held together by tamarisks, where even the life which sustained the hills in place itself seemed dead. He had seen a bowl of rock a hundred feet across, with a nipple in the centre, like pictures he had once been shown of the craters of the moon, and all the surface of it was cracked into lozenges and shrunken apart, leaving great fissures between. They told him, some who professed to know, that the basin was a volcanic product, and had once been as active as Vesuvius, but it looked to him as if it had been dead since the beginning of the world.

"What do they call this place?" he had asked, watching the sun dance madly on the broken hills to southward, in the noon hush of that first day.

"They don't call it anything," Charlie Smith had said. "Why should they? Nobody lives here. That's the beauty of this sort of country; you can call it whatever you like, it's got no name." And he had christened everything himself, from Petrol Magna and Petrol Parva to the highest rock south-eastward of their position, which he called Jebel Kebir, because it looked from one angle like a crouching lion. "But," said Charlie Smith, "if you mean your question in the larger sense, this is a little bit of the land of Egypt that nobody wants, and on the map it lies, though you won't find it, somewhere in the centre of the northern segment of the Libyan Desert—double-top, so to speak."

"Desert?" said Jim. "Who're you kidding? Deserts are all sand—miles and miles of it. I may not know much, but I've lived long enough to know that."

"Deserts," said Charlie Smith, his hollow eyes contemplating the shimmer of the skyline palsied with mirage, "are those stretches of the earth's surface rendered by chronic drought uninhabitable, for man or beast. They may be miles and miles of sand, or miles and miles of clay, or—as in the present case—simply miles and miles of sweet beggar-all. There's not much difference—they all reach much too far, and are all equally unpopular. But if it's sand you want, there's plenty of it over yonder." And he nodded towards the south-east.

Because he had never talked like this before, Jim knew that he was on familiar ground, perhaps with one eye upon his audience, but quite certainly with the other upon a distance in his memory. "Go on," he said, "tell us about it. What *is* over yonder?" But his indicating nod was careless, and turned the deep bright, contemplative eyes due west.

"Over there," said Charlie Smith deliberately, "is about thirty miles of this, littered with troops here and there—some barbed wire, a few guns, thousands of Italians, and the frontier. But where I pointed, due down that wadi, and off beyond those ridges, is the real thing. First you come to the top edge of this warped shelf we're sitting on—you can see it from here, that saw-tooth edge up there wobbling like the top of a jelly. From there there's a sheer drop of a thousand feet or so into a trough, and you can look down into the beginning of the sand you're so keen on. Miles and miles of it, right enough, all fawn-coloured and dun, with nothing to break the monotony, but maybe here and there a greyish-green patch of *terfa* scrub, or *heskanit,* not far from the cliffs, where there's a drop of moisture still left in the soil to feed it. But mostly even in the hollow there's no good water, it's all so dried up that the ground's caked with salt where it's been, and sparkles like mica. It's impressive, that bit, but it's fierce. Not my style. And after that—well, you can walk out into the biggest, deepest, goldest, God-awfullest stretch of sand you ever saw, with no sea to it, except that they call it the Great Sand Sea. They have dunes there as big as mountain ranges, long, straight, parallel dunes running the way of the wind. *Seif* dunes, they call 'em— that's the same as saying 'swords'. Round the edges of the Sand Sea you can see 'em lying tidily along with bare spaces of rock between 'em, their rims finished off with a nice ribbon edging, just as if somebody'd swept the stray grains up with a broom."

"Go on!" said Jim. "How could they possibly stay so neat as that? Why doesn't the first wind that comes up scatter the sand all about again, just anyhow?"

"Why does anything happen the way it does? Why do thousands of migrant birds travel south by the hard way across here, instead of down the Nile Valley? Why do the Italians want this pestilential country? Why do hundreds of antelope down there choose to live all their lives on poor grazing, with never a single drink of water to wash it down, instead of lighting out for a more Christian sort of country? I don't know that I'm afflicted with any urge to know why. I like to see how, that's all. I know you can live through the wildest sandstorms, and the first calm day you'll see the old *seif* dunes still lying

3

along north-west to south-east, the same as ever, all polished and burnished and swept up in between."

"Go on," said Jim, "tell us more."

And the mood had been on the silent man, and he had told them more; about the crescent dunes that march along in the south, beyond the Sudan border, march horns foremost downwind, over tracks and railways and rocks and villages, never advancing one symmetrical foot a yard before the other, and engendering, in their own infinitely patient time, baby *Barchans* the exact copies of themselves to march ahead on either flank; about the long gash under the cliffs south of the coastal plateau, where a hundred and fifty miles of glittering salt river lies petrified into crusted waves, with here and there little shrivelled pools of salty water, and starved patches of grass; about the distant paradisal aspect of any oasis from the edge of the cliffs, jewelled blue and rich dark green of water and date palms, limes and pomegranates, and emerald of fresh turf under the trees, and how this miniature heaven dwindled with a nearer view into a brief, grateful coolness and shade, everywhere gnawed and withered at the edges with the inescapable destroying salt of evaporation; about the Arba'in slave road out of the Sudan, sown with bleached bones of men and camels, where now no one goes but the enthusiast looking for fresh worlds to discover and unveil.

When he had talked himself out, and leaned back flat into the shadow of the escarpment, his audience of three had sat silently looking at each other, wondering how much to believe; for Charlie Smith was known to be a princely liar when he chose. And how had he, a mere English private soldier, if an unknown and incalculable one, seen and learned so much of the unmapped wastes of Libya? Few of his fellows had even heard of it until they landed at Alexandria. The whole voyage had been an adventuring into an unknown world. How, then, could this long, lean, sober-faced and vagrant-eyed philosopher from nowhere have discovered so much concerning the desert, even though his years were perhaps forty instead of the twenty-two which was the battalion's average age? No, he was just spinning the yarn, making it up as he went along, partly from things he'd read, and partly from his inexhaustible imagination. They decided to wait and see for themselves. The two youngsters, eighteen and twenty-one respectively, made no bones about calling him a liar on the spot. He took that placidly enough; he took anything from the kids, had done ever since

4

Jim had known him, rather after the manner of a benevolent
St. Bernard complacently enduring all kinds of indignities from
a litter of puppies. It wouldn't have done between contem-
poraries, but coming from Charlie, who could have pulverised
the Ballantyne brothers one in either hand, it was all right.
Occasionally, to show there was no ill-feeling, he exerted himself to bang their heads together, or shove a handful of *heskanit*
burrs down their necks, condescensions which they accepted in
the joyous spirit in which the same puppies might accept an
exasperated swipe of the long-suffering St. Bernard paw; but
most of the time he just opened one bright black eye at them,
and smiled, and said, as now:

"All right! You know it all backwards. You wait and see!"

But Jim Benison wasn't a simple eighteen-year-old Curly
Ballantyne, fresh from Caldington, seeing the world outside
Midshire for the first time in his life. True, his experience was
not so wide nor so deep as it might have been, but he had waded
into the sea and lost his footing, and he was willing now to go
with the tide. The old things, the confining things in which
these cheerful children were still bound, had broken away and
left him naked and adrift in that first venture; he would never
again be confident that he knew everything, or quick to reject
as lies what was alien to his experience. That phase was over.
They could look at the dazzling colour and strangeness of the
world with round, inquisitive, entranced eyes, and measure it
against Caldington, and half-reject it as a fairy-tale, opened to
them only by wildest chance and for a brief time. They hadn't
lost their footing yet. As for him, he might have viewed it in
much the same way, in spite of all the revelations of Flanders,
if there had survived a single substantial tie to keep Midshire
in his mind. He thought of England sometimes as a pleasant
but elusive dream, something so far away, and obscured by so
many bright colours and dazzling incidents, that he could not
keep his hold upon it by any magic of longing or discontent.
When he came back to it at last—though of this he never
thought now—it would not be as one drawn by a cord in its
recoil, but as one completing the circumnavigation of the
world, and coming upon it unaware. It was not that he had
willingly relinquished it, but that it had been taken from him.
She, if she had been the woman he had thought her, could have
given him England in his arms, to carry with him wherever he
journeyed, and herself in the gift. But that was all over. He
had, instead of that sharp, delightful pain, this brightness with-

5

out and emptiness within; and a lifetime doled out to him one day at a time, for that continuity of nostalgia and desire.

But he knew he would get over her. You can get over anything in time. The process is bad, but the end is pretty sure, human nature being as resilient as it is. And at least, all the past being taken out of his eyes, he could see and take a detached interest in the detail of the present. Nobody's face came between him and the arid limestone skyline now; no drifting hair, pale gold or red gold, dimmed the radiance of the sun. He saw what he was looking at, clear and full, and knew that he possessed nothing more. People at home would think of him and worry about him, no doubt, as he did sometimes about them; but that was all a long way off. The Great Sand Sea was less of a fable now than the green Sheel Valley, and the taller stories of Charlie Smith more credible than the quiet of Sheel woods in the gossamer light of the English moon. So he was silent, waiting until he should see with his own eyes, but nevertheless already willing to believe.

And then he saw. It was on a longer than usual run south with ammunition to an advanced battery, one day, with Gyp Ballantyne beside him in the cab, and Charlie under the awning of the lorry behind. They spent the night in the rear of the battery, and for the first time Jim saw the tangled, deep lines of British wire, insignificant in the stony waste, and in the infinite distance puffs of hazy dust marked the positions of the invisible enemy. Until then he had seen, since Alexandria, no glimpse of the war, except for an occasional plane wheeling in the cloudless expanse of the sky.

"We're pretty near the cliffs here," said Charlie, "if you care to take a walk before it gets dark. Only it's now or never, because the night comes with a whizz around these parts."

"I don't mind if I do," said Jim. "How about you, Gyp?"

Gyp stopped whistling long enough to shout, from inside the tool-box, that he had no intention of walking anywhere but the twenty yards or so back into the bosom of the battery, where he had a drink, a smoke and a game of pontoon lined up already with a bunch of the boys. So the two of them set off southward and left him to his own interests.

"He's too young," said Charlie Smith tolerantly. "No soul above pontoon, that's his trouble. In half an hour the gunners will have skinned the pants off him, but he doesn't know that yet. They learn by experience. Come on, let's you and me go

6

out into the wide open spaces. Plenty of time to skin young Gyp's pants back off the gunners afterwards."

It was a longer walk than Jim had bargained for, and he had heard enough about the difficulties of retaining a landmark in that uniform scene, and the sudden descent of the desert night, to be cautious about going far from his base at sundown; but it was apparent to him that Charlie knew what he was about, and the light was still brilliant and the set of sun not yet immediately threatening. They walked as directly south as they could, over rising, broken ground sown with outcrops of rock, between which the yellow pools of sand grew rarer and shallower; and suddenly they were standing on the rim of the lucid air, and the ground reeled away dizzily below them to a depth of seven or eight hundred feet in sheer faces of rock. Jim had known the pull of space from other belvederes, but never anything like this, this breathless, still, exultant surge of radiant air plucking him forward into space. What should have been a golden void was a world of positive and stimulating light, light that sang and sparkled and troubled the senses like the rising spring, a potent thing and beautiful. Looking out through this ecstatic shining air, he saw reach out from under the cliffs, and deepen, and grow golden, and undulate away into the infinitely remote skyline, the beginning of the sand. Near to the rocks it was a mottled sweep of brown and grey, brushed bare in places by the winds; but beyond, he saw the dizzy march of the dunes begin, monstrous and strange, mile upon mile of sinuous golden creatures, with burnished sides and fringed backs, moving south-south-east over the horizon from the rim of the sunset to the silken edges of the twilight, an irresistible army. He saw the sun glitter along their arched necks and narrow, tawny crests. He saw the wind play over them with long, rippling shudders, as if like racing stallions they shook their streaming manes in the storm of their own speed. He saw and wondered at the restless illusion which made them seem at once so motionless and so fleet, a whole world of mirage made tangible, yet evading knowledge. The light swam over them unceasingly in flashes of amber and blue and pearl, like the changing heart of an opal, and dissolved between sand and sky into a honey-coloured lustre in which the wind lost itself and died. It should have been repellent, this arid, monotonous, uni-tinted plain; instead, it was breath-taking.

He stood there fascinated, near to the edge of the limestone plateau, staring at the play of the threshing manes a thousand

7

feet below him and a score of miles away. Charlie Smith sat down beside him upon a rock, and filled his pipe with leisurely, abstracted gestures.

"Kind of surprising, isn't it?" said Charlie Smith. "You'd expect fifteen thousand square miles or so of nothing but sand to be a pretty depressing sight, and a lot more than enough of it. But when you see it, it's like looking at the jasper sea, or something—or a woman you don't know as well as you'd like. You can't look at anything else or think of anything else until you get better acquainted. But the desert takes longer to know," said Charlie pensively. "Most women last you such a short time."

"You should know," said Jim mechanically; but he need not have bothered to speak, for Charlie was launched upon a tide of reminiscence in which his friends had no part, even as audience.

"Come to think of it, there is something about all this that's like a woman," he said. "Not the easy kind—the other one, the thousand and first, the one you never do get to know. You can't get her out of your mind, and you can't get yourself into hers. She makes love to you in her fashion, and you think you're getting somewhere. All the time she treats you like hell, and half the time you're sane enough to know she's ordinary, and hard, and generally no good—not even specially good-looking—but you can't leave her alone. Then you get wise to it that you're getting no forrarder, but still you can't get away. She hasn't got you blindfolded any more, so by all the rules you ought to be happily quit of her. Are you hell! You get to know damn well that she's cheap, and shallow, and nasty, that half her looks are paint and the other half nothing to write home about, but still there's something in her you hanker after and never can reach. That's the sort of woman men murder in their beds in the end. I didn't wait for that," said Charlie Smith, with his lean, satanic smile. "I was fly. I saw it coming and got out in time. If you stay around that sort of woman indefinitely, either she'll be the death of you, or you of her, and I didn't fancy swinging for her. But it's a bit like that with this country. I can't think of a fouler, more deadly place, and I've been in plenty. You haven't seen what it can do yet. It isn't only the heat, though that's bad enough in all conscience. It isn't only the loneliness, and that feeling of being deserted by God and man. It's the little spiteful physical things she does to you that drive you desert-mad in the end; the scorpions, and

8

the flies, and the beastly sand-fleas, and the sand that scores your eyes raw and makes your lips split and dries the spittle in your mouth—those are the mean little things she kills you with. You wait a little while, and you'll be cursing her like all the rest for the bitch she is, and never a foul word she won't wear like a ribbon in her blasted yellow hair. But when she catches you at sundown, like this, all golden and sleek and still like a marmalade cat winding herself round your shins, you'll fall for it the same as ever. You're the kind. There'll still be something in her you hanker after and can't reach, and she'll still be able to kid you she's putting it in your hand. Look at me! I spent the better part of four years getting kicked around by sand and heat and thirst in these parts, and an evening wind over the dunes and a good sunset still has me talking in blank verse."

"It doesn't get everybody that way," said Jim stolidly; but his eyes did not move from the amber distances. He had never seen such air or such light. That was enough for the moment. He hadn't supposed he was coming to a paradise, anyhow; all the tales leaned the other way.

"No, very likely you'll never run to talking about it. That isn't your style. But from the way you're using your eyes I'd say the germ's bitten all right"

"It's new to me, I never seen much. Naturally a chap's curious. And, anyhow, how do you come to know so much about it?"

"I was four years in Cairo with a firm of engineering contractors, and I kind of got a liking for the desert; spent all my off time and holidays with a handful of other fellows who had the bug worse than I had. I know the Egyptian side best, and the north of the Sudan, but I've been in Siwa, too, once, a long time ago. It is a long time ago, but Libya doesn't change much. Did you see that stone young Curly was toting around the other day to chock his back wheel? That was a diorite axe—Stone Age or thereabouts, I'm not well up in palæolithic periods. And if ever you go into the captain's little cubby-hole, take a look at that long, flat bit of rock he's using as a paper-weight. It's a flint knife from away back three or four thousand years ago. And that scratched drawing of an antelope in the shady side under Jebel Kebir—that dates from much the same time. It's like that here. Everything lies on the top of the ground together, yesterday's bones and bones from centuries back, they're all equal. Nothing's new here, and nothing's really old,

9

and nothing matters very much. You and me and Wavell and the Eyeties—it's all one."

"That makes this just a silly waste of time," said Jim. "Why don't we drop it? You make it sound easy."

The long brown cheeks were dented again with Lucifer's gaunt smile.

"So you haven't noticed that about men! Only the wise few realise how unimportant their activities are; the rest find their back-gardens at home bigger than all that ocean of loneliness down there. We have to tag along with the majority, naturally; that's the way a human society is run."

"You can talk, all right," admitted Jim, "like nobody's business. But don't count me in, I'm in the majority this time. I want a back-garden at home, the same as the rest, and so do you, for all your humbug."

Afterwards he was never sure if this was true. How could you know what Charlie Smith really wanted out of life? He didn't seem to want anything; he just drifted along with the days and nights as they came and went, talkative sometimes, sometimes silent, managing the youngsters, twisting the officers, evading promotion, making a sort of dark, high-flown fun of most things, travelling without any apparent desire to arrive. He didn't seem to have any people, he received very little mail, and wrote next to none. His profession was an unsolved mystery. Sometimes they made stabbing guesses that he had been this or that, schoolmaster or lawyer or even parson, something involving brains; but none of their blind hits squared with the contracting engineer's agent from Cairo with a passion for the wilderness. How could you guess what a man like that wanted from life, when you'd never met the like of him before? Even Jim's own longing for that back-garden was now more a matter of getting back to what fitted him than to what he desperately wanted. The wilderness was too big for him, he needed something of a comfortable handy size, with a hawthorn hedge round it.

"I tell you what, my lad," he said, "I don't like your desert."

"Oh yes, you do," said Charlie. "I can see it in your eye."

"Oh no, I don't. And the sooner we start moving west across it, the sooner we'll be out of it, so I'm all for starting an advance right away. I like my country green, not tawny."

"Now you're talking like all the rest," said Charlie Smith sceptically, "like the Lathams and the Bells and the Warriners, like Robbie with his sweetheart in the A.T.S. and Vin with his wife on the land. And I had you down for the one chap who came with an open mind, and might be able to see straight in front of him. Don't tell me you've got a sweetheart in the N.A.A.F.I. or a wife making brackets for Bren guns, too. I can't bear it."

"No," said Jim, "don't worry, I've got nothing like that hanging round me. But I still like the looks of England, and I'm even partial to a place of my own, with a roof and a bed and a chair by the fire, and a few people around who know me and speak the same language. Don't let it discourage you; by the time we've been here a few months I may be converted. What soured you, anyway? You're mighty set against folks having families. I suppose you were quarried?" If he didn't like being asked about his own people he shouldn't have set the ball rolling; he couldn't complain if it rolled in a direction he didn't like.

Charlie Smith continued to look into the lapis lazuli blueness of the southern sky, and did not smile. "Sour grapes!" he explained, without resentment. "I could be as domestic as the best of 'em if I had the chance. I could hand out photographs of my missus and the kids, and tell the same yarns about the baby's teething troubles seven hundred times over, until you had to sit on my head in relays to shut me up. Only it so happened we never had any kids, and I walked out and left my missus before she could drive me to murder her. We were a very happy couple, as you may guess. That's why I can't stand the sight of a married Benedict. Sour grapes, like I'm telling you. It can't be any good—*I* never had it."

"All right," said Jim. "You're not the only one." But he thought he knew more about Charlie Smith already than he had ever expected or wanted to know, and he felt as if he had been looking at him through a keyhole. This crazy country, this incredible country made you open your uneasy heart and let someone in, anyone to share the emptiness with you. The Ballantyne brothers, twined together like children, sharing the same hollow of soft sand as once they had shared the same bed, fended off from each other the awesome loneliness; but the masterless man who had no brother nor companion from home must needs look round and choose his friend from what company he could, and carefully, for you lean hard upon your friend. Charlie Smith had chosen Jim Benison. So much was clear to Jim, and he felt young, and astonished, and flattered by the revelation, for in the extreme rawness of the re-constituted 4th Midshires, Charlie Smith stood out head and shoulders, with something of a perverted greatness about him.

"Hadn't we best be moving?" said Jim abruptly, half afraid of this tongue-loosening, enchanted hour. He didn't want to talk yet about Delia, not to Charlie nor to anyone. She was still too near. The time might come, much later on, when he could discuss and dismiss her as Charlie did his wife, but he hadn't reached that stage yet. "Don't want to get lost out here —at least, I don't, you can please yourself. I've heard there's no twilight around here to speak of. Is that right? You're the man who knows!"

Charlie arose and stretched himself mightily, and cast a last long, deliberate glance into the golden abyss where the stallions of sand shook their smooth locks. "It's right enough. Yes, I suppose we should get back. Gets a bit chilly, too, once the sun goes, and I shouldn't wonder if there's a swine of a cold wind up here in an hour or so. All right, come on with you. Even the disillusioned have to go home some time."

The disillusioned went home; silently, companionably, home to a battery hut under mottled grey-brown camouflage netting, where the fug of cigarette smoke made the air blue and bitter, and Gyp had already lost his shirt to a poker-faced gun-layer, and was beginning to look a bit worried about his shorts. There was even a species of beer to drink, or something by courtesy called beer; at any rate, it was better than the odorous water they had here. Take it all round, a man could be in worse places. Once they were on the move—the younger ranks still confidently expected it to happen at any moment, poor mutts— the mess-hut in the limestone desert might appear in retrospect as a sort of sub-paradise. None the less, Jim found himself reluctant to go in. Maybe there was something in Charlie's verdict, after all, and he did instinctively like the wilderness. "Like" was a queer word for it, perhaps; but it did have a fascination, the size of it, and the quiet, and the freedom. If it was hell, there was at least elbow-room in hell, and the stars were bigger and more in number than anywhere else in the world. Yes, there was something to be said for it.

He had not as yet seen it, of course, in anything but a good temper. It remained to discover the worst it could do. He was making allowances for that. Take it all just as it comes—that was the only way. Don't look behind, or you turn homesick for what you once had; don't look ahead, or you grow afraid of what's coming to you. Stick to what you have in your two hands, and never be sure of anything else. That was how he was going to conduct the rest of his life, at least until the war was over. No emotions at all, no feelings; you can't afford them. Just five senses, and whatever intelligence God and costly experience have given you, should be able to make the desert habitable and your fellows endurable. He'd finished with that impulsive habit of transferring all his geese into swans; from now on they had to work their passage. Delia had taught him so much sense.

Actually he had altered very little. Not all this chilly resolve to distrust all men could change his nature. Charlie Smith was already in his grace, and could do no wrong.

2

From Petrol Parva to Fort Nibeiwa was somewhat over forty miles of undulating sand, without any considerable dunes, and broken by outcrops of naked rock, and occasional patches of starved terfa-scrub. This stretch of ground, or the greater part of it, they set out to cover before daylight on December 8th, and it was the beginning of an Odyssey. The rumours of action, so persistent and so little trusted by any but the optimistic young who had never yet seen action, had crystallized for some days past into a form more definite and exact than usual, and mysteriously, before ever they were officially endorsed, had become better than rumours. The desert army was moving; the deadly dull and tedious winter they had feared was not, after all, to be their fate. They were going to Sidi Barrani. No one could have given those unblooded boys a more welcome Christmas present. Any step forward was a step towards home; and they were already heartily sick of sitting frizzling in the sun and listening to the desultory exchanges of the batteries. Wait till they got at the Eyeties, and see how the beggars would run!

They left their bases in lorries, round about four in the morning, in a darkness becoming luminously blue round the edges, and drove due west out into the lustrous starry night instead of taking the north-north-westerly direction they had expected. They passed through British wire, and somewhat later through Italian, and someone said there were bodies lying by the track, but it was too dark to see very much, and there were no delays, for as yet all their work had been done for them. There were tanks ahead, blazing the trail. All they had to do was sit in their lorries, and keep silence, and go where they were taken. Shadowy, even to each other, insubstantial in the disguising dark, they were ghost soldiers going into battle, not men but afreets. No barrage attended them as yet. They swung in their wide quarter-circle west and north, far into enemy-held territory, with only the noise of their own transports to carry word of their coming; and the vast, level, monotonous noise flowed across the vast, level, monotonous desert and was dwarfed and lost. They moved steadily but swiftly, shaken together like dice in a can, cushioning one another against the worst of the jolts. The ground and the light improved as they went, and they were able to see the clear-cut edge where land and air divided, paling to a translucent jade-green along the eastern horizon behind them. Through that shimmering slit light flowed into the black inverted bowl of the sky, and in a while filled it; a light between dove-grey and shallow green, not strong enough as yet to cast any shadows.

They could not talk now, it was too late for all that. All this time they had been hoping for action, and now it fell upon them out of a clear sky, and they were whirled into it before they could consider what it was, what it demanded of them, where it would lead them. Certainly they had known for some hours the rough outline of the intended move. Up north-north-west of them, on the coast, was Sidi Barrani, the first objective of any westward drive against the Italians; and south of it lay a group of fortified posts, covering the approaches, Tummar East and Tummar West, Nibeiwa, and more remote to the south-west, Safafi. The lay of all this enemy land had been explained to them in some detail, and Nibeiwa, for which they were bound, had become more than a name to them. They knew that it was large, and populous, and likely to be very strongly held. Well, it was their job to reduce it, and they had no doubt they could do it. They had no doubt they could do anything, never yet having been given anything considerable to do. It was not uncertainty nor fear which made their faces, seen dimly in the eerie distilling light, glisten and stare with straining skin drawn taut over jutting bones; it was simply the astringent excitement of impending action. However ready you were, however you had schooled yourself, when the thing happened this breathlessness took you by the bowels and wrung you, so that you felt as if there were birds in your belly. Even when you had been through the same thing already, it still got you; but at least then you had control of it, you knew what it was, a mere physical reaction, not to be taken to heart. Easy to see, by young Curly's anxious eyes, that he was wondering what was the matter with him. Was he scared? Or what was it that had got into him? Was he going to let himself down, after all, at the first pinch? He did not recognise this as the same feeling which had punched him in the wind at school, before every sprint, belying the secure knowledge he had that he could and would win. Well, in a day or so young Curly Ballantyne would know how he stood, and he wouldn't be taken in again by any amount of breaking sweat or any leaden weight in his chest.

Jim could just see, against the lightening east, Charlie Smith's gaunt profile, unmoved, as still as one of the limestone rocks south of Petrol Parva. He had most certainly known it all before; where and how, was his business. That was why, in the company of these raw boys, he had felt the need of someone else to restore his balance, and chosen Jim Benison to fill the bill. Well, it worked both ways. If he was getting out of that companionship the half of what he was putting in—well, he was not doing so badly, Jim thought.

The light grew. The rim of the sun showed; and now they were able to see the column of lorries ahead, demurely spaced, creeping forward steadily across the shadowy grey face of the desert, where the stones and rocky outcrops lifted themselves now from the dead level and put on a third dimension. But for themselves the dawning world was void. They saw the tracks of caterpillars in the pools of smooth sand, and once they passed a derelict Italian car, the shell of a Fiat, burned out days since after some lucky long shot.

"I think we've finished for the day," remarked Charlie, and made a wry face. The lorries ahead were drawing in among the *terfa* scrub. "This is our billet, Jimmy, my lad, for the next sixteen hours or so."

"What?" shouted Curly in an explosion of disgust. "Rot! I thought we were going all the way? I thought this was the big kick-off? You said yourself——"

"So I did, and so it is, laddie, but this is all for the day, you see if I'm not right. To-morrow maybe we'll see what we can do for you in the way of battle, murder and sudden death. Right now you'd better hop out of here and give a hand with all that camouflage netting, same as the rest of us."

Curly hopped, though with no very good grace. Once out of the warmth and cramp of the lorry, they found that the dawn had teeth, a biting, stinging wind blowing low across the arid plain and bringing sand and gravel with it. They were glad to occupy themselves with the disguising of their lorries, though that exercise did not last long. Curly continued to grumble as he worked, out of the fury of his disappointment; another day was an age to wait for what he had promised himself now, at once.

"What's the point of staying here, anyway? The first Eyetie that comes over, and we're spotted, and then bang goes the whole business. They'll be waiting for us with all they've got, and by all accounts that's plenty. Why don't we go ahead now, before they know we're coming?"

"Because we're moving in on our terms, not theirs, my bucko, that's why. We're already well inside territory they think perfectly safe, and we can afford another night to finish the job properly and walk in on them at dawn all fresh and un-expected. Yes, unexpected." He looked up the length of the column, a series of gentle, neutral-tinted hummocks in the neutral-tinted plain. "Try and find that from the air!"

"Oh, the transports! But how the hell are we going to keep 'em from spotting *us?*"

"The hard way," said Charlie Smith. "By keeping still."

Curly demanded with horror and alarm: "What, all day?"

"I said it was the hard way," said Charlie, not without sympathy.

He was right. Their orders, received a few minutes later from Sergeant Lake, were to find the most sheltered positions they could, dig themselves in, and prepare to spend the whole of the daylight lying flat, with as little movement as possible. They were advised to get some sleep if they could, and to go easy with their canteens, which would be refilled at night. As if the Ballantyne brothers and their kind could sleep in cold blood on the eve of their first battle! But Charlie Smith could and did, once having settled himself into a pocket of soft sand under the propped-up tailboard of one of the lorries. The selection of position was a matter of some importance, for though the wind was bitterly cold at dawn the noon sun would be savage, and to choose the lea of a transport now in many cases meant to leave oneself shadeless later. Jim crept in beside Charlie, and scooped out hollows for shoulder and hip, and after much trial and rejection settled upon what he considered to be the easiest possible position. In two hours it was intolerable, but so would any other have been; and by then the air was warm enough to help him into an uneasy doze, which at least passed almost an hour of the interminable day for him.

Captain Priest—he looked as if he should have been one, with a long, sad face and a long, cadaverous body—came down the line before full daylight was come, and exchanged with them, here and there, a few words meant to be encouraging. He wasn't good at making contacts with his men as yet. An administrative soldier, they said, one who'd never been in action, for all his rank; he wasn't to blame for that, of course, but it didn't make his position any easier, and his efforts at *bonhomie* were a bit embarrassing, especially when Charlie Smith, who alone seemed able to go seventy-five per cent of the way to meet him, was fast asleep under the tailboard and couldn't fill the pauses. The Captain had Second-Lieutenant Stringer with him, a fat, fair, earnest kid from Caldington— his father owned a quarter of the town's house property, some of the worst-kept and highest-rented, too—with a commission so new it was visibly stamped on everything he did or said. A nice enough kid in his way—fancied himself rather a lot, but that would wear off in time, and he honestly meant well by every one of his men, and had high conceptions of his duty. But it was a far cry to the old A Company days under young Brian, a far cry indeed from this conscientious, obtuse, humourless youngster to that slim, underweight, fiery little hero. No one was left in this company now to remember Second-Lieutenant Ridley. That was another thing Charlie Smith might be told some day.

The officers said their little pieces and passed on, and all along the column of motionless men the gleam of the sun struck suddenly with a perceptible abrupt warmth, and the long day began. Considering the sand-flies, and the heat, and the small ration of water, they got through the hours fairly well. Gyp had a bad moment with a scorpion, and being taken by surprise let out a yell before he was touched, and at least afforded Curly some amusement. The ribbing went on for half an hour, too long for Gyp's temper, until Charlie rolled over and rubbed Curly's nose in the sand, and told him in no uncertain terms to lay off. There were other embarrassments. Towards noon the wind changed, and came at them across the open plain stiflingly hot and laden with sand and *heskanit* burrs, which silted into the necks of shirts and the legs of shorts, and played merry hell with the little comfort they had found for themselves. Several times aircraft passed over, but none lingered or showed any undue interest, so they considered that they had not been observed; but there was always the possibility that they had, and the thought that they might be gunned and dive-bombed to pieces here without ever so much as contacting the enemy was a background nightmare to Jim at least, if it failed to occur to many of the others. Sometimes, too, they saw their own 'planes cruising overhead, presumably to report on the quality of their camouflage. There were desultory bursts of gunfire in the distance on both sides, the normal exchanges of the day. They talked a great deal, to allay the irritations of the sand and the prickling of camel-thorn, and to keep themselves sane against the slowness of the time. In the heat of noon they played impromptu games in their slender patch of shade, and in the first sudden cool they could have slept again, but by then there was no time for sleep.

In the deep night the column stirred again and reassembled, the nets were stripped from the lorries, and new issues of water made; and they were off again, and on the last lap. Very steadily they moved this time, with as little noise as possible, feeling their way across country very indifferently known to them, for few of them had ever been farther west than Siwa before. The cold came down upon them with the darkness, witheringly chill after hours of sweating in the sun. They were glad to avail themselves of the warmth of the packed lorries, though it was only the exchange of one cramp for another; and inexpressibly glad to be moving in at last upon their objective.

They travelled for over four hours, and in the later stages of the journey they were aware by the starlight of the squat dark beetle shapes of tanks moving with them. While it was still dark they halted, drawing into an open line facing north-east, and they knew, though as yet it was out of sight, that there lay Nibeiwa Camp. They had made a great half-circle about it, to approach from within the enemy defences, and from a direction entirely unexpected. All they needed now was the dawn, the hour of the traditional Arab attack, according to Charlie. Well, there was more than tradition behind that idea; there was sound psychology, too. Jim had never found any hour in the day so dispiriting as that first light, or less conducive to strong resistance against a surprise attack. And this would be a complete surprise, he was sure of that; they would not have lain so long undisturbed if the Eyeties had known of their existence.

Major Jerrold and Captain Priest came down the line again, and talked to Sergeant Lake earnestly for a few minutes, and passed on. Making sure all the non-coms. knew what was expected of them, he supposed. They needn't have bothered; Lake knew his business as they would probably never know theirs. He'd lied himself into the army at sixteen in time to see the finish of the last war, and had joined up again with the territorial battalion of the Midshires in 1938, at the time of Munich; and if he hadn't been so fond of an occasional roaring, berserk drunk he could have been sporting pips himself by now. As it was, he was far too good to be pushed lower than sergeant for anything short of murder. No, Lake might be able to give them tips, but he doubted if they could give Lake any.

The first light began, almost imperceptibly, along the skyline ahead of them, and suddenly there were outlines there, mere distant undulations in the rock and sand, crescent-shaped swellings like baby *barchans* with their horns pointing east, and probably either machine-guns or riflemen tucked snugly into the inner curve. And beyond these, on the skyline, a long toothedge, as yet formless but for the silhouette against the first gleam of light, the outer wall of Nibeiwa. Overhead the stars paled and faded, and beyond the fortress of the enemy the saffron and silver of the dawn began to mount slowly.

"What will the walls be?" wondered Jim. "They look almost like rough stone from here."

"Dry-walling," said Charlie, "with stones gathered on the spot. They couldn't bring all that with 'em from Italy, there's miles of it. Tanks will make easy work of that once we get there."

"Must be time to move. What happens now? Do we hoof it from here?"

"Shouldn't think so. We go as far as we can awheel, surely. Hold tight, we're moving now." The tanks had nosed out of the line and shot ahead. The lorries roared forward and after them. No stealth now, only speed. This was it, the last run, and the blow at the end of it.

The noise of their coming streamed across the desert, a wave rushing to meet the wave of light. They stood up, leaning forward against the thrust of the air, and heard before them the first crackle of rifle-fire, from the outlying trenches, and a shout, and the stutter of a machine-gun. They had been observed at last, too late to stop them, too late even to impede. They saw one of the tanks ahead roar straight for the nearest trench, driving in the broad parapet over the defenders and clambering over them and on with only a momentary lurch and check. A thin stream of men, not more than five or six, shot out of the column of dust and sand, and ran screaming across the path of the lorries, dropping their rifles as they ran. No one troubled about them, though they held up their hands and ran a few stumbling yards alongside, shouting over and over that they surrendered. The possibility of prisoners had not occurred as yet to anyone. They had come to fight, not to receive surrenders.

They were through the first circle of outposts now, and there was wire ahead, and the usefulness of the lorries was over. They drew up, and decanted the Midshires and their fellows in the wake of the careering tanks, and from then on it was a simple matter of every man for himself, and the quickest way into the fort was the best. They fixed bayonets, and they ran, a few down into the tatters of the outpost trenches, but most of them headlong for the heaped earthworks and the stone wall. A random and hysterical fire met them, but they scarcely noticed it, and because of their speed it did them little damage. They kept to the paths the tanks had battered out for them, running like furies, angry when they had to fall aside to pick out stray snipers from their holes with the bayonet like winkles with a pin. Nor was this always necessary. A few fought it out until they were hand to hand, but most, when the stream of shouting, racing men threatened to roll over them, came scuttling out of their narrow trenches and gave themselves up wherever they could find any astonished youngster willing to encumber himself with prisoners.

The wire, on this side of the camp at least, had never been meant to keep out tanks. They had crashed it at speed and carried it in with them by whole sections, raising a cloud of fine white dust that clogged the nostrils and filled the mouth and eyes with gritty particles. The double stone wall, raised with weeks of labour, had simply exploded where they had nosed into it, and scattered stones in diminishing heaps along their tracks for twenty yards within. Over this debris, through this stinging dust, Jim Benison climbed into Nibeiwa.

The picture he had of this battle was always confused and blinded, a whitish mist through which loomed and flashed fantastic figures, and crazy incidents leaned to him and sprang away again half seen. It was less a battle, indeed, than a collection of individual actions, many of them so ridiculous that it was difficult afterwards to believe they had actually happened. It was like nothing he had ever seen or dreamed of. It was so

funny that periodically he had to stop and lean upon the nearest
solid thing that offered, and laugh and cough and gasp the sand
out of his lungs. And yet quite a number of people died while
he was laughing. What had got into him that he could find the
whole thing funny? He didn't know. It was all very well for
young Curly to double up and hoot his head off at the sight of
an Italian officer bolting half-dressed from his tent with his
trousers precariously held up by one hand, and the other arm
pumping madly to help him along. Curly had never seen the
other side. But what possessed Jim Benison to laugh like a
lunatic as he ran through the dust-fog for the nearest tents?
He knew what it must mean to a lot of the fellows, even if at
first glance it had its amusing side. Maybe it was the sheer unexpectedness of it, as astonishing in its results to the attackers
as to the attacked; or the dizzy fall from what he had conceived
to be the normal aspect of war; or merely a manifestation of
nervous excitement in himself. He reasoned about it as he ran,
but came no nearer understanding it.

As the dust cleared he saw the opening aisles of the camp
before him, acres of tents, mounds of cases and cans, a vista
of strange luxury. Men, some half-dressed, some in elaborate
field uniforms, ran about among the tents and slit trenches,
shouting incoherent orders and getting no attention from anyone. Native troops leaped into the shelter trenches dug against
bombardment, and stood to their rifles, but did not stand so for
long; unled, uncertain what had happened, some broke and ran,
and some were ploughed bodily in as the trenches caved under
the rush of the British tanks. Smoke from cook-house fires,
richly scented with breakfast, blew across the scene, and one of
the cooks, screaming indistinguishable Italian, tore down the
slope to the nearest gap in the wall, and rushed out into the
open desert with his apron gathered aside in one hand, until a
corporal coming in with prisoners flattened his rifle across his
path and added him to the bag. The noise was indescribable.
Above the shrill Italian shouts the shriller screaming of horses
and mules rose, and the drumming of their hooves was like
distant thunder. Somewhere in this square mile or more of
madness they were broken loose, and rushing about among the
tents and huts to the danger of Italian and British alike. Who
herded and quieted them at last Jim did not see. Some, probably, rushed away into the desert and were lost; for after a time
they were heard no more.

In that first rush for the tents, Jim lost his companions. Whoever fought, fought singly, and many, at the end of the business, wondered if they had really fought at all. In spite of isolated stands, it was all too easy, incredibly easy, the whole incident finished in under three hours, and only the clearing up left to be done. An ex-deep-sea-diver from the Adríatic coast put up a redoubtable show with a machine-gun for over half an hour, until Sergeant Lake ran along the crest of the wall behind him and dropped upon his shoulders from eight feet up, and all but brained him against his own gun; but that was the most determined resistance they encountered, and they were almost childishly pleased that this one man of spirit should, after all, live to tell the tale. He did so within an hour of recovering consciousness, at great length, and in rapid, indignant Italian, of which no one understood a word until Captain Priest turned up. The incident came to Jim afterwards; his part in the morning's work was not so orthodox, and in spite of a string of prisoners it did not seem to him that he had anything to show for it.

It began with a swerve and a plunge into a trench on his left, where an Askari soldier was training a rifle steadily upon the attack from the main gap. They went down together into the stony soil, tearing at each other with their hands because there was no room to manœuvre rifle and bayonet; and a passing tank lurched over the end of their battle-ground with one track, and shook down a considerable weight of stones on top of them, and did Jim's job for him. He was sorry and angry. He had no feeling against the Askari. This was not like Flanders, where he had hated the Boche so insatiably that he could not do enough against them. Here he knew, but did not feel, the urgency of the fight. Moreover, this was not even an Italian, but a poor devil who didn't even know what it was all about. He dragged himself out of the trench in a sick rage, and made for the tents.

The first he entered was empty of men, but full of excellent wireless equipment which tempted him mightily. From the second, someone fired at him as he came, and screamed as he fired back. A small man, elegantly dressed, shot from behind a table and all but fell at his feet in haste to surrender his revolver and be safely made prisoner. An officer of sorts; Jim looked at the shaking, jabbering creature and wondered in what particular it was different from a man. He'd heard they were like this, but he hadn't believed it. Even seen thus at every disadvantage, surprised, disorganised, he couldn't understand

22

how men could behave like this. These were the people who had made a spurious outcry against the Abyssinian slave trade, their voluble tongues in their greasy cheeks, and had then proceeded to humanise the administration with mustard gas and high explosives. On top, they were bold, arrogant, cruel; this cringing, ingratiating thing was the reverse of the victory medal. At least the Boche, God blast him, could fight. Jim's flesh crept. He wanted to close his finger softly on the trigger of his rifle and blow a hole clean through the pretty uniform, but that wouldn't have conveyed his feeling, either. Anger came into him, anger against the enemy, whereas until now he had felt only anger against the fantastic futility of the encounter. He knew now that it was the same battle. He wasn't likely to forget it again. Here or in Flanders, against Boches or Eyeties, it was all one war.

Italian and Askari prisoners in great numbers were being herded out of the tents and trenches and lined up in the open. It did Jim good to make his captive walk half across the camp in line with one of the Askaris. The coloured man bore himself better of the two, and was half as big again, but perhaps his calm was due rather to bewilderment than courage. Jim rid himself of them both, and went on through the fort with the rest, accumulating prisoners by scores as he went. The fighting was already over; they were examining their spoils. Italian tanks, never brought into action because in the brief and shattering bombardment from the desert their crews had never had time to reach them, began to roll slowly through the aisles of the camp and assemble outside the broken walls. The number of them struck their captors silent with astonishment. Rank upon rank they wheeled into position, and still they came. Half a square mile or so of undamaged vehicles, neatly arranged in files along the flat sand, made the desert fantastic. Within the walls, the number of prisoners taken began to stream into thousands. There was too much of everything.

Jim grew weary of it. The very Arabian Nights richness of the place sickened him, the stacked tins of olive oil and canned foods, the wickered bottles of Chianti, the white bread, the elegant silver ware, the pieces of elaborate dress-uniform, all those details which ravished the simple souls of the Curlys and the Gyps. His anger, which was no longer baffled or undirected, embraced the prisoners and all that was theirs, their pretty clothes, their scattered, tawdry, pretentious medals, their elaborate food, their polished equipment, their plentiful wine.

23

They were sitting there waiting to be led triumphantly along the victory road into Alexandria, were they? Ready and waiting to make a gilded parade of it, with drums and banners and prancing horses. Well, that was one bubble pricked. This was the most they would ever see of the land of Egypt, except from behind the wire of a prison camp. He wished he had hit the wretched little officer when he fired into the tent. That would at least have been some satisfaction, whereas now he had nothing to show for it all, not a wound, not a kill.

The sun rose over the camp, and its heat struck suddenly upon their flesh, dry and brittle and fierce. The turmoil was already over. It was now a matter of assembling and sorting the spoils and the prisoners, and then on to the next obstacle, for by the tales they heard, Sidi Barrani was ringed round with Nibeiwas. The delectable breakfast smells continued to float across the tent roofs, for enterprising amateur cooks had taken over the lavish cook-houses and the half-cooked meal. It was now past eight o'clock, and here and there about the camp soldiers of three British and one Indian regiments were pausing for food wherever they could find it. Jim saw young Curly, excessively pleased with himself, like a kid at a party, standing guard over probably around two hundred Italian and Askari prisoners inside the shattered wall. Gyp, who was helping to assemble captured transport out in the level desert, had seen him, too, and at every journey leaned out to heave some brotherly wise-crack at him as he passed. He could get on with that. Curly wouldn't have changed places with Wavell himself.

Charlie Smith had disappeared into the disorder of the camp from the time of their entry, and was not seen again until Jim, tired from an hour of packing and loading wireless equipment in the sun, shouldered his way into one of the abandoned mess-tents, and came upon him sitting very much at his ease at a trestle-table laden with silver-ware, in the company of an elderly Italian officer. They appeared to be very comfortable together, sharing a silver coffee-pot and a leather-bound book which passed from hand to hand across the table. No one would have taken them for captor and prisoner. Jim stood with the pale blue of the sky bright behind him, and the grateful cool shade before, and stared at the two of them as if they were of a flesh alien from his own. Certainly this tall, quiet person with the grey hair and the thin, lined face was no fellow to that miserable little demoralised creature who had first enraged him, yet Jim could not have sat at a table with him, nor spoken to him as one man to another. He was still the enemy.

A fierce disgust possessed him, against them both, but against Charlie Smith in particular, who could talk like nobody's business, but was not ashamed to touch the pollution he professed to hate. He said, in the blackest, bitterest voice he had ever heard from his own lips:

"What are you doing here, sitting around having heart-to-heart talks with a dirty rat of an Eyetie while we work? You're supposed to be on our side."

Charlie Smith looked up mildly, and lifted his satanic eyebrows, and a queer, dry smile touched his mouth. "I am discussing Boccaccio," he said, "with Captain Desorigimenti, who speaks—and understands—English as well as you do."

"What I said still stands," said Jim Benison, "in English or Italian. Better bring him out to the others; or I shall."

The officer stood up. He was very tall, and ascetically thin, and his face was as tranquil as if he had been enjoying breakfast with an old friend, but it was not a happy face. No one could guess what was passing in his mind. He did not look at Jim, but gave the slight shadow of a bow towards Charlie Smith, and smiled, and held out his hand for the book.

"What more we have to say of 'Olympia'," he said, "must be deferred to a happier occasion. I am quite ready. It will be well if we go."

They passed by Jim, in the flap of the tent, and went up towards the enclosed area where the prisoners were herded; and as they went they talked, softening, as it seemed, the violence of the transition from that illusion of companionship in the tent to the hard reality outside. They walked side by side, with even, unhurried steps. Was that any way to bring in a prisoner?

It was astonishing how the incident haunted him, how the two of them, still talking together courteously and coolly, came back again and again into his mind all through the day, and tormented his senses constantly. He couldn't understand Charlie. That was the hell of it. He never had understood him; and now even the idea he had conceived of him was smashed to pieces. A man who would be smooth and suave in all circumstances, yes; but not as smooth as that. His code, perhaps, made it all the more imperative that he should be punctilious when his enemy was defeated. Yes, you could put it that way if you liked, but it wasn't convincing; it wasn't straight. Jim's code impelled him to set up his hate like an impassable steel barrier between himself and the thing he hated; to keep his hands from it except by way of fighting, to make it aware of his feeling, without exaggeration or emphasis (if either were possible) but without deceit. He had to know where he stood, and they had to know it, too. That was the only way he could live. But not everyone was like that. Some liked to keep their feelings bottled inside, pretending they had none; maybe because they felt naked and outraged if they were suspected of having human emotions—as if they were some secret part of the body covered by a rigid tabu. But that wasn't Charlie Smith, either; little as he knew him, he knew him too well for that.

All day long he was galled and goaded by the dissatisfaction of his own warfare, and the dubious grace of Charlie's. They did not say a word to each other on the subject, even when they were thrown together again in the forward dash to Tummar West, and shared the noontide heat of that brief struggle arm to arm. That at least was more of a fight; the shock element was still good, but its sharpest edge was gone, and the defenders stood and shot it out, having little hope of withdrawal. But even when this encounter, too, was over, and the afternoon sun found them inside the fort, the shadowy barrier remained erect between Jim and Charlie. They sat down under the wall together as if they had nothing whatever on their minds, and swopped cigarettes, and begged a light from a passing High-lander with a long string of prisoners; they talked, as everyone else was talking in this first breather, of the morning's work, and all the work ahead, of the stinking heat and the blistering dust and their monumental thirsty dreaming of English beer; but they did not talk of Captain Desorigimenti and his little much-thumbed "Olympia" which he read over breakfast, nor of the correct attitude towards the enemy. Charlie behaved as if he was unaware of anything amiss between them; but Jim, having said to him something for which any other member of the company would have knocked his block off, knew better than that. He was in no mood to try and put himself right, though; let Charlie do that first, if he could. It was doubtful if he could; one step into that indiscreet sophistication was enough.

Jim sat with a handkerchief draped over the back of his neck, and smoked, and sulked because even on this first day of success, when every objective fell into their hands like a ripe

plum, the fruit did not taste as it should, nor as he had believed
it would. In the beginning it had all looked so single and simple,
a straight fight between right and wrong; if you died, well, in a
way even that was satisfaction; and if you lived, well, you went
on fighting like that, straight white against straight black, until
it was over. But here he had been in both overwhelming defeat
and astonishing success, and in neither of them was there any
satisfaction. Everything was unstable, everything shifted, the
ground under his feet, the friends around him. Everything,
everyone, sooner or later, shifted and let him down; himself
most heavily of all.

3

In the evening of that day a dozen men of the Midshires,
under a little corporal, were sent foot-slogging it back to Nibeiwa
with a long column of Italian and Askari prisoners who were a
nuisance of the first magnitude at Tummar. Not that they had
any intention of making trouble; most of them seemed only too
glad to have finished with the war, and had, to all appearances,
nothing but affection and gratitude for their captors; but they
were too thick on the ground, cluttering up the field of action
in all directions, making, as Curly said, their nice desert untidy.
So an escort party was told off to march them back to Nibeiwa
on their way to the rear, where they could no longer be either
a danger or an embarrassment.

The corporal took Charlie Smith, partly because he had some
knowledge of Italian, but more because he was known to be
able to deal with the most complex and difficult circumstances
without turning a hair; and he took Jim Benison because he was
Charlie Smith's lesser half, and for no other reason. The job
gave no pleasure to either of them.

It was late evening, but still full daylight, when they set out,
the twelve disgruntled Englishmen and the eight hundred-odd
happy Italians. Twelve, said the corporal with disgust, was too
many by ten; only two were needed, and even then the second
was only to keep the first company. Charlie held that it was
not really necessary to do more than give the cheerful column
a workable description of where they were expected to report,
and they would make the best possible time there on their own.
However, it was more in accordance with custom that an escort
should walk alongside its charge at suitable intervals, rifle on

arm and ready for anything. And so this escort did, back to Nibeiwa in the cool of the evening, and reached it some little while before the abrupt, glossy night came down. All the way along the dusty road they met guns, and cars, and columns of mechanised infantry moving up to forward positions; and everywhere they saw spread across the desert the wreckage of Italian transport, from ten-ton trucks down to little six-horse-power Fiat runabouts, and Italian material, from ammunition dumps disguised under mounds of *terfa* scrub to huge barrels of Diesel oil rolled alongside the track. At this discarded plenty the Italians did not look. They wanted no more of the war. Captivity was safer and pleasanter; they made for it with all speed.

Jim, marching with his rifle slung ready on his arm, looked them over as he walked, and found them a motley lot. All ages were here, and all sizes. There was one fellow, in a rakish Tyrolean hat, who must have topped six feet by a couple of inches; but of the others most were small by English standards. There were middle-aged men with greying hair and heavy beards and big-eyed boys who could not have been more than seventeen. One of these kids, and a good-looking one at that, walked close at Jim's side. He had lustrous, black, womanish eyes in a dirty face, and ebony curls dulled now with oil and dust; he looked tired, but quite unabashed, and deeply interested in everything under the sun, and most deeply in Jim. And what Jim found most disturbing about him was not the bright, covert glance which was fixed so steadily his way, but the grubby little mongrel puppy the boy carried hugged to his chest. He held it as if he had made up his mind that nothing on earth should wrest it from him; no one was likely to try, of course, but the kid didn't know that. Jim tried to tell him, but was not sure at first if he understood.

He pointed to the pup. "He's O.K. Get it? O.K. you keep him. We like dogs, too."

The boy looked doubtful still, but smiled. "Nice dog," he said suddenly, and displayed the lamentable scrap proudly in his extended hands, fishing for an ally in the event of difficulties ahead.

" 'Strewth!" said Jim, "of all the bastardly mixtures!" But he grinned as he said it, and scratched behind a dusty yellow ear, so that it passed for a compliment, and the kid flashed a brilliant white smile out of his dirty face, and was wonderfully cheered. Seventeen? He could have been fourteen just then, and nobody would have known the difference. He could have been one of the leggy lads who played football in the remote back-alleys of Caldington, but for his dark good looks. It was as well to remember, though, that he was an Italian.

Jim drew away, and lengthened his pace to move a rank or two ahead. So that was how it happened. "It's dogs with you," he thought. "It was poetry with him." There was not the simplest, most direct issue in this war that could not be so confused within an hour that no man should any longer be able to find his way through it, or remember which direction he had meant to take. No man—but perhaps, here and there, a woman. They had long memories, women; not, perhaps, just minds, but long, accurate, retentive memories. Miriam would have known what troubled and disgusted him; known it, though it could not trouble her. She would have been able to show him how to dispose of it. She had grown so that in his mind there was nothing she could not have wiped out from his path, leaving the issue clear and clean.

He wondered, for the latest of many times, what had happened to Miriam. Had she got away out of France? Or was she still in Boissy, still taking upon herself the burdens of other people's lives, and rearranging implacable circumstances to make stepping-stones for other people's feet? If she lived she would still be doing these things. If she lived! He had never thought of her with any such qualm before. He was tired. He had begun to imagine things. Of course she was alive.

At Nibeiwa they got rid of their unwieldy charge, and in the cool darkness went gratefully to whatever ground they could find, intent upon getting as much sleep as possible before haring back to Tummar by limber or lorry at dawn. Charlie and Jim found a corner of the outer stone wall still unbroken, where there had been a deep embrasure for a look-out post. The scattered stones which cumbered the sand had been flung from fifty feet away, where tanks had crashed through at the assault: and these they built up into an additional wind-break within. and with purloined Italian blankets and half a bottle of Chianti contrived to make themselves more than ordinarily comfortable. But they still did not talk about anything that mattered a tinker's curse. Jim couldn't; his tongue stiffened at the thought. And Charlie wouldn't, though he could have started the ball rolling any time he pleased, damn him, with any one of a hundred slick gambits, because it suited him to let Jim fry, and take it out of him that way.

How would it begin, when it did begin? Something cool, and patient, and faintly amused, but calculated to get him in the wind at once.

"Well, have you got over your burst of white-hot patriotism yet?"

"If you mean have I thought better of anything I said, no. Why, are you still trying to put me in the wrong?" Maybe he wouldn't lay himself quite as wide open·as that, but whatever he said the results would be much the same.

"Put you? Little man, for all of me you can place yourself gently but firmly wherever you want yourself. All I'm wondering is why I didn't take you apart at the time, and shuffle the pieces. Can *you* think of any good reason?" Inviting him to say: "You and who else?" or something equally childish, and be annihilated; but he wouldn't, he'd say: "It must have been out of consideration for your friend, Captain Desori—whatever his name is."

No, he wasn't good at that sort of thing, but he'd keep his end up as well as he could, and maybe in the end Charlie would hit him, after all, and then they could get it over. Big as he was, he suspected Charlie would know enough tricks to lick him. He hoped so. Then the air would be clear again. For now he remembered this rare and heavy mood. It was the same in which, as a kid, he had occasionally gone round with mischief and malice in both hands, insufferable to others and a misery to himself, until someone had had the sense to lick hell out of him; and then it had been suddenly, queerly all right again, the tight dark wretchedness gone out of him, his temper as buoyant as cork, and no grudge left in him against anyone. Some sort of growing pains. "Well," he thought, "maybe I'm still growing."

But the encounter did not start, that way or any other way. He gave Charlie a smoke, and Charlie gave him a light, and they finished the bottle between them; and with the aplomb of a child, Charlie rolled himself firmly into the softest corner of sand, and went to sleep. An excellent example, but hard to follow. There was a continual activity about the whole space of the camp, a ceaseless flow of voices subdued and purposeful, so that the senses were always at strain to decipher this event from that, and sleep would not come. Some time after midnight Jim did drop into an uneasy doze, only to be awakened sharply by the spurting roar of one more motor-bike going into action; only this one was different, for it was immediately echoed by the crack of a rifle-shot.

Jim rolled over and reached for his rifle in one movement, and peered out into the lofty darkness from one of the peep-holes. Charlie was on his feet, and craning over the wall.

"Some stray coming in?" said Jim.

"Some stray going out, if you ask me. Keep a line on that clear track south-west."

"Think he's heading that way? Why, what's down there?"

"Safafi. Nowhere else he could be going. Looks like one of em had some guts, after all."

The motor-bike roared suddenly out from under the wall to their right, a rocket of sound crossing their field of fire obliquely. Jim hugged his rifle-stock and followed the sound blindly with his sights as another shot, and another, followed the fugitive. From the open desert well on their left, where the rows of trucks stood, headlight after headlight sprang out, and in another moment a searchlight followed them, cutting a lane of dazzling white through the darkness, and caught the escapist full, blinding him so that he swerved and paused for a second to recover his balance. A long, thin man, an officer; difficult to be sure of a likeness at that range, though he had jerked his head round in their direction, but he looked like the Boccaccio captain. The range was not great. Easy enough to pick him off now, before he regained control and managed to get out of the searchlight. Jim had him in his sights. His finger contracted steadily upon the trigger.

"What are you waiting for?" said Charlie Smith, levelling his own rifle across the irregular edge of the wall.

Yes, what was he waiting for? He dropped his sights and he fired; not at the man, at the motor-bike. He could do it; he knew he could do it; he was ten times the shot Charlie Smith would ever be. And wasn't it better to get the prisoner back undamaged, if it could be done? It's all very well in an attack, when your blood's up, and it's either the other fellow or you; but you can't pick people off in cold blood, like thinning rabbits.

The fugitive straightened his body, put his head down, and ripped the bike into high speed, wheeling sharply to elude the glare of the searchlight. A miss; what could you expect by that tricky, shifting, complicated light, even at a moderate range?

Jim clashed back the bolt and reloaded, but he knew he was going to be too late. Too damn clever, that's your trouble; you've given him a clear ticket now.

Charlie Smith took his time over that shot. The rider, in wheeling the bike, had turned his back upon them fairly and squarely, and his front wheel was boring at the sharp-cut edge of the darkness when Charlie got him between the shoulders. He seemed to jump clear up into the air from his mount, throwing up his arms as if for flight. The machine went over sideways in a flurry of sand; the man leaped upward and forward into the darkness, and disappeared before he fell.

Charlie Smith lowered his rifle slowly, and stood looking over the wall. The searchlight went out. By the subdued glow of headlights men ran out towards the spot where the body had fallen, and were presently seen bringing into camp what was left of Captain Desorigimenti. After the sharp sound of the shots it was very quiet.

"Did you see who it was?" asked Jim.

"I saw who I think it was," said Charlie Smith; and he sat down and re-lit the cigarette he had half-smoked before he fell asleep. They looked at each other narrowly through the darkness and were silent for a moment. "Well?" said Charlie, in a voice as acid and dry as the silence. "Are you satisfied?"

Was he? He was more at sea than ever. He could make no sense of any of it. "I don't know," he said helplessly. "I just don't get it."

"You don't know much, do you?" said Charlie Smith, in that knife-thin voice that flayed him at its leisure. "You don't know your job. How can you expect to do it properly when you don't understand what it is?"

"If that's my job," said Jim violently, "I want no part of it."

"Do you suppose I wanted it?"

"What's the good of asking me that? How am I to know? How's anyone to know, when you kid him along you're blood-brothers one minute, and shoot him in the back the next? That may be one way of making war; it isn't mine."

"No," said Charlie, "it isn't yours, or mine either. Yours is to keep a hundred yards' distance between your fastidious self and him, but to baulk at bringing him down in cold blood when it's your obvious duty. And mine——" He drew at the cigarette stump, and his cheek-bones started sudden and red out of the darkness. "There was no deceit," he said. "There

32

was only one person deceived, and that wasn't Desorigimenti. Think it over!"

He got up suddenly, and ground out the spent cigarette under his foot, and turned away, curtly, as if he had finished lecturing an irresponsible schoolboy; but in a moment he looked back. "The trouble with you, Private Benison," he said deliberately, "is that you're trying to conduct your war on an emotional basis. You want to be able to indulge all your little natural urges to hate, and pity, and spare, and relent, to freeze a middle-aged scholar who makes no pictorial appeal, and warm towards a nice-looking kid hugging a mongrel dog. It isn't as easy as that. Even your feelings have to go into battle-dress, my rugged individualist. That's one of the peculiar small hells you land yourself in without thinking in this racket. It looks simple from the outside. Once you're in you begin to find the snags. It gets worse as you go on. You haven't got very far yet."

"And you have?" said Jim bitterly.

"That's as may be," said Charlie Smith equably, and walked away into the dark.

But he had, he had! Goodness knew how, but he had. Everything that was hitting the others now had hit him and glanced off him long since. Maybe it was his age that got him by; or maybe he'd been born with more ballast than most people, and could afford to swear by reason because instinct failed to torment him as it did them. Or maybe, at that, he was wrong and Jim Benison was right. Either way, it was something talking couldn't help or change, something every man had to work out for himself as best he could, unswayed by another man's reasoning on his part as on Charlie's by another man's emotions. Logic was nothing. The only truth of it was inside you; it might change, it would change, but even its changes would not be forced. And all he had learned between Petrol Parva and Sidi Barrani, all he had discovered as he sat there alone with his back against the stone, was not the rightness and wisdom of Charlie's views, but the loneliness and helplessness and secrecy of his own.

4

Within two days they were in Sidi Barrani. The issue had never been in doubt since the first impact at Nibeiwa gave them an indication of their power; nevertheless, the last struggle before the sand-dunes, in sight of the sea and the broken white remnants of the town, was a taste of hell while it lasted. They spent hours creeping forward dune by dune, maddened by the blue of the water and the glimpses of British ships lying ever closer inshore. The defending fire was very strong, and throughout the battle wind and sand together flayed the skin from their faces and arms and knees, while the enemy in his trenches among the dunes enjoyed the only shelter possible in that barren stretch of country. But tanks on the left flank and artillery on the right broke down the wall of fire; and in the centre the Highlanders, losing patience, went in with steel and obtained the same result. After that it was a race down the scrubby slopes and into the smoking shell of the town, and a brief hand-to-hand clash, and a sudden fluttering from cover of shirts and handkerchiefs and rags, anything that would pass for white. The defenders came out in swarms, with hands raised. *"Ci rendiamo,"* they shouted, *"ci rendiamo!"*

That was the true beginning of the most delirious journey the 4th Midshires had ever made. There was no pause, no rest, no halt to assess the dizzy rise in their stock. From Sidi Barrani it was hell for leather along the coast road—the Victory Avenue designed to bring a new Cæsar to Alexandria—after the armoured brigade and those remnants of the Blackshirt troops which had withdrawn intact; on to Sollum, and Capuzzo, and so into Libya itself. By December 20th they were outside Bardia, feeling at the perimeter of the town through southerly gales in which no ship could draw inshore to repeat the bombardment so shatteringly successful at Sidi Barrani. During that siege the attackers fried by day and froze by night, but theirs was the better fate. In the first days of the new year began the most furious bombing Bardia had ever seen or dreamed of; in improving weather the defenders were blasted from air and land and sea at once, and on January 3rd the Australians went in eastward through the Italian wire, and bridged the wide defence ditch, launching a flood of British tanks and infantry down the Wadi Gerfan and into the rear of the perimeter forts.

It was not the luck of the Midshires to go in gloriously in that thrust. They were busy playing the more conventional part of poking at the southern defences from the outside, a façade behind which the Australians could operate unsuspected. They made little impression; they were meant to make little, to raise as great a commotion as possible and lose as few lives. They helped the gunners to raise a perpetual and stifling dust, made a few convincing holes in the tank obstacles, and took a number of prisoners. They did not enjoy themselves at all.

On one of these spurious expeditions they lost Charlie Smith. They had gone forward in a cloud of dust and rooted out a couple of machine-gun posts covering the perimeter; and as they fell back with their handful of prisoners, Jim suddenly missed Charlie from his elbow. It was not a matter of seeing; he had not consciously seen him for a quarter of an hour; it was rather that he felt the loss of him, as if he himself had gone lame. He turned back for him, but found no trace, and having all but presented himself into the hands of the Italians, thought it better to retire at last without satisfaction. No one could give him news. Curly and Gyp were themselves looking for Charlie, and concerned about his absence. They were sure he had been with them, and unscratched, when they moved back from the demolished gun-pits; nor did they know the moment when they had lost him. Sergeant Lake had spoken to him just before they broke from cover at the attack, but had lost touch with him immediately afterwards; he came to the reluctant conclusion that Charlie had let himself be taken prisoner, and was disposed to hold it against him that the adept of the platoon could be so maladroit. Besides, his job was to be as great an inconvenience as he could to the enemy without actual loss to his own side, and there went his best man and his unspotted record in one blow. So Charlie was mourned in many keys.

As for Jim, he couldn't believe it. It didn't seem possible that anything could happen to Charlie, whatever might go wrong for lesser men. Yet he was gone, prisoner or dead, who was to know? All night he lay sleepless in the sand, with one hand on his rifle, waiting for the possible alarm, and wondering where Charlie was, and if he was hurt. One good thing, the Eyeties had no means of getting their prisoners away from the town, for they were surrounded on all sides, from land and sea alike; whoever was in Bardia would still be securely there when the British walked in. But suppose he was already dead? Or worse, suppose he was wounded, and lying somewhere in the scrubby gravel gullies at the mercy of exposure and thirst, and sand gangrene? It didn't take long for that ghastly putrefaction to set in, once there was an open wound, however slight, to receive it. He lay and listened to the ceaseless din of shelling from the sea, the dull reverberating thunder upon thunder which could not now normally disturb his sleep. Somewhere

35

over there, beyond the fortifications, the Aussies were already fighting. He wished to God they would hurry up and let his crowd in. He wanted to find Charlie.

Towards dawn they saw flares fired from the rear of the Italian positions opposite to them, and knew with an inexpressible relief that they would soon be launched against the outer side of those fixed defences to meet the wave of Australians from within. They had spent days playing tip-and-run, but now they would go clean through with the full weight of that punch they were so tired of pulling. And if Charlie was in Bardia, he would soon be free again; and if he wasn't—— Better not think of that. Time enough afterwards to worry about the worst. But what was the platoon going to be like without Charlie Smith?

It was barely daylight when the expected order came, and the Midshires picked themselves happily out of the sand and scrub and ran like hares for the enemy positions. Since that first dash at Nibeiwa they had changed, had become, by comparison with that raw, undirected eagerness, old campaigners, the cautious borrowing dash from their neighbours, and the hotheaded learning judgment, so that the impact they made upon the enemy was co-ordinated and forceful, getting its effect by calculated power instead of by happy chance. Individuals, too, had burst into astonishing flower. Little Stringer would always be conscientious and uninspired; but who would have recognised Captain Priest in the long, lean greyhound of a man who scoured over the rocks ahead of his company shouting like a happy fiend, and leaped clean over the first Italian rifle trench as if it was game too small for him? Who would even have thought his precise and nervous throat could utter such eldritch shrieks? Or his gangling legs cover the ground with such a seven-leagued stride? He had surprised himself, as well as them. He would never be nervous of his men again, never unsure how to talk to them. The condescending note, the shying-horse approach, quitted him once for all at Sidi Barrani, where he came back to his reassembled company at dusk with his arms bare and his shirt in rags from the wire, and a curious, astonished, reminiscent grin upon his soiled and sweaty face, and having meant to compliment them in his usual pedantic manner, found that he had said quite happily and easily: "Well, chaps, was it all right?" It was very much all right, then and now. They knew where they were with him now. Anywhere he cared to go, the company would go with him.

36

Here was one officer, at least, whom his men had literally to follow, for nothing could have held him back, and no one could outrun him.

Jim made it a point of honour to keep as near to him as possible; it gave him something to fill the blind spot in his mind, the queer vacuum that came still with the first instant of action; besides taking him inevitably to the hottest centre of the encounter, which was where he wished to be if he must be in it at all. Jim could run, too, when he chose, though he had considerably more weight to carry than the lean captain; and he was close behind him when they tumbled in upon the Italians in the second line of trenches, and the close and nasty work began. There was never very much of it, they had found, where the Eyeties were concerned; even the best of them—and not all were quick to give in—had little appetite for that kind of fighting. Neither, in cold blood, would Jim have had, per- haps; but after that gap in him filled at the first impact he had no spot of cold blood in him. Afterwards, yes, marching along- side a column of unabashed, undejected prisoners, he could be cool enough, distributing his cigarettes among them with more of disdain than charity, perhaps, but still giving all and leaving himself none; but while the pinch lasted they were the enemy, the hated thing, the thing that had destroyed Tommy Goolden and ruined Miriam Lozelle, the thing that kept the 4th Mid- shires from going home. They had messed up his world beyond reclamation. He sailed into them with the bayonet as if he meant to regain his own out of their bodies; it was only after- wards, when the distorting mist cleared, that he saw that nothing he could take that way bore any likeness to anything he had lost. That was the peculiar tragedy of it, or perhaps, as Charlie would have had it, the peculiar virtue, that even victory could restore nothing, but only offer them the spare and barren earth where the house had stood, and leisure and love to build again. And better, said Charlie; but to Jim what was gone looked good enough.

Charlie kept coming back to him while he fought that day, at his elbow as he leaped down into the rifle trench, and in his mind as he climbed out of it with the shirt half torn off him, and blood—not his own blood—smearing his knees. What if he was dead? What could you do for him then, knowing him so little? No Nancy to face this time. The chaplain, poor devil, might make it his business to find the wife, but Jim never would, unless it was to satisfy a sort of morbid curiosity in himself. A chap might well wonder what sort of a woman Inez Smith was, to keep a man like Charlie reluctantly faithful even after he walked out on her. Not that she'd care if he lived or died. But the platoon would never be the same again. Who was to know the right minute to slap the kids down, before they tormented each other into a real quarrel? Who was to interpret Stringer to the rank and file, or them to Stringer? Who was to cover up for Sergeant Lake in his inevitable raging drunk when next he got within arm's length of liquor, Christian or otherwise? They couldn't do without him. He had to be alive.

A neat little range of concrete tank obstacles suddenly went up in a torrent of dust and stones fifty yards before Jim as he ran; and although he dropped flat and hugged the rock tighter than a sweetheart, a shower of stones came down on him and knocked him silly, so that he lost two minutes or so of precious time collecting his senses before he could pick himself up and go on. But for his hated tin hat, the inverted frying-pan under which his brains sizzled in the sun, he must never have got up again. As it was, his head perceptibly opened and shut at every step, and his back felt as if he had been thrashed, but he could still run.

Run he did, through the wire, which had been pierced in several places, and over the rocky brow of the escarpment, hell for leather into the struggle round the inner ramparts. From there, dimly through the haze of smoke and sand that hung upon the air, they could see by thirsty glimpses the harbour and its deep, sheltering headlands, and the soiled whitish ruins of the town three miles away down the broken slope, and beyond, the Mediterranean darkly blue, and their own ships. They knew then that it was theirs, that they could finish the job that day.

With the Australians battering at their backs and the Midlanders closing in from before them, the Italians holding this second ring of fortifications had little hope of putting up a successful resistance. They acted according to their nature. There were places where they surrendered wholesale before noon, and places where they dug themselves in as if for a dogged stand, only to flash a white rag or a shirt from their cover within half an hour, and come tamely out to join their fellows. There were even occasional pockets of real resistance, where they kept up a withering fire until late afternoon, and broke only when they were rushed with the bayonet and pricked out of their holes. Then they threw down their rifles and surrendered themselves, with relief, as if they rid themselves of a load. And while the Midshires absorbed prisoners to saturation point in this southern section of the approaches, the Australians, shortly before dusk, made the final assault upon the town itself.

It was a wonderfully brief affair. The fighting was already over. At sight of that last wild rush downhill, the defenders came streaming from cover with their hands raised. The Midshires, limping in sweaty and black from their heights a mile and a half away, saw the Italian flag flutter down from over Government House, and the Union Jack sail up in its place; and Bardia had fallen.

Entering the town at nightfall with an accumulation of prisoners picked up by the way, they encountered another long column emerging from a narrow street, with a single escort lounging alongside, rifle on arm; a tall man, this, with a feathered Italian hat worn at a rakish angle over one eye and shadowing his face, so that it was his walk which first made him recognisable. He was rolling a cigarette with the fingers of his left hand, and his attention was divided between this operation and the masonry and rubble over which he picked his leisurely way, so that he was seen before he saw them. Curly's yell made him look up sharply, and the smile was unmistakable Charlie.

" 'Strewth!'' said Curly, "look who's here!"

"The old war-horse in person," said Charlie Smith. "What offers, Sergeant, for this little lot?"

"You tote your own rubbish," said Sergeant Lake crisply. "We've got plenty already." And he took the jaunty hat by the brim and pulled it down over Charlie's eyes by way of welcoming him back to the fold. It was rather as if he had never been away. He unbonnetted himself with the most placid good humour, and fell into step beside Jim, leaving his prisoners to follow or not, as they chose.

"You're a cool one!" observed Jim. "Suppose that lot decided to walk the other way, and try and find some guns?"

The black eyebrows lifted ever so slightly. "My dear boy! Them? They wouldn't let me out of their sight for all the coconut palms in Hawaii. I've guaranteed them my personal recommendation for a quick, safe trip into Egypt, and a peaceful pastoral life till the end of the war. What do they want with guns? They've just carefully stacked all their own rifles in an open space back there, and mighty glad to get rid of them, too. I've got a *ghaffir* standing guard over 'em, an old patriarch by the name of Suleiman—looks like Suleiman bin Daoud, but probably not the same guy." He added dryly: "Don't worry, if he takes it into his head to try 'em out, it'll be on Italians."

"You're pretty darn sure of yourself, aren't you?" said Jim, between admiration and anger. Hadn't he spent the whole of the night tearing himself apart over this exasperating devil of a side-kick of his? And all the time Charlie Smith had probably been snoring in an Italian blanket, unscratched and completely unshaken. Jim could have kicked him. But what wouldn't he have given for a measure of this experienced and sustained assurance which tamed everything to its own designs?

"Yes, pretty damn sure!" agreed Charlie, with a furtive smile. "Weren't you?"

"Oh, I knew you'd turn up again. Your sort of old wangler always does. I haven't lost any sleep."

And Charlie laughed. That was what he would do, of course. What was the use of trying to pull the wool over his eyes? He could see clean through Jim any time he liked, and out the other side. He threw back his head and let it go, a big, clear, echoing laugh that made Italian heads turn and Italian teeth flash in sycophantic sympathy.

"Remind me to take you apart, some time," said Jim, himself reluctantly grinning.

"Oh, I will, I will! Whenever you like! Maybe I owe you that. Seriously, though," he said, over-stating his own gravity, "it was money for old rope. They don't believe in fighting for lost causes, these people. From the time it becomes impolitic to hold Bardia, Bardia's a gone coon. I was more scared of those damned ships and their confounded gunners than of all the Eyeties in Libya."

They tramped along together in the dusty evening through narrow, overhung streets towards the harbour, and of the two it was Jim who limped, Jim who hunched sore shoulders to lessen the pressure of his rifle-sling. He felt by then as if his back had been carefully flayed from shoulders to waist.

"What happened to you?" asked Charlie, suddenly turning upon him the disconcerting gaze of his clairvoyant eyes. "Seems to me you fared worse than I did by a long way. What was it? Blast?"

"Half the damn tank barriers went up in dust and fell on me. It's nothing but bruises—nothing broken, but I'll be stiff as hell in a few hours. Better if I kept on the move, I suppose, but lord, could I use some sleep!"

"Fall yourself out of this Lord Mayor's Show, then, my lad, or be dragged out. I'm going to work on you with my own hands. When I've finished with you you'll be fit for the next Libyan Olympics. Come on, we're going to turn over this little job and go back to see how many rifles my *ghaffir* has palmed up to now. I know where there's oil for the looting, and I'm not so bad as a masseur. We might even manage a drink, with a little finesse."

"The pubs are shut," said Jim, abandoning the idea of putting all the sensible questions he had meant to put.

"Black market, laddie. I've got a nice little racket all worked out."

Yes, whatever he did, whatever happened to him, Charlie would always fall on his feet, and whoever came up against him, Charlie would always get his own way. Queer how he'd failed with the shadowy woman, his wife! He had no difficulty with men. He abstracted Jim from that escort, with Sergeant Lake's blessing, inside five minutes, and within half an hour had him laid out at ease upon a heap of rugs inside the shell of a partly-ruined house, while the *ghaffir*, who was enjoying himself hugely, sent one self-important small boy for olive oil in a chipped pottery bowl, and another to abstract wine from a half-demolished and abandoned shop; which he did with complete success. It was raw, heady stuff, with a bite like a rabid dog, not worth pinching, except that it cleared their throats of the dust and smoke of the day; they discouraged, not without difficulty, both the *ghaffir* and his boy from presenting them with unlimited quantities of the ghastly stuff, but at its worst it was better than the water. With a roof over them, and comparative quietness, they were very comfortable together all the evening. The pause, they knew, could only be brief.

Jim lay on his belly upon the piled rugs, his head in his arms, while Charlie kneaded at the stiffening muscles of his back. He lay in a pleasant, dreamy state, half asleep, drugged by the wine buzzing in his brain and the sensuous soothing rhythm of the fingers in his back; and being half drawn out of himself, was ready to talk most freely when speech was most difficult.

"What *did* happen to you last night?" he asked. "You didn't get hit? One minute you were with us, and the next I couldn't find hide or hair of you anywhere. I came back to look for you." He could say that now without realising that it was an admission of the human weakness against which Charlie had warned him with so much severity. Nor would Charlie remind him of it now.

"No," he said quietly, "I wasn't hit. It was a stone that did

for me. We were climbing that weathered slope on the way back
—remember?—and I stepped on a rounded stone—sand action,
I take it, it could hardly be water—that rolled and brought me
down a purler. Didn't bust a thing, just winded me and slid
me back forty feet or so; and when I got back on my feet there
were Eyeties all round me. So I went like a lamb. I'm all for
caution. They sent me down here. I didn't see any more of our
chaps, but there must be some around. The shelling from those
ruddy ships got so damned hot that everybody went to ground,
and took me with 'em.''

"I hope you spent a comfortable night," said Jim, flinching
from a too shrewd probing of a more than usually tender spot.
He was thinking of his own. He hadn't felt like that since the
first few nights in hiding at Boissy-en-Fougères, when he had
been morally certain that Tommy Goolden was going to
die.

"Oh, not so dusty, really. We were in a cellar under a big
block, well on the landward side of the town. Plenty of grub,
and heaps of bedding, but they were getting pretty windy.
Don't suppose I was much help. I kept telling 'em we had
over a hundred thousand men outside, and lashings of armour
and guns, and it was a cinch we'd be in Bardia by to-night. I
told 'em they were fools if they fought, because if they
surrendered they'd be treated well and sent off to a nice safe
camp in Egypt, and anyhow the town was as good as gone, so
they had nothing to gain by making us mad. They were feeling
that way to begin with, but harping on it discouraged 'em even
more. So when they heard you chaps were inside the defences
and coming in hot and strong they gave up. Asked me to
accept their surrender and do what I could for 'em. They gave
me my rifle back, and I told 'em to pile arms down here in that
little court, and took 'em along to meet the rest of you. That's
all about it. Hold still a minute, kid, you've got the heck of a
bruise along your ribs here. Do me a favour, will you? Yell if
this hurts worse than the rest. I want to know; if all's well it
shouldn't; if it does, you're booked for the M.O. and no bones
about it.''

The flexing fingers, gentle but quite relentless, hurt like hell
everywhere, and soothed like honey at the same time; but this
was no worse than the rest, and got no more than a grunt out of
Jim.

"That's all right. A bruise is all it is. No Blighty for you,
no nice Egyptian base hospital, no convalescence in a frilly

dahabieh on the Nile. Just another spell of sand, and scrub, and flies, and more sand."

"I'm not complaining," said Jim. "My ticket says all the way. I didn't take a return."

Charlie sat back at length with a sharp sigh. "All right, you'll do now. Put your shirt on again, and then you can go to sleep. You're half-way out already. I'm going to sit and watch my watchman."

In the verges of sleep, stretched out on his face, Jim saw clearly the paradox he had passed by. He had a nerve, had Charlie Smith! He was a nice one to preach against the indulgence of human instincts, and the swaying of reason by inordinate affection, wasn't he? He, whose loss was not to be contemplated; he, who himself was a house where all whose lives touched his, even for a moment, might go freely out and in for shelter and warmth. They did it, too constantly, making use of him, sustaining themselves by him, copying him, using his calm when their own was frayed away, and his endurance when their own was exhausted, and his hard sanity when their own fretful foolishness was getting them into deep water. It took some thinking out, this aspect of Charlie, because it came from so far below the suave surface of him. It was not deliberate. Who would deliberately go to the endless trouble of trying to increase the quality and stature of every person he met? It flowed out of him, without his concern, out of no personal regard for the people it influenced and no earnest desire to do the world good. It flowed out of him because it was there and must have free outlet, because it was an inexhaustible energy and must be put to work. And in following its nature it did something very strange and unforeseen to his. There might be a sort of love from the benefited to the benefactor, certainly, but suddenly Jim knew that it was nothing compared to the love that went the other way.

He lay there with his face in his arms, not quite sober, not quite asleep, unshaven, unwashed, his nostrils full of the sour, warm smell of the rugs under him; and he saw what he could not remember next day, what he could not keep more than a moment; he was shaken by the revelation of God's love for the world, the astonished, humbled, exalted love you have for the thing you have comforted and served. In little things and great things it was the same. He recognised it in people who had seemed until then as commonplace as himself, as if little flames had leaped up within their flesh to make them glow like lamps

43

in his memory. He knew how Charlie Smith felt, kneading the twists from Jim Benison's back, and the creases from his mind. He knew how Miriam had felt, when she held him against her cheek at parting, and her heart beat upon his heart. He knew in the last moment of all, just before he slept, that once and again the same astonishing happiness had been in his own mind and passed unrecognised. The rapture, the arrogance of martyrdom, these hung very fitly upon some people, but it took raw Libyan wine to make him see himself in them; and upon this ludicrous vision he fell asleep, grinning, and slept all night without a break, and did not dream at all.

5

Most of what they remembered afterwards of Tobruk was sand; thirteen days of it, eating sand, drinking sand, breathing sand, and the two days of battle at the end of it did little to distract their minds by graver issues from that exquisite discomfort. It was bad enough while they were on the move by the coast road from Bardia, before they had to sit down and camp in it, before they moved inland from the comfortable blue sight of the sea to encircle the outer defences of Tobruk, and scratched themselves homes in the earth, and settled down to endure it in comparative stillness. From then on it became steadily worse. During those thirteen days and nights while there was no air to breathe, and no sky to illuminate their world, no sun nor moon nor stars where so many stars had been, nothing but a dun-coloured fog and an acid, abrasive wind, their battle was with Libya itself rather than with the Italians.

They had fondly imagined that what they had experienced at Sidi Barrani was a sand-storm, but this was the real thing. Their skins were raked raw in every exposed spot as if they had been scrubbed with coarse emery, and grains of sand found their way into every fold of clothing and chafed even the covered parts of their bodies so that they erupted in red, raw weals. *Heskanit* burrs came down the wind also and added their prickly irritation to the leisurely tortures of this minor hell. Sand improved upon what sand had begun, settling and clinging in the sore stubble of beards, and the inflamed creases of ears and lips and eyelids, aggravating tenderness into rawness, and rawness into festering sores. Sand filtered into their nostrils, and stripped the membranes within, leaving a watery agony that would not heal. Sand made lime-kilns of their mouths and sulphurous

44

chimneys of their throats, so that they were further weakened by being unable to swallow. Fortunately they had been, at the outset, in the very pink of condition and the highest of spirits, so that apart from the discouraging effect of the delay they were in good case to sit down doggedly and endure all with stubbornness. A few who had more serious skin wounds became gangrenous, and were taken away, and some of these died; but the rest made themselves what shelter they could, and stuck it out, shaving in the dregs of their tea, washing once in four or five days if they were lucky, and then in a cupful of water between two or three of them, and with much cursing and pain. Without wishing to be morose they reached the point where the agony of speech was too great to be invited except for an end even greater, and for the lack of human conversation grew morose at last against their will. There was nothing the Italians could fire from guns or pack into hand-grenades to match this misery. None the less, they knew Tobruk was theirs once the wind dropped and the sky cleared; there was never any doubt about that.

Towards the tenth day the dun darkness thinned, and the earth steadied under their feet. There were periods of blistering wind still for two days more, but between these the sun and the stars returned in their courses, and there was air to breathe. The fiery eruptions subsided, though the noon heat and midnight cold plagued them still and made the healing slow. The sand settled again, and the earth resumed solidity and shape. It was firm enough by the thirteenth day to carry them forward; and they were panting to go.

That night no one in or around Tobruk slept at all. The noise of the bombardment went on all night long, wave after wave of 'planes sweeping across the town; and at dawn all the groupings of British batteries poured in from the desert the heaviest barrage of the Libyan war. When it subsided, the sappers suddenly sprang out of cover and went tearing across the open for the enemy wire. Theirs was the first and the worst job. The wired area was full of minefields and booby-traps. Jim would rather have trotted into a box-barrage he could hear and see than into that harmless-looking sector of desert, but then, that didn't happen to be Jim's line of country. It cut both ways. He remembered a nonchalant sapper sitting beside an exposed booby-trap in the ruins of Bardia, very much at his ease with a cigarette, who had asked him how things went as he passed, and being told that he had just come from the final and fiercest bayonet charge against the Italian batteries in the southern perimeter, took all the gods and devils to witness that hell should assuredly pop before he would go poking the gunners out of heavy batteries with a ten-inch splinter of steel. Yet he could and did, so placidly that only afterwards did the chill of realisation contract Jim's spine, dismantle and carry away in his hand the detonator that should have set off a considerable charge of gelignite, enough, probably, to have wiped out a platoon. He did it whistling, as if he had been removing a worn-out washer from a tap in the kitchen sink; and yet he didn't fancy the quick run-in and the short scrap, which was so easy and thoughtless by comparison. Yes, it took all kinds to make a war.

After the sappers the infantry went in. The wire was breached at intervals for a distance of several miles, and the Aussies, first to be launched against the outer defences, went through the first positions joyously, ravenous for action after the demoralising delay they had endured. The Midshires, moving forward steadily at some distance behind, could just see the quivering tremor that seemed to pass along the perimeter as the impact came, and then there was only smoke and turmoil ahead of them, and the converging rush of British tanks passing the wire. They would have liked to be forward there among the real action, but their job was to follow on and finish whatever the Aussies left undone. The ground ahead was uneven in detail, barren and brown, rising somewhat to the ridge which marked the perimeter. The town, two miles or more distant, they could not yet see, but its position they knew by the column of black smoke which poured upward and splayed writhing hands against the sky. The oil reservoirs were ablaze in the port.

Inside the wire, they began to meet a few walking wounded of the Aussies, and very soon the first hurrying columns of Italian prisoners. One of the escorts, an Australian private with a bloody left hand buttoned into his shirt, but the right exceedingly competent upon an Italian revolver, advised them cheerfully to watch their step on the road ahead. There was a spot nearly half a mile up, he said, where the rocks limited the field of advance, and the surviving batteries on the ridge had the range pat and were playing hell there. He said the cussedest thing was that he had a throat so badly inflamed that he daren't smoke, although he'd sell his immortal soul for a cigarette. He said he'd knock the block off any bloke who offered him one.

46

He was right about the road. They were advancing in open order, at a walk, as their instructions were, and suddenly young Curly, who was on Jim's right, swerved inwards like a baulking horse, and said: "Oh, my Gawd!" and his face went greenish and sick. Ahead of them, winding like a serpent along the easiest track, a long column of Italian prisoners came; and their own batteries, playing that range for all it was worth, caught them in their intermittent barrage, and blew the column to shreds before the Midlanders' eyes. Jim took Curly by the neck and pushed him down to ground, since he was past hearing the word of command for himself; but even so he stared ahead with eyes like organ-stops, and you could hear the breath whistle between his teeth. You couldn't wonder. He'd seen nothing like that at Sidi Barrani, no, nor at Bardia. It had been like a sort of tough game to him up to now, but he didn't like this. And Gyp was yards away from him, close by Sergeant Lake, craning anxiously after his kid brother like a hen with one chick, and being told for his pains, and with quiet but paralysing profanity, to keep his qualified head down and his mind on what he was doing. How could he, knowing what Curly was going through? Half the time he played up to the kid, and from sheer high spirits they drove each other mad; but the other half he stood over him like a tigress over her young, trying to keep even the wind from blowing on him; and here they had to be yards apart when the nastiest thing either of them had ever seen hit Curly in the pit of the stomach and knocked all the guts out of him. Almost as if he was suddenly transported from his own mind into Gyp's, Jim found himself thinking, with rage and impatience and protest: "My God, if he's sick he'll never forgive himself or me or any of us."

It was very dreadful, the more dreadful because it was paraded before them like a scene upon a stage, in which they had no part. They counted, one after another, seven shells that burst among that column, and as many more that struck within damaging distance upon one side or the other. Showers of sand and small stones came down upon them, and fragments less harmless than these. They saw between the eruptions of smoke and soil, turning slowly in mid-air like leaves rolled in a wind, the bodies of men. They saw them fall, and drift, and lie, like mere discarded rags, and the survivors trampling them, living and dead alike, as they ran madly to escape the inescapable slaughter. They ran in all directions, sightlessly, dragging mutilated limbs and crushed bodies, and the air was full of a thin, horrible screaming.

Jim put his hand out and took good hold of young Curly's shoulder. He could hear how little whimpering breaths came between his teeth, and the sweat was standing on his forehead and lips as heavy as dew. It was touch and go with Curly. He might break if you touched him, or he might turn round and ask you who the hell you thought you were patronising; but if this tension went on he would break for certain, and that would be as near as damn-all the end of him. So Jim took hold of him and shook him, and said: "Snap out of it, kid!" in a voice so dry and authoritative that it sounded to him more like Charlie Smith talking than Jim Benison.

Curly turned his head, and fixed his eager, agonised eyes upon the speaker, and asked, as if he thought he was talking to God Almighty: "Ain't there anything we can *do*? Why don't they stop firing? Can't we stop 'em? We could, surely! There must be some way."

"Talk sense!" said Jim. "They can't see what's happening. You don't think they're doing this on purpose, do you?"

He sounded all the more acid about it because he felt pretty sick himself. But there was nothing anyone could do, as long as the barrage continued. Run as they would, they couldn't get out of range. The bursts went on, and the pathetic, horrible crying. There was no getting it out of your ears.

Curly said: "I can't stand it!" His voice went up. He got his hands under him, and made to lever himself from the ground in a cat's spring, but Jim took him by the neck and forced him down again, not gently.

"Where the hell do you think you're going?" he said. "You stay here and stay down. There's nothing you can do there except make one more. Ain't there enough already?"

Curly's cheek was bleeding a little where he had cut it on a stone as Jim jerked him back, and he was winded. He wiped away the blood on the back of his hand in a dazed fashion, and took a minute to draw breath, and suddenly Jim could see by his eyes that he was as mad as hell. That was a good sign. Curly had the sort of temper that took up all his time once it was roused, and all other people's, too.

"You take your hands off me," he flared. "I'll do what I damn well like for all of you. If you're scared, I'm not. We could get some of those chaps out, sure, if we weren't a lot of white-livered rats. It's only because they're Eyeties. You don't care what happens to 'em! You don't give a damn if they get shelled to bits——''

"Why, you gutless little perisher!" said Jim. "You'll do fine things. You'll go trotting slap-bang into a heavy barrage, will you, to fish out an Eyetie or two or get blown to pieces? You fancy yourself, don't you?" He stood back amazed at himself. The likeness was unmistakable. The words were not the right words, but the tone was the chill, incisive tone Charlie Smith had used to him by the wall of Nibeiwa. "You know why you want to chuck yourself away like that, don't you?" he said. "Because you know damn well it'd be a sight easier and pleasanter than this is. Because you haven't the guts in you to stick it out here, and have to remember it, and still carry on as if nothing had happened to you. Because you're scared as all hell of just standing by and seeing it, that's why."

Curly made a noise in his throat like a cat growling, and rolled over in the sand, and hit him. There wasn't much force to it because he couldn't get any weight behind it, but it was well-meant enough, a left-handed swing as vicious and desperate as a cornered leopard's leap, and almost as dexterous. Jim rode it, and was curiously pleased to feel the hard young knuckles split his lip; pleased and angry at the same time, so that he thought first: "Well, that ought to do the trick!" and in the next breath: "All right, my lad, I'll take that back out of you some other time!" He brushed away a smear of blood, and looked steadily over his massaging hand into Curly's furious and frightened face. The smoke of a nearer explosion went over them, and neither of them knew it.

Jim grinned, and that fictional anger of his went by the board. "Well," he said approvingly, "that's more like it!"

Curly's face went suddenly quite white, and he began to shake; and then that stopped, and it was all right. All right, except that he knew he'd been hefted over a bad patch on somebody else's power, and therefore somebody else had been very well aware how things had been with him; but that would make it the more surely all right. His self-love was deeply offended; you could feel it drawing itself together in him and becoming rigid. Jim Benison had known he was going to make a fool of himself, and had presumed to put out a well-meaning hand and fish him back from the edge. Even the muscles of his face went stiff, but this time with another tension.

"He'll never forgive me," thought Jim, astonished how

much he knew of it. "It's like watching him through a keyhole, and being caught at it. Ah, well, he'll get over it!" And he was quite undisturbed; for the kid was a sensible kid, the kind that loses very easily all prints of mortification and self-consciousness and resentment, and comes out smooth and buoyant again, like a Sorbo ball. Not to-day, perhaps, not even for a day or two, but pretty soon he'll get tired of being on his guard, and come scrambling down, and act the way he's always acted with me, as if I was a collie dog he'd grown up with. You don't have to put on any sort of appearance with a dog; he knows you through and through anyhow, and it still makes no difference with him.

Opportunely, the barrage ceased then, abruptly, leaving a sudden vacuum of quiet in the surrounding din. They did not yet know what had happened to put an end to the slaughter, but afterwards it was made plain that some of the Australian infantry, working round behind the Italian positions, had rushed the batteries with the bayonet, and virtually wiped out their crews before they had even time to realise what was happening, and react with the usual scream of "Ci rendiamo!" The incident was over. It was between the two of them, one of those clear, shattering things which stand out strangely among the confused fog of battle, so much smaller than their environment, and yet so enduringly remembered where the rest is forgotten. Remembered by one person only; Jim knew enough by now to know that Curly would forget it as lightly as a girl kissed out of turn, or one drink too many on Saturday night, and Sunday's resultant headache.

Well, he thought, as they picked themselves up out of the stony sand and went forward at the double to overtake their time-table, you take from people, and you give to people, in equal measure. What you receive from one you give in turn, some time, somewhere, to another. Very seldom can you return anything to the person who gave it to you. That's the way it is. But you have to bestow it somewhere. It has to flow. It can't be stemmed. It goes on and on from link to link, the continuity of human wisdom and human affection, too strong to be dammed, too stubborn to relent. That's the first and most inexplicable secret of survival. If it stopped, humanity itself would die. People like Miriam Lozelle, people like Charlie Smith, they are the life-blood of the world.

This he thought as he ran, and having entered, it quitted him as swiftly, and he was left doubling up-hill towards the still smoking batteries, and the sentimental revelation was gone like a dream, vivid but unremembered.

They made the crown of the ridge, and ran into the tail of the Australians. There was little left to do there. One gun still defiantly firing, but it fired its last before they could reach it; and a number of prisoners to be sent back under guard, but a few of the walking wounded could handle that assignment with ease; and that was all, except the grim job that awaited the advancing medical columns.

They were now inside the defence ring, and could spread themselves to mop up the successive ramifications of fort and earthwork and gun emplacement within, more or less at leisure. It was barely noon, and they were somewhat ahead of their time-table, with many hours of daylight in hand. Tobruk was not expected to be a one-day job. There remained, studded here and there upon the high ground in the irregular gradient falling to the edge of the coastal escarpment, several formidable forts to be reduced before the town itself could be even sighted; in the eastern sector a group of three, Boella, Nuovo and Markuchi; farther west, in the centre of the inner defence ring, Pilastrino and Solario; and north-west near the road to Derna, Fort Airente. But once within the inviolate line of the perimeter all these could be circumvented and reduced at ease, even if the process was a slow one. Between Nuovo and Boella the attackers flowed, between Boella and Markuchi, and early in the afternoon settled down to the task of possessing all three. It took the Midshires all day to get into Markuchi, but they were past the stage where all must be done in a hurry. It was their job to finish what had been roughed out by the Australians of the spear-head, and in an area honeycombed with Italian booby-traps, mines and gun-pits that might fairly be considered a full afternoon's job.

They adapted themselves with surprising facility to this cautious work. The greyhound Captain Priest became a ferret, ingeniously careful in approaching the innumerable bolt-holes, patiently ferocious in depopulating them. He had his short-comings in the world of army routine, but in a battle he had only one fault, that he conceived it his duty to keep his men out of situations into which he himself would gallop enthusiastically without a qualm; rather as if he thought himself invulnerable, but that they knew he did not in these moments think of himself at all. Little Stringer, painstakingly modelling himself on his captain, was rather a liability than an asset, because he would hurl himself into the same dangers, with nothing like the same aplomb to get him out again, so that they had constantly to keep one anxious eye on him and stand ready to effect a rescue; but still he meant well. They couldn't all take to it like ducks to water.

There were losses, of course. Apart from the normal tale of dead and wounded inevitable in the teeth of such a fire, they left outside the earthworks of Markuchi a corporal and seven men of the company, all victims of a booby-trap the sappers had missed. All of them were written off as dead, but Jim heard afterwards that Bob Calder, whom he had seen with his own eyes blown twenty yards through the air and to all appearance smashed against the ground, had been salvaged by the ambulance men still alive and voluble, and was safely recovering in an Egyptian hospital. The medical columns were doing a good job, and one Jim thanked God he didn't have to do. It was all very well sticking a finger on a pressure-point now and again until the stretcher blokes arrived, or shoving in a strip of wood or a discarded rifle as a temporary splint to stop some poor devil from wriggling himself into permanent cripplehood; but as a full-time job—no, not for him, thanks. He preferred the fighting end of the business, however tough, however unsatisfactory.

Late in the afternoon the forts began to fall. They had made, on the whole, a good resistance; but when the Australians, two miles or more away to westward, lost patience and cut their way into Solario the enthusiasm of the surviving garrisons cooled rapidly, and they surrendered one by one. The Midshires walked into Markuchi just after six o'clock, and were detained there for the better part of an hour more before they were satisfied that no resistance and no mines remained. There were a great number of prisoners. There were very many dead. It was, Jim reckoned, the best show he had yet seen the Eyeties put up; but like all their flashes of spirit it had petered out too soon. They had no stamina, that was their trouble

At dusk the attackers had reached the edge of the coastal escarpment, and could look down the sharp slope into the town itself, two miles away. It was theirs, Tobruk; they had it between their hands safely enough, and could afford to wait for daylight to finish the job. In the meantime, the steady barrage from the desert went on, but the P.B.I. could take a rest, and what scraps of sleep they could find; and food, for they had not eaten all day.

Jim found himself a sheltered angle of rock, and sat down to watch the play of fire and smoke over the harbour. The coils of black, thick smoke pulsing upwards from the burning oil-reservoirs in the town blotted out the headland beyond, so that he could only guess at the positions of Fort Perrone, and the airfield, and the wireless station; but in the harbour itself it was light as day, for an Italian liner stood well out in the anchorage, blazing from stem to stern, and the old warship *San Giorgio*, whose guns had plagued them for thirteen days in the desert, lay off the lighthouse at the harbour-mouth, burning more sullenly, with a red lustre, and not yet abandoned. Beyond this fantastic oval of dark water and fiery reflected light the billowing smoke, oily black above and lurid red below, made a towering back-cloth, cutting off earth and sea and sky so that Tobruk lay isolated and fiercely glowing in the heart of a great void. It was fascinating and appalling. This was what they had waited thirteen days in abject misery to see. For this, also, the people of England must be waiting. He imagined they were getting excited by now, looking eagerly for the headlines in the morning, poring over maps. A success is always a success. They would probably forget that all this meteoric trail of glory arose from the desperate need to remove the threat from the borders of Egypt. It was a defensive gesture, not an offensive one. Queer he should suddenly think of it like that now, but it was very clear to him. They had struck, not to destroy the enemy, but to deliver themselves; and the result, however successful, would not be to bring victory so much nearer, but to set defeat so much farther away. "My oath!" he thought grimly, "what would Joe say if I told him that? Or Dad, for that matter? They probably think we're winning the bloody war hands down."

A year ago he would have thought so himself. He had learned a lot since then. Maybe you're better off if you don't.

Charlie Smith came silently to his elbow, and bending over from behind the rock against which he leaned, stuck a cigarette between his lips and held a match to it.

"Oh, it's you," said Jim, inhaling. "I thought you were miles away chivvying the supply chaps. Don't tell me they were on time!"

"They were so! Ahead of time, in fact. Oh, there's been nothing the matter with the arrangements for this trip." He looked down into the abyss, where Jim's eyes were fixed. "So that's Tobruk!"

"That's Tobruk. How long do you give it from the kick-off in the morning?"

Charlie sat down and considered the problem at leisure. "I'll be generous, and make it four hours. That's on distances alone. As far as resistance goes it could be done in one. Actually, it's all over bar the shouting now. The town really fell when the Aussies got peeved with Solario."

"Well, and what happens next? Where do we go from here?"

"Derna, Benghazi, Sirte, Tripoli, Tunis——"

"You don't believe that," said Jim suddenly, "any more than I do. They can't afford to let it get to that stage. If the Eyeties can't stop up, the Germans will come into it themselves."

"And you think *they* can?" asked Charlie casually.

"They can do a damned sight better than this with half the numbers. With what they can easily afford to bring—yes, I figure they stand well above an even chance of stopping us. We'll do bloody well if they don't."

"Can it be," said Charlie softly, "that you are not satisfied? Haven't we done well? Aren't we making the first successful advance of the war? Isn't it a pleasant change from retreating?"

"All right, you can leave it at that. I know you're speaking what are supposed to be my lines, you supercilious devil. Yes, it is a pleasant change, but I'm not kidded into thinking it any bigger than it is. Say we make Derna—say we make Benghazi —we can do it; what's to stop us? They can't land enough German stuff in the time. But after that they've *got* to do something, before we get too good a hold on the Mediterranean. It isn't a matter of saving face. Think they care what happens to their little tame Musso and his prestige? No, they've got to stop us because we're going to be too damn dangerous if they don't. That's why I'm sure we'll be fighting Germans as well as Eyeties before many weeks are out."

"And you don't like the idea?" asked Charlie, with a furtive smile; producing out of his friend's mouth, as he had a queer, constant way of doing, words no one had known were there; not even Jim himself.

"Like it? I'm living for it. We've got to meet them sooner or later, and I want it sooner. I've got scores to settle with the Germans. No, what I don't like is the way most of us, here and at home, are jumping to the damn-fool conclusion that the war's half-over, just because we've pushed the Eyeties back to

54

Tobruk. I'm all for meeting them, but not with both eyes shut; and I've got a horrible idea that's what we shall be doing."

Charlie narrowed his eyes against the smoke of his cigarette, and looked across the valley into the coppery, quivering sky. Sometimes he knew what was coming; sometimes it was an echo of something within himself; but sometimes, as now, he did not know. He just sat there to receive whatever confidences emerged, and troubled the standing waters with his gentle, provocative questions, and the elicited thought came out and dazzled him as if he had had no part in it.

Well, what if this was a true presentiment? Was Saul also among the prophets? Why not? Even Saul could learn.

"That being the case," he said deliberately, "what do you, whose eyes, I gather, are wide open, propose to do about it?"

"My eyes," said Jim, "are not by any means wide open. Only sometimes I see a little out of one of 'em. Having been there before!" He paused. Between the reverberations of gun-bursts the night was full of small, sibilant echoes, like voices. He thought of Miriam. That was not strange; she was never far from him, he thought of her whenever he could pause for a moment to look beyond the immediate present. There was something she had said—had she? He couldn't recall the occasion. She or someone. Speaking of the first horrible enlighten-ment, when you despair of the world and want only to gather what comfort you can, and run away and hide somewhere, and make-believe that nothing exists but yourself and your little goods. "I tell you, this also passes, as the blind confidence passed." Yes, that was Miriam, it could be no one else. There was more, if he could only recapture it. "There is nothing that cannot be borne." Yes, that was Miriam. That was the fourth-dimensional way she had of containing the world instead of being contained by it, of deflecting circumstances instead of being mauled by them.

We take, and we give. Now if you could give that—to every-one, to every soul in this army, to every soul at home! If you could issue it from stores, like a tin of Blanco, to every man drawing his kit: one article of faith, untarnishable. That would be worth doing.

But to attempt to superimpose it upon them in words—no, it could not be done that way. They would listen and not believe; or they would believe and not understand. And at best, for the near-blind to venture to lead the blind——!

"Do about it?" he said. "Nothing. What is there to do?"

They took Tobruk, and went on to take Derna with even less trouble. All these North African towns, they said, were alike, white outside and dirty and smelly inside, sitting between the escarpment and the sea, with a few palm-trees and a few piers and stages to pass them as ports, and all with the same eastward-opening anchorage. This, of course, was before they hit Benghazi. Some were bigger than others; Derna was the most of a town they had struck; but otherwise the monotony was as complete in its way as the inland monotony of sand. Never mind, said the optimists, after Tripoli and Tunis there would be Italy, for a change from this endless desert. Why not? What was to stop them? Half the Italian forces in Libya were either destroyed or taken, and the other half on the run hell for leather with old "Electric Whiskers" Berganzoli in the lead, and quite incapable now of turning in time to make any considerable stand. It was no longer a series of battles, but a point-to-point race, with the Eyeties always one jump ahead. There was no difficulty whatever in beating them; but they were hard to catch.

In the breathless intervals of the chase, the Midshires talked a good deal of optimistic rubbish about where they were going and the things they were going to do. Who could blame them? For most of them it was the first campaign, and no one could wonder if they were a little drunk with its success. As for those who had been in Flanders, and known the dizzy feeling of top-speed retreat before this taste of headlong advance, they kept their mouths shut and their minds open, and made the most of the hour. No use trying to depress the youngsters. It might never happen. But their own fingers were crossed.

From Derna the pursuit went on by the coastal road, the Australians in full career for Cyrene and Benghazi; but certain units, and with them the Midshires, were diverted, for no good reason that they could see, south-westward at a sudden angle, inland of the Jebel Akhdar, and full across the desert. South of the mountains the mechanised columns converged with and followed convoys of tanks which had crossed the desert from Egypt parallel with the coastal advance, and had seen fighting in the northern villages of Kufra while the Midshires were closing in on Capuzzo and Sollum. They swopped attack stories with the tank crews over the increasingly brief halts for food, and agreed that something extremely urgent was calling them cross-country at this breathless speed.

"Reach the coast!" said one of the tank drivers, gulping tea. "That's what our old man says. Reach the coast south of Bengazi, he says, that's our only order of the day, and reach it pretty damn quick. There's no roads, he says, and not being a bloody camel I'm not interested in cameltracks. I'll set a compass course, he says, across this go-damned country, and I'll *sail* the go-damned convoy in. Crazy, our old man is, but if he says he's going somewhere, you can bet your life he's going there. The coast south of Benghazi it is for ours. 'Strewth, but I don't like this blind flying. Give me a road every time!"

The Midshires, who had already suffered from the fiercest burst of speed of the whole trek, rubbed their bruises and agreed with him fervently. They did not yet know how fast nor how blindly they were to travel before they reached the coast again.

"I suppose," said Jim, "that means we shall be taking a poke at Benghazi from the south while the Aussies crash in from the north-east."

"Don't ask me. I just drive where they tell me. But we're in such an almighty hurry it looks as if they mean to shut the back door this time. The sooner the better! I'm sick of chasing the same Eyeties in and out of the same old towns. Maybe if we finish that lot off we can start fresh on the next."

"You've put your finger on it," said Charlie. "Ever since Sidi Barrani they've salved a certain amount out of every town we've taken. Our job is to cut Graziani and the Benghazi divisions off from Tripoli. We want the army this time, not just the city. Lord, that means some jaunt!"

"And your old bones ache already," said Curly irreverently. "You should carry an air cushion among your kit." He was quick in rolling aside, but Charlie was quicker, and one loudly-ringing slap got home on the seat of his dusty shorts before he was safely out of range.

"Listen to that!" said Charlie disapprovingly, shaking his fingers. "If I were upholstered like you I should need no air cushion. Padded like a blooming girl, so help me! You ought to take more exercise, my lad."

"Leave him alone," said Jim. "I use him as a cushion in the lorry. Don't you go putting ideas in his head."

He could talk that sort of tosh now with the rest of them, and get no sudden, wary, reminding looks to set him aside. The irrepressible Curly, whose straightness was like the straightness of a larch sapling, and his flanks as flat and hard as boards, accepted these and other such libellous pleasantries from him as complacently as from any. He had forgotten the shameful occasion when he had put Jim Benison clean out of his acquaintance; or if it was not forgotten, all the sting was gone from the facts as he remembered them, which was the same thing. Nothing rankled for long with Curly.

Round a large mouthful of the inevitable bully-beef, Gyp asked indistinctly: "How many men should you say Graziani has left? I mean, in Benghazi?"

"Dunno. Maybe twelve to fifteen thousand and a fair amount of armour, I'd say."

"And how many have we? Here, on this little trip?"

"I wouldn't worry," said Charlie. "With you and Curly we should be all right."

"No, but seriously, how many?"

"Don't ask me! Not above three thousand with armour and guns and infantry and all."

"Might be good," said Gyp, his eyes brightening.

"The Henry V touch!" remarked Charlie. "Personally, my appetite for glory isn't developed to that extent. I wouldn't complain if they sent us another couple of divisions. But they won't, not having 'em to send; so we'll have to rely on you two, after all."

They grinned at each other, the two brothers, unimpressed and unpersuaded as ever, and visibly meditated a combined reprisal upon their elder; but there was no time, for already the halt was over, and here and there along the lines men were picking themselves up out of the sand and scrambling back into their transports.

From now on there was no time for anything but to move and keep moving. The rare ten-minute pauses for food and drink left no spare moment for the careful to spend in speech, even if the careless must be talking. For sleep there was no pause. They drove by day and night, and at each re-loading assembled themselves into a complicated human jigsaw puzzle, and slept upon one another's shoulders and loins and thighs like a litter of puppies. The ground became increasingly bad as they travelled, and they drove within twelve hours into a head-storm of full gale force, which scoured their faces with fine sand, and worse, cut down visibility to three or four yards and forced their speed down to a mere seven miles an hour. Under these conditions they drew in to their night formation, bonnet to tail; and even so, at intervals a stray would wander off the track and head away into the desert, to be fished back by its neighbour with much profanity, and restored to the reckless profession moving blindly south-west.

When they had given up the losing battle with the silting sand, and allowed it to cover every surface of flesh and khaki and canvas and wood with a layer of fine grit, the nature of the storm changed. Out of the invisible sky frozen rain came suddenly sheeting down the wind. The sand became russet-grey mud, and bitter cold. They were coated with it, unrecognisable under it, before they could take refuge inside greatcoats and tarpaulins and anything that came handy. The unhappy drivers disappeared behind leather coats, goggles and masks of mud; but they at least had something to do. Their passengers had nothing to take their minds off their acute discomfort; they had simply to sit in it, and write it off with cramp, and weariness, and cold as another of the incidental horrors of war. It made them all the madder, and all the more eager for the end of the journey, no matter what odds might be waiting for them there. They endured twenty hours of this stabbing rain, and then, in the small hours of February the 5th, they saw a few stars between the squalls, and the force of the wind slackened. By daylight the rain was negligible, and they took heart of grace. They had covered about a hundred and thirty miles; there could surely be little farther to go.

Throughout this forced march their radio had been absolutely silent; but towards midday of that day the advanced armoured units spoke them. "Have reached coast and contacted enemy, thirty-five miles south of Benghazi. They're packed along the road. Hurry!"

Hurry! They had abandoned already several lorries and the Commanding General's car in their haste; but in that last burst of speed they all but tore the guts out of every transport they had. The whole trip, they worked out afterwards, had taken them about thirty-six hours. Two more, or three at the most, and they would have been too late.

The Battle of Soluk—they called it that in the reports for want of a better name, though most of it was fought in a blank space on the map, a nameless sea of mud—was not primarily the infantry's battle. Such mechanised units as followed the tanks and guns were there as a background only, a form of insurance, during the earlier stages. The action had already begun when they reached the edge of the coastal belt, and began to catch distant glimpses of the sea ahead. There was a great deal of noise forward, where high-speed tank clashes had already been in progress for an hour or more; and wherever an outcrop of firm ground offered, British guns were deploying and firing. From these vantage points they could see in the distance a light streak running inland of the sharper gold of sand dunes, and the blue-steel glitter of sea. This was the coastal road, running north to Benghazi and south to El Agheila. They saw it only as a flat hair-thin line, speckled with dark movement, and even this only by snatches as the ground under them rose and fell; but they knew that they were looking at Graziani's armour, artillery and infantry on the retreat intact from Benghazi, the force they had been sent to intercept. British tanks were tearing ahead over the soggy ground to straddle the road before them. British guns were moving round nearer to the sea on both flanks to complete the semicircle of fire. Already they had the range; their shells were bursting among the confused mass of transport on the road. Already, too, the Italians had made the decision to stand and fight; made it, or accepted it when it was forced upon them, for there was now no way for them to run except into the sea. They were deploying their guns and opening fire; and by the noise ahead they had plenty of guns. Plenty of tanks, also, and they began an outward and forward push with them, so that the clashes came nearer, through the sea of mud, and soon the shorter-ranged anti-tank guns were able to go into effective action.

For the duration of the daylight that was the battle, tank against tank and gun against gun; and the statisticians worked out the odds afterwards as five to one in tanks and three to one in guns in favour of the Italians. There was little as yet for the mechanised infantry to do. They crept round in two horns upon the flanks, ready to close the semicircle; but they were held back from the range of the enemy shell-fire until night, for there was no longer any need of haste. The Eyeties couldn't get away; there was no hurry about the job of annihilating them, and no justification for risking British lives in the process. All they could do was watch from their scattered cover the prowess of the artillery, count the major bursts which meant ammunition or transport had gone up, and keep the rising tale of Italian tanks left bogged and burning in the mud. By nightfall there were over forty within their range of vision.

They were not troubled very much by enemy aircraft, though once or twice, they had to take cover from casual bombs, and once a dive-bomber began a determined run, but pulled out of

his dive and made off with all speed when a British fighter came
tearing happily in to intercept him. Soon after this solitary
alarm the dusk slid down over the scene like a drop curtain,
and the strange lights of the battle burned up in the darkness,
expanding orange flashes of gun-bursts, sullen, pulsating glows
of burned-out tanks, pencilled lightnings of machine-gun fire,
and distant, ephemeral reflections of broken lights thrown back
from the sea. An instant activity broke out, urgent but unhurried. The night was full of movement. Both arms of the
British crescent stretched out steadily towards the sea, enfold-
ing the enemy in a closing embrace. The Midshires went south,
splashing through the mud, south to the road, past the sector
where the sappers were busily mining. Not even in the darkness were the enemy to be allowed to slip through the cordon.

On both sides the guns kept up their continuous fire. All
night the exchanges went on; and by their flashes the Italian
guns were patiently marked and systematically wiped out, one
by one. By dawn, when the hopelessness of the position became apparent, the number of the enemy's field-guns had considerably diminished, the shells of their tanks littered the mud,
and from north and east the attackers were closing in upon
them. In desperation they launched the expected counter-
attack, and with more resolution than the Midshires had ever
yet seen them display. Their tanks, and they still outnumbered
the British, launched a thrust at once east and south, trying by
sheer weight to cut a way out for the columns to follow. Eastward they were fought to a standstill, picked off one by one
by light guns brought in daringly near during the night. Southward they ran upon the new minefield, and such as survived
the Midshires took apart. In the centre the steady process of
reducing the odds went on all that day and all the following
night, the semicircle of the attackers contracting gradually.
They marked their target, tank or lorry or battery, and took
their time over obliterating it, and chose another and repeated
the business, and did not tire of it. It had been a workmanlike,
economical affair from the beginning, and should be so to the
end. They were well aware that it could not go on much longer.

There was one more attempt at a counter-attack, made next
morning, and far too late. It was savage while it lasted, but it
collapsed within an hour, and on both sides they knew it for
the last burst of energy of which the demoralised body was
capable. The Midshires followed its recoil, recognising their
moment. And suddenly in the centre of the contracting ring

men ran out from cover, waving handkerchiefs, throwing down
their rifles in the mud, screaming surrender. The last contrac-
tion of the British circle carried the Midshires clean through this
clamorous importunity, and on across the road into the sand-
dunes, where rifles and small arms were still firing. But there
was no heart in the enemy to go on fighting any longer. From
every rock shadow and every patch of scrub they came out
in their thousands, the fantastic tatters of an army. Seven of
their generals were picked out of the sand and taken under
escort to the village of Soluk. Their armour and artillery, perhaps half of it still serviceable, lay scattered over the miles
of cratered mud as far as the eye could see. Only one or two
tanks and a handful of motor trucks and carriers had slipped
between the meshes of the net, and made away for Tripoli to
carry the news. Not only the battle, but the campaign, was
over. The British would need another enemy before they could
fight again. This one was wiped clean off the board.

7

Benghazi was an eye-opener. They had expected something
ruinous and dirty like Bardia, and here was a spacious white
town, the centre of a complicated system of roads, railways
and lakes, with a fine harbour and impressive buildings, shops
and cafés and hotels all in flourishing operation, and only a few
scattered shell-scars here and there to remind them that it had
until two days previously been in Italian hands. The electric
light was still working, and there was hot water, genuine hot
water, for baths and shaving; you just turned the appropriate
tap, and it flowed. The trees and gardens pleased them, and
the sight of good-looking girls of their own colour was a joy;
there was limitless drinking water, and cheap wine less raw
than the Bardia brew, and fruit and vegetables and sweetmeats
after endless bully-beef and hard tack; but it was for the baths
they made their first bee-line, and there they dallied longest.
After that three-day wallow in glutinous russet mud, with only
a hand-basin wash in a Soluk farm-yard to dislodge the caked
layers, and that in cold well-water, half an hour in a full-sized
bath with steaming water and plentiful soap was pure heaven.

In other ways, too, the entry into Benghazi was an astonishing experience. It was all very well for the Bedouin along the
Soluk road to run alongside as the transports passed, diving out
of their half-sown millet fields and leaving their early plant-

ings of melon and cucumber to cheer the conquerors. They bore no love to the old regime, and therefore might well raise a cheer for any which displaced it; besides the plain fact, as stated by Charlie, that they would have downed tools to applaud the passing of anyone who afforded the thinnest excuse for quitting the job half-way, especially if he had a few cigarettes left. But why, when all the Alis and Husseins and Ibrahims were left behind, and they were driving along the first streets of the town, should the Italian children cheer and wave, and the Italian girls come out on their balconies, and smile, and flutter eyelids and handkerchiefs at the victorious enemy? Even when the enemy happened to look like young Curly, with his copper-coloured hair and his wildly innocent eyes, it was scarcely understandable. The curiosity Jim felt in this particular prompted him to ask Charlie's opinion; he, after all, knew a little about the Italians.

"There are three reasons," said Charlie, at his most didactic. "Firstly, sheer relief; they've had the Aussies here for two days, and it isn't a tenth as bad as they thought it would be. By the way, don't make the mistake of confusing that with gratitude; there's no connection. Secondly, they hope we're susceptible to flattery, and mean to stay on the right side of us by any available means. Thirdly, they're only too pleased to have us; we stand between them and the Arabs now their own fighting men have hopped it. They feel safer that way."

At the time Jim doubted the justice of this cynical view; but on the third evening of his stay in the town he saw one of the not-infrequent clashes between Italian and Arab boil up at a dark street-corner into an unsuccessful knifing; and he wondered. It was on the English that the shrieking little Eyetie merchant called for help, and it was Jim who picked him unhurt out of the gutter; though he was scrupulously careful, as the only witness, not to remember anything at all about the appearance of the assailant. It was no quarrel of his, and how did he know what provocation there had been from before-time? The victim was still intact, and he was damned if he would get the other chap into trouble. Maybe, at that, Charlie was right, and the smiling welcome the British had got in Benghazi originated not in the sunny, unretentive temperament of the Italians, but in their fervent devotion to their own interests. From then on the thought, at any rate, was always at the back of his mind, and put a different complexion upon the beguiling looks he got from some of the promenading women in the streets. Now if just one girl among them had stared scornfully through him, he might have been interested. But he could never fall for that honeyed stuff of drooped lashes and fulsome smiles. He couldn't fancy a woman with so little spirit. In Boissy-en-Fougères, the women had walked with fixed eyes colder than ice, drawing their arms tightly to their sides to avoid the polluting touch of the invader. Even those who broke under the strain, as perhaps Eliane Brégis had broken, could not disguise the death in their hearts. The wheel had come full circle now, but what had happened to the conquerors and the conquered, that they should sit together in the cafés as if no warfare stood between them?

No, Jim left the townspeople alone. Only the kids wormed their way into his graces, and on the whole he preferred the grubby little grinning Arabs to the Italians. They were scared of nothing and nobody. They found their way into every privacy, and took their welcome for granted with the most disarming arrogance. When you picked yourself a sunny corner of a roof to indulge in an afternoon nap you were sure to wake up to find a ring of them squatting on their heels all round you. When you went swimming in the sea they appeared from nowhere, shooting from between your knees like eels and leaving you labouring behind. They were always under your feet, and you might as well resign yourself to it. The best thing you could do was to pick out one or two of the most entertaining and give them the job of keeping the others away. They would do it, too, with tooth and nail, making you their express possession. That way you got some peace.

They were in Benghazi for nearly a month, though other units had gone on to El Agheila, and patrols had pushed even beyond that point. But it looked as if for the moment the lightning advance was over. Communications were strained already, and would be stretched to a very much more dangerous degree if they ventured the Sirte desert and the journey into Tripoli. What they had set out to do was, in effect, completed; the shadow of Italy no longer menaced Alexandria. Moreover, the force they had was being mysteriously thinned these days, this armoured unit being withdrawn, that infantry brigade vanishing overnight, the other battery suddenly packing up and moving back at speed for Egypt. Where were they going? Some said to Greece, but the Greeks were doing all right by themselves. Some said to India, or Singapore, because somebody in high places was getting cold feet about the Japs. But nobody knew the rights of it. So the depleted Army of the Nile would settle down to hold what it had. The Italian army, after all, was wiped out, and it would take time to assemble another one on the borders of Cyrenaica to trouble the Britannic peace.

In the meantime, what with hot water and cold sea bathing, heady drinks and comfortable billets, this rest was a sort of minor paradise, where Sergeant Lake could black himself out decently for a couple of days and not be missed, and Charlie, having seen him safely through this expected lapse, could disappear for a night or two in his turn upon some curious ploys of his own, and return with a reminiscent light in his eye but no visible signs of a hangover, at least of the accepted type; where Jim could explore the mysteries of the Arab town at leisure, and teach his small partisans the intricacies of English football, and get comfortably tight at night whenever he felt like it; and where the Ballantyne brothers, after their kind, could get themselves into deep water, and fish each other indignantly out again, a dozen times a day. It was not, take it all round, particularly good for any of them, but it did not last long enough to do them any great harm, and at least it was something different, something to remember, an oasis in their interminable Libyan desert.

All the same, Jim was glad when they moved out. He didn't much like watching young Curly doing the round of the cafés with Italian women old enough to have had the decency to leave him alone. He picked the wrong ones with an infallible genius. Sometimes even Gyp could see it, and Gyp wasn't much more competent himself. Sometimes they were so bad that Charlie, doing things his own way as usual, exerted himself to lift them from under the kid's nose and remove them before they could get their teeth into him. With Charlie's experience and finesse it was as easy as taking candy from a baby. As for Curly, he took it as a compliment to his taste, and bore no malice. Now if Gyp could have handled him like that they might have got along together without quite so much wear and tear; but Gyp would always lecture him, implying that he was still a kid, and couldn't look after himself, and as a result they fought bitter battles up and down Benghazi, and the obstreperous child continued in his courses.

There was this, too, to be said for Charlie's diplomatic tactics, that when occasion demanded, and he threw them suddenly overboard, the contrast was awe-inspiring, and even subdued Curly's exuberance, which was a giant's achievement.

65

It happened only once or twice in Jim's knowledge, and the first occasion was a week or so before they left Benghazi, when Gyp came tearing into the café where they were sitting, and reported that Curly had gone off with one of the worst specimens yet, into a filthy-looking house in a back street which was most certainly no place for him. He wouldn't come away. Gyp supposed he was just being big. He was rather drunk, if that was any excuse. Gyp was always able to find an excuse of some sort.

"I didn't want to start a fight in that dump," he explained apologetically. "Suppose a patrol broke it up? He'd be in the soup. And anyhow, they all look as if they sported several sorts of knives. But I don't think he'll come out without being dragged."

Charlie finished his beer, and put down the glass with a crash. "Won't he, by God?" he said, in a most uncharacteristic voice. "He'll walk out on his own two feet, without a hand being laid on him. I've had about enough of your Curly to last me for the present. Now for once he'll do as he's told, or else! And there'll be no argument about it." And he pushed back his chair and stalked out of the café, leaving them to follow as the tail follows a comet.

There was no argument. It was the most completely neat thing Jim had seen. Charlie halted for nothing, but pushed his way through the narrow outer door and the greasy curtains, stood off with one hand the curious hashish-soaked apology for a man that acted as porter, and walked into the private office of the proprietress. She might have been anything, French, Italian, half-Arab, Levantine, there was no telling. He tried Italian on her, without apparent result, for her face remained expressionless, a mask of drooping curves of fat, with hooded eyes.

"*Le jeune soldat Anglais!*" said Charlie. "*Où est-il?*"

She said nothing, but her immense satin shoulders lifted, and she made an indifferent gesture towards an inner door. They went through into a large and garish room, lit only in a subdued, insidious fashion, and full of alcoves in which small tables stood. There was a bar, and a cleared space for a cabaret, but at the moment the only entertainer in sight was an Egyptian gentleman in a greasy dinner-jacket who was playing anæmic jazz on a grand piano. A number of people were sitting at the curtained tables. Some of the girls were white or near-white, but the only white man present was Curly. He was at a table in a dark corner by the stairs, with the worst specimen yet, as Gyp had called her, draped round his neck; but at the sight of Charlie marching upon him like a one-man patrol he sat up with a jerk and pushed her away, and made, and visibly abandoned, one desperate attempt to muster his dignity and behave as if he had every right to be where he was.

Charlie said, in a voice like the quietness just before the crack of doom: "Come on out of here, and look sharp about it."

Curly took one look at him, and came on out. Jim thought he would have done the same in Curly's shoes. It's one thing to turn a deaf ear to a brother whose business it is to nag and worry you away from any dubious excitement; but quite another to retain your assurance in the face of such cold ferocity in the most tolerant person you know. Curly walked out on his own two feet, without a hand being laid on him, according to schedule; only when he had him safely in the street did Charlie take him firmly by the arm and march him back to billets at top speed, and in grim silence. There he dumped him upon his cot, and went for him, as the victim said afterwards without resentment, like a tiger.

The flow went on for ten minutes without a pause, and Curly heard himself called by several highly original names, but happily was in no state to memorise them. The tone, however, registered with a vengeance. The breath was knocked clean out of him. He listened meekly to all the kinds of irresponsible fool he was, and all the things Charlie proposed to do to him if he ever was put to the trouble of fetching him out of such a sink again. He believed it, too; Charlie meant every word of it. Curly, who had not liked the back-street dive in the first place, ceased even to think his gesture sophisticated. No such outburst from anyone else could have achieved that result.

Charlie ran out of breath and adjectives together, and stood for a moment surveying the crushed remains. "Oh, go and wash your face!" he said disgustedly. "You've got cheap lipstick all over it. And get rid of that stink of freesia before you come near me again."

All of which, with astonishing docility Curly did, and for a full day thereafter went about his business in a subdued silence; upon which phenomenon, though not from awe of him, no one ventured to comment. No one, indeed, thought fit to refer to the affair again, except Curly himself, who at the end of an evening of fatigues suddenly looked Charlie Smith full in the eye, and remarked surprisingly: "There was nothing to it, anyway. Even the gin was lousy!"

And Charlie laughed. But for all that, they were not sorry when they moved out from the town and took over a section of the coastal road towards Cyrene, a week later. With plenty of work to do the place might have been all right; but as a rest billet it was too disturbing. Even at the cost of swopping their abandoned hotel for a bunch of tents between the road and the sea, the exchange was for the better; and the sea bathing was still theirs, if everything else went with the town. And as for dangerous company, there wasn't a girl within miles except the two small, shrill daughters of Ibn Radwan, who farmed the redstone homestead sloping down to the sea, and whose goats and camels wandered in and out of their camp at will. Their greatest excitement was helping Ibn Radwan to sow spinach and complete his second plantings of cucumbers and melons, and at the extreme end of March watching him fertilise his date-palms in the grove dropping down to the shore. It was like the quiet time at Petrol Parva, but three months and four hundred and fifty miles nearer victory, and with the sea thrown in for good measure.

Then, halfway through March, a great homesickness came on them. In part it was due to this strange quietness after violent action; but the spark that fired the fuse was the coming of the migrant birds on their way north. The chaffinches came in clouds, and the willow-wrens, and the warblers; and then one morning there was a fluting of soft, hesitant notes about dawn, down among the bushes below the palm grove, and Jim dropped the boot he was about to put on, and said: "Hush!" and in the silence they all heard him trying out his first call, the solitary nightingale. Charlie might have to pin the names on the redstart, and the crested lark, and the cream-coloured plover, but Jim knew a nightingale when he heard one. In a country where so many of the native birds are mute, the low, repeated notes, tried over and over call by call, were a music poignantly lovely. He was rehearsing for England, running through the song he would pour out in May and June upon the quiet of Sheel woods, water-clear across the river in the magic night, for listening lovers to hear in the lane as they walked home toward Morwen Hoe.

Suddenly he wanted to be home as he had never wanted anything on earth before, not even Delia in the days of his weakness, not even safety in the days of his captivity. They

68

had to move again; they must go forward; how else could they
ever get home? He could no longer bear to be still, even in
the ripening heat of Spring, with the lapis-lazuli Mediterranean
at his feet, and the flowering date-palms over him. To stay
was to stay for ever, or so it seemed to him. They must
move on. But the advance was over. Sheel woods were a
dream.

After that sudden peremptory enjoinment of silence he himself
fell silent; and he took, deliberately, the longest journey that
offered that day, a trip south with supplies to one of the inland
ammunition dumps. A day to go, and a day to return, and
the worst might be over by then; and if not, the respite would
be worth having for its own sake.

Charlie went with him, of course. He did not ask any
questions until they were a good three hours out from the road,
taking it easy over a clear but bumpy track through mile upon
mile of scrub. Then he asked, without subtlety:

"Well, what's your trouble?"

"That blasted nightingale!" said Jim. "I don't know—
they just start you thinking at the wrong minute." He looked
at the track ahead, tawny between the grey-green *terfa*, and
he said: "What happens next? And when? I want to go
home."

"Who doesn't?" said Charlie.

"Oh, I know, I know—I'm not complaining; there's plenty
worse off than me, married men with families, sons of widows,
all manner of fellows with more excuse than me for getting
homesick. But you asked me, didn't you?"

"All right, all right! I asked you." But the oracle was mute
of comfort. Perhaps, underneath that homeless, citizen-of-
the-world pose of his, there was some corner of the earth that
had him by a string.

"It's all right while something's happening," said Jim
fretfully. "It's in the pauses you have time to notice how this
year's slipping after last year, and us no nearer home. I
reckon they all get it pretty bad some time or other. Well,
this is mine. Looks like you'll have to put up with it this.
trip. I wonder why you bothered to come."

"Go ahead, let off steam," advised Charlie. "I can face it."

But Jim had no more to say. It was enough that he had
admitted the nostalgia. No more was needed. He said more
cheerfully: "Oh, forget it! It's not that bad. It just gets
over you sometimes, that's all. All the chaps are in the same

boat. Skip it! Talk about the weather, or the scenery, or something."

Nevertheless, it gnawed him still without ceasing, as a tooth gnaws for days after you have bitten on the nerve. It wasn't a question of reason. He knew he had to put up with it, not only for this year, but probably for at least two or three years more. The thing was too big now to be reversed all in a few months, even by superhuman efforts. He had sense and judgment enough to realise that. All he wanted to keep him content was progress, however slow, however costly; just an inch on the way, and never to be still, and never to be without a job of work; so that at least he could look forward to arrival some day, somehow, at the place where he would be. Not, perhaps, a little house in Caldington; however, the nightingale called him back, that was not the whole of it. No, it was rather a place in the soul where he wanted to be, a quietness, a spiritual security, a snug place, warm with friends, comfortable with habit and use. The way to it could be as long and hard as it would, and he would not complain; the only satisfaction he asked was that his feet should be firmly set on it, and not withheld from movement, as now they were.

The clairvoyant beside him said, looking for the words as he went: "The trouble with you, though you won't believe me, is that you're hankering after the wrong thing. What you left behind, what you look forward to reaching again in the end, doesn't exist any more. Oh, I dare say the house is still there, and the people, and the place, and some of the habits and customs; but the thing itself, the binding agent—that's gone. It had a lot of shapes, local usage, national usage, the habit of mind that keeps lads like you tangled in your forebears' roots, thinking as they thought, taking for granted what they took for granted, living by their standards, measuring by their scale of values. When you wake up to the impossibility of pushing yourself back into that mould you'll quit thinking it a loss. Can you get a grown man back into the clothes he wore as a kid? Or steam back into a kettle? No more can you get yourself back into the shape of the man you started from, or your world—or your village for that matter—back into the circumscribed quietness you remember and are homesick for. You'll have to put something else in its place; it's clean gone."

"I suppose you hold," said Jim, "that we've got to aim

at putting a new order of socialism in its place—make a new world fit for heroes to live in, and all that. I didn't know you were one of those."

"I'm not. I wish I was. To be a revolutionary you have to believe in the future of the race, as embodied in the revolution. A cynic can't be a revolutionary. I wish I could believe in human beings enough to be one of those. But I don't, you know. Still, you've got to have something to hang on to, something to orientate yourself by. You can set to work to build your Utopia if you're one of the lucky ones; or you can simply drive your own heels into the ground and concrete yourself upright, and hang on to that—as I do. Or you can get religion, and shake a tambourine with the Salvation Army, and dose yourself along that way. Me, I haven't the temperament. I could never resist the temptation to analyse what goes on inside me, and reject the bits I didn't like. No, I'll stick to myself, the only thing I do believe in—myself and my capacity to endure anything that can happen to me in this world or heaven or hell or limbo—out of sheer cussedness, if for no better motive. The one article of faith I'll never let down, and the only one that'll never let me down."

"Either you flatter yourself," said Jim bitterly, "or you're damned lucky. And anyhow, what good are you to the rest of the world, at that rate?" But he knew well enough without an answer. Hadn't he ridden to the same anchor himself more than once? And hadn't the others, great numbers of them, seized and held by Charlie to draw themselves upright again after slippery steps? "Besides," he said, "it sounds pretty bloody lonely."

"It is," said Charlie with a sigh. "Pretty bloody lonely."

But that would never be his trouble, thought Jim, torn between envy and gratitude; he would always be one of the crowd, reaching out for possessions and company, hankering for things he could hold in his hands; neither capable of achieving, nor big enough to desire, that solitary integrity. No, he was born ordinary. If what he had had could not be regained—and in his heart he knew it could not—he wanted in its place something as like it as he could find, an unexciting job, some leisure, a surrounding world not too dizzy with change; all this, and as much for other men.

He drove on in silence through the noon heat, his eyes fixed ahead, where the gravelly streak of the track swayed round outcrops of rock and then settled into an arrow-straight line across the face of the scrub-desert. There were increasing patches of hard sand, level and finely-packed, on either side, for they were now well out of the coastal belt, and the softening influence of the shore rains was left behind. In the brilliant sky, in the eye of the sun, two 'planes drew feathery circles after them like trains of gauze, weaving intricate white patterns against the hard blue, so gracefully and tranquilly that it seemed impossible they could be engaged in trying to destroy each other. They were so high, and whirling in such dizzy convolutions, that it was difficult to pick out the R.A.F. machine or recognise to what type the other belonged. They watched the spinning patterns with a narrowing interest. It was something actual, something outside themselves, this distant battle in the sky. They saw the loser heel over suddenly and drift down the wind with a long plume of smoke at its tail, and the winner straighten and recover, and drop circling, to watch his victim fall. It was a thing they saw most days; except in this blank scene they would not have bothered to watch it.

"One more written off," said Jim.

"Could be two. I believe the other chap's having trouble. Which is he, anyway? Italian or ours?"

"Ours, for sure. There goes the Eyetie, look!" His going was a meteor-flash on the horizon, and a spurt of dust and smoke that hung upon the air for fully thirty seconds. The victor lost height in a series of silent plunges, like a hawk swooping, and glided down towards the road, which showed as a pale ribbon across the desert. They heard his engine sputtering and cutting out by turns and saw him shudder and heel in his course.

"He's looking for a patch of firm sand to put her down on," said Jim, and stepped on the accelerator. The 'plane was coming down ahead of them, lurching above the scrub to the left of the track, perhaps half a mile away, dropping until they thought the pilot would dig his nose into the sand and somersault into wreckage; but at every last moment he picked himself up, with a desperate spurt, the few yards he needed to clear the next ridge of scrub. He gained on the lorry, and was a full three-quarters of a mile away when he finally put down his machine in a wide bed of hard sand, five hundred yards or so from the track. Of the landing they saw only the waving lift of one wing, but they heard the impact, and knew that he had wrecked his 'plane beyond reclamation, and possibly himself as well. Happily there was no flash of fire after the hissing gravel shower and the echoes of the crash had subsided. They were both of them watching for it anxiously as they bumped along the last stretch that brought them alongside; but it did not come. They jumped out of the lorry together, and plunged into the scrub, jumping from one clear patch to another to avoid the *terfa* thorns and *heskanit* burrs, and cursing them mechanically as they got home none the less. But by the time they reached the wreck, the pilot was already out of it, and sitting upon the ground a few yards away in a very bad temper, tying up with his left hand and his teeth a jagged scratch in his right forearm. Apart from this tear, and the loss of half his flying-suit, which hung upon him in picturesque ribbons, he appeared to be perfectly intact and extremely capable of managing his own affairs. As for the 'plane, she had landed without any undercarriage to speak of, and tilted over upon her left wing, snapping the tip into splinters, and ploughing the remnant deep into the sand. Still, he had landed her.

He looked up sharply as he heard them come crashing through the scrub, and dropped the corner of the handkerchief from between his teeth, and gaped. "Well, I'll be damned!" he said.

"I don't see why," said Charlie, mildly. "I should say somebody on the other side had an eye on you, all things considered. Are you as sound as you look?"

"I'm O.K. But for Pete's sake, where did you spring from? I was just putting a small blast on yon bitch for chucking me overboard miles from anywhere. Seems she didn't, after all. What's round here? Where are you from?" He gave up the attempt to finish knotting the handkerchief, and stuck out at Jim a thin and very oily hand. "Here, tie this up, I'm damned if I can."

"Lucky for you she didn't fire," said Jim, making a neat job of it. The hand trembled a little, but after that crash who could wonder?

"Are you telling me? I thought my number was up, all right. You wouldn't have a fag about you, would you?"

They would, and did. The sergeant-pilot drew on it breathlessly, and shivered a little, but not from cold, and said he felt better now, but he wished he had a double whisky. They grinned at each other above his head.

"Take your time," said Jim, "but if you can cover the stretch back to the road we've got a perfectly good First Aid kit in the lorry, complete with brandy."

The pilot sat up abruptly. "Lorry? Did you say lorry? You mean I don't even have to walk back?"

"Lorry is what I said. Didn't you see us on the road?"

"Too damn busy to see anything but the patch of sand I needed. Where are you chaps heading for?"

"Post M, three hours south yet. But to-morrow we go back to the coast road, if you like to tag along. How about it? Suit you?"

"Suit me? Lead me to it!"

They led him to it, and gave him the drop of brandy they had, and sat him between them in the cab as they went on southward. He was shaken, but it was not his first crash, and he was a resilient youth. Inside half an hour he was giving a spirited account of the dog-fight they had witnessed. It was his second that day, but the first beggar had sheered off at high speed before he could get a decent chance at him. It was a pity; he would have liked to be able to report two in one day.

"Still," he said contentedly, "the one I did get was the Jerry. The Fiat ran like hell, and I was too far out over the Sirte to feel like chasing him. Besides, I wanted to get back quickly and report. Nice mess I'd have been in if you blokes hadn't happened along. I guess I ought to make for the nearest 'phone. What will this truck do?"

"Most of what I ask her," said Jim, opening out to top speed. "We can get to one of the batteries inside half an hour, and drop you off there if you like. I dare say they could loan you a motor-bike, and the daylight will last you to the coast all right. How about it?"

The sergeant-pilot opened his grey eyes wide. "What, me on a motor-bike? Not on your life? I tried it once, but never again, thanks. I don't feel safe on those things. No, if you're coming back to-morrow that suits me, so long as I can get to a 'phone pretty quick. I can do with a night off."

"O.K., hang on to yourself, here we go!" And he shouted across the noise of their going: "Did you say that was a Jerry you fetched down?"

"Ju. 87 as ever was. You knew they were around, didn't you?"

"Knew they were supposed to be. They used to come over Benghazi every few days, when we were there last month, and take a quick blast at it, and buzz off again before the Aussies could really get going. They said those were Luftwaffe 'planes."

"Oh, yes, they're up regularly now. But that's not all.

74

There's a lot of shipping in at Sirte that I don't like the look of; more than there was yesterday, and they thought it worth bombing last night. And there's transport along the Tripoli road, loads of it, tanks and all. It could be German. I think it is German."

"You reckon they're landing at Sirte?" asked Charlie. "In strength? German armour, and infantry divisions as well?"

"Sirte, and Tripoli, and maybe half a dozen places in the Gulf besides. In strength? Well, I don't know, I couldn't hang around, but it looked a hell of a lot of stuff to me. And they've got advanced patrols along the coast east of Sirte, too. They're not on the move just now, but all I know is they weren't there yesterday. It looks as if they're heading for El Agheila."

Charlie said: "So they're here! Well, you wanted action! It looks as if you'll soon be satisfied."

He looked across at Jim, whose eyes were fixed steadily upon the road ahead, and caught the sudden, shadowed look, as if smoke had blown across his face, dulling the first fierce anticipation of renewed activity. He wanted the Germans there; he wanted to meet them again, whatever it cost him; and yet the shadow crossed the fixed eagerness of his eyes, like a memory of the blown, oily smoke clouding the escarpment above Tobruk, where he had prophesied the landing and the clash. It had been slower in coming than he had foreseen; it might also be more thorough. As for the end of it, that was the one thing he had not prophesied.

8

They drove back the next afternoon into a denuded camp. The little city of tents had disappeared, and all that remained was three long files of lorries already loaded and facing outward towards the road, and a great number of disconsolate men sitting along the running boards and standing about in the sand, some silent, some vociferous, waiting for the word to leave.

"What, already?" said Charlie, raising his eyebrows.

"It doesn't take us long," said Jim, with a wry smile. "It looks to me as if I'd better go over this hussy's motor and get her filled up again pronto, ready for off."

Charlie sat still for a minute, surveying the depressed faces of the Midshires. "Off," he said thoughtfully, "in which direction?"

"Need you ask?" said Jim, and laughed unpleasantly, for

this was a thing he had not bargained for, a feeling he had almost forgotten. Nevertheless, they did ask. They asked Gyp, when they happened upon him sitting upon an empty petrol tin with his chin on his fists, watching Ibn Radwan and his small son at work in the date grove, as if he was witnessing rather the preparations for his own execution than the harmless necessary marriage of male and female palms. He looked up at them in a preoccupied fashion, but the wretchedness of his face was not eased.

"Oh, hullo!" he said. "Good job you're back, we're moving out any minute now."

"So we see." Charlie sat down in the thin grass beside him, and asked firmly: "What goes on?"

"All I know is, we've got orders to move, and all we're waiting for is the word go. But they say German and Italian patrols are in El Agheila, and moving north. We've seen some fairly badly-mauled armour coming back through here; I should say it must be right."

"And we," said Charlie delicately, stabbing a finger westward, "move—that way?"

Gyp jerked a savage thumb eastward. "Don't kid yourself. We move *that* way. Derna's where we're going."

"That," said Jim, grimly, "is what we thought."

And to Derna they went. There was no help for it, however they might rage among themselves at the double disappointment of moving back at all, and moving back without a blow struck. It was all very well for Sergeant Lake to insist that their withdrawal meant nothing, that other units were holding Benghazi, that El Agheila and Mersa Brega, where the enemy were now disporting themselves, had never been seriously held, but only manned as antennæ to detect the first probing touch of the inevitable counter-attack; which they had effectively done, and so served their purpose. That sounded reasonable enough, but lost its virtue when they reflected that Sergeant Lake had himself the look of a man cheated and bereaved and had been heard, in an unguarded moment, anathematising the order to retreat to Derna in unprintable terms. It was the indignity of being removed to Derna while others fought off the attack behind them that annoyed the younger element most sorely. Jim took the side of reason on this point, and assured them acidly, as they drove along the coastal road towards Cyrene, that it was impossible, even in a full-scale retreat, for every unit to get a job in the rearguard. He was sorry afterwards that he had used

76

the word "retreat", however apt it might be; for he saw Curly
blink as if it had hit him in the face, and swallow it down with
a wry gulp; and there were a good number in the company not
much above Curly's age. They were not used to retreating;
they had known only one campaign, the dazzling advance from
Egypt to Benghazi, and they were prepared for no other kind
of warfare, however they might theorise, and however attentively
they might suffer the lectures of the veterans.

Still, thought Jim, if they had to learn no more of it now
than this single move back to Derna they would do well. A
pity so much of the stiffening of the defence had been filtered off,
but surely what he could half-foresee they had not failed to
provide against. Surely they would stake everything they had
to hold their gains. If the thrust was heavy and hard they might
have to recoil even beyond Benghazi, and their defence had to
be as elastic as possible; the force sent back to Derna would
have the job of preparing a second rampart, and the satisfaction
of holding it. Though Tobruk, but for the loss of face and
ground in moving back so far, would make the better defensive
base. Perhaps it would not be necessary to take the threat quite
so seriously. The withdrawal of patrols from El Agheila was
nothing; whether Sergeant Lake believed his own statement or
not, Jim knew it to be accurate enough; Agheila had been a
nerve, not a fortress. No, this depression that settled upon
them was a personal business, a fit of sulks, not over the possibility of disaster, but over their exclusion from the front line.
So, at least, he persuaded himself, and so he swore to them,
throughout the seven days they spent in the desert south of
Derna, wiring and concreting, and watching the daily sorties of
hosts of 'planes overhead, and envying them.

He even convinced a few at last, or so Charlie informed him;
but he did not deceive Charlie. Whenever he caught those
bright, incurious eyes upon him he was clearly aware that they
saw through that hardly-erected shell of reason and moderation
to the furious impatience within. Not one of those enthusiastic
boys suffered as he did from the withdrawal. How could they?
They had no Tommy Goolden to remember, no personal terrors
to avenge, no host of the murdered clamouring in their minds.
Their hate for the Germans, if they had any, was a conventional
thing imbibed from the headlines and the B.B.C. news broad-
casts. He had not realised, until the Herrenvolk came so nearly
within touch of him again, how his own hate rooted and grew.
To have them come within a few miles of him, and then to be

77

restrained from taking any action against them, even if the ban did not last more than seven days, was a form of hell; and by some process of sympathy Charlie knew how it burned, and kept silence before it, neither asking nor offering companionship beyond what was now implicit between them.

They were bombed often, but sketchily, for the R.A.F. were very active and seemed numerous enough to hold their own. They were short of water for some days, but were more worried about the shortage of accurate news. But on the 3rd of April, when Benghazi was abandoned in the face of increasing German pressure, the bad news travelled far and fast, and reached them before nightfall. Convoys of tired men began to come in, streaming along the coast road, lorries and limbers, guns and Bren-carriers, even some damaged but workable armour. Much of the gunners' stuff could not be moved in the time; some they had destroyed on the sites, some they had abandoned. It was all distressingly familiar to Jim; he had seen it once, and hoped never to see it again, but wherever the Germans came, came also this procession before them. There was for him one comfort, though he himself did not recognise it as such; but Charlie saw it clearly in him, the one point of eager hope behind which suddenly all his energy was gathered. Where the defeated went before, the conquerors would come after; and this time the Midshires would be in the rearguard. When the shelling began, and they crouched in their slit trenches listening to the bursts falling short of them, Charlie could see him counting the hours before the impact must come, telling off the minutes to assuage the insatiable desire he had to embrace his enemy. Already in anticipation his hands were round their throats. Fear, even the sane, useful fear which is merely a normal care for one's own life, was gone clean out of him. Several times Charlie watched him, flat on his belly in a niche of the rocks, as high as he could get, staring out westward over the face of the desert with ravenous eyes. Shelling would not fetch him down then. He came when he was ordered, promptly but impatiently, and returned as soon as the eye of authority was off him. What did the disgruntled boys know about an obsession like that?

On the 6th of April, when it seemed that his hunger must soon be appeased, the Midshires were ordered eastward again at three hours' notice. They raged, but he was silent. Things like that had been done to him before. He had not bored the company with his hate, nor did he burden them with his disappointment and frustration. It was Jim who told Curly, in

78

the most reasonable of tones, to shut his trap and get on with his job, and leave tactics to the tacticians. It was Jim who worked like a fury at the loading of equipment, and without offering any argument against pessimism, cut short complaint whenever he met it with the calm platitude that there was nothing they could do about it, so they might just as well shut up. But that was not what he said as he looked back in the dark just before they set out, with his hand on the wheel, and his eyes on the nearing gun-flashes along the western horizon.

"All right, you bastards!" he said through his shut lips, "All right, you swine! But I'll get at you yet!"

He had hoped they would turn at Tobruk, but Tobruk was already garrisoned in strength. In one long journey they were swept back to Bardia, and there moved into the desert again, having seen by the way not one living German, only a few corpses dragged from burned out bombers. That was their warfare. The Luftwaffe swooped over them in increasing numbers; time after time they were dive-bombed, until the traffic upon the coastal road was thinned by the use of all the desert tracks for forty miles south to lessen the risk; and in all this time they saw not one German, and could lift no hand to help themselves or strike at their enemies. In a grim silence now they drove along the interminable tawny tracks, past protest, past hope of recovery, picking up crumbs of news where they could from dispatch riders or scattered posts which had not yet packed up and bolted for the Egyptian border. Derna was gone. It had been occupied the day after they left, not without considerable loss on the enemy's part. Tobruk? No, according to present reports Tobruk was held, and the German Africa Corps and the four divisions or so of Italian hangers-on were by-passing it and racing after the main body of the retreating Army of the Nile. But they couldn't keep up that speed indefinitely, seeing they had to import all their transport and supplies by sea from Sicily, and then bring them hundreds of miles overland. There was bound to be a pause for stock-taking, but it looked as if they were bent on reaching the borders of Egypt before they halted.

There was other news too. They heard it at Bardia, before they swung south. Germany had attacked Yugoslavia and Greece on the 6th of April, the very day the Midshires left Derna in such anger and grief. It was too big to be seen whole. The ripples of war ran outward, catching this one and that one into the eddying swirl. Pretty soon every country would be in it, on one side or the other. Already they said that Belgrade was bombed to pieces, and the Germans were in northern Greece.

"This," said Charlie, indicating with a pass of his hand all the course of their unwilling retreat, "was timed to coincide. The 'Drang nach Osten' from north and south of the Mediterranean together, meeting at Suez."

"Maybe. Is that where our reinforcements went?"

"Some to Abyssinia, so Lake says, but most to Greece."

"Well balanced," said Jim; "too little to do any good here, and too little to do any good there."

"Unfortunately none of us know how to be in two places at once."

"If we did," said Jim, "we should still be in the two least useful places, I expect. It seems to be a gift of ours." But he did not talk like that when any of the others might hear. He held his peace right up to the gates of Egypt and beyond, when the rearguards were fighting back step by step from Bardia, and at last, at last, the main body of the Army was turning to make a stand. As if the feel of Egyptian soil under their feet put new anger into them, the retreat ceased there. They turned along the high ground south of Buqbuq, and Sidi Barrani, deploying southward, picking their positions. And on April 14th the Midshires came to their camp, well inland, out of sight of the sea by many miles, unsearched as yet by the Luftwaffe, a barren stretch of hard sand in the mottled grey waste of the limestone wilderness. They did not at first recognise it; but as Jim and Charlie walked out together from the shadow of the outcrop rocks, where the transport was drawn up, Jim suddenly stopped, and looked forward, and said in a sharp breath: "My God, no, it isn't possible!" and began to laugh, and as suddenly fell cursing, half under his breath, with a dreadful, unaccustomed felicity.

"No," said Charlie. "It isn't possible; but it has happened."

It was all there, just as they had left it, the broken limestone escarpment, the smooth expanse of sand which disguised their water tank, the scratched faces of rock in the shadow, the lion-shape of Jebel Kebir sharp against the shivering of mirage on the southern horizon; Petrol Parva, and no other place. They had travelled some nine hundred odd miles, and left thousands dead of their companions, and many thousands in captivity or wounded, all to get back to this.

"Two months to get there," said Jim, in a low voice, "and just ten days to get back. A mere bloody pleasure trip! All

80

for this! Not one chance at the bastards! Not one solitary sight
of a blasted German along a rifle barrel! Not one chance to get
my hands on 'em, me that was waiting for just that one thing!
Three hundred miles of running from 'em, and never a chance
to turn and get just one sweet minute of satisfaction. And me
that said I hadn't got a return ticket! I should have known!
Every time we go forward quick we come back a damned sight
quicker. I should have known! All those chaps thrown away,
all that stuff gone, and five months out of our lives—and back
where we started from, with the whole bloody thing to do
again—every step, every sore, every drop of sweat——"

He looked at the russet and grey of it in the noon sun, the
heat shuddering overhead, the arid, blazing blue of the sky
threaded white here and there with the trails of aircraft, and
the plumes of gun-smoke along the western rocks like aigrettes
in a smoothly folded turban. Already, perhaps, the nightingale
was in Sheel Woods, trying his song from the deep green of the
trees, over the coolness of the river. The wind in the leaves
made a small, soft noise there, continuous as the whispering of
the water. Here, as he turned his head, the breath of a furnace
blew in his face, laden with scalding sand; and the humming
of aircraft was in his ears, the soft voice of the enemy. He had
chafed at being still. Movement, he had demanded, progress,
an inch on the way. Well, movement he had achieved, and with
a vengeance, movement that turned upon itself, self-binding,
self-devouring.

"And I wanted to go home!" he said. "Oh, my good God
Almighty!"

PART TWO

MALAYA

"——or fever-airs
On some great river's marge
Mown them down, far from home."
ARNOLD: *Vision of the Strayed Reveller.*

I

A CTING (unpaid) Lance-Corporal Benison was the only man in A Company who didn't like Singapore.

He didn't know quite what it was that had decided him. He'd come there heavily prejudiced in its favour, for whatever it was like it would be a change from the interminable monotony of Egypt. After they were moved back from the edge of the desert into the least interesting bit of the Nile Valley, where there was no contact with the enemy, and not enough work to keep them content, Egypt became intolerable. The stalemate went on and on, disguised as war by a slight façade of patrol activity, and there seemed no possibility of another drive against the Germans. True, they lived there, by comparison with the hard existence at Petrol Parva, in conditions of green luxury; but ennui hung on them like a drug, and the little unnecessary jobs cooked up for them by an anxious Battalion H.Q. did nothing to allay their boredom. They were not deceived. They knew when they were being nursed and kidded along. From there any move was a good move, and they set out for Singapore in September like a peace-time school party going on a pleasure cruise. From Alexandria to Suez, southward through the Red Sea, across the Indian Ocean and through the Straits of Malacca, they took everything as it came, and enjoyed most of it, discounting the heat and the cramped quarters as unimportant, though it grieved them that they were not allowed ashore at Port Said. About that heterogeneous town they had heard very intriguing reports, and they would have welcomed a chance to investigate its possibilities for themselves; but a cautious adjutant thought otherwise. They were the more ready, after long repression of increasingly high spirits, for the due enjoyment of Singapore. At any rate this would be something new. They were leaving, they knew, the seat of operations; but then, there were no operations; and it was less maddening to be

82

thousands of miles away living in peace-time ease, than to sit in the sand month after month through the summer heat, knowing that your enemy was not forty miles distant, and yet unable to get at him. Anything rather than that. They would have preferred to move into action, but there was no prospect of that; the only fighting in the world just now was being done in Russia. Yugoslavia and Greece were all over, nothing left of them now but a memory of splendour and sacrifice, and an indescribably bitter taste in the mouth. And in Egypt all they did was spar like a couple of terriers on a rubbish-heap. No, if that was war, the sooner out of it the better. By all means let's sail a few thousand miles aside from it, and take whatever we find there and make the best of it.

The best promised, on the face of things, to be very good indeed. Coming in from the Straits of Malacca, between Singapore Island and Blakangmati, past Keppel Harbour and into Singapore Roads, with the first glimpse of the city opening out on the port bow in a vista of bright buildings and rich dark foliage and bluest sea and sky, the place appeared to them as a paradise, lush with all the greens they had missed from their lives for a full year. Plenteous trees, unbelievable flowers, a thousand greens gentle to the eyes, and water everywhere; this they had in exchange for the arid brown gold of Libya and the salt scrub and the sparse palms. It was very well done. They approved it. And at this time Jim had no doubt whatever that it would surpass expectation at a nearer view; as it did, but after its own fashion, and not to his taste.

Once ashore, they saw how far, how very far they had travelled from Libya. At least there, even if they never came within sight of it, they knew there was a war on; but here in Singapore City the people knew nothing of any war. The streets were wide and gracious and full of traffic and trade; and along their tree-lined shade walked and rode elegant, decorative women, whose whole and obvious object in life was to please the eyes of men and beguile their own interminable leisure. They were exquisitely dressed, and everything about them was so lacquered with expensiveness, from their hair to their scarlet toenails, that it was a wonder their menfolk were not afraid to handle them. It was impossible to imagine how such polished porcelain figurines had produced children, but children there were in considerable numbers, though usually attached to their *amahs* rather than to their mothers. And the men themselves carried upon them an aura of superhuman assurance and unlimited ease, as if they were proud of having built an empire and retired upon the profits of the building venture. Jim supposed that all these civilians—he hadn't seen so many for eighteen months or more—worked at something or other for some part of their time; there were plenty of imposing offices in the business quarter of the town; but at almost any hour of the day or night the hotels and cafés and streets and clubs seemed to be full of men, as well as women, with unlimited time to spend in play. And it became gradually clear that they held themselves to be a class apart from those who were compelled, either by necessity or war, to work. In this respect the Midshires found themselves somewhere very low in the social scale, the Other Ranks just above the Tamil labourers and Chinese artisans, the officers between the wealthy Eurasian merchants and the minor—the very minor—white officials.

This complicated sliding scale of values in humanity was not, of course, apparent at once to even the most hypersensitive among them. Some of them never awoke to it at all. They saw at first only the richness and exuberance of the scenery, the vivid redness and whiteness and greenness and blueness of town and sea, the flowering trees, the oily-leaved frangipanis and shimmering golden mohurs, the curved clean lines of pagoda roofs, and the white opulence of city squares, the hundreds of craft of all kinds lying in Singapore Roads, and the fringed palms and clustering sampans of Singapore River; a whole shining compact world of peoples and tongues and customs waiting to be explored. All one night they lay in the Roads, crowding the rails, watching the starlight gilding the water between the swinging ships; and the next morning they docked, and were marched through the city to a transit camp near Bukit Timah, six miles or so out of town.

It was on this march that the first paradisal impression of Singapore which had filled Jim's mind was suddenly shaken by a tiny tremor, as still water is shaken by one more drop of rain. They had provided timely amusement for the pause before lunch, he thought, and did not grudge that; though it was a queer feeling to be part of a side-show again, after so long of places where the man in uniform was the normality, and it was at the civilian one looked a second time. Up from Raffles Place and through the town, a wave of impersonal curiosity followed them, and the opaque stares of hundreds of pairs of eyes, and a civilised silence. In France, where last he had figured as part of a show, people had smiled, Jim remembered, and waved, and cheered, and even thrown flowers. God forbid the battalion should be tangled a second time in such a welcome as that; it was too beguiling, too discomforting to remember afterwards if things went wrong. But there was an indifference about this which chilled him more nearly. They were curious, these people, only as one species is curious about another, without friendliness, without emotion. Their life was an established, an immemorial thing, upon the polished surface of which neither wars nor rumours of war could make any graze.

The platoon was halted for ten minutes at one point, under the windows of a fashionable hotel, and a woman and a man came out upon the veranda to look at them. She was an orchid of a woman, slender and vividly coloured, with black hair piled up high under a tilted coolie hat, and eyes like amethysts, iris-shadowed under purple-black lashes, and thin brows arched high in perpetual sleek amusement. She held a half-empty sherry glass in the emaciated fingers of her left hand, and gestured with the right as she talked, little outward passes that floated her petunia-tinted nails like shed petals upon the air. And her voice —her voice was like ice being dropped into a long cool drink in the thinnest tapered glass ever made in Venice. The man was not quite middle-aged, smooth, going rather bald on top, and his face was as exact an ivory colour as his tussore suit. They stood together, these two, and looked the Midshires over steadily; and the woman said, in that piercingly clear, cool and brittle voice of hers:

"My dear, how drab! Not even Highlanders! What *are* they?"

"Not sure, m'dear. Some county regiment from the Midlands— ex-territorial battalion, too, I'm afraid. Gwynn was telling me they were docking, but I didn't pay much attention."

"Oh, *no!*" she said, between a laugh and a disappointed sigh. "He promised me some new blood, too, the beast. I expect all the officers are sons of publicans, or secondary schoolmasters, or rural district councillors, or something equally deadly. They look the part, don't they, poor lambs. So utterly *worthy!*" She went on drinking sherry, her smooth lips smiling against the glass.

"Nothing very glamorous about 'em, certainly!" agreed the man, his disparaging eyes passing over the ranks in a long, leisurely stare. "A little solid virtue will be good for you, Joy. Go to work on 'em. See what you can really do against all the handicaps."

"I?" Her amethyst eyes opened wide. "Oh, I resign! I know my limitations. After all, one must at least have a working knowledge of the language. Why, I don't suppose there's even a bridge-player among them. Oh, no, my sweet, I draw the line. This silk 'purse from sow's ear legend doesn't make the slightest appeal, thanks. Let's go back to lunch."

They went in from the veranda, the swish of her hyacinth skirts leaving a faint sweetness upon the air.

That was the beginning of it, and at that time it was nothing, only a second or so of discomfort, and an itch to show that exquisite, supercilious bitch what a war was really like, and how little her values counted in it. She was only a solitary bat-brained female, not a symbol, not even a type. It was only afterwards that the pin-pricks began to add up and make sense, amounting in the end to something more formidable than any one woman's clearly stated disappointment in the 4th Midshires.

From Bukit Timah it was easy to get into Singapore City whenever they were off duty, and as yet they had no work to do. In twos and threes they streamed back into town every evening, swelling the already considerable crowd of seekers after pleasure. They found Raffles Hotel and all the reputable ones of its kind rigidly reserved for the use of officers, and themselves pointedly directed to a series of non-committal establishments calling themselves cabarets, and blessed usually with some such name as the Golden World, the Happy World, the Halcyon World. The feminine company there was what they might have expected, and most of it Eurasian into the bargain. They were nobody's concern. It was nobody's business to offer them hospitality or provide them with congenial company. The petunia-coloured woman in the coolie hat was not alone, it seemed, in rejecting them. They were not, to the people of this city, equals, but only retainers. Except as a barrier against Japan, a kind of costly insurance, they did not exist.

If the questionable respectability of the Golden World palled, there was always, of course, Lavendar Street and the Rangoon Road, about which there was no question of respectability. Jim and Charlie walked down Lavendar Street one night, just to see what it was like; past the pickets standing waiting to remove the inevitable evening crop of casualties, and into that rustling roadway of girls and their patrons. Along every yard of it their sleeves were plucked, and soft voices poured improbable pidgin-English sales-talk into their ears. The girls themselves seldom talked; they stood posing in the roadway before their doors, almost as immobile and expressionless as Charlie's description of the Ouled Naïl of Algeria, and probably as bored, permitting their charms to be displayed and expounded by their old woman patrons, and appraising the prospective customer with glittering, painted eyes, but with no apparent eagerness or reluctance. There were girls of every colour and description, some even near-white. Most of them were young, and some were attractive even by Jim's narrow standards. Chinese, Malay, Burmese, Dusun, Murut, they slipped forward indifferently out of the shadows, and suffered themselves to be shown off like cheap jewellery on a Woolworth counter. Only once did Jim see any of them display any sort of feeling in the matter, and that was when a young Burmese girl, whose manageress was extolling her charms volubly into Charlie's left ear, suddenly took a voluntary step towards him, and put her small hand against his breast with a soft, wild gesture, and stood so, close, studying him as she was accustomed to being studied, as unembarrassed as a cat, and with the same acute, unwavering interest.

She was tall, as Burmese women go, and still neat and fresh, for she was very young. Perhaps she had not long been proficient in her trade, for that sudden fearless, candid gesture had none of the laboured grace of the professional, and her eyes, under the broad forehead, were vividly awake and aware. Also, when she put the artful folds of her veil aside, she could almost have been beautiful, there was so distinct a personality within her. The Burmese, so Jim had heard, were a very moral race. Clearly she was not. To sympathise with her situation was to waste your time. If she had not wanted a room in Lavendar Street she would not have been in one. For here was one who knew what she wanted, and reached her hand for it imperiously; just as she had reached her hand for Charlie Smith.

He put her aside then lightly enough, and she stepped back without apparent disappointment, and let him go; perhaps because she knew he would come back. Jim knew it, too. There was just that something about her which retained a challenging quality even when she offered it for sale instead of bestowing it as largesse, as by nature she was intended to do. Not for three or four days did the remembrance of her achieve its object; but one night Charlie Smith went off on his own, and Jim knew that the Burmese girl had got what she wanted. The next time he walked down Lavendar Street, Ma Hla was not there. In any case she would have stayed there, patron or no patron, contract or no contract, only so long as it suited her obscure and incalculable purposes.

Jim was neither bewildered nor troubled by this lapse on Charlie's part as once he would have been. He didn't expect consistency now from any man; much less, of course, from any woman. The Charlie who had warned off Curly from the stews of Benghazi with horrible threats merged without difficulty into the Charlie who succumbed to the fascinations of Ma Hla in Lavendar Street. He still kept his north eye on the kids, and they still responded. Even if they had known about Ma Hla, as he took good care they should not, they would still have held him in the same regard. He was one of those rare people who move with assurance even when they make no pretence that their feet are anything but clay.

So Charlie Smith, who might have chafed at the Singapore mentality more bitterly even than Jim, was side-tracked into Ma Hla's green cotton lap, and turned an indifferent shoulder upon the vexations of his kind. Besides, he had expected what he found, and could afford to pass it by with his cynical smile instead of breaking his head against it. And as for the youngsters, they grumbled and groused at being shut out of this place and that, and treated like an outbreak of plague; but they could and did look round at once for the pick of what was left, and settle down to have a very comfortable time with it, only momentarily piqued at the limitations imposed upon their enjoyment. Jim Benison was concerned with more than a good time.

It was a new kind of disquiet to him. He had been hurt before, but that was the least of troublings. He had gone through a lot, one way and another, and never whined—or at the worst, only momentarily in his weakness, and not for the world to hear. He'd wanted, of course, the whole war to stay as brightly divided into black and white as it began; but he'd survived the shock of finding that it didn't. For always he'd had the rock at his back, the rightness and excellence of England, its generosity, its sincerity, its disinterested goodness, and its unity; yes, above all, its unity to which all the weaker countries might cling and reach salvation. He'd believed—looking back now he saw that he had believed implicitly—that all must go right for a cause in itself so right. Well, that didn't last long. Flanders finished that, Flanders where the black swept the white off the board, where the Jerries fought like heroes and devils, and the British and French like blindfolded animals. All the vigour, and vision, and conviction which should have fought on the side of the angels seemed to have passed over to the powers of darkness.

It was a long time since he'd let himself think about Flanders, but it came back to him vividly now. Was it possible that these toy women existed in the same world?

Right will prevail, will it? It needs more than just the quality of being right. It needs tanks, and guns, and men, and realism in the use of them. You can be as right and good as you like, and remain hopelessly incompetent at running a war. And who could honestly claim that Britain had handled hers well? But still there had never been any doubt of final victory, because the rock, the immovable rock was there.

So he had felt, and while every other illusion was stripped from him, this was never shaken. Never until now. Suddenly, in this summer city where war-time values did not exist, where exclusive European clubs froze out Chinese and Indian alike, and the private soldiers who were good enough to fight for democracy were not good enough to drink under the same roof with the local inhabitants, he felt the rock dwindle and recede, leaving him naked. He felt a knife-point in his back.

2

It was in November they went up-country. A few Jonahs were taking a black view of the Japanese situation and the obscure reactions of the Thai government, and batches of reinforcements were being sent north to join the unhappy units stewing in the mangrove swamps of the Kelantan River and being eaten alive by red ants and drunk dry by leeches in the jungles of the Thai frontier. With them went the 4th Midshires; and back to another room in Lavendar Street, as composedly as she had left it, went Ma Hla. Jim saw her, the last time he ever walked down that joyous thoroughfare, posing before the doorway of her patron's house, a flower in her black, lacquered hair, and her face as sleek and indifferently content as a cat's before the fire. He wondered if she would ever become like the rest, or if she would always retain that independence of heart which had prompted her to select where it was designed that she should only be selected. He could not imagine her submitting absolutely where she had no inclination, nor ever suffering her fancy to be too deeply caught. She moved from one objective to the next, losing interest in each as she achieved it. She was past Charlie Smith. No one, not even herself, knew what the next objective would be; but the odds were that it wouldn't be located in Lavendar Street.

As for Charlie, he'd had what he wanted from her, and it wasn't companionship, and it certainly wasn't love; and having had it, he was quite ready to move on, just as she was. It was a queer attitude, thought Jim, but at least it did nobody any damage. If there had been any affection on either side, Charlie could hardly have withdrawn himself so blithely from her, or she have relinquished him so philosophically. As it was, he could have boarded a train for Timbuctoo instead of Kualakrai for all she cared.

So they went north, and in their innocence were glad to go. Curly and Gyp were like kids let out of school. They'd enjoyed Singapore, everything about it, from the bathing to the iced drinks, and from the flowerlike women to the feline flowers; but they were quite ready to move on to the next thing, and get as much fun out of that. The tedious rail journey north from Johore Bharu, through Gemas and Kuala Lipis to Kualakrai, which was their railhead, was to them a perpetual entertainment, a moving picture of flooded paddy-fields and mountain and jungle, huge-leaved trees, tall grasses, white villages, strange flowering shrubs, canna and hibiscus and flame-of-the-forest, bougainvillea and orchids, and ferns. The snags were scarcely apparent until they left the train and set off to foot-slog it forty miles or so through jungle and swamp to the coast south of Kota Bharu, but they were not unprepared for them. There always were and always would be snags. The heat, a moist heat not at all like the withering, sandy, stunning heat of Libya, had taken all the stuffing out of them for a time, even in Singapore, and they knew it must be infinitely worse in the green, enclosed darkness of the jungle. They knew there would be mosquitoes and other pests to put up with. That was all in the day's work. They under-estimated it, of course, they under-estimated everything unknown; but at least they had open minds on the subject, and were ready to accept the worst without surprise.

Nevertheless, in their ignorance they laid themselves open to all manner of discomforts. On the first halt in the hilly jungle young Gyp wandered off from their camp in the grassy clearing, to look at the tall ferns and the glittering parasitic orchids, coloured like jewels and vicious as poison, the like of which he had never seen before. He came haring back twenty minutes later, his face comical with outrage and disgust, trying desperately to pick off several grey, slug-like creatures from between his fingers, and staring in consternation at the bloody smears they left when he crushed them in the effort. He knew about mosquitoes, and he'd learned about red ants, but on the well-made roads of Singapore he had never met leeches.

It was a little thing, but curiously disquieting. Gyp would go, in the way of business, wherever you cared to send him, and neither German nor Italian nor Jap would frighten him off; but from leeches he recoiled in horror, their loathsomeness sending him into a shuddering revulsion. It was Charlie Smith, as usual, who knew what to do. How he knew was a mystery, for he was as much a stranger to these parts as the rest of them; but he had a way of establishing contact with the country wherever he went, letting himself sink into it, learning from it, living off it mentally as well as physically, so that it did not seem particularly strange that he should reach out a large hand and pull Gyp down beside him, and casually prick off the beastly creatures with his cigarette-end, as if he had been dealing with leeches all his life. They curled up and dropped off at a touch, leaving tiny punctured wounds which oozed and itched for hours afterwards, and when Gyp by ill-luck stepped upon the fallen bodies he saw his own blood squash out upon the trodden grass-stems, and was almost sick at the sight.

For a time they went fastidiously among these alien evils, arming themselves with little bags of moist salt which acted even better than a lighted cigarette, but in a very short time they forgot to care, and let the leeches feed until they dropped off. A messy business, for they walked often with their shoes full of blood and left dark smears along the trails after them; but there were no ill-effects, they found, and they had more important things to think about than mere ugly discomforts.

There were other pitfalls, too, as Jim discovered during their first day along the small river which wound northward through the mangrove swamps to empty into the Kelantan. It would have to be Jim Benison who took a risk on what looked like solid ground, and bogged himself to the waist, and had to be hauled ignominiously out by the two kids, of course! Not that he grudged them the laugh; it was worth something to have them ribbing him, for a change, and leaving each other alone, since they had to be plaguing the life out of someone. But to tell the truth, that ten minutes of floundering deeper and deeper into the mud, covered with red ants and mosquitoes, wrapped about with the sleepy stench of heat and rottenness, had brought him up short against the sharpest fear he had ever known for himself, the fear of a lingering, lonely death, in the embrace of an earth no longer familiar and kind, but monstrous and obscene. From that day one at least of the battalion walked with great circumspection in the swamps, and feared the quivering of the green ground under his feet more than all the Japs across the China Sea. To be cut down clean by machine-guns or blown to pieces by bomb-bursts—that was one thing, a legitimate thing; but to be smoothed and smothered and folded to death in warm, odorous slime, like a half-digested meal—no, that was a nightmare at which he could not look without shuddering.

They learned a great deal, though afterwards he knew they had not learned fast enough. It seemed to Jim, after three weeks of the "impenetrable" jungle, that there was precious little of it a man couldn't penetrate if he put his mind to it. Given a good *parang* and a little determination he could get through all the tangled growth of creeper and grass and fern, impossible though it looked at first glance; and where he couldn't go on foot, shallow-draught boats would take him, the Chinese sampans and the little Malay craft that rode in a few inches of water. But he was worried about his rifle. What good was it? What was the use of being able to bring down a man at long range with it, when there wasn't a long-range field of fire to be found within eighty miles or more? What he would have liked was a nice, handy little Tommy-gun cuddled into his side, something that would get off the mark in the fraction of a second when he bumped into his enemy round a clump of bamboo; because if they ever fought at all, it was going to be that sort of fighting. Once he would have put by all these dubious thoughts with the comfortable reflection that the men at the top knew what they were doing. Hadn't he said so in France, while they waited fretfully for the day of action? Once—earlier still—he would not even have noticed the possibility of doubts. Now they went with him step for step through the exquisite horrible, breath-taking jungle, through the limestone hills where the lizards sunned themselves, through the ordered, monotonous rubber plantations, through the smoothly-washed alluvial mounds of the tin mines and the butterfly-haunted swamps, to the beaches of Kelantan.

That was a sight worth remembering, the first glimpse of the China Sea through the casuarina-trees; creamy beach and sapphire sea, the whiteness of foam lipping the sand, the undertones of jade and emerald along the shallows, and far out the cobalt deeps; and above this jewelled blueness that other blue of the sky, breathlessly lofty and without a flaw.

They were there for just over a week, working at the final gun emplacements and wirings which were to hold this paradisal coast from assault by sea. Already there were concrete pill-boxes all along the fringe of the palms, and wide stretches of the beaches were mined, but there was still considerable activity inland of this first line. Every night of that week Jim would go down to the mouth of the little creek, where there were no mines, and watch the dusk come, the beauty of it in flame, and after, the sudden, sweeping, plunging dark. He didn't know why he withdrew himself from his kind to walk alone, nor why the night sucked his spirit out of him. It was like a kind of strange sickness that possessed him against his will. Something was passing from him into the magical earth, into the warm darkness and the stir of the palms, into the silence of the Chinese village across the creek, and the pallor of the houses up the hill, the rich white houses glowing in the dusk like a necklace of moonstones round the throat of the night. He leaned to his lotos-land, and yet he hated it. He was homesick for the mythical land of England, and yet he was in love with Malaya. The rest, they just took it as it came, bathed in its streams, ate its bananas and mangosteens, cursed its insects, and its heat, and waited to get out of it. As for him, he was tired, and the thing had got him which had got Charlie Smith in Lavendar Street in the body of the Burmese girl. The desire to shut up his senses and shield his mind, not from pain or the remembrance of pain, as once he had longed to do, but from the world's stupidity and inconsistency and feebleness; and from his own. Most of all from his own. Nothing went as it should; everything, in success and failure alike, was mucked up out of all recognition for the thing you had meant it to be. In hospital in England he had seen the ghosts of the warriors; in Kelantan he saw the ghost of the war. But in Kelantan he saw it across long, dreamy distances, an ugly, a ludicrous thing, but very far away.

He went down to the creek one night, and there was a man standing under the casuarina-trees, a strange little man in a tussore suit of immaculate European cut, and a white hat. It was the 6th of December. The Chinaman was standing in a demure attitude, leaning a little forward, his hands clasped across his waist. He looked across the China Sea intently, and seemed to be waiting for something in a resigned way, but

93

whether in hope or foreboding could not be guessed. When Jim came on to the edge of the beach, and the soft sound of the sand under his feet brushed the fringe of the silence, the man turned round gently, and showed a mild, smooth, yellow face, unexpectedly young. He took off his hat, and gave a solemn little bow, and: "Good evening!" he said in a soft, reedy voice and the most correct of English. "A beautiful night, is it not?" As if he had known Jim Benison all his life, and fully expected to see him here.

"Yes," said Jim, "it's a nice night."

"I have seen you walk here at this hour on other occasions," said the little man. "You care, perhaps, for the beauties of nature?"

It had never struck him that way exactly, but he grinned, and said that he supposed he did. At any rate he found it pleasant to come down to the creek in the cool of the evening. "But this is the first time I've run into anyone else here," he said.

"Ah, yes, I do not come here often. I am a busy man. My house is the white one on the hill, with the flame-of-the-forest-tree beside the gate. I am Mr. Ling Hsu Tai."

"Another admirer of nature, I see," said Jim, unconsciously sketching a larger version of the other man's bow. Upright, he stood head and shoulders over him, and yet in some inward way it was as if in observing him he found it necessary to look up. Here was a dignity unlike anything your strutting Singapore City whites had.

"My interest," said Ling Hsu Tai, with a smile, "is, I fear, purely practical; I was looking for something."

"Oh, something you've lost?" Though it had been at the sea he stared, and not at the ground. "Pity it's getting dark," said Jim. "Not much hope of finding anything here to-night."

The lustrous brown eyes behind the gold-rimmed eyeglasses looked at him steadily. "No, you mistake me. I was looking for smoke on the sky-line. The ships, when they come, will, I think, come this way."

"The ships? You mean the Japanese?" Nor had he said "if they come", but "when they come".

"Yes, the Japanese"

"You think they'll attack, then?"

"I reason that they will. Of what advantage is it to lay down a paved path if you do not intend to walk upon it? Yes, they will attack."

"And on this coast? All the best roads are on the west, so

they tell me." Still, he wouldn't be surprised if the little man was right. They had French Indo-China, away over there, hadn't they? A grand spring-board for a blow at this eastern coast, that would make. If they couldn't attempt much southward from here they could try to smash Kota Bharu, to the north; that alone might be worth the risk of the landing. He laughed, it was a crazy thought. In Libya there was another push on; the boys were making progress against the Germans, the whole front was moving west. He had longed for that more than for anything in life; now it was happening, and here he sat on the beaches of Kelantan, waiting for the coming of the Japanese. "My God, it's crazy!" he said. "I've fought the Jerries once, and I've fought the Eyeties once. Every time I turn round I seem to be up against somebody I've never seen before. Now it seems it's the Japs. For God's sake, who will it be next time?"

"I am unable," said Ling Hsu Tai, courteously, "to suggest a fourth antagonist. For myself, I am a timorous man, but I too have fought. There is, I believe, some difficulty for you in perceiving that you have not been diverted from the war, but only directed to another front. May I with delicacy point out that this is the oldest front of all? The first action was fought in Manchuria, very many years before what is considered in your country to be the beginning of the war. Even if you could confine your warfare to one enemy, you would still have the others to reckon with afterwards. Why, then, regret that it is against one partner you fight, rather than another?"

"There's something in that," agreed Jim. "But while I know all that, I can't feel the same way about it as you can. This is your part of the world. You know what's gone on here; I know what the Germans have done over yonder. It's them I want to reckon with."

"To contest one is to contest all," said Ling Hsu Tai. "For over two years I fought in China what was as much your battle as mine; as you have now fought for me, as well as for yourself, in Europe and wherever else you have been. The war is one, and indivisible. It may be, perhaps, that the debt between us is heavier on one side than the other, but who speaks of debts where all are giving as they can?"

The line of silver up the creek narrowed and faded. There was a stirring and quivering of leaves, like a deeply-drawn breath, and perceptibly the purple shadows dropped seaward, and swung in curtain-wise upon the dull gold of the shore.

"Feeling that way about it," said Jim slowly, "how do you come to be here, instead of still in China? Don't take me wrong; it's none of my business; I just need to understand, that's all."

The Chinaman smiled. "I am here on China's business. I was sent here to raise money; perhaps I am more successful at that than at fighting. You have heard of the United China Relief Fund? I am one of its agents in Malaya. I must confess I have had more success with dollars than with guns; as I have said, I am a timorous man."

Not so timorous, thought Jim, or you'd have packed up and left here the minute you decided they were coming. The first man they'll want in this part of the world is Ling Hsu Tai. But he couldn't imagine this little man running from Japanese or devils or both. He might retreat to a new line at a discreet walk, but he would never drop his dignity nor lose his grip of the purse he was holding for Chungking.

Because it was the sort of encounter in which you can ask almost anything, Jim said: "Is it that you don't think they'll ever make any headway here? Or don't you care a lot about going on living?"

"You over-rate," said Ling Hsu Tai in his precise English, "both my courage and my confidence in the British. Certainly I think the attack may be successfully held; but I have an open mind, and I have seen enough to know that it may not. As for my life, I attach very considerable importance to it. No, I have taken all reasonable precautions. My wife and son have gone to Sumatra already, and I intend to follow them when I have cleared up my business here, and when—and if—my agency ceases to be of any value. Not, however, until then. It is folly to close the eyes and assert that the worst will not happen, but it is also folly to run before it is clear that it must happen. The wise man stops up every available loophole and awaits the event in arms; but having taken these precautions, he continues the orderly business of living with equanimity. I, perhaps, have not been very wise. I ask myself if it would not have been better to realise all possible securities a month earlier, and so ensure their reaching China intact. But miscalculations in time are apt to occur in all matters of this kind, and if at the end unseemly haste should be necessary, at least no one remains to suffer the consequences but myself, who am the responsible party."

Jim asked, softly in the clear dark: "Is there much more to do—before you can go?"

"There are papers to be destroyed; the rest of the business is all but concluded, and most of the assets have gone south. My wife will know what to do. But these vital papers, you understand, must not be destroyed unless it proves necessary. That is why I came down to watch for a sign of activity at sea, but as you observe there is no sign. It is not yet time to take extreme steps. I can go back and work through the night now."

He turned towards the shadowy path between the casuarina-trees, and paused there, looking back over his shoulder. The oval lenses of his glasses caught out of the obscurity some glimmer of innate light, and shone faintly upon Jim. His gentle smile could no longer be distinguished, yet Jim knew that he was smiling then.

"You are wondering why I tell you all this," he said. "Perhaps I am stepping, as you would say, out of character. It is the desire of man to perpetuate himself. In three days I shall be either gone or dead. It is pleasing to me that you will remember in what circumstances and with what sentiments I either fled or died."

Jim was silent. Remember? Yes, he thought so. It was rather as if he had been talking to China in one man.

"Good night to you," said Ling Hsu Tai, and raised his white hat, and walked away between the trees until the darkness took him.

"Good night," said Jim, to the vague dissolving pallor of the tussore suit; and when the curtain of the dark had swung back fully between them: "Well!" he said to the quiet night, "what d'you know about that?" For he had talked to Chinese from the villages before, in pidgin-English and signs; but never until now had he encountered so closely the finished product of east and west which he supposed was the motive power of the new China. A country could go a long way on the stamina of that little man, he thought. If there were many like him it was not so queer that Japan had been unable to force a decision in five years. They wouldn't finish that kind in fifty years, let alone five.

But how right was he about the prospects of attack? Jim couldn't see that the position had changed at all, or the possibility of war become more imminent, in the last month. No, he didn't blame Ling Hsu Tai for getting out; but surely it would all blow along indefinitely like this, in vague threats and shuffling deceptions, rather than come to open action. The game was to hold as many as possible British troops helpless in the Far East while Germany wiped up Europe and Africa.

Japan was playing partners in Germany's hand, that was all.

So he told himself; but he wondered. He wondered all the next day, as he worked in the fringe of the jungle clearing yet more ground; and now and again he looked up at the roof of the white house, shimmering between the branches, and the blazing red of the flame-of-the-forest-tree, and wondered if the agent of the United China Relief Fund had been down to the creek again to watch for Japanese smoke upon the horizon. Three days, that was all he'd allowed for a decision; and here went the first of the three, out of the sea to eastward and into the jungle to westward, with never a sign of change to-day, to-morrow or any day.

He lay that night in the darkness of the hut, and was long in going to sleep. He heard the Ballantyne boys breathing as sweetly and evenly as children, close beside him, wrapped up in their single blankets. He heard the sleepy, high singing of mosquitoes, and the rustling and sighing of the night outside the thin wooden walls, and a medley of snores and mutterings within. In the dark the world became an index of sounds, time and vision rapt away together. By sounds he knew who slept and who stirred, and by the silence beside him he knew that Charlie Smith was awake and aware; but with which of them that infection had originated he could not be sure.

They were awake still when the 'planes went over, some time after midnight. They knew the sound of them, and the direction; they were going up from Kota Bharu, and heading out to sea. Jim raised himself on his elbow, and lay listening intently. Flight after flight, a good number of them, and at speed. Where were they going at this unearthly hour, and in such haste? And what was the sudden flurry of feet and clash of voices outside the hut, and the heavy hand of Sergeant Lake at the door? This was it. It had happened, the improbable thing. The whole room sprang to life at that sharp, dry shout. The kids fell apart and sat shaking the sleep out of their heads, one hand already reached out for their belts and kit. It was stand to, was it, and be ready for action? There had been smoke on the horizon, after all.

No one spoke; it was waste of breath, and an offence against the silence which had closed in again upon the camp. They simply groped their way into their equipment, and fell out into the clearing in a fever of haste and curiosity and eagerness; and as they went, they heard the first of the eighteen-inch guns on the shore give tongue.

3

There were four ships lying off-shore. From the fringe of palms they could see them, as the deepest shroud of the dark lifted, mere distant black specks smudging the purple of sea and sky molten together. No one could yet guess how considerable a force they carried, or what their tonnage might be, though along perhaps twenty miles of beaches innumerable eyes were straining upon them. Far out over the sea the invisible combat of 'planes circled with a distant insect-hum, curiously soothing and detached, impossible to associate with struggle or death; and yet more than one flashing descent had marked the end of a machine and a man together. Jim had seen three such falls as he lay in the deep grass within the arc of the palms; had watched the comet-plunge, the fiery curve of light flowing down the night, so gradually, so gracefully, until it was quenched in the sea. Hudsons or Japs, no one could tell which the victims were; but the Hudsons had made one ineffective sortie already, and seemed to be having no better luck this time. To judge by the recoil, they were out-numbered fairly heavily, even here, over their own flying-fields.

Jim had that old feeling in his bowels again, and worse than ever. He stood against his palm-tree, pressing his flesh against its hardness, keeping fast hold, with foot and hand and flank, of the material world and substantial things. Not more afraid than of old, for everything becomes a habit in time; but more reluctant. It was a long stride from the warmth and softness of Malaya to the violent iron of war, farther by far than the first dizzy leap when the heat within him had been new. What he had done then with ardour he did now with effort; but he did it better. Was it only that he was sick of the whole dreary business, or was the root of it in the crumb of responsibility he had incurred with his promotion? Maybe it was. He had had only himself to answer for in Libya; now he was here in command of a couple of machine-gun teams and a handful of men, covering the narrowing of the creek, where there were no mines. All those lives were his to worry about. The new anxiety goading him, the new lassitude drugging him, he found a new kind of pain; and to combat it, he had only the same old weapons of stubborn guts and fatalistic helplessness. He could do what he had to do.

Yes, the others, they were the heart of it. When Charlie Smith said in his ear: "Well, Temporary Acting Unpaid Lance-

Corporal Benison, this is it!" he was doing a hell of a lot more than pull his friend's leg. A hell of a lot more! They both knew it. There was a stab of resentment, even of dislike, the first and last he ever entertained against Charlie.

"Permanent Over-paid Play-Acting Private Smith!" he said to him in a sudden savage whisper, "it's you, not me, should be doing this bloody job."

"This way you gain," said Charlie's satanic, soft voice. You heard that sweet, small note from him, and you knew the devil was in him. "You carry the stripe, and I carry you!" Oh, yes, the fiend was in him, the acid that burned, the goad that drew unsuspected things out of Jim. What was he fishing for this time, that the bitter mischief struck out of his voice like a cobra, and bit, and was certainly venomous? At this moment, of all moments! Keep fast hold of the main issue, he told himself. No sense in letting your attention be diverted now, with those small black blots upon the paling night putting on form and shape. This is no time to do what one bit of you has always wanted to do, and all of you wants to do now, and smash his face in. Nothing he ever said, nothing he ever did, was quite obvious, and even this has three dimensions; you have to walk all round it before you know how to answer, and even then there are other ways of answering. Don't react to every thrust of his. Stand on your own feet if you want to prove you can; what better proof?

"No man carries me," said Jim Benison; but he said it with an astringent quietness, trying to convince no one, not even himself, because the very utterance was a charm, being true. Charlie might chuckle to himself as he slid back into the shadows, but the thing was said, and was seen to be fact. Hell, if he had to be a blasted non-com. he was going to be one, all the way and with all his weight, and no asking for quarter.

He looked across the creek to the deserted Chinese village, and surveyed his position with critical eyes, but it seemed to him that he could not improve upon it. If the enemy found this inlet they would almost certainly try and land men there. For one thing, by doing so they would avoid the obvious danger of land mines upon the beaches, where the sappers had sown certain death thicker than cress in a window-box; and for another thing, an inroad made here by shallow-draught vessels would bring them well into the rear of the Sikhs in the beach positions to northward, and do half their job for them before they started. So he reasoned, and so had Sergeant Lake reasoned in putting him there. The only wonder was that they had left it to him.

Well, it looked innocent enough. The two machine-guns were disposed so as to bring a converging fire to bear from either bank upon any boat attempting the entry of the narrows; the near one in the long grass under the palms, and the far one among the bushes overhanging the water, near the first tottering, mat-screened mud hut of the abandoned village. Beyond these, in the village and the forest fringes, the rest of the men lay over their rifles, and waited for the attack. The defenders, like the attackers, were invisible.

But they might not find the inlet; it was small, and bent upon itself here so that to boats coming in from the sea it would present no inviting gap. More likely the Indian troops on the fixed beach defences would take the worst of the shock. The eighteen-inch guns were going now at settled intervals, in an orderly fashion. Nothing smaller could yet hope for a range, even if it were better than half-light. But from the last spur which helped to mask the creek Jim could see the enemy ships standing gradually inshore, creeping upon the land with a deliberate stealth, so that the range was perceptibly shortening. Straining through the clear grey distances, he believed he could distinguish more ships beyond; but they could have been mere flecks deluding his eyes from too much staring; he was not sure of them. One of the nearer four, the most northerly, had, he thought, put off boats, some sort of water-craft, though it was not the boats he saw, but their tracks across the water, arrow-straight and palely luminous. Between the sonorous bursts of the heavies the staccato chattering of smaller automatic arms began.

"Going to be pretty noisy later on," said Jim, watching the explosions of water far out from shore grow iridescent in the first sudden, soft light

But it was the 'planes, not the guns, which scored the first success. He saw the bomb burst, amidships in one of the transports, veiling her in smoke and spray; saw the fire spring through the veil, expanding wonderfully in a double image of royal scarlet colouring air and sea. Not so many would come ashore from that ship, though barges put out in haste. She burned so fiercely that he thought the display would be brief, and the hulk presently settle and go down with half her load; she burned all day with the same persistent brilliance, and at night was burning still, though sullenly. An unconscionable time dying, she was, but from their point of view she was as good as dead by dawn. They hoped for more of the same fortune. Ancient Wildbeestes laboured over valiantly with their torpedoes, and tried for more deadly hits upon the other ships, but they had no luck. Where was the Jap getting his aircraft from. The sky was full of them. Were they from carriers? Some of them, maybe, but certainly not all, unless he had a fleet of carriers lying out in the China Sea. They weren't long-range 'planes, the bulk of them, they couldn't all be from Indo-China. Thailand, then? It would account for them. If only one knew what was going on up there, across the border! If they were using Thai airfields they would soon be heading over the border with infantry, and light armour, and everything they had.

He was expecting the dive-bombers. They came with the dawn, the first wave of them, in short, shallow dives over the beach defences; and having cast their load, with what degree of success Jim could not gauge, flew up and down the nearest stretch of coast machine-gunning in random swathes from the rear turrets. The creek came only under the extreme rim of this methodical area of fire. Twice the 'planes banked and roared north again full over them, where they lay flat among the bushes, and they got a good look at the familiar silhouette of the Junkers JU 87.

"Translated from the German," said Charlie Smith. "I don't know that they've bettered the instruction, exactly, but it's more than good enough." He dropped his head into his arms as the second flight passed over. The bombs were nearer this time; fragments crashed among the trees, and sent up threads of smoke from the grass; but to judge by the impacts the stuff itself was not heavy. The pattern of the bombing was working gradually south, following the arc of approach of the barges. They could see them clearly now, though they were still out of machine-gun range; motor-boats, big and moderately fast, towing slant-ended iron barges that seemed to ride on the water like sleds rather than cut through it. How many men would they hold? Fifty, probably, or even more; and there were a good number of boats.

The dive-bombers heeled again just south of their position; they heard the machine-gun bullets spatter through the flimsy mud-and-mat walls of a Chinese hut, and a ruled line of small fountains hissed across the creek. The moment passed, and left them untouched. They raised their heads again. Every time there was a queer moment of lightness, almost of wonder, to find themselves still alive.

"Anyhow they stay out of the back of your neck," said Gyp

clearly from the long grass. "Remember the Jerries in Libya?
I used to feel 'em getting knotted up in my back hair."

"No wonder," said Curly's voice, a shade higher than usual
with excitement, "it was always standing on end." And they
were at it again, even in this hard moment, shaking the bushes
with their wrangling. That was all right. Never let any raw non-
com. be such a fool as to call them to order because they took
their horse-play to war with them; those two could wrestle like
badgers, and still keep their eyes on the ball. The time to worry
about the Ballantynes was when they let each other alone.

They were on their mark, all right, when the first impact
came. They saw the black shape of the boat nose into the mouth
of the creek, and froze into quivering stillness behind their sights.
There was a minute or more of amazing quietness, while the
barge swung into view, and silently they fastened their eyes upon
the strange enemy faces, the flat, featureless, narrow-eyed faces,
seen for the first time. No one moved, though the Japs were
beginning to climb upon the sides of their craft for the leap
ashore, until Jim shouted and the whole thorny volley broke
together. The creek was swept clear. The motor-boat listed and
poured out oil across the brown water; the barge was brought up
sheer, rocking in dirty, reddish foam, spilling live men and dead
overside. Some, wading ashore, were picked off at ease by the
rifle-men. Some, on board still, and untouched, took what cover
their iron craft afforded, which was shallow but stout, and
opened fire with automatic-guns, killing one man and wound-
ing another; but the barge, bereft of way, swung broadside with
the small inshore tug of the current, and Harry Bridger, who
was nearest, lobbed a grenade into her, and that was the finish.
Except of course, that the next wouldn't be long.

Jim slid forward on his belly out of the bushes, and scrambled
down to the wounded man's side. The other one was gone; he
was certain of that already, and a near sight of him confirmed
it. But Creagh was good for years yet, only torn through the
fleshy part of the arm without a vein or artery the worse for it,
and the bleeding nothing to speak of. He said he was all right,
as good as new, not even in need of bandaging; but who knew
how long this spell of work would go on? Pumping away at
the bolt of a rifle for hours on end at more or less short intervals
is apt to lose a man a lot of blood even from a superficial wound.
Jim made a quick but workmanlike job of him, and got him
back into the deep grass, where he could rest between rounds.
Not that he would. He was Midland Irish, hotter than the one

and more mulish than the other. Jim knew that mixture.

He wished he knew what was going on up the beaches. There was a lot of noise, and far too much of it was from the dive-bombers. They seemed to be having things all their own way. He thought the Sikhs were having a pretty thin time of it. But his job was to keep this strip of dirty water clear of Japs, and not to worry about the rest; nor had he got any too many men for the job. If two or three boats made in together a solid number of the enemy might get ashore, and then there would be hell to pay. In the meantime it was getting uncomfortably hot in the enclosed places under the trees, and the creek, churned up into thick, oily mud, stank to high heaven, the jungle stink of ripeness and rottenness. He made another trip out of cover, and brought back Hayward's body into the shade, and covered it from sight. This was a longish pause. The longest for a hell of a time, he was afraid. Here came the bombers again, nearer this time, and in greater numbers. Maybe they did stay out of your hair, but you knew they were there all right. It was beastly stuff they were using, too, not heavy but with a terrific radial range, lawn-mowing fragmentation stuff that threw red-hot metal splinters well over two hundred yards. They lost another man that way. One minute Charlie was swopping yarns with him behind the near machine-gun, and the next the grass was smoking dully round his head, and half his scalp was ripped off. He wasn't dead, maybe he wouldn't die; they got him away from there still breathing, anyhow, and still unconscious, thank God, before the next wave of bombers came over. They weren't so lucky that time. One of the Junkers dropped his load just inland of them, and but for the trees half their little force might have been wiped out in that one burst. They heard the razor-sharp fragments thudding into earth and trees and mud, tearing the bushes to shreds, casting up hissing fountains from the stained water of the creek. Two men were hit that time, badly, one in the shoulder, and one in the loins, besides several superficial flesh wounds. Jim didn't have time until afterwards to notice that a sliver of metal had taken a long strip of flesh out of his own right forearm; he was too much occupied with salving what was left of Mike Summers, and beating out the fire that had started among the flimsy matting huts of the village; sticky jobs both, for the boy could be moved only with difficulty and pain, and the reed dwellings burned like tinder.

The boy was the worst. He was only a kid, not much older

than Gyp, and he had it bad. He kept hold of himself as long as he could, but he fainted when they moved him back into the pathway under the trees, and came to five minutes later screaming so lamentably that Jim wondered if he'd done right to move him at all. Then the assault boats came in again, nosing round the spur close under the bank to avoid the fire from the pillboxes on the edge of the sand; two, three of them this time, close behind one another, but coming in more cautiously, with less way on them. He knew then that he'd done well to clear the field. They could go in now with steel, as they would have to go, and no wretched wounded boy under their feet. But he wished to God the ambulance chaps would hurry up and come and put him out. It was awful to hear him. They were unspeakably relieved when he fainted again, which he did just before they opened fire on the advancing assault boats. Or was it simply that after that they were raising such a din that his cries could no longer be heard?

They knew it couldn't be done with guns only this time. However good the shooting, a certain number among so many were bound to get ashore. Some made the attempt upon the spur, standing up on the steel sides of their craft as they passed close, and leaping for the bushes. That lessened the odds, for the neck of the spur mounted another machine-gun, and whoever got ashore there was well taken care of; but there were still far too many left. They dealt with them according to their necessity. The machine-gunners were doing pretty well, keeping a steady stream of fire playing fanwise across the creek, lopping off anything human that showed himself too rashly; and the slow approach of the boats gave them time to be effective; but constantly the Japs rolled overside and plunged for the shore, and some of them made it safely on the near bank, where the field of fire was less open and the landing easier. Once in cover they were dangerous. They had to be wiped out now, before they faded into the background. Not one must survive in freedom.

Jim stood up and went for them in a roaring charge, and his handful of men shot out of their scattered cover and followed him gladly. They were outnumbered several times over, but they had the impetus, and he had timed the attack so that the impact came at the crest of the bank, before the Japs wading ashore had adjusted their balance. The clash was brief but bloody. The mud of the short slope, which had helped to repel the landing, grew dark crimson in a moment, and many small bodies rolled back into the water and lay swinging loosely with the current. But though they obviously didn't like the bayonet, they still came on. Queer creatures, not like human beings at all, persistent, automatic, clawing their way through fire and water and oil and slime towards their objective; not with the arrogant suggestion that they had a personal stake in the balance, which was the Nazi way, at least in success; not like the Eyeties, with the implication that they were driven to fight and would happily slide out of it if they could; but rather as if they pressed forward in response to a dreadful blind instinct inherent in their very flesh, like the frenzied leeches writhing through the grass to fasten on the traveller's foot, and feed themselves fat on his blood. Probably generations of leeches lived in those forests and never tasted human blood at all, but the instinct did not weaken on that account; when the desired food at last presented itself, they thrust forward to it madly, and nothing would stop them but the destruction of their obscene bodies and the incredible lust which was their only intelligence. These little, flat-faced unhuman creatures were like that. You stuck your feet in their middles and heaved them back winded into the water, you smashed their jaws in with your clubbed rifle, you bayoneted them, you all but cut them in two with a swathe of machine-gun fire, and every time they dragged themselves up again and came back at you with whatever speed and vigour they had left. They were uncanny and terrifying. They returned again and again, until you finished the job; and they took a lot of killing, being improbably tenacious like all primitive forms of life. And they came at the prompting of something obscure and repulsive in their own natures, not of courage, which was a clean, understandable thing you did not think of in connection with them at all. They neither had it nor lacked it, any more than the leeches had or lacked it when they came back again and again until you stepped on them and squashed them flat.

There on the banks of the creek, in the moist, steamy heat, they at last stepped on and squashed the Japs flat. But a lot of blood had been drained from their own body by then. When they drew together at the end of the effort, and recoiled upon the village to lick their wounds, they carried seven dead with them, and several badly injured; but there were no Japanese survivors. The heat of the sun upon the stained mud of the shore was heavy and foul; the boats, one capsized against the crazy piers under the village, one listing and filling slowly with a wash of dull brown water, one swinging in mid-stream, spilled bodies upon the current, and sent them floating down towards the spur, where they lodged, and lay rocking gently, a dirty red foam washing round them. From the iron hulls a fetid steam went up. That was the sum of it. The earth trampled into raw slime, the water stirred into bloody foam, the air fouled with the heat and stench of blood; no more to show for that hour's work.

But at least young Mike was quiet. They got the rest of their casualties back to him, and found a cocky young doctor on the scene, and the boy already covered up upon a stretcher, and under morphia. Captain Priest came along between the trees as the stretcher-bearers were carrying him away. He looked at him, and said: "What, young Summers? How is he? Is it bad?" And suddenly you loved him, because of the concern in his voice, and the wild kindness of his eyes, and most of all because he had the name right. If it had been any other man of them, he would still have known the name, and the history, and the next of kin; and a year ago they would all have looked alike to him. He was the kind that learns by touch, not by precept, a whole world falling suddenly into his knowledge as softly as the shed feather lights. They knew where they were, Priest and his company. Everything else, everyone else on God's earth might let them down, but he never would. That was one secure thing they had, one land-mark standing bolt upright in all this shifting confusion. Not every company could lean on its commander as they could.

The doctor, rather pleased with himself for reaching such an advanced position, said that it was bad enough but he'd seen plenty worse. He said the kid was good for years yet, given even ordinary luck; he didn't yet know, they none of them knew, what it was going to be like getting the wounded south through that lovely, cruel country. All he knew was nice, smooth doctoring in sterile hospital wards; that, and the queer something inside himself which made him lie forward over Mike's body when the dive-bombers came playing hopscotch again down the creek, the queer something that makes you think now and then that a man may have it in him to be better than just a man.

They took the wounded away, and the dead, and there were only the marks on the ground and the unpleasant Japanese flotsam in the creek left to record the progress of the battle. Sergeant Lake came down after Captain Priest, and cast a professional eye over the set-up, and said he couldn't let them have any more men, they'd have to stick it out. He said he thought he'd come and give them a hand; but Captain Priest looked at Jim Benison, and said abruptly that it was out of the question, he wanted Lake, they'd have to carry on.

"We'll do that, sir," said Jim.

Yes, a queer chap, this captain of theirs. His family would never recognise him when he got home again—if he got home again. It brings out some surprising things, this business. You loose a pigeon, and home an eagle. It wasn't only the surprised, bewildering courage of him; there were these other things, the way his smoke-reddened eyes looked at you and through you, and saw your very heart lusting after his confidence; and the way he filled your hands with it on the instant, without any provision or warning or reserve. He wanted Lake, did he? They'd have to carry on! Oh, yes, they'd carry on, until they dropped in their tracks. He knew he could stake on that; he was staking on it, the biggest way he knew, and he did things big.

They carried on. All through the heat of the day, in the steam of vegetation and stink of blood, they held their battered, collapsing village. Time after time boats came in, until they grew ingenious in devising means of stopping them, means more economical than the rush into the open with the bayonet. They stood waist-deep in the water among the bushes, and lobbed grenades into the barges as they passed the spur. They made little mat rafts, and built clay nests on them, and let them dry hard in the sun; and on these, when the enemy reached the curve of the creek, they launched charges of gelignite, grenades, anything they had, and sent them spinning down the current to burst against the bows of the landing-boats. There was little movement in the water, but there was a sufficient tension in midstream to move the explosives well clear of the rattan and teak piers from which they were launched. Some of the charges failed, some of the fuses were washed clear, some lodged against the bodies and debris swinging in the shallows, and exploded there; but some went directly home, lifting the boats out of the water, and spilling a rain of men into the mud, where the machine-guns finished such as were still whole. They had not, however, the means to continue this defence very long. Worse, early in the afternoon one of the machine-guns jammed, and while Charlie sat coaxing and soothing it, the rest of them had to beat off an attack with bayonets and clubbed rifles and sheer cussed ferocity. That was a bad patch. Costly, too. They couldn't afford to pay out at that rate again.

Curly and Gyp went for more ammunition in the late afternoon, and brought back no cheerful news. The Indian troops had fared pretty badly, being dive-bombed all day without ceasing, and with scarcely a sign of an Aussie or R.A.F. fighter to stand up for them. They had repulsed landing after landing, but the hell of it was there were always more; and nobody quite knew what was happening, but the Japs had almost certainly made good their beachheads to the north, nearer Kota Bharu. As for the aerodromes—well, all they knew was that the sky had throbbed with bombers all day over that direction, and the British air cover now was practically non-existent.

"The same old tale, eh?" said Jim, keeping his sweat-rimmed eyes fixed upon the opening of the creek. This, after all, was his job, not the defence of the flying-fields to the north. A man can only do one thing at a time if he's going to do it properly.

But what had happened up there? Had they had so little from the start that it could all be fairly accounted for in one day? Remember those ancient Wildbeestes blundering over to meet the Mitsubishi-built bombers and midget fighters light as gnats! Remember the way the Japanese fighters made rings round that first squadron of Buffaloes! What had happened at Kota Bharu? Had they lost the bulk of their remaining 'planes on the ground in that terrifically savage and sustained bombing? Was it to be that all over again, that old wearisome business of the man on the ground trying not only to hold the earth in place, but to stem the sea and sustain the air as well? Had they learned nothing in two years of being out-thought and out-fought?

"It looks bad," said Charlie, lying by him in the trodden grass.

"It looks bad. It looks like hell." He wiped the sweat out of his eyes. "Where do they get this idea that all we need is men?"

"And a good cause," said Charlie, in his voice of a famished devil. "Don't forget we have a good cause. The Lord will provide for His own."

"It begins to look as if hell does these things better," said Jim.

"Hell carries no passengers," said Charlie.

Suddenly Jim remembered with a horrible, blinding, bitter anger the woman on the hotel balcony at Singapore, the iris-coloured, glistening woman with her assurance, and her disdain, and her damnable, damning condescension. "So utterly *worthy* !" Priest, and little Stringer, and Lake, and poor Mike Summers—"I don't suppose there's even a bridge-player among them!" "My dear, how drab! Not even Highlanders!" He sank his nails into the hot, moist earth, and felt the burning of it beat back into him like a reflection of his hate. Hell carries no passengers! No, but we do—we do! That bitch and her kind, piqued at being deprived of a favourite brand of gin or a shade of lipstick, while we try to carry them in one arm and fight with the other. And other women—Imogen, at home, tearing her way into a smashed ambulance to get out a dying child—old Simone risking her life for two English fugitives, her face so grim and so serene—and Miriam—Miriam—Miriam—the very name of her—the mere sound of her name——

"How long can we hold this?" asked Charlie. "How long is it worth holding, if they've made good their landings north?"

"I don't know what it's worth," he said. "I know we shall hold it until either we all go west, or until we're told to move."

"That won't be long," said Charlie, and swung to his gun again as the trees forward of them rustled over the coming of the next assault.

It was not long; not long as they knew time now. It came in the dusk, before the reflection of the sunset had left the sea; and it came while there were still a baker's dozen of them alive to obey it. They were in pretty good shape, considering all things, but deeply troubled because there was by that time an effective Japanese point upon their spur, and they could not throw it back into the sea. The machine-gun which had held that position inviolate was some hours out of action, and its crew dead. But the reason for the abandonment of the village was not there; it was down on their right flank, where an earlier landing had been made across the beach, and the enemy was suspected of filtering through to the rear. To close the thinly-held section they drew in their line, silently moving backward step by step with their two beloved guns and their few grenades, back through the hot darkness of the jungle to their new position on the southern side of a clearing from which the huts had been swept flat to afford a field of fire. It was a short withdrawal; but it was a withdrawal. As they accomplished it, the night came down, purple and soft and cool. They lay down at their guns, and got a few mouthfuls of bully and biscuit down throats raw with heat and smoke. They looked for their friends as the rest of the company closed in on their left. There were many gaps. He knew by then, he knew from beforetime, that no gap like that is ever filled. You can put another man there, but there is still the emptiness where the other one was. You can't fill that.

He was very tired; they all were. No use thinking of that yet; this was only the first day, they hadn't yet stood up to twenty-four hours of it, and there might be as much as twenty-four days, rather than hours, before they could get a decent relief. In any case, only the very young among them, whose resilient spirits could speedily put by all but physical weariness, could possibly sleep now. Curly fell asleep over his rifle, with his head upon Charlie's lean flank. He slept like the abandoned child he was, suddenly, shutting the door against the world, his breathing soft and deep. Even Gyp, with only two and a half years between them, couldn't close his eyes and turn his back on realities like that. But maybe there was more than merely two and a half years of time in it; there was a whole lifetime of taking the responsibility for both of them, of trying to keep step with the adult world on one side and Curly on the other. That makes a kid grow up early. If there'd been a third son, now—Curly must now be just about a month short of the age Brian Ridley was when he died; but Brian had acquired in his platoon so many younger brothers.

Strange, the gentleness of the darkness upon eyes prickly with smoke, and bodies stiff with sweat. Strange, to find suddenly this island of leisure and rest within oneself, this silent place full of remembered faces; to have time in the middle of battle to touch again old loves, and recognise and make welcome new ones. There were a lot of people in his calendar of saints now. That was how a man kept himself alive and unbroken among devils, by looking at his own particular saints, and remembering that they too were men.

He turned his head upon his arm, and saw Charlie Smith looking at him, with a peculiar contemplative smile which reached him even through the dark. Charlie Smith knew everything. He could show you things you didn't know were in your mind; sometimes Jim thought it was he who had put them there.

"Well?" said Jim bitterly, "what did we do wrong this time?" As if he didn't know! As if they didn't all know!

"The same thing," said Charlie. "We undervalued the enemy. We mixed up condemnation with contempt—we always do."

"And what about the rest? What about the natives here? They'd have helped us if we'd let 'em. They'd have done things for us if we'd told 'em what to do. They'd have followed us, if we'd offered 'em any lead. But no, they're only natives! It isn't their war! They only live here—the running of it's nothing to do with them. The defence of it—that's no business of theirs, either. My God, the things we've thrown away!"

"Yes," said Charlie, "we do that. Everything that isn't clearly stamped 'British Made'."

"And what about the other passengers? They made this mess. They were the ones who should have known what to do, the ones who should have seen what could be used. They haven't lifted a finger. They're still passengers."

"Yes," said Charlie again. "But they're going to find it a rough passage."

Jim laughed. "Here, yes, maybe, if they don't wake up pretty soon. But some of their kind are riding first class back home, too. They'll come out of it with fortunes—and most likely decorations, as well."

"Even with them," said Charlie Smith softly, "the whirlwind may catch up this time."

He laughed again, pressing his shaking mouth into his arm. "What makes you think it's going to be different this time?"

"You do. Have you ever thought about these things before? Haven't you changed? Haven't you made discoveries? And do you think you're the only one? Oh, yes," he said in a very low voice, "it's going to be different this time. Even I believe in the possibility now. I haven't believed in anything for the last ten years, but even I have hopes now. That's your doing, my true-blue, bred-in-the-bone Tory countryman! That's your miracle, and it's you that'll have to answer for it." And suddenly he put his hand upon Jim's shoulder, and wrenched him round to face him as easily as picking up a windfall. "God help you if you let me down after this!" he said. "Dead or alive, I'll never leave you alone."

Rigid against each other in the grass, they felt the sky over them shuddering with 'planes. And suddenly, from the position they had left, they saw flames go up, licking between the trees upon the terraced hill where the white houses were, the quiet white houses behind the flame-of-the-forest-trees. The second of the three days Ling Hsu Tai had allowed himself was barely dead. Remember him? Yes, very clearly, very faithfully. He was a part of that inner place, too, a little bit of the strength of the world, the little man encountered once in the dusk; little, but of equal stature and dignity with death.

To-morrow, back to the beach; to-morrow—to-morrow——

<h2 style="text-align:center">4</h2>

There was no going back to the beaches of Kelantan, on the morrow or any other day. Instead, there was what he had foreseen in taking the first step back, a continuous recoiling struggle to maintain their front and keep the Japs on the northern side of it. Clearly it was no use fighting stubbornly for an isolated patch of ground when the enemy had by-passed you and pushed on southward towards the vital parts you were trying to cover. The Midshires, or small parties of them, were continually in danger of making this senseless gesture. The only alternative was to go on retreating. They were ordered to leave Kota Bharu, and they went; and from that spring flowed the later sickening stream of retreats which thrust them back by the end of December to the southern jungles of the Pahang river, not so far from the borders of Johore.

By then all pattern, all plan had gone out of their fighting. They had fought without ceasing for twenty days, snatching drunken moments of sleep where they could, eating and drinking when they had the means, out-numbered, out-run, out-flanked, dive-bombed to stupefaction, with no effective air cover. They no longer knew where their friends were, and their enemies were everywhere, in the grass, in the reeds, among the branches of the trees, before them and behind. They did not know what steps, if any, were being taken in the rear to relieve them, or to re-establish some sort of a continuous front which could be held. They no longer thought of that possibility, but fastened their exhausted and befogged minds upon the only stable objective they knew. At least they could not go wrong by killing every Jap they could find, and conserving what they could of their own forces. Their senses, dazed and darkened and bludgeoned into numbness, clung to that one ferocious purpose like a bull-terrier to his opponent's throat. It was the only thing they could still comprehend, and had still the strength to do.

The conditions in which they now fought were increasingly fantastic. The enemy were a disease which had spread across the country, a virus which fell on them from the trees. It was nothing out of the ordinary to have a grenade dropped among them from the branches overhead, or to drag out a human frog from the swamps, a thing painted green and smeared with mud, but still a man. They were everywhere. Jim thought if you dredged the paddy fields you would bring up Japs, and if you shook the fruit-trees you would get Japs instead of mangosteens and bananas. Beset by so many independent incidents, at every turn faced with the unexpected encounter, it was difficult to maintain contact at all times with the other platoons of A Company, let alone with the other companies of the battalion; the retreat—what else was it?—had become a series of isolated rearguard actions and backward leaps, undignified, maddening, shattering to tired men. Often they maintained touch only by desperate effort. Many small parties were lost during December. Some cut their way back to their units after days of wandering in the jungle; some never came back at all, and their fate was a matter of conjecture. Of those who returned, all had confused stories to tell of Malays who were not Malays, and Chinese who turned out to by anything but Chinese. A sarong was no test. The Japs wore anything that came to hand, coolie dress, singlets and cotton shorts, steel helmets, rough-rider hats taken from British dead, Malay sarongs, anything from more or less full uniform to a loin-cloth and a few leafy twigs. But most of all they wore the jungle, its colouring, its light and shadow, the habit of invisibility.

It was in the southern jungles of Pahang in the early days of January, that Sergeant Lake, the infallible, the unshakable, lost himself and ten men in the swamps. It was an excusable lapse, considering the circumstances. The party had deployed and settled down in cover to defend the ford of a wide creek, while the main body of the company made the passage. By the time they had all crossed the move had been located by Junkers 87's and three of them were cruising up and down over the ford, machine-gunning the last of the troops viciously, and continuing the exercise long after the survivors had all taken cover in the forests on the farther side. The rearguard wisely remained invisible. To attempt the crossing then was suicide. They lay low, and waited until the sportive pilots tired of raising fountains of mud, and made off in search of more fruitful hunting grounds. By then, though they crossed in haste, and made all possible speed after their fellows by the one practicable path they could find, they had lost all contact with the company; but they were sure of their direction, and confident of overtaking them in a little while.

That was on the first day. By the time darkness fell they were less sure, and their speed had perceptibly decreased, partly because of the slackening of their conviction of competence, but chiefly because there were two sick men among them. Curly was shaking with the first ague of malaria, his eyes bright and hot, his hands dry as bone; and Hughson had a bullet-wound through the fleshy part of his thigh, and had lost a lot of blood. Reducing their speed to carry these two without shaming them, the party sacrificed yet more ground. When they halted for the night they knew themselves isolated; it was not pleasant knowledge.

"I'll take this party back into the line," said Sergeant Lake, placing his sentinels for the halt, "if it kills me!" And with this prophetic oath he seemed to shake from him all concern for himself or any of the preoccupations of living, and all his energies of mind and body flowed into this one channel. He would take that party back or die trying.

He drove them for five days and nights, steering by sunrise and sunset and the conviction in himself that he could get them through. He put into them something of the power he had, and the singleness, so that Curly continued silent long after he was dropping with fever and fatigue, and Hughson fought to stay on his feet when he could not even maintain himself upright without holding by his neighbour. After that they made a rough litter with branches and belts and vines, and carried him; but he still insisted on taking his turn with the rest as look-out on the halts, and they humoured him because it satisfied the need he had to consider himself justified in continuing to live.

They lived off the country now with a vengeance, eating fruit, and what rice and meat they could get from the occasional Chinese and Malay villages they encountered. There was not enough of it to satisfy them, but it sufficed to keep them alive and in command of their bodies. Those very bodies had changed. In the course of that tortuous march, in the darkness and sultry heat under the trees, in the steam of the earth, they lost much that had been in them, and gained strange things in return. They had long ago discarded all their useless equipment. During these days they stripped off and threw away the rags of their shirts, and such steel helmets as had been retained, and anything else which was no longer of use. They had sweated away all the flesh from their bones, and went in leanness, hard and copper-coloured and very filthy, with bushmen's beards stippled with sores and prickly heat; they wore nothing but their boots and shorts, and their heads were bared to the sun, or wrapped in cloths of coloured cotton torn from sarongs, like Malay pirates. They had lost some of their rifles; Curly's had slipped out of his shaking hands and sunk in the bubbling red water of a creek in the mangroves, and Lake had traded his at a Chinese village for a *parang* and a *kris* which were now of infinitely more use to him and to his friends. He had acquired, besides, from a dead officer by the ford, a revolver, and all this formidable armament in his belt made him look more than ever the complete desperado.

They were, take them all in all, a queer bunch to find themselves cutting a way through the jungle together. There was Lake himself, the best sort of professional soldier, so deeply learned in his subject that he could afford to ignore the preliminary rules and adjust all the others to suit the local conditions; a hard, intolerant man, but wise, and jealously considerate of his own. There was Hughson, a useful man when he was whole, a butcher by trade, like his father before him, when every man returned to his place, but a botanist by nature. He lay in his litter, when he became resigned to being helpless, and filled his hands full with fronds of fern, and speckled orchids, and flowering vines. "You don't get them in Staffordshire," he would say. "I raised a primula that colour once—took first prize at the 'Bulls' Head' Show. They wouldn't half open their eyes if they could see these." There was Gregory, who taught art in a secondary school before the war—in several secondary schools, in fact, until he got into trouble every time for propagating his particular gospel of individual liberty. He was a thin, rangy young man with red hair and lively eyes, who could no more keep out of hot water than a bear can keep away from honey. Under any government he would find something to contest; it was in his nature, it was what made him function. With nothing but Japs and jungle in sight, he could make do with Japs, and when they failed, with jungle. There was Farrar, a collier in peace-time, a family man who fought well only because he wanted to get home and dig coal on a slightly better wage for the rest of his life. When the belated newspapers reached them in Egypt, and the kids raged about colliery strikes at home, he was quiet, and once, when he heard an indignant twenty-year-old declaiming that all the strikers ought to be shot, he shut them all up by saying slowly: "Well, I don't know. They ain't going the right way about it, but those lads reckon they're fighting my war back there just as much as I'm fighting theirs here.

They're doing it all wrong; maybe they ain't so smart, at that; but I haven't done so good myself, to say very much. And then, they ain't been handled all that smart, either." He was the man who knew both sides; that was the hardest part to play in this business.

These three, with Charlie Smith and Jim Benison, were the responsibles on whom Lake chiefly relied. The remaining five were all youngsters, not one of them above twenty-two. There was Garland, who had quit a comfortable job as his father's bailiff to join up, not for any high-flown reasons of ideology, but because he was bored, and this was a heaven-sent opportunity of getting away from home. There was Chick Foulds, straight from unskilled labour in an iron works, a boy who had never had enough to eat in his life by Garland's standards, nor any money in his pockets; and these two were as thick as thieves, though in peace-time their paths would never have crossed at all. There was the ex-cowman Parnaby, slow but assured of speech and movement, and very deft with his hands; and the slick little builder's clerk Tremlett, a smooth fox-terrier of a lad, full of cheek and guts and quivering curiosity. And there was Curly Ballantyne; but just now Curly was a dead loss.

They made, during those days, some progress southward, but by such devious and difficult tracks that they could not gauge the distance they had travelled. For three days they did not see anything of the enemy on the ground, though occasionally they heard 'planes passing over, and recognising the note of bombers, wondered what was happening in Singapore. But on the fourth day, and the fifth, they made unexpected contacts with isolated small parties of Japs, and shot it out without loss, being the stronger in numbers in spite of their two sick men. Sergeant Lake grew terribly handy with the *kris*. He preferred it for its silence, and because it gave nothing away.

They were helped, too, by Chinese, and sometimes by Malays; at almost every village they touched they were given rice without asking; and it was a Malay boy who ferried them across a river in southern Pahang, and another Malay who showed them the hill-path on that fifth evening, and offered with every expression of partisanship to guide them to a village for the night.

They met him in a clearing, just as the light was failing, and at first glance he turned and ran from them, diving into the underbush in panic, as well he might, for they were a fearsome sight. But they waited, and he came back, caution and curiosity alternating in his face. He examined them at length, and said unexpectedly: "You English?"

Satisfied on this point, he explained himself, in very moderate English helped out by signs. He had been, it seemed, donkey-man at the processing plant of a rubber plantation some miles away, nearer the coast, and after holding the job for over ten years had lived to see the day when he was told to smash up all his machinery, take his share of rice from the godown, and his wages, and get out. He had left the latex burning fiercely, and the plant wrecked, and had come back to his inland village, where at first sight of the Japanese he could disappear into the jungle. He said he would take them there if they liked. He said there was an Indian doctor not far away, who had also left the coast, his practice having evaporated, and his own record being too advanced for his life to be safe where the Japs came.

It was the offer of a doctor that decided Sergeant Lake. The little man told a convincing tale, of which quite certainly the greater part was true, or where had he got his English? Hughson was in pretty bad shape, and they were all pock-marked with bites; and if there was a chance, even the remotest, of getting hold of quinine and other drugs, they were bound to take it.

"All right, chum!" said Lake. "Go ahead and bring us to this village of yours. We're right behind you."

The little Malay—he was as lean and brown and hard as the branches of the trees, and even his face might have been cut from teak—led them by a narrow track which climbed the hills westward, and carried them away from the mangroves into dry ground. It was easier going there. He set a pace they could not keep because of Hughson, and twice Lake called him back to them; and after the second time, he went more easily, constantly looking back to assure himself that they were at his heels. The journey was not long; there was still a faint grey shimmer of light when he brought them to the edge of a small clearing, and they saw the mat huts of the village before them. They had already received welcome and help at many such. There was nothing different about this one, except that it was more than usually opportune. They advanced into the open eagerly, confidently, foreseeing rest for their wounded, and food, and possibly a guide on the next stage, or news of other British units ahead of them. The Malay went smiling and bending before them, inviting them in; this until they were clear of the darkness of the trees, and he well ahead of them towards the huts. Then he suddenly uttered a thin, high cry, and ran from them, and plunged into one of the dark, low doorways and disappeared.

It was less the unexpectedness of the movement than some innate and ready distrust in himself that made Sergeant Lake halt in his tracks, and wave back the tail of his procession with a long, brown arm.

"Get back into the trees," he said, "and stay there." And without waiting for their obedience or protest he went forward over the short grass, straight for the huts, the revolver braced in his hand. Farrar, who was next to him, followed him step for step, no one afterwards knew why. Whether he was tired past understanding, or would not stand to let Lake go forward alone, after him he went, and died with him. For they had not gone ten paces when the dull brown of the mat wall ahead of them shook as if in a gale, and the stuttering rattle of an automatic-gun broke out, slashing the silence and the dusk to shreds. They fell together, and rolled along the grass, and lay still.

In the dark aisles of the track the survivors dropped to earth, and pressed their bodies into the steamy mould as the semi-circle of fire swept back and forth over them, searching the recesses of the forest for the last of them. Jim, on the edge of the clearing, lay with Hughson in his arm, where he had dragged him down, out of the litter. He was the nearest to the dead; he had seen the bullets thudding into their flesh. He lay now watching the emptiness of the air above them, and the spitting flashes of the hidden gun turning fanwise across and across the dusk; and a drift of confused thoughts went through his mind, numbed, limping thoughts, sleep-walking in and out of his brain. He was not yet angry; that was to come. In such weariness it is difficult to feel quick reactions even to treachery. He only thought, over and over, wondering at it: "Lake's dead—they got him clean through the chest—pretty near cut him in two. He's dead! That leaves me—that makes it my job from this on. Lance-Corporal Benison, you'd better think fast. You've got to do something about it. What are you going to do?" And he didn't know, and he couldn't think for a full minute, because of the suddenness of the betrayal, and the painful exhaustion of his mind.

And then the anger came, the cold, clear anger that blew through him like a great wind, and tore him erect against the batterings of chance. Over and over again he saw the two deaths enacted, until the pattern of them was branded into him with an aching, acid intensity. It was his move now, was it? It was up to him now. Well, what Lake had begun he would finish. They were nine men still, and seven of them were whole. That was enough for the job. "I'll get them," he thought, "the Japs and their bloody decoy—I'll get every man of them, if it's the last thing I do." And he began, inside the ice of his mind, to consider how best to do it.

Hughson, beside him, whispered: "My God, the sergeant!" as if they could do anything about Lake now! No, it was of the others he was thinking, it was the others he moved about like chessmen in his brain. Charlie Smith was just behind them in the grass. "You carry the stripe and I carry you!" That was the way it went. The old devil, who wouldn't lift a hand's load of responsibility himself, and yet was willing to put himself to the infinitely greater trouble of raising up men to do it for him. Jim drew inch by inch back to him, and said in his ear: "Pass the word back—nobody fires till I give the order. I'm doing no damn-fool thing like shooting it out on these terms."

And Charlie Smith passed the word back unquestioningly, withdrawing his gaunt body silently through the grass. In a few minutes, between the vicious stammerings of the automatic-gun as it raked the underbrush close above them, his cool voice came: "Well, it's all yours. Now what?"

What, indeed? It wasn't so easy. Seven whole men and two sick ones against a number unknown. But it won't be great. They hunt in small formations, these creatures; they have the secret of it, the inconspicuous, new, sudden, treacherous warfare. In a place like this there will be only a handful. As for arms, they have an automatic-gun, and we've got rifles, and exactly three grenades. They have one pull—they know how many we are; their blasted Malay stooge will see to that. Or do they? Not one of us has fired a shot or made a sound since they opened fire. All they know is how many we were, not how many we are now. If we keep silence long enough, they'll come out to see. All we want is one clear sight of them; even a darker thing in the dark, a thing that moves instead of being still. That's where we hold the cards; we can move, and they can't. From them every way is open ground, and from us every way is jungle darkness. We can go right round them. We will go right round them.

He said to Charlie: "Now this! You see that stretch of bushes to the left? How near can you get without being heard?"

"Near enough," said Charlie Smith. "What then?"

"Then you stay invisible until they come out to see what

they've got. When they're well out, pick the nearest. And take one of the grenades—you'll be the best-placed to use 'em."

"Suppose they don't come out?"

"They will," said Jim.

"All right. Anything else?"

"Yes. Take Tremlett half-way with you. Find him a good spot, and tell him to wait till they come into the open and then pick 'em off the safest way. Where's Gregory?"

"Right behind you," said Gregory's voice. "I heard all that. What's mine?"

"The same, but you go right. Take Chick along—he's the lightest of the bunch. Give me that last grenade, and get moving."

He was left with the remnant of his force, Parnaby and Garland and the two sick men. Hughson could shoot, if need be, but Curly was no good. Get him back, well out of range, where nothing bad can happen to him; because you've still got Gyp to face if any harm comes to him; and anyhow he's the Company's kid. Jim stationed his three serviceable rifles, and himself edged back into the close, leafy tunnel of the track, and dragged Curly back fifty yards or more along it, and stowed him into cover. He didn't realise what was happening, anyhow; he was burning hot, and the sweat stood on him like quicksilver. When you put him somewhere, he stayed; he couldn't get far without somebody's arm under him. He was another reason—but they needed none—why they must have cover and food, and if possible, drugs.

Jim went back to his battlefield, and in the silence of the night, immense and smooth after the fraying chatter of the gun had ceased, he lay down to bide his time. Nor had they very long to wait. It was a foregone conclusion that the troops in the huts would come out, as soon as they were satisfied that they could safely do so, to examine their kill. The only difficulty was to resist the temptation to let fly at them as soon as they showed themselves, before they came well out of cover; but the others would hold their fire until he called the tune, and he was in no hurry. He felt their weight behind him, the burden of trust. He meant to get every man of the group that held the village, every man and most particularly the Malay donkeyman. Why had he betrayed them? What did he stand to gain? Was it only an old hate he wanted to satisfy, or was he a professional agent, or had money passed to buy his services as you buy cabbages in a market, without emotion of any kind?

It was very quiet. The gun did not speak again. For a time it was so silent that he thought he could detect the rustling movements of his own men circling upon the village to left and right. He lay nursing his sights, and saw the darkness of the nearest doorway, a narrow rectangle purple-black in the night, shake and change its shape, bulging outward towards him. That was the first venture; it was either a man, or an attempt to represent one. He lay still, and let it alone. It left the doorway altogether, and came a few steps forward, and he saw it for a man, the man with the automatic-gun. Small, in what looked like a sarong and a light-coloured cotton coat, the more fool he; fool to outline the vital parts of him with the only pallor in the clearing, and doubly fool to come out with the gun and leave his fellows behind. That made it easy. Only let him come well forward, where a fellow could pick him off at leisure, and keep any of the others from reaching the gun. If he really believed there was no survivor to lift a hand, why should he hesitate? He paused twice, and looked all round, and listened, and appeared to be satisfied, for he turned and called back over his shoulder into the hut, a sudden small explosion of sound in the silence, though the high-pitched voice was probably tuned to no more than a whisper. Then he walked briskly forward, right into Jim's hands.

Jim waited. He let the creature reach Lake's body, and turn it over with his foot, and stoop over it. He let one, two, three more figures appear from the huts, and patter forward through the grass after the first. Then, because he did not dare to wait too long, he chose his moment, and killed his man at leisure. He crumpled in the waist, recovered himself for a second, and then bowed forward over the sergeant's body, and lay upon the fallen automatic-gun. That was perfect; that made all safe. The rest, even if they had not been picked off from left and right, could not reach that gun and live; and there was no other, or it would have been in action by now. He had them now; he was sure of them. From his right, Tremlett had got the second/Jap; and from his left, both Chick and Gregory were firing briskly. Garland, on his own initiative, was off through the grass on his belly, like a snake, reaching out for the coveted gun, rolling the body of the Japanese out of his way greedily, and kneeling up with the stock gripped into his hip, the fan of fire circling outward from his body. Charlie, who had not fired a shot, took his time over making his contribution, but made sure of its usefulness. The grenade—it was the first of the three—burst just within the doorway of the hut, under the very feet of a man. The mat hovel dissolved into fragments of wood and reed and clay, exploding outward, spilling bodies. There were a lot of Japs, more than Jim had thought likely. Afterwards, when all was over, they counted seventeen dead among the ruins of the village. There were no survivors. There had been two who were taken living but wounded; they both died of their wounds before they could die of other causes, which was considerate, for in any case they would have died. The party could carry no wounded prisoners southward with them when they moved on.

The end of it was brief, a sudden inward rush upon the clearing, with Garland's gun blazing ceaselessly, and the rest of them plying whatever steel they had. Brief and very bloody. It wanted only the first wind of their own running to fan cold into hot. Jim, with Sergeant Lake's *parang* in his hand, fought as a man might fight in a trance, unaware if they opposed him or offered surrender, until he found no more of them to destroy, until suddenly he was standing in the midst of a smoking, quivering stillness, and all the shrieking, and stamping, and hacking and thrusting had ceased, and there was no sound but the monotonous, stricken howling of some creature surely not human. He stirred himself out of his red paralysis, and looked, and saw the Malay donkeyman writhing in Parnaby's big hands.

"He was for running," said Parnaby. "I got him just among the trees. The only one who ain't even scratched." He held out a dirty, knotted rag of green cotton. "Look—he's got money in that—paper money, I reckon."

Jim took the little bundle, and felt it rustle under the cloth with the tissue sound of thin paper. It it was money, it was a lot of money. He heard the betrayer fawning upon him, calling him "tuan", babbling that the Japs had forced him to help them, that he had done it under threat of death, that he had worked for the British, and wanted only to serve them; while all the time Jim held in his hand the price of Lake's life, and Farrar's. He untied the greasy torn strips of cotton, and straightened out the thin bundle of notes, and Chick Foulds held a match for him to examine them. All the while the shrill chattering went on, the terrified, lunatic gibbering he did not heed, and scarcely heard. The colour and pattern of the notes he had seen before; they were the familiar palms and fruits and dangling bunches of bananas, but the lettering of these said, in English type: "The Japanese Government promises to pay the bearer on demand Ten Dollars." There were a good number.

He did not count them. He stood with them in his hands, and lifted his head slowly, and looked at the donkeyman; and he knew, horribly, that he was about to kill a man, in cold blood. It was the first time he had ever done that. Afterwards it would come easier.

He could have evaded it, of course. He could have given the job to one of the others; it was his right to depute them to perform any duty, however unpleasant. But he knew he would do it himself. How can you ask a mere kid like Garland or Tremlett or Chick to do what ties your own bowels into cold, rigid knots? Nor should Charlie Smith, for all his adroitness in man-making, lift this thing from him. He looked at the two youngest, and he said: "Go and get Curly. You'll find him down the track. Bring him in careful, mind—he's just about out." But they knew why they were being sent away. Parnaby knew it, too. He did not even protest nor hesitate when Jim said: "Loose him! We'll take care of him. You go and rig some sort of a bed for Curly and Hughson. See what you can salvage. There were over a score men here; there should be food."

Parnaby loosed the Malay and went quickly upon his errand. The donkeyman sagged as the big hands dropped him, sagged and fell down at Jim's feet, embracing his ankles, moaning that he was a poor man, and had been tempted by much money, shrieking that he could not die, babbling for mercy, mercy, mercy, with Lake's body not ten yards distant in the stained and trampled grass. Charlie, with Lake's *kris* in his hand, stood back in silence; the steps and voices of the young men, low and frightened and subdued, receded gradually from them.

The smoothing, frantic hands writhed upon Jim's calves, encircled his knees. He drew the sergeant's revolver slowly out of his belt, and shot the creature through the left side of the head, the muzzle of the gun not an inch from the temple. On the instant the incoherent shrieking mutter was snapped off short. The body stayed erect against him for a moment, and then slipped slowly down, and the shattered head, as it sank, left a smear of blood and brains down thigh, and knee, and shin, scalding hot, like a slow, deliberate wound.

He was slow in disengaging himself, for the power of movement seemed to have gone out of him, the mere step backward out of the limp embracing arms was an effort that drained him of strength, and caused a heavy sweat to break upon his forehead and run down into his eyes. He felt all his body molten into a deadly sickness of disgust and loathing and outrage; but that also passed. He remembered the others, both the living and the dead. Stooping, he lifted the traitor's body, and carried it to the rim of the clearing, and threw it into the bushes. With the edge of the dead man's sarong he wiped the worst traces of the execution from his own flesh, and went back to meet the youngsters as they carried Curly in from the track; that leaden, destroying heat all the while dragging at his bowels, and in his mind the empty coldness in which nothing human lived or moved. He felt Charlie Smith's eyes upon him, and was aware of something strange in that regard, an incurious peace, a satisfied passion; but he did not, because he dared not, pause to consider what passed in the mind behind the eyes. He had to be occupied, hands and heart and body, or his world would reel under him and let him fall, and the tension that held him upright would be snapped asunder, and he would break as the tree breaks in the wind, and so no more of him. There was work to do, and more and more of it, work for the corporate body of them, his world within a world; work for something bigger than himself, the sole salvation of man. He looked for exhaustion, for himself and them, as a salve for the trouble and horror of doing their duty. He looked forward to the end of his strength, the spot where the load he could not lay down would be taken away from him.

So he drove them. They made one hut habitable, and salved what they could from the rest, rice, and fruit, and ammunition for their captured gun, and some dried meat. There were also two small mortars, for once of no value, and some field dressings of sorts, and some small supplies of drugs, though most of the hoard was crushed and soiled beyond the possibility of use. There was quinine, with which they dosed Curly, and got him into a restless sleep; but there was nothing to stand between Hughson and the haunting dread of gangrene. His thigh was monstrously swollen, and he was in constant pain and some fever. They had no morphia, and though quinine reduced his fever it could not end it.

They put their two sick men to bed, and buried their dead, and the enemy dead, but well apart, having it in their hearts that Farrar and Lake should not sleep in the same soil with the inhuman sons of heaven. They made provision for a stay of perhaps two or three days; to go forward at once was impossible, and to remain too long was madness. Late in the night Jim posted Gregory in cover on the northern rim of the clearing, and himself took the southern side, and settled down to keep watch for the first half of the night. That was what he wanted, what he must have, the last consuming weariness, the end of endurance, past thought or feeling. The whole night, if need be, and endless nights after, to reach that blank darkness at last.

He sat on a tree-trunk, long fallen and overgrown with moss and fern, and strained his senses against the immensity of the night. He was not surprised when the hand came upon his shoulder, and the voice in his ear said: "Get in, you fool! Haven't you done enough for one night? Get in, and sleep, and leave this to me." Where had Charlie Smith found, among so much of violence and anxiety and pain, his exquisite tranquility? The voice—he had never noticed it before—was soft and sure-footed and inevitable as great music, and the hand had more of power than was in the practised physical strength of it. Because it was now so dark that vision had utterly ceased, inwardly he saw his friend as if for the first time, above life-size, fixed like the trees, masterless as the winds, an elemental, not a man. His tired mind could not contain all that was Charlie.

He said: "What are you doing here? You're supposed to be getting some sleep yourself. Get to hell out of this!" No, that was what he had meant to say. What he had said, so quietly, so wearily, was quite different. "Well? Are you satisfied?" he had said.

The hand stayed upon his shoulder. The strange body, so familiar and yet so new, sat down beside him with a rustling of ferns. The voice said: "Who am I that I should expect to be satisfied?" But he had never heard in it so profound a contentment. "Who are you," it said, "to want to break in the whirlwind singlehanded? Go to bed, like a sensible fool, and get the world off your mind for a few hours. Isn't your cup full enough yet?"

Suddenly, for no reason, he turned himself away from the body and the hand, and stretched himself along the log with his head in his arms, and lay shuddering, with the over-rich green smell of bruised leaves in his nostrils, and the rank taste in his mouth. Everything went out of him except the sick grief and the grievous sickness. He gasped: "Shut up, for God's sake shut up!" but with so inarticulate a passion that no words reached Charlie's ears. He was no more good. He was finished now. The tension was broken.

"All right!" said Charlie tranquilly. "All right! Let it go.

126

Why not? I know you, and you know me. Nobody on God's earth can stand bolt upright all the time. Nobody but the very young wants or expects to. When you're more adept at it you bend and let the storm go by you. Me, I learned that a long time ago. But then, I was never a superman." The voice halted there; it was as if a curious, sad smile drifted over the invisible lips and was gone. He did not touch Jim again; he was too wise for that. "Go and get some sleep," he said. "I'm staying here." And he settled down with his rifle beside him, and did not speak again, not even when Jim dragged himself out of his stupor and went wearily away to the hut, and lay down there with his face to the wall. If he could not accept help from Charlie, from whom could he accept it? "You carry the stripe, I carry you!" No sting now in that deliberate goad. He had found him out now; he knew him through and through, as he himself was known.

He slept, obediently, having no resistance left in him. The anger and the self-disgust flowed away from him like dividing waters. He went down into the darkness he had desired; the only difference was that even there he was not alone.

5

They stayed three days in the upland village. It was not safe to linger so long, but neither was it safe to go, with Hughson very clearly dying, and Curly Ballantyne still raving. By the fourth morning, when Hughson died, Curly was on his feet again, thin and wobbly and clay-coloured under his ruddy tan, but sane and sullen and ashamed that he had delayed them so long. It was then imperative that they should move on. Though they had refreshed and rested themselves there, the place had other memories not good to dwell upon. It was Jim's whole design to get them away from it.

Therefore he was glad when Hughson died; first, because that was the only conceivable end to pain in which he would not have suffered a dog to linger an hour; and second, because it gave the others at least a moderate chance of rejoining their own people. It was no use being sentimental about a life now past saving and infinitely better ended. Without him they could make twice the speed and reserve their strength intact. They buried him, and went on, steadily at first until they saw how much Curly could stand, but pressing the speed as he came back to normal and began to see that they were nursing him.

On the first day they stayed in the uplands, though the paths became more tortuous and difficult as they moved south, and they found themselves wasting hours upon tracks which advanced them very little in the direction they wanted to go; so that on the following morning they ventured down towards the coast again, thinking a dash through easier country well worth risking. The realisation of their mistake cost them Garland's life. He was at the rear of the line, and they lost him to a sharp-shooter operating from the roof of a hut in the paddy-fields below the track. There was just the crack of the rifle, and he gave a sudden hard cough, and Gregory, who was just ahead of him, turned to see him pitch slowly forward, and roll down into the liquid mud of the fields. He went back for him, and himself narrowly escaped the same fate for a man already dead.

Jim took that death to himself, most bitterly, though he said no word. All the day it haunted him that he had taken an unjustifiable risk, and young Garland had paid the score. But by night, after they had withdrawn themselves into the jungle, and still the presence of the enemy was constantly about them, he knew that the venture into the lower ground had mattered very little one way or the other. The forests were full of Japs. They operated in ones and twos, armed and equipped as lightly as it is possible to be, and in almost every case dressed as Malays or Chinese. One dropped a grenade among them from the fork of a tree as they passed beneath, and by the wildest freak of chance killed none of them, but blew himself from his perch and was promptly dispatched by Charlie with the *kris*. He was naked but for a loin-cloth, and shadow-painted in greens and browns; very small and to all appearance sub-human; but he had broken Parnaby's wrist and cost three of them painful flesh wounds, inconveniences they could ill afford. However, he was dead, and they were still alive; that was the greatest good. So much they had learned.

They halted for the dark hours with the conviction that other such creatures were about them at no great distance. There was nothing to be done about it, except to keep good watch, and be ready to shoot it out at any moment. They had chosen their ground in a thicket beside the curve of a stream, a mere thread of water, but giving them at least a modest field of fire on three sides. Jim himself elected to cover the fourth side. He was not built for arboreal tactics, but here there was ample cover even for his big frame, and on the ground the choking under-growth deadened sound, whereas from above he could detect the movements of an approaching enemy more readily. He climbed into the crotch of a tree, and made himself as comfortable as he could with his back flattened against the main trunk. Parasite ferns and orchids cushioned him. He could feel the flowers crush under the hand with which he eased his position; the texture of them was like silken-surfaced wax. Hughson had nursed just such flowers in his hands as they carried him to his death through the jungle, marvelling at their beauty and strangeness, and the dispensation which had so jewelled the world. And the same power—God or whatever it was—had been lavish with Germans and Japs, red ants and leeches and horrible, venomous flies, with the seed of disease and the generation of corruption. Well, he was not going to let his mind play with a puzzle which had driven wise men mad. It was bad enough to have to live with the paradox, without trying to solve it, above all without trying to reconcile himself to it unsolved. All he knew was that there were leeches and there were Japs, and they must be reckoned with.

It was not that he heard anything as yet but the night and the leaves and the water sighing in its bed; but he was increasingly aware that the jungle was full of their enemies, all about them and closing in, that they were outnumbered, outrun, outendured, that the odds against their ever getting home were long and growing longer. Towards dawn he began to hear what all night long he had sensed, the patient and stealthy movement of men among the grasses and ferns, hunting them like big game, with caution but without respect. He knew then that they would have to fight, and they were in no case to fight. He supposed their ammunition, sparingly used, might last them for the greater part of a day; after that they could not last long.

He watched the light come. Over his head, among the branches where the sunlight filtered in, birds began to circle and call, flashing back the radiance of the morning from vivid wings. Brilliantly-coloured birds they were, with feathers of tinsel and metallic, burnished heads; but for the most part they were either dumb or strident-voiced, far divided from the inconspicuous singer who had ravished his mind in Ibn Radwan's date-grove by the Mediterranean Sea. Remembering it, he felt homesickness less acute, less desperate than then, because he was now past any reasonable hope of recovering what was lost. It was like looking at the picture of someone who was several years dead, and remembering how gentle and charming she had been.

He watched the birds, he listened to their calls, because by them he knew something of the movements of the enemy; but he watched them, too, because they were innocent and handsome and joyous. He filled his eyes with the beauty and diversity of creatures all the more ardently because all concern for himself was slipping away from him. The jewelled butterflies, swaying languidly about the lush ground growth, where was the rich and odorous decay they loved, became to him as touchingly significant as human creatures. Even the monitor lizard which crept out upon a branch of his tree and lay sunning itself and staring at him mildly with its unblinking eyes had something lovely and pitiful about it. There was a heart in the green, soft body. The pendulous throat shook violently to the beat of it. Even cold-blooded things could feel, and had in them the desire that life should be enjoyed, and the fear that it must be endured. Jim was moved towards them all, with kindness, with compassion. He was glad that the lizard should palpitate in the sun unalarmed, even if he and his friends were not to outlive the day. Every happiness, however small and humble, was so much good to set against the evil. Every little thing that lived and enjoyed and did no harm was a part of himself that went on living.

He dropped out of his tree as the light increased, and sent Tremlett up in his place, for he judged that it was time to plan his battle. Not that all the planning on earth could make much difference to the end of it, if the invisible circle now closing in was as strong as he believed. But in the sight of his fellows no appearance of despair was possible. They would fight as they always fought, as men to whom defeat is a distant myth, infinitely more remote than death. Tired, under-fed, poorly supplied with ammunition, and in desperate physical case, they would fight so. They were the fire and the fuel both; they glowed and they were consumed.

He found Charlie at work with the *parang*, clearing himself a field of fire at leisure. The ground on which they had halted was a little knoll round which the stream circled, a knot of ground very richly overgrown. With this luxury of cover about them, and a clear space, however narrow, upon all sides, they might continue for hours seeing, but unseen. Charlie had made some impression upon the long grass and vines, though there was not time to do the job as he would have liked. He stuck the *parang* back in his belt as Jim ducked through the edge of the curtain of vines. "Well?" he said.

"Any time now," said Jim. "You want to stay this side."

"I know. I can hear 'em across the brook. Yes, I'll stay here." He added: "Have a word with Curly, Jim. He thinks this is all his fault."

"He would!" said Jim. "The conceit of the little devil! I suppose he thinks he's lost the whole damn' Malayan war for us single-handed." But he went to look for Curly, as Charlie had known he would go. The boy was lying under the bushes by the stream, watching the opposite bank, where the green, steamy gloom rustled, and the dark, oily leaves of shrubs glistened. Into these deeps no sunlight came, and little of the day. It was twilight perpetually, a hot, stifled dusk dewed with the tumult of the earth's breath, and wrapped in a terrifying silence. In the air Jim had opened his mind to the world; but here on the ground the world rejected him.

Curly rolled over on his side as Jim crept into the bushes beside him. He was still pretty weak, and the motionless, breathless heat played hell with him. He was running with a heavy, quicksilver sweat, face and body standing in great, bitter rivulets of moisture, and his breath laboured and noisy; and he was as skinny as an adolescent boy, with hollow eyes sunk deep into his head, and the marks of many leech-bites on his legs and arms. There was not much left of the sturdy kid who had kept them alive on the troopship coming out, except the damp coppery curls now grown long and falling over his eyes. Jim wished him out of it with all his heart. He should never have been there in the first place. It was no country for clean young men.

"Hullo!" said Curly briefly, and rolled back over his rifle. It had been Gregory's until they acquired the automatic-gun, and Curly, since the return of his reason, had never stopped comparing it with his own lost gun, and mourning the loving care he had lavished on a thing now digesting miserably in the stomach of the earth. "This is a hell of a do!" said Curly. "D'you reckon we'll ever pull out of it?"

"I think the odds are a hell of a length against it," said Jim, "but we may, at that. We'd have had a better chance if we hadn't lost so much time earlier on."

"That's what I thought," said Curly, just audibly, and the struggle of his breathing shook the leaves, like the panting of an animal hunted to death.

"After he began to get really bad," said Jim, "he asked me to leave him and go on. I never let on to the others, so keep your mouth shut about it. You wouldn't think it possible, would you, that a chap could be driven to thinking seriously of taking another chap up on an offer like that? Well, I did think about it. I don't mind telling you now. He's dead now. I reckon he knows all he needs to know about it, and anyhow he'd never hold it against me. Hughson was dead straight. When he said a thing he meant it."

"'Yes,'" said Curly painfully, "he was never anything but on the level." And he asked with a palpable effort: "Why didn't you take him up on it, then?" Remembering, as he forced the perilous question from his lips, who had been most constant and enduring about the hideous death-bed. That was a burden Jim and Charlie had shared between them when the younger men turned tail. Curly supposed it needed a special sort of guts to stand somebody else's pain, especially when it was ugly. He hadn't been alive enough to know the worst of it, but he remembered the sickening closeness of the hut, and a stench that was horrifying, and the incessant muttering moan. They had had to lie in the same hut for safety's sake, a nucleus about which the rest of the force gathered protectively. Curly shook at the memory of those days. He had helped to bury Hughson; it had been the least he could do, and he had been so insistent that they had found it wise to humour him. He wouldn't forget that in a hurry.

"Don't talk as if it was so bloody easy!" snapped Jim. "Take him up on it! You're so damned hard-boiled reasonable, are you? I don't suppose you could walk off and leave a kitten in the lurch, let alone a man. Oh, shut up!" But he knew that Curly wouldn't leave it at that, and very certainly he didn't intend that he should.

Curly was more easily discouraged now than once he had been, but what was nagging at his mind had to come out sooner or later. He was quiet for a minute, narrowing his eyes upon the stirring grasses that leaned over the stream, pretending that he had no personal interest in the subject; then he burst out suddenly: "But if it's a question of the lives of several other men—not just for yourself——"

"Yes," said Jim grimly, "that makes a difference, you think?"

"Well—surely——"

"That's what I thought, too. That's why I nearly let him stay behind, the way he wanted." He parted the bushes before his face, and looked up the creek, and down. There was as yet no movement but the dipping flight of butterflies over the dark red mud. "I wish I knew just what we were up against here. Wonder how far we are from the others?"

"Well, what made you change your mind?" asked Curly, his voice shrill with urgency.

"Eh? Oh—that!"

"I suppose you were just plain bloody sorry for him," said Curly, in a burst of anguished bitterness, and laughed to cover the unintended self-revelation; but the laugh was not a success. He scrubbed his soft red beard along the back of his hand, and peered along his sights, and shivered.

"My God, as if you'd need to be told that! But that wasn't what did it. No—I might have stood out against that—I don't guarantee it, but I might. No—it was coming up against it suddenly that if we left him we were chucking away everything we stood for—putting our side on the same level as theirs. Because that's what they'd do, without so much bloody palaver about it, either. Well, if we bring our side down to balance theirs we might as well not be fighting at all—we've got nothing to fight about. Because that bit of difference—between standing by the unprofitable and helpless—and throwing 'em overboard—well, that's it. That's what it's all about. So I wasn't having any. No, by God! I've come too far with this job to drop it now. I said: 'To hell with that for an idea! You're coming wherever we go.' I don't go back on that now." He turned his head suddenly, and looked full into the sunken anxious eyes. "D'you reckon I did right?"

The locked glance held for a few minutes, and Jim saw Curly struggling to find words for something more he wanted to say, something more difficult than the plain answer to that point-blank question. Then he relinquished the unformulated anxiety, visibly letting it slip away out of his mind. The wild hurt of his eyes was softened and darkened. He said slowly, almost incredulously: "Yes—I suppose so. Yes, I reckon you did;" and seemed to wonder at his own relief. He had never thought of it in that way, but it was true enough. If you sacrificed everything, even human feeling, to expediency, you smashed the very thing you were supposed to be fighting for, the sacredness of humanity. How easy it would have been to be tricked into that very course! And thinking all the time that you were doing the best thing! It was damned difficult. He couldn't cope with it. He always seemed to be getting hold of the wrong end of it, somehow; he wasn't very good at it, or else he was just too tired. Better leave it to Jim; Jim knew what he was doing all right.

He sank his head into his arm with a sharp sigh, and breathed all the rigid self-reproach out of him with that one grateful breath. He was quite sure he was going to die, and he didn't want to die; he found himself reluctant and frightened both; but the worst of the load was off his heart now. He was an equal partner with the rest in their eyes; he could be so in his own; not the occasion of their ruin, but a sharer in their prowess, whatever the end of it might be.

"Nice place you picked here, kid," said Jim reflectively. "I tell you what I'm going to do. I'll get young Chick to come over here by you. Keep an eye on him for me, will you? I'm worried about him since Garland went. Make him keep in cover. I'm not saying we've got above a dog's chance, but I don't want any of it chucked away."

"O.K.!" said Curly eagerly. "I'll keep an eye on him as well as I can. How long d'you think it'll be before——"

"Before the balloon goes up? Any minute now, I should think." He withdrew himself gradually from Curly's side, the oily olive-leaves swinging back between their faces. "Look out for yourself, kid. If there's any sort of a to-morrow, I'll see you then. I shall be up on the knoll there, so I guess we'll hear more of each other just now than we'll see."

"So long, Jim," said Curly, meaning good-bye; but he had got something out of that quarter of an hour that took the fever out of his mind as quinine had cooled it out of his body, so that even good-bye meant less than a separation. Queer, thought Jim, circling his minute, invisible army, that he who was crystal to Charlie should be so opaque to the kid. Queer, too, how miracles flowed out of him, and he the most ordinary of men. Now that it was too late—probably because it was too late, and he was therefore loosed from the necessity of doubting or deprecating it—he was aware of power in him. There was no knot in the mind of any man of his that he could not undo; except, of course, in his own.

He went back to Charlie; the two of them, with Gregory and the automatic-gun on the ground, and Tremlett, the lightest and smallest among them, in the trees, would make shift to hold the side of the knoll which was not circled by the creek, while Parnaby, Chick and Curly kept watch over the water. Parnaby's left wrist was tied up between two slivers of bark hacked from a tree, and the fingers of that hand were useless, but he had rigged himself a notched log to take the weight of his rifle, and was capable of controlling his fire, even though he would be slowed up considerably. He was a good, steady shot. Let Curly, with his alarming conscience soothed by curious means, kid himself that he was exerting a steadying influence over Chick Foulds; Parnaby would keep an eye on them both, and they would never be any the wiser.

He was glad, now that it came to the point, that he was with them; glad that he had fought with them, and commanded them, and must continue with them to whatever end might come. You get yourself tied up with people, and can't get loose again. That's the way it is. He was glad even when the first shots were fired, in the mid of the morning, and the blue, strangling mist under the trees shook to the reverberations.

It was Tremlett who set the ball rolling. For fully thirty seconds he had been listening to dim tremblings of movement in the brush below him, at a distance of perhaps a hundred yards or less. He waited for a reasonable target, and presently saw a hand and naked arm part the trailing vines and a face, copper-dark in the quaking twilight, peer out towards him, considerably nearer to his tree. Still he did not fire, though he braced himself along the broad fork of the tree, and drew a bead on the spot where the chest below the face should be; but when the arm swung a *parang* and cleared, for a moment, the veil of green strands from a small mortar, then he thought it was time to do something about it. He was a shade hasty on the trigger, and missed his mark, besides drawing into the trees the instant reply of two sub-machine-guns hidden somewhere in the leafy gloom. He hugged his tree as the storm swept by him, and swore horribly into the *keringah*-haunted furrows of the trunk, steadying his indignant nerves with every scandalous word he knew, and he knew plenty; but finding as the staccato bursts passed that he was untouched, he returned cautiously to the attack. The profusion of vine and fern was an unbroken darkness by then, no movement shaking it; but he knew the position of the mortar because there was a frangipani, starred with big white blossoms, just to the left of it. It presented no target now for a rifle. He wondered if he dared risk a grenade. They had salvaged a few out of the wreckage of the Malay village, and he had two with him, but he was a little queasy about getting a sufficiently clear throw. How if he should fail to get it past all the tangle of growth, and smash up Jim and Charlie instead of the mortar team? None the less, he risked it, venturing out along a branch towards the frangipani to make certain of his aim. The explosion almost shook him down like an over-ripe fruit, and tore a whirl of blasted leaves over him in a dark-green hailstorm as he threshed about in mid-air with arms and legs clamped about the branch, and his eyes tight shut against a roaring darkness. When the air and the earth steadied about him, and he dared to look down again, he saw a ruinous tangle of leaves where the frangipani and the trailing vines had been, a hole in the web of the jungle, and smoke rolling and rocking in dull brownish clouds round the void. He saw a body, naked, lying along the edge of the circle of destruction, and he believed he saw the mortar twisted and smoking beside it. At least it never went into action, so he considered himself justified in believing he had destroyed it.

That was the beginning of the interminable day. After that first sparkle and crash of combat there was no pause. From every side the crackling echo repeated itself, ringing them in with fire. The hell of it was that they had no target, apart from elusive glimpses; whereas they themselves, though invisible, were securely pinned down into their small circle of ground, into which the contracting ring of attackers could pour everthing they had, and be sure of getting some results. At every movement of leaves within his sight Jim fired, for where movement was, in this monstrous stillness, there was most certainly a man or an animal; and from this area, he was sure, all the animals must long ago have withdrawn themselves. There was little indication of the success of his fire, though once or twice the ferns threshed upon the shots as if he had plugged someone; and at least once a thin brown body leaped upright out of cover and crashed backwards into the leaves. These steady but cease-less exchanges lasted for a long time, past midday, he thought, for the heat had become appalling, so that every movement of a hand was suffering; and it was worse suffering to be out of sight of the others, and not to know how they were faring. His mind misgave him for the three boys back on the creek, but he dared not call to them because that would have been to betray his own position and theirs. At the first lull he would get back to them for a moment. But there was no lull. He went back to them at last for another reason; the mortar that Tremlett had destroyed was by no means the only one the enemy had. Gregory and his automatic-gun had prevented them from moving up another one in a frontal position; but they had brought one up across the creek, and the first shell burst full in the red mud between Parnaby and Foulds, raising a dull fountain of earth, and water, and leaves, and bleached white tree-roots like slivers of bone.

The impact threw Jim flat upon his face. He picked himself up, shook the standing sweat from his forehead and eyelids, and crawled through the smoking tatters of the underbush to where the dirty red water of the creek was slowly creeping into a new crater in its bank, and the torn bushes lay in swathes along the ground. He found Parnaby on his face, with one arm trailing down the raw mud into the sluggish eddies, and his back spattered with blood and slime and leaves. If he was not already dead, he died under Jim's hands as he felt at him, for he found neither pulse nor breath. A dozen yards away a tumult in the bushes marked the spot where Curly Ballantyne was dragging Chick Foulds back into cover.

Well, that left six. He supposed they'd done well to avoid loss for so long, considering they were all almost inevitably bound for the same end. He was glad Parnaby had been killed outright; this was no place and no time to make a slow business of dying. He could almost find it in him to wish Chick had been as thorough, especially when he took him quivering from Curly's arms, and felt the blood start from three long, jagged gashes in his shoulder and chest. Chick was out of it. At every move he made the welling blood would drain out of him. They had no dressings, not even a strip of a shirt to tie his arm in to his side and lessen the flow. Jim sent Curly back to the stream, and himself drew Chick into the best shelter he could find, and strapped his left arm across his chest with his belt. The boy was out, but only stunned. Heaven alone knew what he might not do when he came to and found himself expected to remain a compliant casualty; but no one could spare the time to look after him. Jim left him still unconscious, and went back to where Charlie was.

"Get over with Curly," he said in Charlie's ear. "The mortar's somewhere back over the brook, a bit to the left. If you can get it, get it. You and the kid are on your own."

When Charlie was gone loneliness came in and lay by him, so that the chattering of Gregory's gun and the steady, deliberate crack of Tremlett's rifle overhead conveyed no impression of human company. It was then early afternoon, and they were almost beyond fatigue, parched with smoke and stifled with humid heat, having touched neither water nor food since dawn. The invisible circle of the enemy had perceptibly closed in, and the range was now desperately short, so that Gregory's gun

137

was doing the lion's share of the work. If it jammed, God help them all. In any case the supply of ammunition would not stand up long to this pressure. When the Japs came to the same conclusion they would rush the position, and it was plain to be seen that five whole men and one helpless one couldn't do much to prolong the business then. Maybe they could be induced to believe that the breaking-point had already come; then at least, if the lost men of A Company had to die, they might take a handsome number of the sons of heaven with them. It was worth trying. He made his way across to where Gregory was raking the brush ahead in sweeping arcs of fire.

"Let's get 'em out of cover," he said. "Cut down on your fire for a bit, and then stall, the way you'd run out of ammo. If they think we're finished they may give us a look at 'em." He thought, but did not say: "They may quit firing that blasted mortar, too." The second and third shells had fallen short, to judge by the sound, and certainly he had heard rifles crackling between the impacts, so that as yet there was no further damage or loss to weaken them; but if once the mortar team got the range fair and square it was all up.

Gregory obediently shortened his bursts of fire, and began to lengthen the intervals between them. He was, if anything, too carefully artistic about the process, taking a quarter of an hour or more to slacken his fire to the point where he could reasonably let the chatter of the gun tail off into ominous silence. The two rifles continued to fire, every shot a small puncture in the sudden pall of quietness. "It might bring 'em," thought Jim with a start of hope. "It would get me, all right, but then I'm not a Jap. But it might—it might bring 'em."

The minutes went by, and the strange silence endured. Then, deliberately, the enemy began to show themselves; the mere glimpse of a head and shoulders for a moment above the long grass, an arm parting the lush parasitic creepers, in several places at once palpable man; and when this invitation produced nothing more than a frantic haste on the part of the two riflemen, the attackers ventured the move Jim had longed for. They came in a wave of men, the jungle suddenly spawning them from every bush and vine; they closed in at a run, with bayonets poised, and sub-machine-guns on the hips, shouting as they came, half-naked bodies darkened with sweat and oil to a deep bronze-brown, and hard as teak. Jim pulled out the pin of a grenade, and braced himself back for the throw.

It was a successful move enough, if you counted your score

in enemy dead. Gun and grenade sounded together, and the circle of racing men was broken in pieces; but the trouble was that several survived and came on. They'd held their fire a shade too long; there was no time for another grenade; it was out with the *parang*, and five minutes of cut and slash, with sweat running down their bodies at the effort, and their hearts pumping agonisingly. They beat back what was left of that attack, and dropped back into new cover, and there was a pause of exhaustion. One more such encounter would finish them; flesh and blood couldn't stand that struggle for long. Moreover, in a short time, the gun would be out of ammunition in all seriousness, and there would be nothing to stop the next attack. In the meantime, they lay flat in the grass, peering forward with sweat-scalded eyes, watching the steam quiver upward from the bodies littered among the trampled bushes, and trying to find a clean and satisfying breath where no air was. Behind them another mortar-shell struck, nearer this time. God help Charlie and the kid if they improved much upon that range.

There was another interval of sniping from cover, gun against gun, with no clue to what the enemy was preparing. Then Tremlett, from his tree, saw what Jim on the ground could not see. They were moving up another of those beastly accurate little two-inch mortars into a frontal position. There seemed no limit to the enemy's numbers or the arms he carried. Gun and *parang*, between them had just harvested, by his rough count, some twenty-odd Japanese dead, but still they came. If he called down to the men on the ground they could do little about it. He would try his former move once more, and maybe the luck would hold. It was his last grenade, probably the last among them all; better make a good job of it. He crawled out far along the branch this time; farther than was safe, but the safety-line seemed to have erased itself in his mind, so that there was no barrier between the things it was politic and impolitic to do. He pulled out the pin with his teeth, and stretched back his arm; and a Japanese sharp-shooter got him clean through the chest and toppled him from the tree with the grenade still clutched in his hand.

He was dead before he hit the ground, crashing from branch to branch and bush to bush with a snapping of twigs like rapid fire; but in dying he had shut his hand so fast upon the grenade that it was still between his slowly-relaxing fingers as he struck the trampled and bloody grass. Jim, who had seen that plunging descent, ran crouching towards the body, acting upon instinct rather than for any sane reason. The boy could hardly be alive; he was exposing himself for nothing, for a scruple smaller than a thumb-nail, but he went because he had to go. He was still about fifteen yards distant from the body when the grenade exploded.

He was aware, for one blinding instant, of surprise, almost of relief. So this was death; this sudden ascent of darkness out of the earth under his feet, this wiping away of the jungle like a backcloth from about him, and the rushing in of astonished pain that ceased as it touched him; these, and after them only the darkness, only the quietness as of sleep, and the end of having to drive body and mind to deeds they had no will to do, the end of responsibility; and last, not even these; nothing!

6

Pain, which had left him suddenly, suddenly returned. He felt it stabbing at him, and tried to reject it, knowing before he knew anything else that pain implied continued life; that was the one thing for which he had not bargained. But because there was no evading it, he opened his reluctant eyes upon the jungle again, and endured the momentary agony of the light in them, and of vision returning, before he tried to move. It was still the same day; he hadn't even evaded a few hours of the burden of living. Still the same day, somewhat more withered, something more soiled and muddy; and a Japanese soldier, in nothing but a loin-cloth, his bare feet splaying strong, dirty toes against the earth, was standing over him, pricking impatiently at his left thigh with a bayonet, and occasionally kicking him in the side to hasten his awakening.

He braced his hands under him into the grass, and levered himself up to look for the others, though the effort started upon him what he took to be sweat, and found to be blood from two ragged gashes over his ribs. Dark and light swung before his eyes, and for a minute he sat holding fast by the ground until the dizzy sickness passed, and he could see clearly. He saw Charlie; that was the first thing that made him lift himself up out of his apathy and push away from him the nostalgia his flesh had for death. Charlie sat there in the grass with Curly in his arm, and both of them with their eyes fixed upon him, urgently, peremptorily, commanding him not to die. He put his own hurts by him the more resolutely because of them, and focussing his mind upon them, held to that for will-

power and purpose until something of his own vitality flowed
back into him. He was not only alive, but more or less intact,
with nothing but those body gashes and some lesser flesh wounds
to show for it. He must have been out some time, and well out,
for there were at least seven little bayonet punctures in his
thigh, with thin threads of blood oozing from them and dripping
into the ground; he supposed that the explosion of the grenade
had blown him backwards off his feet and stunned him against
a tree. The back of his head felt as if he had been trying to
bore his way through a brick wall, and he could feel a tacky
mess of blood plastering the back of his neck; but there was
no worse damage. Charlie himself seemed to have come through
more or less unmarked; but Curly was in a bad way. He could
see that, by the way he leaned heavily on Charlie's shoulder,
and the way his face was drawn rigid, the skin tight as parch-
ment over the bones, the mouth clamped shut against complaint.
He was a queer grey colour, his eyes enormous and blank with
shock; having started, poor devil, from a long way below normal
at the beginning of the day, and with that queer, unpredictable
conscience of his turning knives in him.

Jim withdrew his eyes with an effort from them, and looked
painfully about him. The soldier who stood over him prodded
him with his foot, and motioned him to get up. He got to his
feet carefully, holding by the tree on which he had left his
blood; he saw the splashes of it in the bark, alive now with
keringahs busily feeding. Upright, even though the ground was
cotton-wool under him and his head span, he felt more his own
man, being head and shoulders taller than the Jap. He crossed
the trampled grass of what was now an open glade, responding
to the ungentle urging of the butt of a Japanese rifle thudding
into the small of his back, and was brought up short before a
man who sat upon a fallen tree, with a map spread out upon
his knees. During that brief and laborious walk he was so
occupied with the difficulty of controlling his legs that he saw
nothing but what was immediately before him, and even that
as if in a dream. He all but put his foot upon Chick Foulds,
lying against the bole of a tree with Gregory squatting over
him; but he saw neither of them. Every particle of energy he
had was working to hold him erect before his captor and
theirs.

The man was short, but very strongly built, with a chest on
him deep enough for a prize-fighter, and no fat anywhere. He
wore nothing but cotton singlet and shorts, his boots, and a

peaked military cap, but he was plainly a man in authority. Jim, his faculties coming back to him, looked his conqueror over with interest, for he was just reaching the stage when oriental faces ceased to seem all alike to him, but he could make nothing of this one. The impression it conveyed was of malignant detachment, but that was because of its peculiar physical structure rather than of any expression it wore. It was as nearly flat as he had ever seen a face, a heavy surface of flesh, with no bones showing except in the jaw; the nose was negligible, broad-nostrilled but of rudimentary proportions every other way, and the eyes had no sockets, but appeared to have been painted on with black enamel in two single oblique strokes. The mouth was short and full, and yet hard as stone, with a long hair-line of a moustache crossing the upper lip. A child might have drawn that face, or modelled it out of wax; a child or a lunatic.

The thin glitter of the eyes began an appraisal at Jim's boots, and climbed his body slowly, and settled upon his face. Out of the pebble of a mouth an abrupt voice said, in excellent English:

"You are the non-commissioned officer who was in charge of this party? What is your rank?"

"Lance-Corporal," said Jim.

"I am Lieutenant Yorisaka. You will answer my questions, please; all my questions. Were you in charge?"

"After the death of Sergeant Lake, five days ago, I took charge."

"You were moving south-westward. With what objective?"

"It's pretty obvious, isn't it?" said Jim bitterly. "We were trying to get back into the line."

"Line? You have no line! Nor was that the reason for your movements. What were your orders? Why were you sent behind our advance line in this particular spot? Answer me!" he said, his voice rising.

So they'd butted into something, had they? One of the mustering-points of the Japanese infiltration parties, by the look of it; and and they were suspected of arriving there by design. If only our intelligence had been that good, thought Jim!

"If you're hoping to get information out of us," he said bluntly, "you're wasting your time. We've been lost for eleven days now. We've got precious little of anything; but literally no information. All we were after was to get back to our own people, where we could be effective again. If you

142

know how to get blood out of a stone, go ahead, but I'm telling you it's no good."

There was certainly a mind behind the unfinished face, for he received this and was silent for a moment. Then he said: "We cannot guarantee you, as prisoners of war, any comforts. We shall be compelled to carry you with us, for the time being, and we are moving at speed."

"We have wounded," said Jim. "You must give them treatment; you know your obligations, as well as I do."

Lieutenant Yorisaka smiled; it could have meant anything or nothing, but it was by no means reassurring. "My sole obligation just now," he said, "is to carry out the job I have in hand. If my own men, wounded or whole, stood in the way of it, I should be forced to disregard them. I cannot afford to be any more sentimental about yours. But if you are not a hindrance to my mission, I shall do my best for you. Rely on Japanese *bushido*."

Jim saw how much that meant, and thought of Curly and Chick, and was badly frightened. It was like asking a cobra to respect the rules of war.

"You could send us back to the coast under guard," he said. "You need detach no more than two or three men for the job. We're only five, and two of us badly hurt."

"What I can and cannot do," said Lieutenant Yorisaka smoothly, "is for me to decide. I cannot do that!"

He wanted to think fast, but how could he, with that empty pain in his mind? He must do better than this. He must get something out of this parchment-coloured soapstone image for Chick, and Curly, and the others. He said, articulating very carefully because his own voice sounded so distant and strange to him: "If it will alter the case I'll give you my parole on behalf of us all."

"It will not. I am not empowered to receive the parole of non-commissioned officers and private soldiers."

"Then you insist on making my lads keep up with what I take it is going to be a forced march?"

"I have no alternative. You would not be grateful if I abandoned them here to be eaten alive by red ants and leeches; nor could I do so if I wished. There is no more to be said."

"I think there is," said Jim. "I want dressings for them. At any rate you can't refuse that."

The round mouth broadened in an elastic smile. "No doubt

you would like a doctor to attend them, too, but I regret that is impossible. We have no doctor."

"That's beside the point. I asked for dressings. I'll do the rest myself. Do I get them, or doesn't Japanese *bushido* run to that, either?"

The answer to that was in Japanese, and addressed not to Jim, but to the soldier who stood behind him. The rifle-butt thudded into his kidneys again, but he stood his ground. "You must have some clean linen and lint," he said. "I'm not asking for any miracles."

"Go back to your men," said Yorisaka. "You shall have what we can give you."

He turned to his map at that, and it was plain there was no more to be got out of him. Jim obeyed the urging of his guard, and went back to where his friends had been herded together under close watch. There was no point in putting Yorisaka clean against them; and besides, he was desperate to find out in what case they stood. And it was bad enough, as he soon found. He walked into the middle of them, and knelt down by Curly, and looked across him into Charlie's eyes, and didn't ask any questions.

"They're moving," he said, "and moving fast. We've got to tag along as best we can. He won't do anything about it. We go or we drop."

"We can't," said Charlie, but it was a plain statement, not a protest.

"We've got to—one or the other. That's all there is to it. But I don't think they'll move till morning. Anyhow," he said suddenly, "thank God you're on your feet."

"That goes for you, too," said Charlie. "You had us scared. But as for making this one get on to his——"

Curly opened his lips and made an attempt to speak, but no sound came. The sweat was standing in globules on his eyelids, and running down into his eyes. Charlie leaned over and brushed it away with his fingers. "It's all right, kid. Why bother to talk? We know everything you can tell us. It isn't your guts we're worrying about." And to Jim he said simply: "His shoulder was out. I put it back. I wonder you didn't hear him scream. It nearly finished me, let alone him. If we could get him properly strapped up I'm not saying but he might give a pretty good show. He's got a gash in the head from a *parang*, too, but it was a glancing knock, luckily. No danger there."

"I've asked for dressings," said Jim. "God knows what we'll get out of 'em, if anything, but I did what I could. Chick's worse still. I'm scared for him, and that's the truth." But my God, wasn't he scared for all of them, the sick and the well alike? When he thought of that stony small man, with the uncompleted face and the adder's eyes, and reflected that the lives of them all hung on whether or not they thwarted his ideas of speed—and Curly with a displaced shoulder newly put back by half-trained hands—and Chick being slowly drained of blood from three undressed wounds—There was one hope for them, and only one; that Lieutenant Yorisaka and his jungle patrol had no long journey to make. He thought they could keep Chick alive and moving for at least one day, if they had to do it by carrying him; Curly might endure a little longer; but if the forced march lasted longer than a day they would all be damned.

He waited for the dressings, and was abjectly patient because he could not afford to be anything else. To anger the Japs would only make certain what was already a probability. He was hot with rage inside, but he waited without a word; and finally, when the light and his hope were failing together, they threw at him disdainfully, in passing, some rolls of soiled cotton and a parcel of lint, obviously all he need expect to get out of them. He was pleasantly surprised to receive even so much, but he wanted water, and all attempts to convey his need to the guards were met by the same gesture. He didn't relish having a bayonet levelled suggestively at his belly, but he meant to get what he wanted. He tried asking for Lieutenant Yorisaka, but the name had no effect, and when he took a step forward as if to push past the guard he was met by the butt end of the rifle clean in the wind, a nicely calculated blow that doubled him up gasping in the grass. After that he learned sense, and did what he could for Chick with the scanty materials he had. It wasn't a satisfactory job, but at least it stopped the bleeding. The kid didn't complain. Asked how he felt, he said: "Oh, not so dusty!" but he would have said the same if he had been dying. They made him as comfortable as they could. He had no colour and no smile; nobody had seen him smile since Harry Garland rolled down into the glutinous mud of the paddy-fields and failed to get up again. Very fond of each other, those two had been. It was like that in this queer life. The friends you had in the company became in time more real to you than all the people you'd left behind in

England, and the loss of them was every bit as bad as bereavement of mother and brother and wife. Worst of all must be the case of the Curlys and the Gyps, because they had everything between them, both peace and war, both England and Malaya; if Curly went, Gyp was as good as dead.

It was mainly shock that ailed Curly just now. Between them they got him bandaged up as securely as possible, though it meant that he was deprived of the use of one arm, and the right arm at that. Something of the blanched rigidity was gradually softened from his face. He ate a little of the miserable handful of rice the guards gave them, and drank what was left in his water-bottle, and surprisingly fell asleep. That was some help, even if it was no more than the reaction from shock and pain, unprofitable refreshment to him and imperfect rest.

When they had done what they could for the two youngsters they bandaged one another. There was not one of them unwounded. By then it was growing dark, and the cool of night had come down upon them chillingly. The activity of the Japanese went on around them until it was fully dark, and two extra guards were added to the two they already had, but they were not otherwise disturbed. They could make no guess at the numbers of their captors, but they knew there was no hope of escape. Weaponless now, without food or water, weary and wounded against large numbers of fresh and well-armed Japs—no, there was no possibility of getting away. Whatever it was, they would have to go through with it. And that was the end of it. Lake had sworn to take that party home or die trying, and he had died trying. Jim hadn't sworn it, but it looked as if he was going to do it no less surely.

"If only we could have got the lads out of it," he said, "I wouldn't mind so much."

"Quit thinking about it," said Gregory sharply. "We did what we could. More, by God, than I ever knew I could. I'm not going back on anything I've done, and heck! I'm not dying until I'm dead. I've been a thorn in the flesh to somebody all my life, and I'm willing to go on being hell's own nuisance to the Japs until Jap or jungle finishes me off. At the very worst you can only die once."

"Once on your own account," said Charlie Smith. "On someone else's there's no limit."

As ever, he had the last word; the last, however long they talked across it afterwards. None of them could talk aside that word.

Jim did not sleep at all. Upon him rested too heavily the burden of them all. He thought, in the darkness, that Charlie slept, for he was very still; he was sure that Gregory did, by his heavy breathing. Once and again during that night he leaned down over Curly's face, and tried by touch and hearing to sense how things went with him. His sleep continued long, but was much broken, and at every change of position pain came newly upon him, and he gasped and moaned. Jim could have wished the hours of darkness to linger for him; but the dawn was early and vivid, and by its light he saw Charlie's eyes wide open and contemplative upon his face.

"I thought you were asleep," he said.

"I hoped you were, but I knew you weren't. How much longer now, I wonder?"

"I don't know. Not long. I suppose we'd better wake them," he said, looking at the exhausted, soiled faces of the young men, "before *they* do it with bayonets." Suddenly he put his head down between his hands in a wave of appalling sickness. "Charlie, I'm bloody tired," he said, as if he was talking to God, "so bloody tired!"

"What do you expect me to do?" said Charlie Smith, with a strange quietness. "Give you permission to die and be done with it? What difference would it make if I did? You say things like that to me, but you go on just the same, and always have, and always will. Nothing could stop you. Nobody could persuade you to stop yourself. All you want from me, and all I've ever given you, is a few words of appropriate mumbo-jumbo here and there to keep up the illusion that I was helping to make your wheels go round. But I know, and it's time you knew, that your machinery is the kind that needs no fuel, the kind that keeps running until it's smashed to pieces. Oh, no, Jim Benison, don't come telling me you're bloody tired! At this late stage I see no need to keep up that game any longer. It's your energy that's going to drive yourself and us all this day, and you know it; and if you don't know it, then learn it now."

It was of the things he did not understand nor even truly hear at the first time of utterance, the things that said themselves over to him afterwards in quietness with a sort of solemn music, but acquired lucidity only by slow and strange degrees. He put it by him just then as irrelevant, the wanderings of a mind grown light with exhaustion and anxiety. Wasn't he talking rubbish himself?

147

"I don't know what you're talking about," he said, "and the hell you do yourself! What are we going to do with these two? Can you manage Curly, if Gregory and me take Chick between us? I hope to God the going isn't too bad. We might manage the dry ground, but any more mangroves would finish us."

"Whatever we propose," said Charlie, "they may dispose. But if I'm let, I can keep Curly on his feet until we both drop."

"I don't think they'll care how we manage it, as long as we make their pace. Their minds are on just one thing, getting somewhere else in a hurry; right now they haven't got time to get playful, or I wouldn't give much for any of us." He looked round the grove, where the increasing light filtered in greenly through torn vine curtains. A silent stirring had begun all about them, the purposeful movement of men. "Pretty soon now!" he said. "They don't waste daylight." And he put his hand upon Curly's cheek; a strange gesture it seemed to him, but there was no other part of him he dared touch for fear of making him stir and hurt himself in his awakening; fingered his cheek like a sweetheart, like one of his platinum-headed cheap pick-ups of the dance halls, and felt every kind of awkward fool, and did not care. They were a long way past that. All that mattered was that the kid should awake gently, and so he did, opening his dilated eyes immediately but not moving, staring upward out of his sunken eye-sockets alert and instant in fear, but as still as death.

"Sorry, kid!" said Jim. "Time to be stirring," and got an arm under him quickly for fear he should try to raise himself. Curly's face knotted itself into sharp lines and when they lifted him he turned chalk-white and leaned heavily across Jim's arm, and was desolately sick. The contortions of that paroxysm all but put him out again, but when it passed, he was somewhat easier. Take it all in all, Chick was likely to be more of a problem. He roused himself, when they awoke him, with the greatest docility and indifference; Jim doubted if he was more than half-present in all this nightmare. He put himself into their hands as confidingly as a child, and tried his legs, when Jim urged him to the effort, with a pliant desire to please, as if all instinct of resistance had been charmed out of him. He said yes, he could go, yes, he would go; but he had become so insubstantial that they knew in their hearts he would not go far. You could almost see through him as he stood.

The Japs were getting ready to move. The guards, who had

148

looked on with blank, incurious faces while Jim and Gregory walked Chick up and down, sprang into life at a shrill shout from the shadows across the glade, and began with foot and rifle to hustle their prisoners into movement. They had been given no food and no water, but neither had the captors, as far as Jim could see, eaten or drunk. The probability was that they were anxious to make an early start, and put a substantial distance behind them before they halted for food; and in the circumstances they were scarcely likely to give a damn about their prisoners. Nor did Yorisaka appear to have laid any injunctions upon his men with regard to their treatment of the wounded. They were as handy with their rifle-butts against Chick and Curly as against the rest, and to argue with them, or protest, was to encourage them to greater efforts. There was no way of coming at Yorisaka; he did not show his face again; and to turn and attempt resistance on their own, as Gregory in a boiling rage was hardly restrained from doing, was only to invite six inches of steel into their guts, and leave the helpless boys altogether exposed to the gentle handling of the heaven-born; which was not to be thought of upon any conditions. There was only one effective opposition, and that was to interpose their own bodies where the blows fell, and obey their uncivil urging as fast as possible. To submit, in face, abjectly, horribly, and swallow their humiliation as best they could.

How long was the procession into which they were compelled they could not see. They simply stumbled where they were driven, across the trampled and reeking stretch of grass which had been their battlefield, and into the green tunnel which had swallowed up the rest of the column; Charlie in front, with his arm under Curly's sound shoulder, and Curly's arm very convulsively tight round his neck; and Jim and Gregory behind, with Chick between them, half-steadied and half-carried; and before and behind and between these two lame formations, Japanese guards padding lightly with bayonets fixed and rifles ready on their arms; and somewhere a long way ahead, where he might conveniently fail to see anything not to his liking, Lieutenant Yorisaka, blast him! that exponent of *bushido*, that descendant of a long line of *samurai*, with his bruiser's body and his accomplished tongue and his enamelled eyes. Maybe he wasn't just a single-minded officer bent on doing his job over the dead bodies of his enemies; maybe he intended them to die anyhow, and had ensured it, once he was convinced they had no information to be extracted, by withdrawing himself from them beyond appeal. During that day Jim began to think so.

There was no halt for food. They were given no water, though their guards drank at will from filled canteens. When Jim asked repeatedly for a drop of water for Chick, they merely pretended ignorance of his meaning, as if even the most explicit gestures conveyed nothing, and prodded him onward at increased speed. When he became desperate, and with a last groan of anger and helplessness laid his hand upon the water-bottle of the nearest man, the edge of a bayonet was drawn leisurely across his wrist, and the start he gave shook Chick, and suddenly for the first time he gave a brief and lamentable cry. No more of that! Once was enough to hear that desolate sound. Jim shook the film of blood from his fingers and lifted the poor body more carefully into his arm, and went on. And he thought: "Oh, God, where are you?" but it was only the last stirrings of a Sunday-School childhood in his mind looking at a picture in a book, and a gaudy picture at that. The man he was looked for no miracle. Things like this had happened before, and not been interrupted by any thunderbolt of divine anger. Why should it be different because it was happening now to him and to his?

At first, while they moved upon a path, it was not so bad. But afterwards the sun climbed and the earth steamed, so that the whole space under the trees was full of stifling, revolving mist, and sweat ran greasily down their bodies, and leeches dropped on them from the bushes and *keringahs* climbed their legs, and bit, and bit again. They moved now along a deep tunnel of gloom; a track only by virtue of the party which had passed ahead of them. There was no longer room for three to cling together, however they cramped themselves. They took it in turns to nurse Chick along for a spell, the odd man moving ahead and easing aside the worst of the obstructing bushes; by which means Gregory lost a substantial gout of flesh and skin from one shoulder to the talons of a thorned palm. They lost touch with time, in this world where minutes were aeons, and hours interminable. They went on only because they had driven it fast into their minds that they must go on, making a single issue of it, as when before battle, that first faraway time, they had told themselves monotonously, that they must not break nor run. They had not broken, they would go on.

Several times, in this green, shadowy, palpitating noon, supported by only one friend because two could no longer get to him, Chick Foulds dropped into a half-faint, and fell, and dragged Gregory or Jim down over him, until they grew dreadfully adroit at stooping over him quickly when the soldier at their heels became playful. There was nothing they could do for him but that, nothing they could lift from him but those bruising blows in the back; and he had already more than he could carry. Small buds of blood, rose-red cactus buds, had begun to show through the dirty bandages, and expand into monstrous flowers. His eyelids were clay-coloured, and rolled back far into his head from fixed eyes, and his mouth was swollen and purple with drought. When at last they emerged into an open track again, and were suddenly halted for a brief spell, and could lay him down in the deep grass, they believed he was dying. Jim knelt down by him and wiped his face with a fragment of bandaging, and again asked for water, choosing the youngest-looking of the guards in case some softness of humanity still survived in him. The soldier looked at him, looked clean through the boy on the ground, spat, and shifted indifferently away.

He was sure then that they had their orders. The prisoners who could not actually be formally murdered, were to be wiped out this way. He must get to Yorisaka if he was to accomplish anything at all. It was not only Chick, though he was the most urgent case; Curly, too far gone to speak for fear of collapsing altogether, hung upon Charlie like a dead weight, his face blank and stupid with pain; and Gregory was beginning to founder like an over-ridden horse; and Jim himself, God knew, would have let himself float away into the roaring darkness that dragged at him, if it hadn't been for the desperate aversion he had for being beaten.

He was not such a fool, this time, as to attempt to push past the guards. He moved as far forward as they would let him go, unobtrusively, and waited with pitiless patience for one glimpse of the peaked military cap moving among the green shadows ahead. At last he must show himself. No man could take a long column single-file through the jungle without occasionally assuring himself that the end of it was still intact and in touch.

The halt lasted half an hour, in the hottest of the afternoon, though by then the prisoners did not know if the day was young or old. And towards the end of it Yorisaka did at last show himself, some dozen yards away still, in staccato conversation with his men along the tunnel of bushes. Jim let him

151

advance until it was clear he would come no farther, and then cried out to him, in that dry, cracked voice which startled his own ears: "Lieutenant Yorisaka! Your men are refusing us water. We have a dying man on our hands. Tell them to help us. Tell them to give us water!"

He knew he was heard and seen; he knew he was understood. The narrow jet eyes passed slowly over him and away, with deliberation, though they could not have missed the tumult about him, the sudden onslaught of the two soldiers who dragged him back by the arms, and the ferocious gesture with which he threw them off. Yorisaka perceived all this clearly and at leisure, and turned his back and moved away without haste.

Jim felt something tear loose inside him, something that numbed his flesh so that pain went out like a candle, and the drag of a man's weight upon his hacked wrist was nothing, nor the battering of a rifle-butt against his blood-caked ribs. He stood up straddling the path, and roared after the disappearing peaked cap: "Yorisaka, you bloody murderer, I'll see you in hell for this, I'll see you paid, you bloody swine!"

One of the soldiers swung his rifle by the barrel, and hit him in the face, and he went down like a pole-axed bull, rolling over at their feet with his hands clamped over his jaw, and blood trickling out of his mouth. He lay there shaking his head from side to side dumbly, half-stunned and stupefied, the darkness perilously near; and being satisfied, they let Charlie come and help him to his feet and lead him back to where Chick was. His jaw was not broken, after all, though both lips were split wide open, and he spat out two front teeth among the leaves. For a time he couldn't talk, and even when that was by, he didn't talk. There was no more use in talking. Everything was asked and answered now.

When they moved on, he lifted Chick bodily in his arms. He knew he couldn't carry him so for long, light as he was; but while his strength lasted it would give Gregory a rest, and come easier on Chick. He knew, too, that the enemy had not expected the boy ever to move again, by his own power or his friends'. They had expected to leave him there, and were disconcerted and angry that he should still be with them upon this second stage of the journey. Yes, certainly it was intended that they should die, of starvation or thirst or wounds or exhaustion, or snake-bite if the jungle did her part. And if she did not, and they insisted on living in spite of ebbing blood and blackening throats——

It was almost dusk, and they were supporting Chick between
them again, when Gregory's feet went from under him in the
first patch of swampy ground, and they all three came down
heavily, and in spite of the encouragement of two prodding
bayonets, were slow in rising. Chick was barely conscious at
all, and the other two walked through an undulating mist,
moving like automatons. The gap between them and the
company ahead was now twenty yards, and they could not
reduce it, they were incapable even of holding it at that. They
were nearly finished.

Jim was out for a minute or two, full out, the desired darkness
cool upon him, and very grateful. He wanted to lie down in
it, and die decently, but he couldn't; something made him shake
it from him, and drag himself to his knees, and reach for Chick,
and start out of his obscuring cloud with a sudden great cry,
because Chick was gone from under his hand, and all he found
was Gregory prising himself up from the water-logged grass.
He wrenched round upon the soldiers, and was met by the
sharp persuasion of a bayonet-point pricking him in the belly.
There were only two soldiers where there had been four, and
Chick was gone; no hide or hair of him left, only a quivering
of bushes, back along the track. He stood his ground for a
minute, feeling the steel bite, shouting at his enemies horrible,
sobbing curses they did not understand, with Gregory dragging
at his arms from behind, and beseeching him in a cracked groan
not to commit suicide, not to chuck himself away; and then
he saw the bushes thresh again, and the two soldiers come out.
He saw the first one grinning, and the second one wiping his
bayonet upon a rag of bandaging, and throwing the rag away
from him as he came. He thought his heart broke then; certainly
something broke in him, for his inside felt full of blood, a heat
and horror that ate away his substance from within, and left
him like a burned-out fire, the smoking shell of a man.

It was not Gregory's urgings that shut his mouth before they
were provoked into murdering him, too; it was not the bayonet
in his middle that turned him and drove him on along the track;
it was because of Curly, who was still alive, and Gyp, who was
in a very special hell for his sake, and Charlie—and all his
communion of saints; because they were difficult people to
satisfy, and had set a strange standard, by which bodily death,
which was comparatively easy, was not enough; because it was
no longer possible to look forward to the breaking-point where
neither flesh nor soul could bear more, where he could lie down

in quietness and let the burden slip away from his back. There was no breaking point; there was nothing that could not be borne.

7

There was no need to tell the others; they knew, and did not ask any questions. They went on silently, stepping precariously upon the tree-roots which threaded the emerald-green swamp, going in to the knees, falling and being battered to their feet again, in exhaustion, in a stupor of pain so comprehensive that it was no longer associated with wounds or blows, but was a part of their very flesh, or the heavy air in which they moved. Charlie knew why Chick was no longer with them; even Curly knew. There was knowledge in their faces. In the middle of that aura of pain and weariness and despair and anger the thought of Chick was like a live coal in them; but they did not speak of it, then or ever. Even when the night halt was called, and they were allowed to drop into the grass and lie still at last, even then they did not speak of it. Only Charlie, having done what he could for Curly, came in a lame crawl across the grass to where Jim lay, and put his hands on him, the hard palms against his breast, as if he would take away the inescapable load; and by that strangely eloquent touch was communicated the thing which could not be said. It passed out of the flesh into the flesh, out of the blood into the blood, anger touching anger and grief upon grief. It did not comfort him, but it calmed him, as company in wakefulness calms a child who cannot sleep. He turned his face into the grass, so that his eyes should not be seen. They were all going to die. Charlie knew that, too, but it might be that Curly was beyond knowing it; and all the better if it came on him unaware.

They lay together through the dark hours, open-eyed, intoxicated with pain. Speech was exhausting, and movement intolerable effort. The proportions of things were lost, their senses had loosed their hold upon reality. Leeches moved upon their hands with the ponderous, dragging slowness of time itself. The *keringahs* were as big as tigers, and the boles of the trees small and very far distant, so that a hand outstretched to touch them extended itself monstrously mile upon mile until the fingers dwindled to threads in the forest aisles a long way off. There were moments of strange clarity, too, when everything, every ache, every memory, every erected nerve sprang back into intensified life; and these were the worst of all. Only Curly, in his shocked, mindless dream, knew no such piercing moments. He sat there in Gregory's arm, his large eyes fixed, staring at the horrible reality through an impenetrable mist. He was past thinking; thought was gone out of him. His capacity for understanding suffering had stopped functioning, like a watch run down, but his capacity for enduring it went on.

In the first hint of the dawn, after only a few hours of stillness, the march began again. When the guards came towards them they arose dumbly, and made ready to move; by what inexhaustible force of resolution they themselves did not know; but this time something was not as before. The little impenetrable naked men came with cords in their hands, as well as Tommy-guns. It was not enough that they should be able, by virtue of carrying arms, to bludgeon men ten times equal to them; they must still further humiliate the obstinate flesh that would not stay prostrate, that refused to die. One of them jabbed the muzzle of his gun into Jim's ribs, while another dragged his wrists together behind his back, and lashed them there. The same gentle service was performed for Gregory, and then they put their yellow hands on Curly, and at the wrench upon his shoulder the breath came out of him in a gasping moan, and was caught back in a nameless, horrid sound neither cry nor word nor sob; but after that, though the red mist rolled over Jim's mind in vast, bitter waves, there was no more from Curly. His wrists just met behind him, and he was drawn into a bow as if by strychine, but he did not utter another sound, only stood where he was thrust, with a heavy sweat breaking on his body like dew, visibly erupting upon him before their eyes. He did not go down, and he did not cry, though a fresh trickle of blood ran down his chin, slowly winding among the dirt and sweat and red stubble of beard, for he had bitten clean through his underlip.

Yorisaka came along to see his men work on them. He did not avoid the appearance of indifference this time. He stood there in the deep green shade under the strange palms, and looked over and round and through them in the first lifting of the dawn, and cared no more for all of them than for one red ant under his feet. There was no reproach nor curse nor appeal that would not rebound from that half-made face of his; therefore they uttered none. He spoke to his men in Japanese, and made with one hand a curious gesture back towards the path by which they had come, back and downward into the ground.

Then he turned and stared suddenly at Jim again, and said in his exact English:

"I find you cannot maintain the pace I must keep. I am therefore compelled to part company with you. You have used hard words of me, I am aware, but you shall see how I return good for evil. I am detaching two men to take you back to the nearest Malay village and hold you there until you can be sent to the rear under adequate escort. You will be able to rest there, and will receive treatment I have been unable to give you on the march."

Oh, it was a pretty little speech, full of *"bushido"*, glib and over-ready, as nimble as the hands of his soldiers when raised against wounded and bound men. Did he think he could talk away the shaking of the bushes by the track, and the blood upon the bayonet? Did he think they were so far gone that a smooth word or two could take away from them the angry, unhealing void in the heart, where Chick Foulds had been? Perhaps he did believe it. Perhaps he had only to say these things in order to build a wall of patriotic hypocrisy between himself and the simple deed, so that unceasing brutality became solicitous gentleness, and bloody murder was soothed away into an unavoidable death from wounds. He looked at Jim for an answer, but Jim said no word. It was Gregory who asked bitterly:

"Why couldn't you have done that in the first place? You said you could spare no men."

"It is a measure of desperation even now," said Yorisaka, far too politely, far too patiently, "and I have spared only two. That is why I regret I find it necessary to have you bound."

"Liar, as well as murderer," said Jim between his teeth. "Why don't you tell the truth? What have you got to lose? Nobody's going to survive to hand on the facts, I suppose? Then why does there have to be a beautiful fiction about it all? You had one of us bayoneted yesterday, and you're going to wipe out the rest of us to-day. It's plain murder. Why don't you call it that? Or don't you like having to look at it the way it is, you bloody little yellow hypocrite?"

He had forgotten Curly for the moment, or he would not have let that known truth come pouring out of him. But Curly was beyond the understanding of words; he had not grasped Yorisaka's version of his fate, he did not grasp Jim's. Both of them went by him faintly in his anguished dream, and touched him not at all. Actions meant something to him still, but words

were so much unprofitable breath. As for the others, they had
seen, as Jim saw, why their hands were bound, and it was not
to ensure that two men might bring them safely as prisoners
into any village of Malaya, that day or any day.

Yorisaka gave an order in Japanese, loudly and very quickly,
and they were herded away from him, back into the green
caverns of the mangroves. What Jim had said bit far too near.
He must not begin to doubt that all he did, being done in Japan's
name, was virtuous and right, an example of chivalry, as of
efficiency, to the rest of the world. The sons of heaven do only
heavenly deeds. Murder must not be mentioned; to hear the
word uttered was to lose face. To answer the charge was to
bring down Japan to the level of human nations who can be
accused and set on trial. He looked fixedly over the flow of
bitter words, letting it go by him unheard, waving the prisoners
away before more could be said, and the duty of forgetting all
became seriously difficult. So he blotted them out from him,
deliberately, as if they had never existed.

They walked back along the tunnel among the mangroves,
and the ground began to quiver under them and suck at their
feet. There was no longer any haste. These things do not take
long. Nor need they be taken beyond the first quaking, steaming
green expanse between the tangled mangrove roots, where the
grave awaited them which had once opened softly for Jim.
They walked to it docilely, being helpless as sheep. They could
not have broken into a run for even the few yards which would
have carried them aside into the brush. They could only drag
one foot after another through the ooze like broken-backed
animals, and wait for the steel in their backs. Steel it would be;
they·wouldn't waste bullets nor risk the noise of a shooting.
Inside Jim's head his mind seemed to be running back and
forth like a caged beast trying to find a way out; but there was
no way out. Time slipping away through his fingers, and
nothing salvable of all that grievous waste; and in his heart
nothing coherent, nothing to which he could hold fast, only a
host of confused memories passing and re-passing and eluding
his hands.

He wanted to think of Miriam; she was there, not far from
him, but even she would not stay, even she, who could make
all things easy, was rapt away from him. The known faces
went by him wildly, leaves in a great wind, a storm of anger
and loss. He found himself praying, in no terms he had ever
heard of before, or ever conceived as fit for prayer; not aloud,

but in the quiet core at the heart of him, in broken, laboured phrases, asking strange blessings. "Oh, God, don't let us be separated, wherever we're going—don't let Curly remember, afterwards, how this happened—don't let what they did to his body do anything bad to whatever it is that has to carry on—because he's going to need us—we'll be the only people he knows—so let us stick together——" But when they were halted at last, even that slipped away from him, and he was left with an emptiness, and nothing on which to assuage his famished hunger of heart. And this in the moment of his most need.

Gregory was the first to go. He felt the prodding of the gun in his back, and suddenly his face became old. He had scrapped over this issue and that all his life, and would never have wanted to live smooth; but to die like this, like a beast in a slaughter-house, tied and held down—— He straightened his tired body, and turned his chin upon his shoulder as he went where he was driven. He said: "So long, chaps!" and essayed to walk straightly and add nothing to what they had heavy upon them. After all, he was used to making effective exits. He'd done it from so many schools, and never, he flattered himself, lost one of his young Socialist converts by the manner of his going. He could surely make a last gesture now in the same tradition. He walked aside through the trailing creepers, and was not seen again. There was only a soft sound as the quivering mud received him, and what might have been a sigh; and then the guard emerging again from the creepers, with his hands leaving red smears as they parted the saw-edged grass.

Charlie Smith felt the prick between his shoulders, and knew his turn. He took one step after his companion, and hesitated, less for fear of what awaited him than of what he left unfinished. He looked back at Jim, and did not move again for a moment though the steel went into his flesh, and made him writhe and draw back his lips from clenched teeth. He saw Jim start after him. He saw young Curly's stony, expressionless face breaking up like trampled ice, breaking piteously into terror and grief and loneliness. He said sharply: "Stay with Curly! What do you hope to do?" though it was little enough either of them could do for Curly now. Still it was wonderfully clear to him that every moment of company was something saved, and what little they had to give to the kid belonged to him by right. Jim accepted his judgment, then as always. He turned back to Curly, and because he could not handle him, made the steadiness of his body do duty for the touch of the hand. Flank to flank and shoulder against shoulder they sustained each other as Charlie was thrust away from them; the right hand lopped and half the heart cut away, crippling them beyond cure, bereaving them at a blow of half the strength that held them upright. For however mysteriously he withdrew himself, however he avoided the burden of leadership, out of him proceeded the tension which drove them, the whips which kept them spinning. Seeing this force withdrawing from them, they were suddenly, desolately afraid. Curly, quivering, toppling, put his face down upon Jim's arm, and little whimpering gasps came out of him; and then his knees gave under him, and he was down in the grass, the emerald green drawing him in.

The long leaves of the trees swung like a curtain, and Charlie Smith was gone. There was a pause in which the silence gathered like lead upon Jim's heart, and then he heard his friend scream.

He did not know what happened to him then. He knew there was pain in it worse than his body could contain, so that it seemed to tear him apart in an explosion of bitter air and blinding light. He heard a roaring as of a great wind rushing past his ears, and through the storm of it the sound of a shot fired, infinitely far away, no longer effective against him, no longer moving in the same world with him. He saw nothing but a redness, at which he tore with his hands, on which he knelt and lay, embracing it, crushing it, bruising it with his weight, ploughing and gouging at it with his fingers. How this could be, when he had been bound, he did not consider. It was enough that he knew it was so, that he had his hands, that somewhere from the middle of him had burned up again the strength to fight and kill before he died. He thought he was mad. He heard himself shouting, raving, clean through the thunder of the wind, not cursing nor praying now, only shrieking wordlessly and ceaselessly, like a berserk Norseman, like a native run amok.

Amok! That was the word. He was amok. He heard voices, impossible voices, echoing his bellowings; that was a sign of the violent madness. He heard a shrill, venomous Japanese chattering; but also there were other voices, big echoing shouts that shook the leaves, and a crashing and plashing of running men in the water-logged ground. No need to run, Yorisaka, you're in time to see the end of me, and of the kid, too; but at least, he thought, I took one of your proxies along with us.

159

That was more than you believed I could do, damn you!
Weren't we all safely three parts dead? Wasn't it a trainee
murderer's job just to run the steel in us? But he shouldn't
have been clumsy with Charlie—he shouldn't have made that
piteous mess of it—to drag that note out of him—and this
miracle out of me. And then he thought, no, it isn't Yorisaka
come back. It isn't that light, barefoot running, it isn't the
slithering of those little naked bodies through the creepers. It's
a big noise, a breaking noise of deep, lusty voices and big,
hasty feet, slashing through the vines, not parting them,
snapping the twigs, not bending them aside. And last he
thought, deep within him: What's the use? What good are
they to me? He's dead. He's murdered. Charlie's dead. What
are they running for? It's too late to run now. It's even too
late to kill. They've finished him. Charlie's killed. And he
closed his eyes, and the madness went out of him with the tug
of an ebbing tide.

He believed that he wept, but neither tears nor utterance
came out of him; the weeping was within, in the lonely darkness
of his mind, in the de-peopled world of his spirit. He felt
hands on him, abrupt and hard, but considerate of his mauled
flesh. He felt himself raised, and held, and carried aside; the
voices were all about him, close and clear, but the words eluded
him, nor could he see who held him, though the dark and angry
red that draped his eyes was paling into the light of day.
Someone put water to his broken mouth, and steadied it there,
and let him drink deep; and with the coolness of it perception
entered into him again. He heard a voice, as British as his own,
bitterly cursing.

"Christ!" it said, "Christ! The bloody bastards! The
bloody murdering swine! Christ, if I could get my hands on
their bleeding throats! Oh, God Almighty!"

Somewhere, as it seemed from very far off, another, a known
voice, said in a breathless whisper: "Shut your mouth, and
cover me up. Don't let him see this—obscene—mess!"

He came back because of that voice. He would have come
back from the other side of hell if it had called to him. He
struggled towards it through limitless seas of weariness and
disgust and regret, and suddenly there was vision again, there
was air, there were greens of grass and vine and tree, and a
coloured butterfly settling upon a darker redness in the dark
red mud under the mangrove roots.

He looked round him dazedly, and he saw big, broad-built

men, what seemed a great number of them, filling his sight. They were stripped to the waist, and burned to a deep copper-colour, but their hair was fair, and their faces were strongly featured and blue-eyed, with a blonde stubble of beard clouding the outline of a big jaw here and there, and here and there a salting of grey in the hair at the temples. They wore broad-brimmed hats, those who did not go hatless altogether. He was slow in receiving the details of what he saw, and let his eyes dwell long upon them before they meant very much to him; but he knew they were friends because they were angry, and because they handled him so solicitously. He saw one of them kneeling, with Curly Ballantyne in his arm, holding the kid against him closely because he shook so, and coaxing a few drops of water from his canteen between the rigid lips. He saw the brilliance of the grass marred by a space trampled and spotted as if two beasts had fought round and round it, and in this ceremonial circle he saw the dead beast, and wondered at the thing he had done. His hands against the bayonet and the gun, and yet the creature was most surely dead, tangled and contorted like a crushed spider, and its face no longer recognisably human, except that large white teeth stood naked and clenched in the midst of it.

He looked down at his own hands, and saw them torn and filthy and black with blood, and about the wrists, scored deep into the flesh, the strands of the cord he had wrenched in two when Charlie screamed. Hand and arm, he was seamed with gashes, for the thing had dropped its gun and clawed him when its breath began to fail between his fingers. There were marks there he would carry for ever, as long as he lived.

That called him back more surely, for it seemed he had to live, whether he would or no. He looked again, and he found Charlie Smith.

He was lying in the grass at the edge of the trampled circle, with an Aussie shirt, the only shirt among the lot of them, thrown across his body from the middle down, and his hands flattened with spread fingers across his belly. Little springs of blood came through the cloth and filled the hollows between those fingers, and overflowed in slow, heavy streams, the brightest dark red Jim had ever seen. You would hardly have known him for Charlie Smith; the hard, lean body looked curiously flat, already slipping back into the earth; the satanic face was the colour of ashes, drained and grey. Good God, he was old! Charlie was old! It was the first time he had ever realised that they were two generations, with every day of twenty years between them. Did that have to come upon him now, when the rest was being taken away? To separate them by so much distance, when a world or two already loomed between? Jim could not bear it, or for a moment his exhausted heart believed he could not; always now he remembered soon that he could endure whatever might be laid on him; but while the moment was upon him he suddenly put by the careful hands that held him, and plunged across to Charlie's side, and knelt there, and finding himself without a voice, hesitated with his hands spread above the shallow-rising breast.

"Don't touch me, Jim!" said Charlie, in the mere tenuous thread of a voice; and seeing the hands drawn back quickly, he said: "Sorry, kid! Anything else you like, but don't touch me. I won't be answerable. I'm no good, Jim!" he said in a diminishing sigh, and his eyes, hollow and hungry, fastened upon Jim's face and clung. "No bloody good! But you'll take Curly back all right. They'll send him home now. He's had his. And I've got mine," he said, and the ghost of the devilish grin came crookedly over his grey mouth. "Habet! Well, he'll be out of it and so will I."

"Don't talk!" said Jim sharply. The labour of speech made the dark blood bubble the faster through the rigid fingers. It had all happened before; he had seen it all before. Two men he had cared for had died like this, clutching their broken bodies together with bloody hands. "Don't talk!" he said. "It makes it worse."

"I'll talk all I want, and be damned to you!" said Charlie Smith. "It's all the same in the end, and if it speeds things up, I shall be glad. I don't like waiting for things. You could give points to Job, I know, but I'm not made that way. I'm dying, and I know it, and so do you unless you're blind and deaf. But what's in that to worry about? I'd have come to it in the end, anyhow, and a few years makes no odds."

"A few of your years makes a hell of a lot of odds to me," said Jim, "and to all the rest of us. Or is that unimportant, too?"

He said slowly, with a reluctant smile: "No, that counts. I'll tell 'em that when the time comes. I never collected golden opinions while there was time, it might help to be able to show one I never asked for. I'm told they consider these things, but I don't know; this is one thrill I never tried till now. Put your hand under my head, Jim, will you? I'm so damned flat I can't

see you. That's a good kid!" He sighed, feeling the supporting
arm shaking violently. "Damn it, this is a war, isn't it? I said
you couldn't run it on an emotional basis. People get killed.
That's all about it. Neither you nor me has any say in it."

"No," said Jim, "no say in it at all. I wish you could
have gone on carrying me a bit longer, though. Remember?"
He saw the ashy face contort, the willing smile jerked suddenly
into a grimace of agony. He saw as it were the body dissolving
away from him into the ground, and himself was shaken with
the pangs of death.

"He's going," said the Aussie who had covered Charlie's
wounds from sight. "Better be quick!"

Jim leaned lower. "Charlie!" he said in a lost child's wail.
"Oh, my God, Charlie—is it awful bad?"

The grey lips, shrunken and writhed, uttered grimly: "It
could be worse—it could be longer." He opened his eyes again.
"Carry you? Never a step from the first I knew of you. That
was bait, and well you know it. I wish—Inez——" The name
came out of him in a wry gasp. "She'd like to think I died
with her name—on my lips—her name—Inez——" The clay-
coloured lids sank again, caved in as if they had no eyeballs but
only the empty sockets. "I seldom do the proper thing," he
said. You could just catch the words if you put your ear close
to his lips. "Too late to start now—a mere bitch, and barren at
that—no kid—could have had—son your age—oh, Christ!" he
said, "no more of her! It's you, Jim, damn your eyes! Don't
like—leaving you—no choice—but you're all right—you're all
right. I wish you'd been—mine—he could have been your kind
—right colouring, and the size was there. She was big, too.
Only her kid—not so straight. Complicated kind—turn in your
hand—and my kid—not so loyal—— No, better as you are——"

He choked there, and blood came out of his mouth, a thin red
trickle running down his cheek. The clasped hands relaxed
slowly, and lay upon his body. Jim put his lips close to Charlie's
ear, and said very carefully, syllable by syllable: "I'll find her
—I'll find her——" What could he promise, what could he
bestow, in the last instant?

"He's gone, boys!" said the Aussie softly, and reached an
arm to take Jim off him, but did not force him away.

"Can you hear me, Charlie? Can you still hear? I'll tell her
—bloody fool to let you get away from her—the best on earth—
I'm telling you, Charlie, there was only one of you——"
Nothing reached him now, nothing. Even pain was loosing its

hold. Suddenly he said clearly, tranquilly: "So long! Be a good lad!" Just that, in a level breath, to the son he had wanted so bitterly; and having said it, he folded up life as a tidy man folds his clothes at night, and composed himself to sleep.

8

After they had buried Charlie Smith and Jack Gregory there was nothing left; no one to love, no one to hate, no one to fight or protect; nothing to hope or fear. The impetus of the world had stopped dead, upsetting every precarious equilibrium Jim knew. Every fire was burned low. Dispossessed of the spring of his warfare, he fell into a silence and a lassitude. Only Curly Ballantyne kept him in motion. Curly was down and stayed down. Stupefied, silent, doubtfully sane, on him at least a man could expend the need he had to care for something outside himself, and above all to be moved by any emotion, pity or affection or anger or grief, where all seemed drained and dead. He'd been a nice kid, a sound kid; everybody'd liked him in the company, and made a pet of him, and borne with his exhausting, mischievous energy patiently, even complacently; they wouldn't recognise him now. And there was Gyp to face, somewhere down south in Johore Bharu; he must be more like the old Curly before they took him back to Gyp.

The Aussies were very good to them. The bulk of the party had gone on after Yorisaka and his muster of Japs, while three took the survivors to the rear. Three were necessary because Curly had to be carried, in a makeshift litter hacked together from bamboos and vines and the pieces of cord with which their hands had been bound. It was a slow journey, because Curly's resistance was so low that he was liable to long faints, and even between these could stand only short spells of motion, however carefully they carried him. Conscious, he looked always for Jim, as being the only face he knew. For the first two days he spoke not at all, but after that he began to talk again, lamely, with great effort, like a man who has been dumb. He talked about Libya, about Benghazi, and the camp by Ibn Radwan's farm, about Charlie, and Gyp, and Sergeant Lake; time being hazy in his recollections and life and death hesitant and interchangeable, so that to be by him was perilous and hurtful to one who had lived through the same experiences and known the same people.

They halted for the first night at a Chinese village, deeply secluded in the heart of the jungle, where they were welcomed and fed, and were able to wash for the first time in many days, and even to make some sketchy attempt at shaving. The oldest of the three Australians—he was a sheep-farmer in a moderately prosperous way in private life, from a lonely farmstead where he had more than once been doctor, midwife and nurse —helped Jim to strip young Curly and bathe him from head to foot, to cut the overgrown curls from over his forehead and eyes, and trim away the soft growth of beard from his chin. He let himself be handled as they wished, and being cooled and comforted, fell asleep between their hands as they rolled him in a blanket and put him to bed. After that they sat down by him and smoked a cigarette together, and for the first time Jim took a look at one of his rescuers as an individual, and no longer as a belated means to an unsatisfactory end.

"What age will he be?" asked Private Sheppard, nodding at the sleeping boy.

"Nineteen."

"So I thought. He shouldn't be here at all, but how can you keep 'em out? You say he's got a brother?"

"Brother, mother, schoolmaster, keeper, all in one, poor kid, and just twenty-two himself. I daren't think what'll happen to him when he's got no Curly to worry about. I suppose they will send him home?"

"If there's a ship to take him, yes. They'll be glad to get the serious cases away before the siege begins, I should think."

"Yes," said Jim slowly, "I suppose that's the next thing. Well, if it gets him back to England that'll be something saved; but you didn't know him the way he used to be."

"He's lucky to be alive at all," said Sheppard. "If you hadn't gone crazy—if you'd even waited thirty seconds more to do it—he'd have been a goner, and so would you. We never knew we were within miles of a Jap until you began to shout, and then we didn't know what we were running into. We just ran. Lucky for you and him we never stopped to think twice. Yon kid of yours was flat out on the ground, and one of the Japs was feeling for you, but scared of getting his pal instead, for hell knows you were so tangled nobody could pick out the spot to plant a bullet. We took care of the one, and by the time we lifted you off him you'd taken care of the other. A pretty thorough job, that was."

"I'd got nothing to lose," said Jim. "Pity I didn't cut loose a bit earlier; Charlie might have been alive now if I had."

"Or the Tommy-gun might have been turned on the lot of you. Don't get to thinking you could have done better than you did. The mystery to me is you were able to do so much. By the way, what about those wrists of yours? Let's have another go at 'em now the kid's off our hands."

"They're all right," said Jim listlessly. "Never mind them." And he asked presently: "What's happened, down there? We've been on our own so long we don't know how things stand. Is there going to be any sort of a stand made? And will it be any good if there is? It looks like Malaya's gone; I don't see we can do much with Singapore. They used to talk about a Johore Line, but I wonder if it's any use trying to stop the rot so far south, especially without 'planes."

Private Sheppard sat quiet for a minute, considering it, his big shoulders outlined against the green twilight in the doorway of the hut. He was no professional soldier, but a sheep-farmer with greying hair and a good solid purse, and a family of school-children left in Australia. He had military opinions only because he was anxious to get the business over, and therefore critical of any policies formed to that end by other men. Besides, with Malaya gone and Singapore in the balance, the centre of the hurricane was drawing too near to home for his liking.

He said: "All I know is, it's taken 'em just over five weeks to get hold of three-quarters of Malaya. We came into action first a couple of days ago with some more or less effective clashes, but all of 'em isolated, so that the best didn't mean much. They talk of a Johore Line, yes, but I doubt if it'll ever come to anything. There isn't any line. Ginger Bennett's in Johore Bharu. The only direction G.H.Q. will ever move from there, so far as I can see, is back over the Causeway into Singapore City. After that, anything can happen."

"What are things like in Singapore?" asked Jim. "We were at Kota Bharu when the balloon went up; we don't know a thing except what's happened to us personally. I did hear they bombed some American Naval Base that first day, and America's in it at last. The only way they ever would have come in. But that's all I've got. How about some details?"

He got chapter and verse, from Pearl Harbour to Kota Bharu, from Kota Bharu to Penang, Penang to Kuala Lumpur, and Kuala Lumpur into Johore. It was a miserable story, with incidents in it not good to talk about. Penang, for instance, where the dead had lain rotting in the streets, and the living had passage out only upon the passport of European blood—— No, better forget Penang. A lot of money had been made out of it in its day, but the one idea at the end had been to get away from it, and leave the native population to look after itself. Better forget it quickly—if you could. Private Sheppard couldn't. Jim could feel very little of it all just now; shame for Penang found no sensitivity in him which was not prepossessed by Charlie Smith; but he remembered, and afterwards the acid began to bite.

"And how's Singapore City taking all this?" he asked, thinking of the indifferent faces which had looked on at the Midshires' arrival, and the bars of Raffles and Seaview closed against them. "I suppose they're finding out how it feels now? Have there been raids?"

"Yes, but not bad ones—yet. It'll come. They run when the sirens blow, but they still sit back with a whisky in one hand when it's over, and do mighty little about getting ready for the next. Most of the bombs have fallen in the Chinese and Malay quarters—especially Chinese—so I suppose it doesn't greatly matter to the Europeans. They're windy at the time, and indifferent afterwards. The women and kids ought to have been sent away long ago, but in December kids were actually coming back from Australia to spend Christmas with their folks. Can you beat it?"

"And I'm still supposed to go on tearing myself apart to keep these people alive," said Jim, in a voice as bitter as gall. "And Charlie's dead!"

"They got me that way, too," said Private Sheppard. "But then I recollect it's for Janet I'm tearing myself apart, and the kids, back at home; not for these beggars. And your Charlie wasn't the only Charlie, and my Janet isn't the only Janet, not by thousands. Still it helps to think about your own, and make her stand for all the rest."

"You forget," said Jim. "I've lost mine. I've got folks in England, but what good's that to me? I don't even know what's happening there. I only know it seems a hell of a long way off, and a hell of a long time ago. If there'd been a Janet it might have been different, but there's no wife to worry about me. I'm one of the thousands that have to get on without any inspiration or find it on the spot; and all I've found I've lost again. Maybe once I could have made do with a sort of feeling about England, but that couldn't survive long among these English here. I hung on by the chaps I knew—by Charlie Smith mostly—— Well, that's gone too! What happens next?"

167

Sheppard shook his head. "It comes. I'm not saying it doesn't."

But Jim was arguing against himself, and to no purpose. All these apologies, all these excuses, he put by as he put them forward. He had to go on, with or without a goal, with or without a purpose, still he had to go on. It was the sentence he had laid on himself, and it was for life. What was the good of turning with this weary longing to shelter himself in his sickness, and disillusionment, and desolate loneliness? At the first mutter of Curly in his sleep, the first sight or sound of the enemy, he would be on his feet again, and reaching for his arms. It made no difference that Charlie Smith was dead. Nothing made any difference. There was no discharge. He couldn't sit there and talk any longer, even to this incurious, receptive Aussie who never put a foot wrong. All roads led back to Charlie Smith. Wherever you started you would find the track turned on itself and brought you back to him. Jim got up abruptly, and went out of the hut. In the quiet dusk a little breeze was stirring, and a rustling of leaves shook the silence. A Chinese woman with a baby astride her hip passed by him from the creek below, where the shallow boats lay, by means of which they meant to move on next day. War seemed a world away, and violent death an impossibility.

In the morning they were taken down-river until the course became too directly east, and put on to a well-used track which brought them in the course of the day to a half-made military road, deep in mud, but carrying a great deal of traffic. It had originally been a drive up to a large rubber plantation, but was now entirely in the hands of the army. They passed through the plantation, and saw a smoking ruin where the house had been, and the godowns deserted, and the plant and latex sheds poisoning the air with clouds of black, acrid smoke which darkened the whole expanse of the sky. On the road below they contacted an ambulance, and were handed over by their Australian friends to the care of a four-square little sergeant who was taking down a fleet of Red Cross lorries to Singapore. Sheppard and his two companions turned back upon their tracks here, and set off upon the return journey to rejoin their party; and since all the ambulances were full, Curly was stowed away upon a mattress in the back of an open lorry, and Jim sat beside him. It wasn't yet safe to leave him to strangers, no matter how well-disposed. Queer things were going on at the back of that shocked and over-burdened mind, and Jim wanted to be by in case of need.

They saw, as they moved slowly southward into Johore Bharu, men of units they knew; and just before nightfall, when the cumbrous procession was nearing the village itself, they were halted alongside the road for a full hour while an overturned lorry was hoisted out of the mashed mud ahead of them, and A Company 4th Midshires marched up from behind full into their tail-board. Jim had been nodding in his corner, and failed to notice their approach. His sleep was pierced through and through by a sudden high-pitched shriek, like a girl's, and he opened his eyes dazedly upon a frantic Gyp, and had his arm stretched out to hold him off from Curly before he even knew who it was who was clawing his way in over the tail-board. Then he saw them, the known faces, grimed and weary, little Stringer, and Instone, and Heychurch, and Stubbs of Sheel Magna, all crowding in on him, all shouting to him, calling his name in astonishment and joy, the first astonishment in all that long march, and certainly the only joy. "Jim!" they shouted. "Jim Benison!" and passed back over their shoulders to those behind the word that it was indeed Jim Benison in person, and Curly Ballantyne with him. Only Gyp, once having given tongue, never uttered a word, but plunged upon his brother madly, panting like a hart hunted to death.

Jim took him in his arms, clean and hard, so that the breath was driven out of him. Curly had opened his hollow eyes, and the wind of that desperate emotion caught him and tore him. He said: "Gyp!" in a trailing whimper, and tried to raise himself and slipped back again with a startled moan of pain as his arm gave under him. You couldn't hold Gyp off him, or he'd try that again; you couldn't let Gyp swoop on him with the full impetus of that stormy affection, or it was liable to blow him clean over the edge of sanity and break him for good. And there was no Charlie to lift the older brat off by the neck and tell him crisply what to do and what not to do if he wanted to save his brother. Charlie could have done it in a few words. Charlie knew every devious by-road of the human heart. He could save a soul in a few choice words which sounded to the outsider like a hearty threat to break the owner's neck. But Charlie was dead in the mangrove swamps, two days' journey away; and someone had to do something in his place, someone had to venture the void that could not be filled.

He thought: "Oh, God, no, I can't!" but he felt the compulsion of his own nature upon him. He took Gyp by the arms, as he struggled to pass and reach his brother; took him

169

by the arms and shook him fiercely, and said in the very voice, in the very intonation: "Take hold of yourself, you half-baked little imbecile! He's all right. Get that into your damn-fool head! Curly's all right! Do you hear? Now, are you going to behave yourself, or do I sling you out of here? I'm having no hysterical nonsense going on round young Curly. He's in no state to stand it. Get that! I mean it!"

Gyp, quivering and breathless, pleaded with his chin on his shoulder and his eyes fixed wildly on the thin face: "Let me get to him! Please let me go to Curly!"

"Stop that!" said Jim sharply, and shook him again. "Damn you, I'll chuck you over the side if you don't calm down. He's been through enough already; I won't have him upset now. You've got to take it quietly. Do you hear? I'll flay you if you damage him now." He felt the boy recoil at the suggestion, and stiffen himself, and stand suddenly mute. "That's better!" he said, and took his hands away. "Go ahead, but go slow."

Poor kid, he was afraid now to let himself go at all. He went on his knees by Curly, and put his arms round him, feeling him all over, piercing himself with wound after wound. He said: "Curly! Oh, my God, Curly! Are you all right?" and held him jealously, as if someone had threatened them with another separation. "I've been worried sick about you," he said. "We thought you—we thought—— Are you hurt bad? You're awful thin——" He looked at the grey, lost face, and a sudden strangling sob came out of him. "Oh, my God, Curly, what have they done to you?"

"I had malaria," said Curly very clearly, puckering his forehead to stare back into the green nightmare of the past. "I was bad—and then we fought, and I put my shoulder out— and Charlie—put it back—— They made us keep going all day," he said, his voice suddenly high and shrill. "They wouldn't give us any water. Chick's dead—they killed him. They killed Gregory, too, and Charlie——" He turned his face into Gyp's shoulder, and began to cry, softly at first, and then with a horrid, rending violence that shook them both like leaves in a wind. Gyp held him the tighter, and looked at Jim over his head with agonised, apologetic eyes.

"I never meant—I couldn't help it, Jim. It's only because he's so weak——" .

"It's all right, kid," said Jim. "As long as you keep steady, this won't hurt him. Do him good! Let him get it off his chest."

He went away and left them together, clinging to each other like children lost in the dark; as they were, as all of them were, in this pagan darkness which had closed upon Malaya. He dropped over the tail-board of the lorry, and a dozen hands reached to touch him as he came down in the grass. Instone said: "My God, Jim, what happened to you all? We began to think we'd seen the last of you. What happened to the kid? So help me, there's *grey* in his hair!"

"Is there?" said Jim, and looked back at the desolate young head burrowed into Gyp's shoulder. "I never noticed, but well there might!"

"What happened to you after we lost you? Where's Lake? Where are all the rest?" they asked him, pressing close around him with question piled upon question, they who had themselves had no easy passage south. "Are any of 'em in this convoy? Is Chick around?" they asked. "We've been hoping to pick up some of you down in Johore Bharu. Is Lake all right? I'd like a word with the old son-of-a-gun if he's anywhere about."

"You're looking at all there is of us," said Jim. "Lake's gone. And all the rest as well, one way or another. There's only Curly and me, and we're lucky to be alive." He did not say: "If you call it luck!" but it was as if he had. "Where's Captain Priest?" he asked. "I'm coming back with you lot, if he'll let me. I'm not hurt—not to speak of——" He looked down at the half-healed gashes down his ribs, and his mangled wrists in their filthy bandages. "One of these chaps can fix me up, easy. I don't want to go on into Singapore until the company goes."

"What about Curly?" asked Heychurch. "Is he really going to pull out, O.K.?"

"Yes, unless something bad happens—clean out, I hope. He's got his ticket home if they know what they're doing. Where can I find Captain Priest?"

Instone looked at him soberly and said: "Priest's dead. He copped it at a little action we had on the Johore border. There's a lot of us gone, Jim, since we lost you chaps. It's been fight and run all the way—every step."

"Yes—I suppose it would be. Christ!" he said. "I'm sorry! Of all people we couldn't spare—Priest, and Lake as well——" He did not speak of Charlie Smith, but they knew that his name was there beside these two.

"How did yours come?" asked Stubbs.

"Oh, the way you'd suppose. We kept going, trying to join up with you again, and after about five days we walked into a Japanese post, and Lake and Farrar were killed. The kid was down with malaria, and Hughson was hurt bad, so we had to halt for a bit—and Hughson died—and then when we went on—well, they were all round us, and we had to fight it out. They took five of us—Tremlett was gone in the shooting, and Parnaby—— They were going somewhere in a hurry, and we had to hold their pace or drop trying—I suppose we got to be a nuisance. They started to kill us off—beginning with Chick, because he was the weakest. The Aussies turned up in time to save Curly and me—and that's all about it. We're here. Five minutes later, and we'd have been feeding the mangrove roots, like the rest."

There was an instant of silence, while all their appalled eyes stared at him, and all their tired faces sharpened. Then Instone said: "You mean they just—murdered the others? Just—killed them off in cold blood? Not in the fighting at all? After they were prisoners? What, unarmed?"

They had fought for weeks on end without respite, yes; they had suffered every conceivable pressure of weariness, and thirst, and heat, and pain; but they had not been prisoners in Japanese hands. They did not know what was known to the grim man with the smashed mouth and swollen hands; they had not seen what the broken boy had seen. They could still feel surprise, they could even feel reluctant to believe. Oh, yes, they had yet a long way to go before they reached the end of this road.

"Yes, in cold blood," he said patiently. "Not only unarmed, but bound. They did it with the bayonet."

"My good God Almighty!" said Instone, and looked at Jim, and looked at Gyp rocking Curly in his arms, and fell suddenly and softly to cursing under his breath, in a flat monotone, as if he was telling his beads. And then little Stringer came dragging his tired feet soggily through the mud along the road, and made for Jim with his hand out, and his round face, stupid with fatigue, lightening with at least some measure of gladness at sight of his lost lance-corporal; and there was the whole story to tell again, and again the exclamations and anger that meant nothing now, falling, as they did, so far short of what he himself knew but neither would nor could express. Stringer was not immaculate any more, though he still had a shirt, and still wore a steel helmet; it was like him to retain the steel helmet. His stubble of beard was three days old, and his face was

marked by purple smears where he had wiped away the sweat
with passes of a dirty hand; and somewhere or other he had
learned to swear in a fashion which did not become his civilised
voice, and only served to degrade the terrifying, speechless
immensity of the quarrel Jim had with the enemy. It wanted a
tongue like the whirlwind and the fire to put his wrongs into
speech; and this inept little man cursed about them with curious,
filthy words only imperfectly understood, like a stray mongrel
worrying a corner of the mantle of the prince of darkness. Priest
would have known. Priest would have felt the stone in his man's
heart, the fire and the crying in his man's mind; and wanting
the tongues of angels, would have been wonderfully silent. But
Priest was dead, too. The other half of that divided unity he
might touch again, but never this one. This one had Stringer
for confessor.

Jim said quietly: "I should like to come back into the company if I can, sir. I'm all right. There's nothing the matter
with me." He was lying, of course, but where they were all
pushed to the limit, what did a few extra scratches matter?
And he wanted to be in action again, doing anything, digging
trenches, draining streams, concreting, anything to be back
among his own and a man again, under orders, with the burden
off his back for a little while.

"It makes no odds either way," said Stringer. "We're all
heading back for Singapore. The Australians took over from us
two days ago. No, you go down with Ballantyne and get proper
attention, and they may let you rejoin in a day or two. We
don't want you foot-slogging it back when there's no need."

So it wasn't worth arguing about, after all. He climbed back
into the lorry, when the sergeant shouted back that they were
ready to move, and with difficulty detached Gyp from his
brother. There was one person, at least, who was only too glad
to part with Jim Benison upon these terms; the company could
do without him, and Curly couldn't; there had to be someone
with him, preferably someone who had been through the same
exquisite hell, and understood how it had broken him. Gyp
hung upon the tail-board as the convoy began to move, and his
voice cut clear through all the others.

"I'll see you in a few days—see you in Singapore. It won't
be long. I'll come as soon as I possible can. Don't forget
now! So long, kid! Be good!" Desperately bright and brittle,
as if nothing dark had come between them and plucked them
apart, and no suffering had changed them.

The lorry moved forward, ploughing through the mud, and jerked into speed. A Company receded slowly in a flurry of valedictory waves and shouts, and the trees closed in upon the road and shut the last glimpse of them away. Curly lay quiet on his mattress, worn out by that storm of grief, his eyes so wide open that they seemed to have swallowed up half his face. Jim offered him a drink; he put it by, but he did it with the ghost of a smile, and something of warmth and feeling had come back into him, so that he looked less like a dead man. Also he was no longer afraid to remember the things that had been done in his sight. He was bent upon looking back at them now, and getting the mastery over them. Jim could see him knotting his brows over the recollection, as they jolted down into Johore Bharu, and waited to cross the Causeway. It was not yet dark, and they could see dimly, in soft and dusky colourings, the long, low outline of Singapore Island afloat upon the water like a purple flower upon a short white stem. It was the end of one phase, and the beginning of another, the battle of Malaya finished for them, and the battle of Singapore about to begin. Curly raised himself to look at it, that dark jewel of an island, still scarcely marked, scarcely blown upon by the smoke of burning latex from the north, still indifferent in its dreaming sleep.

He said: "How long is it since we came out of there?"

"Just over two months," said Jim.

"My God, it feels like a hundred years! You wouldn't think it possible, would you, for everything to change so in only two months?" These were the first coherent sentences he had put together since the battle by the creek; oh yes, Curly was coming to life again, however reluctantly. The very words were familiar; hadn't he used them himself once, a long time ago, after the first lesson of his apprenticeship? Hadn't he said that same thing to Miriam Lozelle? And hadn't he been answered? "I tell you, this also passes as the blind confidence passed. There is nothing that cannot be borne." Curly's feet were on the same road, and there was no turning back for him, no more innocence of what man can do to man, no more faith in the omnipotence of decency, no more refuge in blindness. Charlie Smith had done to him what the pregnant woman of Hainault had done to Jim Benison. Another soldier was being made.

He hoisted him into the hollow of his shoulder, to ease him of his own weight. They moved forward slowly upon the straight, wide roadway, and the mainland was left behind.

174

"Jim——" said Curly.

"Yes?"

"Jim—what happens to people like Charlie? I mean—what happens now?"

He turned his head away. "Christ!" he said, "are you asking me? What do I know?"

"No, but what do you reckon does happen? That couldn't be the finish." And this was not a question; of this he was quite sure.

"Jim——"

"Now what?"

"Jim—being as he isn't around—not the same way he used to be—will you just—well—will you sock me if you see me playing the fool?" He asked it simply, with complete and desperate gravity, his dilated eyes constant upon Jim's face; the poor kid, the poor, fool kid!

"I'll slap your ears down," said Jim, "with the greatest pleasure."

"You won't forget? I shan't have much chance to break out for a while yet."

"I won't forget. Anyhow," he said, "I owe you one for that left hook you handed me outside Tobruk. Oh, I haven't forgotten!" He saw the wan face lighten and flush. There was life there yet, there was spirit; the broken creature would mend again; only there was no returning to the old Curly, any more than he in his time had found a way back to the old Jim.

The convoy swung slowly round the white curve of the Causeway, and they were upon Singapore Island. They looked back to the mainland, a feathery darkness of trees about Johore Bharu, and the ribbon of the Straits between; and in the sky a vast pall of bitter black smoke, many-stemmed, bearing down with an ominous slowness upon the last stronghold, the shadow of siege heavy over the joyous city, the threat of defeat, the promise and threat of death.

PART THREE

SINGAPORE

"Bunglers, bunglers! They ruin everything they touch!"
ANDRE OBEY: *Noah.*

I

THE Hindu doctor came to see him twice, and then left him to the care of a Chinese nurse, who let him wander in and out, and help with the stretcher cases, and load and unload ambulances, but would not let him go back to the mainland and rejoin A Company, which was the one thing he wanted to do. The first thing he ever heard her say was: "No," to that suggestion, and she continued to say it at intervals throughout his seven-day durance in the emergency hospital, always with the same soft, regretful inflection and the same inflexible finality. He never set foot on Malaya again. He was still pottering about with pails and dressings, and burning rubbish in the crater-pitted garden, on the morning of the last day of January, when the whole island quivered to the shock of a great explosion in the north, and they knew without the question being asked or answered that the siege of Singapore had begun.

Jim was helping to lift out cot cases from an ambulance when it happened, wounded of the Argyll and Sutherland High-landers, who had been the last to leave the mainland. There were one or two walking wounded among them, one of them a piper still clutching his pipes under his arm. He looked north-ward as the air shook to that terrestrial thunder, and saw the exquisite pale-blue sky suddenly soiled by clouds of smoke and dust, a towering column of shadow broken slowly apart.

"Yon'll no' keep the wee divils oot," he said darkly. "A mile o' watter wouldna' stop me, and I'll tak' ma oath it'll no' stop them." At that moment men of his own unit were in that mile of water, swimming valiantly from one battleground to the next, since they could no longer walk. They pulled them out of the water at Kranji as thick as May-flies on an English brook.

The piper was a silent man, but restless. Whatever memories he had of Johore he confided to no one, but he took to music for solace, and the sorrows of the Argyll and Sutherlands in Malaya

176

came lamentably in at the hospital windows in strange translation, in ancient mourning airs with grieving names: "Lochaber no More", "The Flowers of the Forest", "Fields of Flanders", "The Highland Cradle". Jim couldn't stand the noise of the drone. It got into his mind like a captive bee, and flew round and round there, and went on long after the piper had ceased to breathe the breath of life into his terrible comforter. But when he offered to discourage the performer, suddenly the little Chinese nurse said more than: "No." She said: "I like his music. Please do not make him stop." And because her word was law, they let him go on drugging himself, only confining him to the compound by the receiving station, where the gravely-wounded could not hear him.

The little nurse brought the doctor in to see Jim again that day. His wrists were still bandaged, but the marks of Japanese bayonets and Japanese nails were healing cleanly, and he had clamoured for days to go back to his unit. His ribs were seamed with brown and purple scars, but that was no matter. Fighting men could not be wasted in Singapore.

He saw the nurse smile, and he knew they were going to send him back, in time for the siege, at any rate; if he had missed the last of Johore he was to be in at the beginning of Singapore. The slim brown hands of the doctor moved upon him, delicately probing, flexing the newly-healed skin of his ribs; and the inexpressibly tired voice said: "Very well, he may go to-day, if he has wished it. It will make little difference in the end." It was not cheering, perhaps, but it was honest, and it set him free to go back to his own, which was what he had pestered them for.

The doctor, as he moved away from them across the room, looked a man worn to death. He was not very old, and broad-built, more on the lines of a fighting man than a doctor, with fine strong shoulders and long arms; but his wife, so they said, had died in one of the raids ten days ago, since when he had worked without ceasing, night and day and twilight, without being known to sleep, or eat, or drink more than an occasional glass of water, so it was not strange that all the virtue was gone out of him. He had a clever, keen face, but his eyes in it were an ox's eyes, patient, mild and grieved. He never spoke directly to his patients, but always through the nurses, as if he needed someone to interpret him to mankind. He had had an English senior here, so it was said, but the Englishman had embarked a week ago for Australia with a shipload of pregnant women.

Someone had to look after them. Jim hadn't been out of the hospital compound since the lorry dumped him there, except to open the gates to Red Cross convoys coming in; but those who had said that Singapore City was full of pregnant women waiting for ships to take them to Batavia or Darwin. Every planter's wife from up-country must have been expecting a baby, they said, by the look of the town now. And the Englishman was that sort of doctor, and the Hindu wasn't; but still they regretted, silently, that it was the white man who had felt impelled to go.

The nurses, too, were grossly overworked. The big, raw-boned Scottish sister, with her iron-grey hair and fierce eyes, and her indomitable toughness, carried half the weight on her own back. Most of the others were Chinese, little light-handed creatures, but strong and tireless and silently kind. Nurse Leong, who closed the door now after the doctor, was the prettiest of them all; and though he had taken her for granted for seven days, his mind being set on other things, Jim could afford now to take a real look at her and feel pleasure in her daintiness, and curiosity about her background. After all, they were all in the same boat now, and the boat was sinking slowly under them. Why pretend otherwise? And having acknowledged so much, why not reach a hand out freely to whoever sat near to you, and at least put some grace of human kindness upon the tragic business? He had only a few hours left in this place; he could take his eyes off the horizon now, and spare a glance for the hibiscus by the dispensary window.

He followed Nurse Leong into the garden, when she took her ten-minute rest in the heat of the day, and sat down on his heels beside her under the flame-of-the-forest-tree. They could hear from over the high white wall a subdued murmur of traffic, but that was only an echo of what had been, no longer a reality. The air was never free now from the reverberations of guns; the aquamarine sky was never clean of that drifting, purple-black rubber-smoke from the north.

"You know they've breached the Causeway?" he said.

"I have heard it," she said. She had a voice tiny like her person, and compactly neat, every syllable a small golden globule of sound. "That means we are besieged, does it not? You do not think they will land here?"

"I don't know," said Jim. "Wish I did. Not if we can stop 'em, you bet."

"But we can," she said firmly. "My people have raised a

178

strong force to help in the defence. There are companies of them in the north now, at Kranji. You will see how well they acquit themselves."

"They will," said Jim, "they have. Only the place to fight for Singapore was on the Thai frontier, not on the Straits of Johore."

"Let us not speak of it now," said Nurse Leong gravely. "In a few hours you will go back to all that, but why should you consider it until you must?" She had a quiet way of speaking, half-sophisticated and half-childlike, and altogether her own. He liked the trill of her r's that nearly became l's, but never quite abandoned their nature. "Rather," she said, "you should be quiet here for an hour, until I must do your dressings again, and consider the flowers of this tree, or the colour of the sky, or the texture of the leaves."

"Or you," said Jim.

She looked surprised at that, but in no way disturbed. "Or me," she agreed, "if it gives you pleasure."

Now that he had time to see her, it did give him very much pleasure. She was only a miniature of a woman scarcely darker than ivory, but so exquisitively proportioned that she had a dignity more complete than he had seen in any white woman in Singapore, for all their extra inches and consciousness of race. Nurse Leong had pride of race, too, but it expressed itself in gentle, courteous and adult ways, in the graciously competent functions of her hands at work, and her civilised silences, and the unhurried moderation of her speech to everyone, from the highest to the lowest. She had beauty also. Prettiness was no word for the thing she had. Her face was a pure oval, fashioned with wonderful delicacy, her features small and fine to fragility; and her eyes were not oblique at all, but only different from occidental eyes in their elongated shape, and the depth of their brilliant blackness. She had a mouth as full and soft as a budding camellia, with such smoothly-polished modelling that there was a suggestion of fragrance in the very look of it; and her hair was soot-black in the shadow, and metallic blue where the glancing sun caught it, straight silken hair parted in the middle and knotted on her neck. As she sat there under the flame-of-the-forest-tree, fondling the blazing flowers with her glossy olive fingers fragile as a dream, it did not matter that she wore a grey uniform frock and a starched apron, or that the red cross of her discarded cap stood up beside her valiantly upon the bench; she might have come straight out of a book of Chinese fairy-tales, or a Dulac drawing of the daughter of Kubla Khan.

"It gives me no end of pleasure," he said roundly. "Now I come to look at you, you don't look a bit like a nurse. Nurse Leong doesn't fit. You haven't been a nurse all along, I'll take my oath, or you wouldn't take the trouble to treat us all as individuals the way you do. We're allies, aren't we? Tell me about yourself!"

"There is so little to say," she said, and was quiet a moment, looking at him steadily with her long eyes. "I am not a professional nurse, no. My sister and I, we had a little shop. You would not, perhaps, know the street; it is down near Raffles Square. We made exquisite baby-linen, she and I, all by hand. All the *amahs* with their beautiful prams used to come to us. Do not look for the shop," she said. "It was hit in a night raid nearly a month ago; so I give all my time to nursing now, having nothing else left. It does not sound much to lose, but when you have made it with your own hands you cling to it jealously."

"What's become of your sister now?" asked Jim. "Is she nursing, too?"

"She left me eight months ago. I am used to being alone. She married an English merchant, and went to Penang with him."

"Penang? Oh, lord! Were they there when it fell? Did they get away all right?" But he knew the answer already by her eyes.

"No," said Nurse Leong, in the same, quiet, serene tones. "They did not get away. There was an English lady, once a customer, who brought me a letter from her. They would not let her embark, you know, because she was Chinese. Her husband, yes, being English, he could leave; but he would not go without her." She looked at Jim, and said with a quick chiding: "You must not take all things to yourself. Remember I have seen your wounds. It was not you who made Penang."

So his chagrin was as obvious as that, or this little creature as clairvoyant! Well, things were past the stage where it mattered that he should admit shame and anger. Singapore was a body already hurt and contorted by the first throes of what he for one believed to be a death-agony. When he tried to look ahead he saw only a blankness, unpeopled except by Charlie and his peers, who were more alive to him now than the living. He was assured that he would never get out of this island alive;

he didn't have to think about it, the certainty of it was in him, part of his being, as obvious as the air he breathed. With that knowledge upon him, why should he avoid confession and absolution?

"I'm English, too," he said. "I have to stand in with the rest of 'em. I made Penang all right, whether I like it or not."

"Then, also," said Nurse Leong in a very low voice, "was it not you who refused to leave her?" And she rose, and went away from him with her quick, gliding walk, her tiny, upright figure flashing through the sunlight and shade under the branches of the trees, until she rounded the corner of the white wall and was lost to sight, having made perhaps the only reply possible to the imperfections of humanity, and made it by instinct, as surely as plucking a flower.

He saw her again when he was discharged. She changed his dressings for the last time, and as always would have completed the operation in silence had he let her. But he looked up into her face as she rolled the bandage round his wrist, and asked her:

"What's the rest of your name? I can't think of you as Nurse Leong."

She smiled; with her it was always a curiously sad thing to see, that little lengthening and quivering of the camellia mouth in so much of tenderness and so little of mirth. "In business," she said, "we were called Mary and Louise Lei; but you will not wish to remember Louise Lei. My Chinese name is Ah Mei." As she said it, it was like a sigh.

He said it after her, trying it on his tongue; it fitted her like the steel-blue sheen on her hair, or the burnished shadows under the curve of her cheek. "Ah Mei—— Ah Mei Leong! Yes, that's more like it."

"Leong Ah Mei!" she corrected him, and finishing the bandage, put his hand away from her. "The family name comes first with us always. And now," she said briskly, "you will wish to see your friend before you go."

"Yes," said Jim, "I was going to ask you that. I must take some sort of news back to Gyp."

Ah Mei, going before him through the long, crowded wards, was hailed from all sides with greetings shy and bold and saucy all at once, but she passed them all by with her serene impersonal smile. It couldn't be easy to stay the same to them all, day in and day out, as she did; never in haste, never still, never out of temper as Sister Mears was never in, the East silently instructing the West. Yes, he would remember Ah Mei among the rest, for as long a time as he had to remember anyone; he judged it would not be long.

She stopped with her hand upon the handle of the last door. "You know they are taking him away?" she said. "Tell his brother he is on his way home. They are embarking all the worst cases from here, all those who can be moved, I think from Keppel Harbour, in a very few days now. Those who are badly shocked, as he is, will all be sent home. You can be easy about him; he will make a good recovery when he forgets the things he has seen."

So she knew that, too, and accepted it into her Oriental calm with the rest. She saw what Jim was thinking, and the quivering smile touched her lips again. "At first he used to talk in his sleep a great deal. That is all over now." She opened the door softly and led the way in.

There were twenty-two men in the ward, many of them in beds screened from sight. Curly, very clean and tidy and young, lay near the door, held rigid in a plaster cast, and propped up at the shoulders with hard calico pillows. His copper hair was brushed and bullied back from his forehead and cut very close, but it still curled. His eyes, in which something of the dazed stupefaction still lingered, were watching the door, and lit up eagerly at sight of Jim. When he smiled he looked almost like the old Curly, but very much thinner, with an incandescent pallor about him. His nerves were not yet under control; the hand he held out to Jim—he had the use of only one—quivered like a highly-strung terrier pup, and clutched like a girl's.

"Hullo, kid!" said Jim, and knelt beside the bed so as not to disarrange its glazed whiteness. He took the shaking hand between his own, and steadied it there lightly. Ah Mei, who knew more than it is good for a woman to know, went away from them and left them alone.

"Hullo, Jim!" said Curly. "I hear you're going back to the boys."

"Yes, they've done with me. I'm off this afternoon."

"Wish I was coming with you! Think it'll be very long? Surely I shan't have to stay in plaster much longer? I want to get back to Gyp. I'm worried about him, Jim," he said earnestly, "honest I am. I don't like leaving him alone so long."

"That comes well from you, my lad," said Jim. "Likely he's

having the easiest time for years, without you to pester him to death. And anyhow you can put it out of your mind. I'll keep an eye on Gyp for you, and see he doesn't do anything you wouldn't do if you had half a chance."

Curly grinned. "Fat lot of use that'll be, you old humbug!"

"All right, I'll see he doesn't get half a chance to do the things you'd do, you little perisher. Not until you're back to do 'em with him, anyhow."

"Straight!" said Curly, "you will take care of him?" And his eyes were suddenly anxious to desperation, and his voice had dwindled to an urgent whisper. He was like all children, and most animals, when it comes to the point. He laid the burden of his trust upon other people without a qualm, unaware how heavy it was, and how it galled; and the victim had not the heart or the guts to reject the load. He could only close his fingers very firmly on the shuddering, beseeching hand, and say:

"Straight, I will!" So easy to say, and so hard to make good; and once having said it, he would go floundering through successive purgatories to hold fast by what he had sworn. It was the same thing when a dog looked at him with melting eyes asking for food and companionship and comfort; their demands knew no moderation nor limit, and yet he promised, like a damned fool, and began to dig away the mountain with his hands. Well, since he had no hope of getting home again, or outliving this siege unless in captivity, at least this gave him something to measure himself against, something to struggle for, an interest in what was left of life. "I'll do what I can," he said, "You quit worrying, and concentrate on looking after yourself; that's your job. And don't you trouble about us, whatever they may do with you. If they send you away by sea, that's all right, see, that's the best that could happen, for Gyp as well as for you. You'll be off his mind, and I'll be keeping an eye on him; and don't forget, if things get too hot to hold here, they'll get us out of it somehow; they always do."

"All right," said Curly pliantly, "I'll do anything you say. Gyp was in one of the days," he said; "did you see him?"

"Yes, we had a word or two together."

"He looked pretty done," said Curly. "They won't send us back into the line again, will they? He looked awful tired."

"They'll give us what rest they can, you may bet. Gyp'll be all right; don't you worry."

That's what they always say, of course, he thought; don't

worry, there's nothing to worry about, everything's going to be all right. No one believes it any more; even Curly doesn't believe it, it just soothes him to hear it said. He knows this island is dying round us while we talk together; he knows there'll be no new Dunkirk this time. There isn't the shipping to take us all off, and the women and kids who should have gone months ago will be embarked first. He knows there's a tragedy beginning; but he doesn't yet know that he won't be here to see the end of it. He thinks we'll all die together, or go together into captivity; and my job, as far as he's concerned, is to make it easier for Gyp; and all Gyp will be agonising about is Curly. Well, he thought, we're queer creatures; but maybe there's hope for us yet.

"I shall have to push off," he said, "if I'm going to get back to the lads. And here's Nurse Leong giving us a time's-up look, too." She came to the side of the bed and stood looking down at them with her grave porcelain smile, and said no word. "Now you be easy in your mind, and leave Gyp to me, and we'll try to see you again as soon as we can. Right?"

"Right! And thanks for everything, Jim," said Curly, clinging to his hand as he rose.

"Get off with you! I'm on a soft thing; Gyp isn't you!"

The old grin, somewhat strained and pale, came back for a moment. "All right!" he said, "I'll have to let that one by. But you wait till I get out of here!" His fingers closed convulsively for a moment, and then withdrew themselves resolutely. "So long, Jim! Good luck!"

"So long! Be a good lad!" That was Charlie's farewell to him, it would do well enough between him and Curly now.

Ah Mei made a little gesture of her hand to the boy, a little ceremonial motion of leave-taking, as if she too had had a part in the scene; and then her creamy fingers touched Jim's arm, and he followed her obediently from the room. And that, he supposed, was the last he would ever see of Curly Ballantyne, unless, perhaps, they met somewhere after the war, when all the killing and capturing was over. He did not bank on that; the blank wall which was the fall of Singapore still enclosed his vision. Beyond that there was nothing.

2

Leong Ah Mei walked out to the gates with him, and said good-bye as if he had, in some way, become rather a special person to her; perhaps because he had understood the things she had not said. When she turned back towards the receiving station he stood a moment to watch her go, taking pleasure in her pliant straightness, and the poise of her head on the slender neck, and the motion of her hands and wrists which had so much twentieth-century freedom and yet retained something of an antique alabaster grace. He wished he had known her better, but time was so brief and so blind.

He walked down into the city. There were a lot of people in the streets. There were queues outside the cinemas. The women were still exquisitely dressed, and still sat about in the windows of houses and the verandas of hotels, smoking and knitting and gossiping and playing cards through the heat of the day and the early evening. Their faces were animated and confident, and yet their eyes were uneasy. They looked at the sky sometimes, but furtively, too arrogant to admit even a sane and moderate fear. There no longer seemed to Jim anything admirable or brave in that. And all the while that smoke of burning latex drifted south over them, and sent paling plumes out to sea. It was rather as if the sacrifice on the altar had declined to believe in the lighting of the fire.

He saw a considerable amount of damage already. Most of it was among the poorer native house-property, chiefly Chinese. He passed close by the ruins of one huge block, where Chinese rescue-parties were working feverishly upon a mountain of rubble, and the smell of death was appallingly strong upon the air. A quarter of an hour later, as he turned in towards Fort Canning to try and hop a lorry going north, he passed by the gates of an exclusive sporting club, and saw a woman coming from tennis. She was in tailored shorts and a white shirt, with her racquet under her arm, but he knew her again in this new incarnation. He'd looked only once at that woman on the hotel veranda, the woman who had sighed for the worthiness of the Midshires, and lamented that they were not malleable; but he would know her again, no matter what the whim took her to be, no matter what she wore to perfect the character.

She had a young man in tow this time, younger by some years than herself, and for all his immaculate whites and open-necked shirt he had R.A.F. written all over him. Maybe she'd found her new blood, after all. She was flushed with the game, and the tan of her legs was smoothly golden, deeper than Ah Mei's skin; and as she passed Jim in the gateway she was busy plucking away some woman's identity with leisurely, charming

185

passes of her hands, as children strip the petals from a flower, leaving her only a cold stem of virtue.

"—but of course, she's ravishing—if you fancy the ingénue. No individuality, though at nineteen I suppose one hasn't—I really can't remember, it's so long ago. If only she would cut herself loose from that lovely but quite too managing mother—but she won't, you know. A charming nature, but the last little thing that makes the difference—it just isn't there. She hasn't enough self."

So some wretched nineteen-year-old had ventured to please a man this woman considered her own; freshness and youth would be no armour to her there, unless she learned how to bankrupt this acquisitive rival of more subtle advantages. A tongue like that could discredit the dew of the morning, and make the evening star tawdry, at least in the ears of a very young man. Whatever darkness drifted down upon Singapore, it was too late for her to change her nature; she would go on playing her little feline games until the last twilight fell on her, and she would conceive that the world had failed her, and accuse it bitterly, having helped in her degree to fret away the pillars of the house.

He went on. Couldn't she realise that she was finished? She didn't matter a tinker's damn now, one way or the other. He didn't even dislike her, or want to see her changed; things were long past that. She was part of Singapore, a facet of an experience which was to prove fatal, and interesting in just that degree. She was there in common with the patrols and prostitutes of Deskar Street and Lavendar Street, the Chinks, drinks and stinks, the Eurasian merchants, the Tamil labourers, the dock coolies, the children grubbing in the fragile ruins of wood hovels outside the town, the grimy rescue squads, the ex-territorial soldiers she despised; and with them she was being whirled round and drawn into a whirlpool of darkness and ruin and desolation whose ripples would shake the world. She was bound breast to breast with him, whether she would or no, for the last swim either of them would ever take. She was level with Ma Hla—lower than Ma Hla because she would not know how to turn with the current, and Ma Hla would. She would die still convinced she was of different clay, but the earth would think her much the same, if she were lucky enough to get burial. Yes, the Japs were great levellers.

He was not far from Raffles Hotel when the sirens sounded the second alert of the day. He saw the women come rushing out to take shelter, women from up-country big with child, women of the smart Singapore set dressed for the daily tea-dance and heavily squired, old women and young, their faces stricken into a blank surprise that their world was mutable like any other. He saw them elbow for places like fishwives, without dignity, without restraint; there was much taking and very little giving. He saw a young Chinese warden trying to bring them into some sort of order, struggling valiantly to make them file into the wretched shallow shelters more rapidly; and having packed in the last dowager, this big-eyed boy trotted away down the empty street calling: "Take cover! Take cover!" at the last few strays, until the 'planes came over with a scream-ing roar, and he lay decorously down in the gutter and folded his arms over his head, and waited the impact patiently.

Jim was lying in the gutter, too, along with a Merchant Navy officer, a Tamil labourer, and two rickshaw men who had decanted their fares into one of the shelters. It was a new sort of bombing to him, not the staggered, recurring, methodical runs he was used to, 'plane after 'plane heeling and dropping in that shallow, roaring dive; this was an affair of perhaps thirty heavy bombers, moving in stately formation across the sky, and all, without leaving their stations, dropping their bomb-loads at the same instant upon a given signal, so that the target area was suddenly spattered with bombs like rain, and in a minute the storm was over. If you survived the minute you could get up and go about your business; but if you happened to be in the selected area the odds were that you didn't survive it; and the minute itself was staggering, as if the bottom had fallen out of a hell of noise and darkness, impact upon impact stunning your senses and battering your body, the world burst asunder in smoke and thunder and fire. Afterwards, as the 'planes sailed majestically on, and the smoke slowly cleared, and the deafness receded, you realised that the block of buildings on either side of you still stood, that you were alive still. Anyhow it was quick, one way or the other.

The Merchant Navy man took his head out of his arms and looked dazedly at the darkened day, and swore a wonderful oath. "If that's pattern bombing," he said, "I'm damned if I like the pattern." And he picked himself up, and raced away into the smoke and dust, and was presently seen hauling out a brood of Chinese children from the tottering remains of a house of which one side was torn clean away. Jim got up from the ground more clumsily, being stiff from the healing of wounds;

he would never, probably, be able to run quite so fast again, nor keep going for quite so long without rest, but he was still good for plenty of this rough work. He followed the Merchant Navy man into the shattered mounds of wood and brick which had been dwelling-houses only a quarter of an hour before, and spent a strenuous hour helping to heft out old Chinese women, and children, and young girls dumb with shock. He was aware through the glittering brick-dust haze, and the stifling smoke, of other men who took a hand in the work: a big Australian private, a Chinese business man straight from his own wrecked office, with one shoulder of his expensive coat torn away, and plaster and wood splinters in his sleek black hair; an American war-correspondent and his Malay driver, who had charged up in a small car and begun to prise up the fallen beams with their bare hands, like enthusiastic terriers at a rat-hole; a couple of English rankers; a Sikh *havildar* wonderfully bearded; a nice-looking young army captain with several decorations. They didn't exchange a word, but sailed in and worked like blacks, extracting the living and the dead from under the wreckage. There were a lot of dead. They laid them in the roadway, and covered them with anything that was handy, and went on; there was nothing else to do; and presently reinforcements of rescue parties and wardens, Chinese to a man like the victims themselves, came and took the orphans and the dead off their hands.

The Merchant Navy man stood up in the middle of the street, black as a chimney-sweep with dust and smoke, and croaked from a throat scoured raw: "Come and have a drink! There's no more we can do here, and I'm a lime-kiln, not a man." He didn't say it to anyone in particular, so that it included them all, except perhaps the Sikh, who didn't come of a drinking clan, and was already taking himself silently away about his dignified business. The two Tommies wistfully regretted that they were on duty; the business man had dived back to the salvaging of his own premises; but all the rest of them made for the nearest bar, and essayed to wash away with long, cool drinks the mortar-dust and bitter smoke that scalded their throats. Even the young captain came. Jim had half expected him to slip away, but he came along and sat on a high stool at the bar, all soiled and speckled as he was, and poured a planter's punch straight down his throat, and came back for more. He didn't say anything; but neither did any of them for a few minutes, until the coldness had had time to bite.

"That little kid!" said the Merchant Navy man, putting

down his glass with a crash. "What was she?—nine or ten, maybe. I keep thinking of her face. She'd have made a beauty some day. If only there were some deep shelters for these people, instead of the wretched little drains they have got. And even those—even those——"

"Are full of Europeans," said the American war-correspondent, very quietly. "You haven't been long in Singapore, have you?" he said.

"Three days, but I'm getting to know. Another three, and I get out, thank God. Even then we shall have Singapore on board. They're so crazy to cash in on the exodus, they've cooked up twelve passenger berths on the tub I sail in, and every one's filled. All women, and three expecting. And lousy with rubber and tin money, or they couldn't afford to leave at all. They're charging God alone knows what for passage to Australia. The Japs can have the poor!"

"The men aren't allowed to leave now," said the Australian. "If they were, you'd have hundreds of 'em discovering urgent patriotic reasons why they should get to hell out of here, the way they made it a point of honour to get out of Kedah and Kelantan down here when the shots began to fly. 'I want to be where I can do some good.' That was the formula. Doctors left their patients, and planters left their work-people, and foremen left their gangs, all from a bloody sense of duty! Christ!" he said. "Get me out of this filthy country full of seven sorts of leeches, and let me die in better company!"

"I'm with you all the way," said the naval man. "I wish to God I'd never seen it. It breaks my nerve. My dad— he was the old kind, God-Save-the-King and Rule Britannia!— he used to stuff me up with the guff about colonisation; carrying the torch of civilisation to the lesser breeds without the law, setting an enlightened example to the poor uninstructed natives—— An enlightened example! God, you saw 'em! The way they run! The way they intrigue and bribe and elbow to get the little bit extra of liquor, or safety, or food, or comfort, or kudos. I tell you straight, I wish I was Russian; and I'm not a Communist, and I'm not kidding."

"You take it too hard," said the American. "If I may say so, you seem to have spent your three days trying to retrieve the position. You've got no need to cover your face."

"No need? I'm English. I want to beg the pardon of every Chinaman I see, and get on my knees to every Chinese woman. I want to start with that little kid," he said. "She ought to have

189

been alive now. It wasn't necessary for her to die."

"You don't say much, chum," said the Australian, looking at Jim.

Jim said with deliberation: "I was thinking: 'So I'm not the only one!'"

"So was I," said the Aussie, "so was I. For a month I've thought it was me that was queer. Now I know I'm not mad, after all. What I've seen, you've seen, too. There has to be something in it. We've all been let down."

The young captain said nothing at all, only sat there with his empty glass in one hand, and his face in the other, and mortar-dust soiling his medal ribbons. They heard the guns sounding, faintly from the north coast; the bottles behind the bar chattered gently, and were still again.

"There was a woman in a car," said the Aussie, fixing his eyes on the whisky in his glass. "It was one of the days last week—we were clearing up after another of these pattern raids, and we got a young woman out, three parts dead, and hadn't any transport just then to take her to hospital. We stopped this car—private chauffeur and all—and asked this woman for the loan of it. The little Malay girl was lying on the ground there; she could see the damage for herself. She said she was terribly sorry, and it was dreadful, and she wished she could do something to help, but she had an extremely important appointment, and there must be other transport. And I was too damned slow to do anything about it when she drove on. I saw her the same night coming out of Seaview Hotel, and the car waiting for her, and she telling the world how much she'd picked up at bridge that evening. The same woman—I couldn't mistake her. The Malay girl was dead then, died on the way to hospital."

"Man and woman," said the Merchant Navy man, "it's all one. There's a bloke here I had to call and see—sort of cousin of my mother's, managing director in one of the tin companies. The day I went to see him he was hopping mad because he'd been asked to make one in a pick and shovel party digging defence ditches in the north of the town. Seems he'd asked for something useful to do, but he didn't mean with his hands. I think he expected to be given a fancy squad to drill, or a labour battalion of you chaps to order about. He refused to go. Spent nearly an hour, while I was there, concocting a sarcastic letter declining the honour. He thought he'd been insulted, being asked to work. His wife took the same line. Said Lady Brooke-Popham had asked her to help two hours a day at the Red Cross, but she was well in the running for the Club singles at tennis, and didn't want to miss her daily practice. The finals are played in March!" He pushed his glass across the bar, and laughed. "That's how blind they are! She hasn't realised yet that she'll never play in 'em." He looked at the American narrowly along his shoulder, and asked dryly: "Well, you're in it yourself now, aren't you? You can talk now, like a partner, not a neutral. Don't be afraid to say it. We've said worse, aloud or under our breaths. Go ahead, this is no Press conference."

The American hesitated, but rather for the right words than the right attitude of mind. "I may be a partner," he said slowly, "but I'm not one of the family. It's not much I have the right to say. I think you're right to be ashamed and angry; but don't forget the boys who flew the Wildbeestes, and fought those incredible rearguard actions, were English too. You're liable to lose sight of them."

That was an echo of Leong Ah Mei saying, so softly, so gravely: "Then was it not you who refused to leave her?" But it was all very well for these others to reason about the landslide, these others whose integrity was not stabbed in the back, whose pride was not stripped naked; all very well for them to attempt comfort, who were not English.

"You've only lived through Pearl Harbour," said the Merchant Navy man simply. "That's only the beginning. You may be right, but see if you think so later. Did you see this morning's manifesto? 'Singapore will be held—— England expects—— Please back us up—— Every man's help is needed, whatever his race or politics——' Yes, they say that now! They want the Chinese and Malays to be partners now. Before that it was: 'You just keep quiet, and stay out of our way, while we get on with our war.' But they still say: 'Together we shall fight until victory is ours; Singapore will be held.' The hell it will, and we all know it! But if I raised my voice——" It was the merest undertone. "—I should be thrown into quod for a subversive for saying so."

"You haven't done so badly," said the American with a wry smile, "for only three days."

"Three days this visit. I've been here several times before. Don't think I'm condemning the place on one acquaintance; only this explains all the rest. The lid's off it now."

"Yes," said the Aussie, "the lid's off it now. I met a bloke in Lavendar Street one night," he said. "He said he was looking for a woman, a very special woman, one of the 'short time two

dollars, long time five dollars, all night ten dollars' kind. He
said it would be cheap at the price if it would take Penang off
his mind. Whisky wouldn't, he said, he couldn't get drunk any
more. He told me a lot about that embarkation. He had to
come back, being a soldier under orders; otherwise he wouldn't
be here now. He said he saw Chinese ladies walk down into
the sea and drown with their children in their arms rather than
stay and be taken alive. He said some day he was going back
to do penance, prostrate himself round the island like the lamas
going round the Potala, or commit suicide where he saw the
women go into the water. He wasn't drunk, either; I don't
know if he was mad.''

The young captain span his empty tumbler away from
between his fingers, and it fell from the inner edge of the bar
and smashed upon the floor with a thin, startling sound. He
took his hand away from his face with a jerk, and suddenly
stood up, clutching the edge of the bar.

"These bloody people!" he said. "These bloody, bloody
people!" and turned and plunged away from them, and
shouldered his way out into the street like a blind man.

"There goes another," said the war-correspondent, at the end
of a long silence, "who has it. Habet, habet! Maybe we talk
too much. Anyhow, he knows now that he's in good company,
for what that's worth." He drew a long breath, and let it go
in a heavy sigh. "You gentlemen will excuse me; I don't feel
like drinking any more, but yours are on me." He went away
slowly and heavily, as if he was very tired; and one by one the
others followed, having no longer any will to talk of what had
already been said too well by half for their peace of mind.

Jim and the Australian came out into the evening together.
The dust had settled, and rolling clouds had covered the sun.
"Rain to-night or to-morrow," said the Aussie. "Heavy, likely.
Well, a storm might clamp down on the air for a bit and give
us a break. I'm going north to Kranji with a draft of Chinese
levies, if they're assembled yet. You aren't by any chance
going my way?"

"Yes," said Jim, "and glad to. My outfit are out in the
rubber north of Mandai, if you can drop me there."

"Can and will. Let's get along to Fort Canning and see how
forward they are. The raid may have held things up."

But when they arrived before Fort Canning they found their
Chinese levies assembled ahead of them, and a young English
officer of the Malayan Police chattering to them in their own

language, round an outsize cheroot like a wax candle. They were not armed volunteers, but a picked labour corps with some skilled men among them, and a half-dozen riflemen attached, expert shots more valuable independently than as part of a body. They were of all types and all ages, from scarred veterans of the China war to eager young Kuomintang students wearing tiny pictures of Chiang Kai-Shek and Madame, and from labourers to officials. They were the most sincerely hopeful people Jim had seen in Singapore. They, certainly, if no one else, believed that the island would be held. They sang Chinese songs in the back of the truck as they bumped along out of town by the Bukit Timah Road, and the squall of rain which came sheeting down suddenly out of the heavy sky did nothing to damp their enthusiasm.

"Hark to 'em!" said the Australian, as the hiss of the rain cut them off for a moment from the jangle of voices behind. "You'd think they were going to a party. And even this is being done months too late. You know they're raising armed companies, as well as these working parties? In a few days' time there should be some of 'em up in the north."

"So they told me in hospital," said Jim. "Somebody must believe the landslide can be stopped, or they wouldn't bother."

"It's plain you don't."

"No, I don't believe in it. Singapore was lost in Kedah and Kelantan, to my mind. It would take two divisions of fresh troop to pull it out of the fire now, and a few squadrons of fighters, and even then I wouldn't do any betting."

"Most of us say in Johore," said the Aussie, "but what's the odds? I wouldn't be surprised if you're nearer the truth, but it's all one in the end. There'll be no two divisions, anyhow, there'll be no squadrons of fighters. What would you do? It's as good a guessing game as any. Given this set-up—this whole bloody set-up just as it stands—what would you do?"

"Fight as long as I could for every yard of this road into Singapore City. There's no option, anyhow. We haven't got the shipping to evacuate properly, and what there is will be wanted for women and kids; and a lot of that, even, probably won't get far. So we're here, and all we can do is fight until we drop. We can't get enough men to be any good to us, or alter the issue; I wouldn't send in one more man to go the same way as us. And I wouldn't arm the Chinese, not because they aren't worth it, but because for every man who fires a shot at the Japs the Chinese population will have to pay the devil's own price after the fall. If it had been done months ago they could have been effective. Now they can't change or delay the result by enough to matter a damn, but they can lay their own community open to reprisals."

"Reprisals?" said the Aussie. "War's war! What do they expect, when they've been playing hell in China for years?"

"War's war, but Japs are Japs. I've seen them in action, I know what they're capable of. I wouldn't give one Chinese civilian a gun."

"You're not so tender about yourself," said the Aussie, and smiled into the slashing rain.

"I've got nothing to lose."

"Nothing?"

"Nothing that matters very much." He had become used now to the idea of putting away life, and was not greatly concerned whether he lived or died, except that he preferred not to live in captivity. Rather than that, he thought, he would run; but if a shell or bomb saved him the decision, so much the better.

"That's it!" said the Aussie, between his half-shut lips. "That's what it was he had in his voice when he went out, and in his look, too. The D.S.O., he was wearing, and bar, and the M.C., too; nobody could say they hadn't tried to do him honour. And all he wanted was not to survive. My God, was there ever a snub like that! They load him with medals, and he turns his face to the wall!"

"There must be many a one doing that at this moment," said Jim. "They won't realise yet what's happened here. It'll look like just another normal mess to them, and a scapegoat or two will smooth things over, or so they'll think. But some day they'll know this is where an account began to be kept—where they lost us." For he knew then that he was with the young captain, one among the great number of the living lost in Singapore, lost not into captivity but into freedom, into an arid and lonely darkness, into a de-peopled twilight without lamp or language. He wondered if there was any place in the world for a man who divorced himself from his country; and if it was possible, however his country failed and estranged him, to cut himself off from the thing that was in his blood and bone, the reality of England. He did not think it was. The utmost he could do was to hold fast to her, like a man with an unfaithful wife, not blindly, not condoning what was unworthy in her, but angrily, reviling her weakness and follies and treacheries, hating her often, loving her always; hold fast to her, and bleed where she clawed him, and die when she murdered him, and never in life or death withdraw himself from her; pay her debts, make good her embezzlements, endure her slights, compensate the wrongs she dealt out to other people, contest her cruelties, as well as a man could, not in ignorance of her nature, nor keeping the world in ignorance, but never lowering his eyes from the creature she could be if she would, and never rejecting her, because she was bone of his bone and flesh of his flesh. What sort of life was that for a man? What hope of happiness did it leave him? And yet what else was there for him to do, being the man he was?

Beyond Bukit Timah Hill the rain became a solid downpour, and began to seep into the cab of the truck at every chink and run down inside the canvas covering at the back. They passed through Bukit Panjong, and Mandai, and turned north-east into the rubber plantations, where the green gloom streamed with greener rain; and there they dropped Jim by the roadside, to walk the last half-mile.

" So long, chum!" said the Australian, leaning out of the cab with his shock-head streaming. "Good luck—whatever way you fancy it."

"Thanks for the lift. So long, and the same to you!" And he waved an arm to the Kuomintang boys in the back of the truck as it lurched and steamed away like a mottled amphibian through the wet twilight; and turned up the rutted roadway between the rubber-trees, and walked into Lieutenant Stringer rustling along under a tarpaulin sheet between the wooden huts.

Stringer was pleased to see him. They were none too well off for N.C.O.s, and had lost just half their officers, besides taking in the remnant of a company of Ghurkas who had been left almost entirely officerless. Jim was another few pounds of weight lifted from Stringer's overburdened back. He was doing his best, but it was hard to step into Captain Priest's shoes, and circumstances conspired against him. As they splashed through the soggy ground together he gave Jim a nervous sketch of the week he had missed, the inaction, the tension, the labour and boredom first, and then the shelling that went on at irregular intervals by day and night without sight of an enemy. He sounded cheerful and confident; his kind would probably swallow the official viewpoint whole, all that guff about winning through with firm resolve and fixed determination, and standing at bay in our island fortress. Fortress nothing! It was a

beautiful swamp, indefensible, flat, soft, with all its guns
cemented in on the seaward side where no enemy was, and an
armourless belly turned to the thrust of the Japanese steel from
Johore. But if Stringer heard General Percival call it a fortress,
that would be good enough for him. If Wavell said help would
assuredly come, though there was no conceivable place from
which it could come in time to be effective, still come it would.

He said they were all in good spirits, which Jim did not
believe, and that the hasty northern defences would prove more
effective than might be supposed, and that the British forces
had reached at last a position in which they could no longer be
outflanked. Then suddenly, turning his streaming face upon
Jim with a feverish urgency, he said a thing which brought down
the whole ingenious erection like a house of cards.

"Benison," he said, "do you think Singapore *can* be held?"

3

After the 5th of February they did not see the sun again, nor
the clean light, nor the deep blueness of the sky. Day was lost
for them in a prophetic darkness. Occasionally, when they
emerged from the rubber-trees, and there was a wind to lift
the pall of smoke and suspend it for a while above the tree-
tops, they could see as far to the north-east as the pylons of
the Admiralty transmitting station, and the big crane at the
Naval Base. But at all other times their world was a gloom
of mutilated rubber-trees, with a roof of black smoke, beyond
which the noonday sun shone invisibly, like a girl in a mourning
veil. There was no light but the light of flares and gun-flashes,
no sound but the intermittent thunder of guns and the plunging
roar of dive-bombers; and under this unrelenting assault, as
once in the trenches of the Dyle, they sat down patiently to
await their part in the battle. The waiting was tediously long
to them, though afterwards those who survived knew that it
had lasted but four days.

On the night of the 8th of February they left their rubber
plantation, and moved northward to the shore, looking over the
Straits towards Johore Bharu. A mile or more away on their
left they could see fitfully by flare-light what was left of the
Causeway, thirty yards of it blown clean out, and a storm of
water filling the gap with gleams of phosphorescence, where the
locks had been. It was then perhaps nine o'clock in the evening,
but it might have been past midnight; and the nature of the

barrage had changed, so that the sound of it was no longer a discernible thunder, exclaiming and relenting, but a continuous rumbling roar like wheels travelling fast upon a rough road. In that incessant uproar the Junkers came and went almost silently, only a sudden spiteful scream out of them as they dived, and the impact of their bombs lost among the bursting of shells. The night had only terrestrial stars, abrupt, angry sparklings of red along the opposite shore, and answering gleams in the black water of the Straits.

They sat down in their shallow second-line trenches and pits, fingering their machine-guns, and crouching low into the sodden earth from the rain of shells. A man needed nerves of iron to stand up to much of this; nerves of iron, and no distracting hopes at the back of his mind, no thoughts of home or kin, no expectation of life. Also he needed all his saints about him, all the lost and all the dead who were the strength of his heart. As for Jim, his mind went no farther away from Kranji than the emerald mound of irregular turf among the mangroves on the north borders of Johore, where Charlie Smith was buried; and he waited for the Japs without impatience or reluctance, nursing his score against them, and looking for nothing but the reduction of that personal debt, and so an end of living. The battering of the bombardment in his ear-drums was a physical torment, but did not reach his mind. He felt in himself, and A Company felt it too, a core of hard quietness about which their shaken endurance gathered and sustained itself, resisting the impulsion of circumstance which struggled to disintegrate it into atoms; and yet it was not in him, but in the bedrock to which he had descended. It was there in the midst of all the hell of noise and danger and darkness, this implacable, barren, stony courage with no fire in it, and no hope, and no possibility of loss or gain; the last courage of man, independent of friends, or faith, or past, or future, or survival this side of death, or survival after death. He felt it, but was without curiosity concerning it. It served his turn, keeping him steady, indeed indifferent, under the mounting tension of the barrage, as the enemy guns stepped their fire inland from the shore, and back to the water's edge, and inland from the shore again, blotting out trench after trench and gun after gun, smashing every searchlight along the shore and killing their crews, blowing trees out of the ground in splinters, raining blasted leaves and the rubbish of bark and underbrush down upon the defenders.

Jim was aware that the attack was imminent. It must be

plain to them all that this crescendo was the prelude to a landing in force, or an attempt at one. They could not discuss it; no voice could make itself heard against that fury of fire; but it was clear from their eyes that they knew the moment was close upon them. They crouched over their machine-guns among the tangled trees, straining their eyes across the beach, watching for boats upon the dark water, while the searchlights went out one by one. What they wished to communicate they conveyed by signs, or merely by a look, for they knew one another better than men can do in easy times, and a look could express all that was needed between them. Young Gyp stayed close by Jim; they both wanted it so, having Curly much in mind. He, at least, was out of this. Every life was something salvaged, Curly was aboard by now, and standing out from Keppel Harbour on the way home; and their minds were eased of him.

Young Gyp had gone through plenty on Curly's account during that separation in the jungle; you could see how it had changed him. If it hadn't been for Jim he might have gone to pieces altogether, for his nerves were in a bad way, and this onset of noise was playing merry hell with him; but Jim was there, and the stony calm of him was something to hold by. It was not like the prelude to any other battle for Jim; there were no birds in his belly this time.

Now and again he came along the shallow trench, stooping under the shell-blast, but moving leisurely as a man does on his own ground, and sat on his heels for a moment beside Gyp at the end gun. All it needed was the feel of him, his big body there, solid and tranquil, and the shape of his lips in the murky twilight saying: "O.K.?" with no audible sound; and Gyp, with the sweat streaking his grimy face, would nod, and grin, and say: "O.K.!" back again; for his neck was as stiff as his brother's when it came to the point.

Along the Malayan coast the fireworks of flash and flare went on in rapid tempo. For nearly four hours now this had gone on, the spring of tension winding tighter and tighter, aiming at a breaking point; but it was never as simple as that. The Japs would possess Singapore; only the incurable optimists thought otherwise; but they would have to take it by force, not sit on the Johore coast waiting for the defenders to fly to pieces like an overwound toy, and let them walk in. They knew that; this pandemonium was merely the overture, as the green flare which soared out of the pitch darkness at eleven o'clock was the rise of the curtain.

It was then jet-dark; the moon did not rise until the small hours of the morning, and even then was only perceptible by fleeting glimpses as the smoke clouds thinned here and there. Most of the searchlights on the foreshore had already been hit, and their crews killed, and across the Strait machine-gunners were playing their fire backwards and forwards for the few survivors. Only one light remained on this sector of coast to pick up the phosphorescent gleams round the passage of the assault boats as they put out from Johore.

The Australian machine-gunners on the beaches caught that momentary vision of the iron barges just before their last light was hit. They began a rapid, blind fire, training their guns low along the water because they had now no visible target; and a flurry of hissing spray went up like a paler curtain in the blackness, and here and there sparkles of indignant red flashed and died as the bullets struck the steel hulls. They could not see what success they had. The noise of the guns obliterated all other sound, so that those who died, died unnoticed; and it was hard to avoid the feeling that their fire was without effect, though Johore Strait might run with Japanese blood unseen, and be choked with Japanese bodies. Certainly they killed and killed; but many of the barges came on into the shallows, and there decanted their cargoes. Jim saw the trails of pallor run shorewards at their heels as they leaped from the boats and came in on foot. The barges, never more than shadows, withdrew to bring over second parties; the men, suddenly possessed of visible bodies, ran in upon the Australians and were mown down in great numbers. Nevertheless, some survived to find holes low in the sand along the water's edge, and there they set up their machine-guns and the deadly little two-inch mortars which had been so effective in the jungle, and began to plaster the Australian gun-positions with a methodical, unremitting fire.

It seemed to Jim then that there was a moment when this landing could have been repelled, and that it was not used. He wanted to take every man out of cover and go down the beach and wipe out that foothold, Jap by Jap, before the barges came with reinforcements and made it impossible. They would lose half their forces, little doubt of it, but he was reasonably certain that they would clear the foreshore. He said so to Stringer, bawling in his ear against the din; and Stringer said he couldn't do it, he had his orders. The moment was not taken. Only a six-foot Aussie sergeant in the sandy gun-pits below sprang suddenly from cover with all his men behind him, and went roaring down the beach to die in the converging fire of two Jap machine-guns at the water's edge. He had left it too late, whether he made his gesture with or against orders. By then the assault boats were in sight again, and more of the enemy were leaping ashore with their mortars and their Tommy-guns and their Rising-Sun flags, and the foothold was concreted fast.

The second wave carried the first forward up the beach; and as none of the defenders moved back, they met hand to hand in the edge of the trees, shadow against shadow in the darkness, fighting blind. The one moment was gone by with no memorial; there would be no second.

In the darkness under the trees they moved back their machine-guns as so much temporarily useless equipment, for in the confusion of struggling bodies, where friend and foe were alike invisible unless you had them at the end of your arm, you were afraid to use guns. Even the Japs, who had no great tenderness for one another provided they reaped a sufficient harvest of their opponents, were chary of firing too freely here, and yet could not bear to put the guns out of their hands. They were natural-born gunmen, less effective at once when they were prevented from using their favourite weapons; they didn't like the Australian steel, and tried to find a way round it, but the Midshires, judging their distances as well as they could in the stifling midnight, filled up the interstices and met them full.

Jim went into that blind and bloody battle with Lake's *parang* in his hand. He had kept it by him for this, preferring it to the bayonet, and in the dismal camp under the rubber-trees they had more than once seen him at work upon it with a whetstone, until its edge was razor-keen. At the end of that long arm of his it had a surprising range. He went steadily into the struggle, stepping lightly, feeling for his enemies with his left hand, and with his right swinging the *parang*. He plucked men apart to find the enemy, selecting and rejecting by touch, and the platoon felt him there, and went with him as one man. He was possessed, with a cold possession. He fought like a machine, not a man, a careful machine built for the one implacable purpose of killing Japs. The fluctuating battle went on all the night, and he did not tire, nor change.

They beat back the first assault; it had been made too soon, before the odds were uneven enough to make the issue a safe one. The first line of the invaders recoiled to the beach, and settled down there to pave the way for another and better-judged advance. They laid their foundations with hand-grenades and mortar-shells; and behind that wall of fire more and more assault boats landed their reinforcements in comparative peace, and moved away again upon the same unceasing errand. The British machine-guns were moved up into line again, but could not make good all the ground they had yielded. Nor would the next attack be long in coming.

While the pause endured, they lay down with their faces to the earth, and covered their heads from the rain of mortar-shells and waited grimly. Jim stretched himself out with his arm across young Gyp's shoulders, and felt the quivering frame grow still at his touch. The kid was in a bad state, all right; he could feel how little flesh there was upon the shapely bones; and when the flash of a gun cast a momentary livid light upon the boy's hand he saw the nails bitten down to the quick, and bleeding. No wonder, after weeks of physical exhaustion, and the endless emotional strain of having Curly for a brother, if in some measure he crumpled now, when his stewardship was virtually over.

"All right?" said Jim in his ear.

"All right!" Gyp nodded back, and stiffened in the encircling arm. Yes, they were a stubborn breed.

"Stay by me!" said Jim, and his tone made it an order.

Gyp nodded again. Half-lost in the dark, there was even something that could be called a smile; good to look at, for that brief and irrecoverable time, and good to remember afterwards, if there should be any afterwards, because when the next pressure came there would be an end of all such human contacts. There would be an end of companionship and intercourse, and nothing left but the mere machinery of body and mind performing to the limit of endurance their last function of killing, until they came to the final expiation of dying. Twin futilities, they seemed now, but with no alternative to either of them, and therefore alike easy to accept.

The mortar-fire was getting too hot to be healthy. There were a lot of dead you could not even see, and worse, a lot who were not dead. When the next rush came, and you picked yourself up and launched your body to meet it, you were as likely as not to trample your own wounded. And as the defenders had been drained of their strength, the invaders had doubled and trebled their number, so that there was little possibility this time of stopping every gap against them. It was either move back and shorten the line, or stand and fight, and run the risk of small parties of the enemy filtering through to the rear. Nevertheless, having no orders, they stood and fought, and staved off for the moment the inevitable retreat. They knew this feeling of being face to face with a hurricane, of struggling head-on against the thrust of it, and being forced back inch by inch. Before them, where the trees began to shut out the broken lights along the Strait, there was an indescribable confusion of struggling men, of threshing and shouting and agonising flesh about the edge of that lost water. The true defence line, the only one in which they believed, was being withdrawn from them gradually, taken out of their hold whether they would or no, their fingers that clung to it prised loose or broken or severed one by one. They were losing the battle as water flows out of the hand, and they knew it; they were losing Singapore.

The order to fall back and re-establish their line came late, for many of them too late. Stringer, hopelessly out of his depth and struggling in vain with a load he could not carry, left Jim to extricate the remnant of two platoons, including a good number of Ghurkas, and bring them back silently to a new position, and there hold them. The move seemed to him more drastic than was yet justified; but then, he knew only what pressure had been exerted here. Away to westward, where the Kranji Creek ran deeply inland, he suspected the position was very much more vulnerable. God alone knew how far the boats had penetrated there, or how much of the west of the island would have to be given up to straighten the line. But to-morrow, he thought, they would at least throw in some of the reserves, and make some attempt to retrieve the position. Those strange composite battalions, remnants of regiments cut to pieces in Malaya, the "Plymouth Argylls" and their like— if the world had their like—would be sent in to give the Australians a breather; and with the Aussies would go the 4th Midshires and their attached Ghurkas, back to a recovery line until they had gathered themselves for another blow. There could be little rest for anyone. There were not so many of them to inherit in turn the weariness and clamour and strain, not so many of them to hand on and take back the appalling load.

The hours of darkness passed so, in a monotonous sequence of contacts and recoils, the recoil always a little deeper, the loss always a little heavier; and the dawn came as a lightening of the gloom only, a soiled grey light under the ceiling of black smoke, as if there would never again be clean daylight, nor a visible sun. Jim wondered if the city had word yet of the landing, or whether they were still being told that all was well, that Singapore would be held. By what dawn-light there was he looked over his diminished company, reckoning the losses they had sustained. Almost half of what had been at best the tatters of A Company was vanished from this exhausted assembly, left behind somewhere in the trampled woods going down to the Strait; living or dead, no one could guess. There were three N.C.O.s left, one of them a Ghurka, and only two officers, of whom Stringer was the senior, Almost every soul he knew well was lopped off from him; only Gyp, who had stayed by him all the night, was still at his elbow now. Of those who remained, known and unknown, not one was without a wound.

This was their situation when the first reserves came in from the rear during the morning of February 9th, and the rags of the Midshires were withdrawn to lick their wounds for a day or two on the Bukit Timah road.

4

With the exertion of battle, and the plying of Lake's *parang*, all the newly-healed wounds in Jim's wrists had opened again, and oozed continually. They did not matter greatly, in this situation, except that they hampered his movements and distracted his attention from the matter in hand; and it was for that reason, and no other, that he went into the dressing-station at Bukit Timah and asked for attention.

There was a great air of competence and calm about that dressing-station; it struck him as soon as he came in. Everyone, the doctor, the orderlies and stretcher-bearers, the Malay drivers and the Chinese nurses, seemed to have complete control of the work in hand, though the speed was the speed of frenzy. By now the wounded in the north-west outnumbered the whole; the procession of ambulances along the cratered road was ceaseless through the hours of daylight; yet this one team of people, devilishly overworked, had not for a moment lost control of the job they were doing. It was satisfying to watch them, and restful to be handled by them. And the doctor, that valiant little hard-handed, soft-voiced man, was English. Any crumb helped to feed this hunger.

The doctor turned the mauled wrists this way and that in his hands in the light from the hole in the white wall, where the window-frame had been. "Where did you get these?" he asked, looking over his spectacles at the big young lance-corporal with the granite face. He had never seen anyone outwardly so impassive in extremity, but he suspected that there was still some violence of emotion shut up within the rock. The eyes, dark and deep-set, had a blankness in which he did not believe; and there were the many and strange scars. "Where did you get these?" he said.

"In Johore," said Jim, "from a Jap."

"Do you usually get so close to your Japs?"

"Not usually. I didn't happen to have anything but my hands at the time, and I was in a hurry."

"So it seems!" said the doctor. He had not missed the implication of the puckered rope-burns round the wrists, scored so deep and so thinly healed, here and there broken and discharging blood and ichor. "Nothing will finish this job except inaction," he said, "and I know better than to order you that. If you will go about tearing Japs apart with your hands, you can expect these weals to burst every day. I don't believe in elastic adhesives, and I won't use them on you. All we can do is renew the dressings as often as you come to us, and keep you from septicæmia as long as we can. The nurse will see to you." He was already half out of the room when he turned back to ask suddenly: "Are you Staffordshire born?"

Jim smiled. "No, Midshire."

"I thought I knew the Midland tongue. I'm from Worcester myself. You'll be one of the battalion that caught it so hot in Johore. It's good to hear the language again."

"There's a few of us left yet," said Jim. "Likely you'll hear it again a time or two before the finish."

"The finish? I see you've got your mind clear what it's going to be. Well, I'll not say you're wrong. Maybe I'll see you behind the wire when it's all over." But he could not imagine that it would ever come to that; certainly this stony young man would not become a prisoner if he could die; it was not captivity he had in mind when he spoke of the finish.

"Maybe!" said Jim.

"I'll send the nurse," said the doctor abruptly, and went out, and was presently heard in the compound directing the arrival of yet another procession of stretcher-bearers; and the nurse came into the room, and the nurse was Leong Ah Mei.

He was childishly glad to see her, to see anyone whose face meant anything to him more than another face. Things had reached with him the bitter pass where most of humanity wore featureless blurs for faces; but hers sprang clear and delicate out of the mists of indifference, recognising him and smiling; for her very clarity he was grateful, but for the smile most of all.

"It is you," she said. "I felt it would be, when he mentioned your hands. You have not been kind to them," she said; and setting down the basin of hot water she was carrying, she took his big right wrist in her small, sleek palm, and looked fixedly at the familiar scars, swollen now and raw. Her porcelain face grew rigid and grave. "It is strange," she said in a low voice, "that a man like you should be put to so horrible a necessity."

"I'm glad you find it strange," said Jim. "What kind of man does that make me exactly?"

"One not made for killing with the hands," she assured him, and went to work upon him with her fine fingers. "Turn to the light, please. There! You have had no rest, I see; I am sorry that it is so."

"Have you?" he asked.

"I?" She seemed surprised that he should bring her into it at all. "Mine is a very easy part, here behind the lines where everything is made safe for us. It would be strange if we should look for rest."

"Is that why you came up here?" asked Jim. "Weren't you doing enough down in Singapore? Seemed to me you were doing three people's work already."

"I wished to come here, yes. It was necessary that someone should come, and I had nothing now to hold me back; having no relatives, I can be a grief to no one. Should I be anxious for myself, at a time like this, when you are enduring so much? I should be ashamed. What I can do is at best but a little. Tell me, how are things—where you have been?" And she looked up for a moment, her dark eyes very near and clear and anxious upon his face.

"Very bad!" he said. He had no heart to lie to Ah Mei, and he knew that even if he made the attempt she would not be deceived. She might pale and tremble like other women, but her impenetrable ivory dignity rejected the protection of lies.

"They are on the island," she said. "We heard that in the city, but there were no details. They will be dislodged, will they not? Have they a very firm hold? Surely, in so short a time—and they must bring everything by boat—the Causeway is gone, you see——"

"They were working on it this morning," said Jim. "Our gunners were trying to stop them rigging pontoons, but I doubt they'll have a workable bridge by to-morrow. No, I don't think they will be dislodged, and that's the truth."

She made a turn of the bandage, fastidiously smooth and firm, passing his wrist from hand to hand in a steady, calm rhythm. She said: "Then they will take Singapore!" Her voice had a soft finality. It was, he knew, the first time she had said that, but not the first time by many times that the thought had been in her mind.

"Yes, they will take Singapore. I don't think there's a chance in a million of saving it now."

She kept her eyes fixed upon her work, and her well-trained hands went on with their unobtrusive ministrations; but it was rather as if eyes and hands belonged to two different people, as if she watched a stranger finishing one bandage and beginning a second. "Down there," she said, "they still do not know that. They are frightened, yes, very frightened, but they cannot grasp that this thing is really happening. It is as if the earth opened under their feet. The bombers come over from Keppel Harbour and bomb the ships as they are loading with women and children; and still people say that everything is in hand, that things will come out all right in the end. They have not yet admitted, as I did then, that Singapore can be lost." She looked up slowly; under her tired eyes the shadows were the colour of irises. "What is to become of us?" she said. "I am young, I do not wish to die." She said it with a great and pitiful simplicity, not complaining, merely saying what was true and deeply troubling to her; and with a dignity as natural to her as the bloom upon her hair, so that he knew she was confronting a considered possibility. He thought of the Chinese ladies of Penang, who had walked into the sea with their children in their arms, and quietly drowned themselves. Doubtless they, too, had been young, and had not wished to die. Nevertheless, they had known the moment.

He said impulsively: "I wish you could get away. My God, haven't we done enough to you?" And he wondered then if perhaps Mary Lei had been one of the suicides. "Have you tried? Why don't you? There must be room for you some-where—— A little thing like you!"

"Do you speak of going?" she said. "Would you go? If you were Chinese, as I am, and had seen what Englishmen have endured here in this cause, as I have seen it?"

He said: "I've got you on my conscience." It did not seem to him a very clear statement, but she found no difficulty in it.

"You forget I have nursed you. I have seen the marks on your hands and wrists. It is not you who are in my debt."

"And yet," said Jim, "a few minutes ago you looked at those same marks with horror. You were right that time; they're not pretty."

"It was not horror of you," she said.

"Not of me, maybe, but of what I've done. Against my nature, if you like, but still I did it."

"It was not horror of anything you have done; rather of what has been done to you." And he knew that she did not mean the tearing of his flesh. "You will not understand me," she said, "because of this—— What has happened has made you cut yourself off from all those who are not injured as you are. But in your heart I do not think you can really believe I recoil from hands marked as yours are marked; and if I should let you into my mind—if I should take your hand, remembering what it has done—and do *so*——"

She closed the pin with a sharp snap, and taking his hand between both her own, dropped her cheek against the palm black with the bruises of the *parang*, and he felt her lips upon it, and the heat of tears.

It was the most unexpected thing that had ever happened to him. That she should condescend out of her remote midheaven, and bend her head over him in a single moment of emotion, was as if the almond-tree should bow and let fall its topmost blossom into his hand as he passed. Among so much ugliness and self-disgust he could not bear that she should so prostrate her loveliness, though she did it with grace and deliberation, knowing what she did. He said in a protesting gasp: "Don't—you mustn't!" But she raised herself composedly and smiled at him, with the tears standing on her cheeks.

"Shall I let you go back without knowing what I have felt? Shall I permit you to go on shutting yourself up in loneliness because you think you have dirtied your hands? My country has a long past, not all gentle nor peaceful. We have known most of the incompatible horrors and beauties that exist side by side in the world; we have learned to accept them all, and understand how they lean upon one another. You can dabble a magnolia in the dust, and the dust will soil it, but it will still be a magnolia. I will not have you make yourself an outlaw because you have put your hands at great pain and anger to purposes unnatural to you. I will not let you build walls around yourself to keep me immaculate, when I would have done as you have done if I had had the courage and the strength—yes, and felt no such scruples as you feel, only joy. I may not have killed with my hands," she said, "but I have done so with my mind. You cannot separate me from what you consider your guilt, and still let me share in your glory. I will not be robbed of my war."

All this she said with more of conviction than he knew how to withstand, so that against his will something of comfort and warmth came into him, and would not leave him even when she was gone. It did not matter that he could no longer see her as he walked away from the dressing-station and up the shattered road, nor that her voice was silenced once for all upon his inarticulate and abrupt farewells. He had her still. He had hastened to get away from her because she was too much of beauty and kindness for a world on which he had turned his back, and because she was mistress of a new and incomparable pain, putting her small hand upon surfaces he had thought impervious as stone, and setting them quivering. But she had taken her stand beside him, claiming her share of his load, in that soft and calm voice which made of her name a sigh; speaking with assurance, and yet with effort, as if she knew what she would say, but not how best to say it. She was his companion in battle; she had said it. So perhaps he had still something more to fight for than the revenge with which he could never be sated, something more fertile, more instinct with hope, than the memory of Charlie Smith's grey face and stained body sinking into the emerald grass; something that had a fast hold upon the future, as well as upon the past.

And with that he knew that he could be hurt again. There was no point beyond pain, as there was no point beyond responsibility. He left the road, because of the periodic visits of dive-bombers, and walked under the double gloom of smoke and crowding rubber-trees, with the stooping roar in his ears, and the incessant rumbling of guns, now so near, fraying at the edge of his consciousness. He didn't want to remember the living, least of all those who would have to go on living after he was quiet at last. He wondered why the hell she had to put her warmth into him and start his blood again, when he was happily numbed. He thought he could more easily have gone on with the grim business in loneliness, but her hand was in his, and she would not go away; and on her heels came the others crowding in, the people who were his, the people of home, from whom he had turned his mind when hope became a folly and memory without hope an unassuageable torment. All that effort of separation was to do again, if it could be done a second time. He didn't know. He only knew he was torn two ways now, all his laborious cold integrity crumbling into this molten sea of pain within, leaving him vulnerable and quivering. There was a creature in him that wanted to die, as the only means of ridding himself of a world which sickened him, and an identity which disgusted him. Like an infected animal, he wanted to use death as a post to rub off the disease of living. But there was a second man in him, too, one who looked forward and back, and had hope in him like a cancer, and wanted at all costs to live and see home again. Ah Mei had touched hands with this man, and the contact of her camellia mouth was in his palm, and he was growing in stature like an idea in a fertile mind, until it was a giant who walked under the rubber-trees, and every inch of him was anger and terror and desire and anguish, and all beyond cure.

So he was flesh again. So he had a mother, and a father, and friends at home who knew him well, and a roof to go back to, and had had a girl once, until she threw him down. He was only a man like other men, not an impervious stock long dry of feeling. The strings of his being, alive and vibrating, drew his heart back to home. He suffered loss upon loss.

It was like that all that day, as he toiled frantically among the rubber-trees with A Company, working upon trenches which would not hold the enemy for long. It was like that in the night, while lorries rumbled uncertainly along the road on their right, and Gyp dozed fitfully against the bole af a tree, and muttered in his sleep; while Stubbs, lying flat on his belly along the ground, suddenly fell to remembering aloud, his voice a lament in the darkness; while Stringer, wobbly with fatigue and shocked into a blank indifference, passed and re-passed along their thin reserve line, ineffective and well-meaning and hopelessly out of his depth, seeking implausibly to instil into his men a confidence he himself did not feel, and a solidity of purpose which had long deserted him.

"You know what'll happen to him, if this goes on long?" said Lockyer, watching him disappear unsteadily between the trees. "He'll go out of his mind, that's what he'll do. He's cracking up now as fast as he can, and what gets back to England won't be worth much, if you ask me."

"If anything gets back," said Jim.

"If anything gets back! But he will; he's that kind."

"His old man owns our house," said Stubbs, looking far through the tropical darkness to a back street in Caldington. "Owns half the town, for that matter. But you know what sort of a landlord he is. There hasn't been a lick of paint on the place, or a new washer on the kitchen tap, or a tile put on the roof, since Adam was a lad. Still and all, I wish to God I was there now. Anyhow my bed's there, and we don't have red ants under the pillows. And just round the corner there's the old 'Hare and Hounds'—remember it? Home-brewed that laid strong men out after a couple of drinks, and draught cider brewed in whisky barrels, that stood up and sang to you. And a lovely crown green at the back—a lovely green! Three years running I picked up the club prize on that green. Wonder if I'll ever see it again!"

"Last time I was ever in Caldington," said Lockyer, "old Farrar and me, we worked a pass up from Hampshire, with five bob between us to do it on. Hitched as far as a little place in Worcester, and then got stuck for the night, with beds at the Y.M. a bob a go, and one and eight left on us. Tuppence for two platform tickets on to the station, and a fill-up at the free canteen, and we slept on the Y.M. rug by the fire for nothing each apiece, and made it next day with one and six still to go. Those were the days!"

"I was in solitary there once," said Stubbs," for telling a sergeant what he could do with his perishing stone-shifting fatigue. Bread and water for seven days, and I come out a stone lighter but tough as a rock. When they paid me the four and a tanner they owed me I went straight round to the 'Hare and Hounds' and poured down a pint of home-brewed. Forgot I was as empty as a drum. Cheapest drunk I ever had! It knocked me flat, and two of the lads carried me home. My God, how Molly laughed! Out cold on one solitary pint—me! I ask you!"

Jim knew Molly Stubbs by sight, a fresh-complexioned girl with iris eyes and a big poppy-red mouth which laughed a great deal, and looked generous and candid in mirth as in repose. Not so pretty as Delia Hall, but still very good to look at. Stubbs was seeing her now, clean through the smoky, shell-pitted, bomb-punctured night, probably the only way he would ever seen her again.

"We've come a long way since that," he said, "and we've got hell's own way to go—hell's own sweet way!"

They went a little of the way that night, when the Japanese began to filter through from the north-west, where all day long encircled parties of British troops had struggled to get back to their own. It began with running feet crashing among the rustling rubbish under the trees, and the nostalgic lament was snapped off sharply upon the sound. Four coolies came scuttling out of the dark, chattering excitedly, and made towards the trenches with their hands outstretched. Stringer rose to challenge them, though perfunctorily, for it was nothing out of the ordinary to see four Chinese making all speed south from the Japs; and the foremost man dived a hand under his loose shirt and shot Stringer dead at point-blank range. Jim took him in his arm as he fell, and eased him down, but he was dead before ever he reached the soggy floor of the trench, his face fixed in ludicrous surprise. They lost two more men, also, before they took the supposed coolies apart. What could you expect when every enemy carried a Tommy-gun or grenades?

After that they were so thinly strung that for a couple of hundred yards through the plantation they were spaced out beyond speaking distance, and Jim had all the authority there was. There were several such incidents during the night; it was Malaya all over again at closer quarters, and with even less chance upon the ground and none in the air. Towards dawn a party of weary-looking soldiers, small men in torn uniforms and wide-brimmed hats, came marching out of the west, and being hailed, announced themselves as Ghurkas; but Jim's Ghurkas were not deceived, and that infiltration party progressed no farther. There could not, however, be remnants of Ghurka battalions everywhere, and Jim doubted that here and there the enemy were slipping through towards the city and the reservoirs. It was round those reservoirs that the next battle would centre, now that the main from Johore was breached with the Causeway.

By the following day the main pressure had advanced like a sea, and was lipping at their line, and all manner of strays from shattered regiments, Aussies, Sikhs, Royal Marines, Midlanders, Ghurkas, Highlanders, came back with the wash of the wave and dug their heels in with the reserve line at Bukit Timah, and would not be shifted. Rumours came in from both sides, with the survivors from the north and the reinforcements from the south. The Causeway, so said the exhausted troops from the north, had been sufficiently repaired to make the transportation of armoured cars and light field-guns a practical proposition, and in a day or so they were reasonably sure there would be Japanese tanks on the island. Only aircraft could break up that concentrating attack, and there were no aircraft. It wasn't superiority the Japs had in the air, it was monopoly. The lads from the city said that shells were falling in the suburbs like rain, and the pattern-bombing went on continually. They said that all the remaining ships, Dutch and British and Portuguese, were loading up as fast as they could, and getting out, but under furious bombing which took no count of nationality, and with every handicap of loss and confusion and mismanagement, tired women and children trailing from pier to pier without effective orders or help, families driving down and abandoning their cars at the dockside as they went aboard, Blakangmati heavily bombed from the air, and in danger of being used to stop the sea exit once for all, and Yamashita's pamphlets raining down upon Singapore City, inviting surrender in arrogant *samurai* terms, "from the standpoint of *bushido*".

So he was as sure of himself as that! Not that any notice would be taken of the invitation, of course. They might not be able to salve the lost island; it was too late for that, had been too late when the Johore Line crumpled into pieces almost as soon as it was formed. The Naval Base was abandoned, a waste of wreckage and destruction, twisted metal and smoking go downs. The transmitting station was blown up; the reservoirs were in grave danger; the multi-coloured city was a desolation. No, Singapore could not be saved; they were fools who thought it could, though hope died hard, and harder than ever in its second death. Nor, in this extremity, could they hope for a chance to evacuate any considerable number of men to fight again elsewhere. Obviously they could not surrender, and fall whole into the hands of an enemy scarcely touched. They could only fight inch by inch along the roads into the town, and kill, and kill, until they themselves were killed one by one; and that was the thing they would do, at such length and with such ferocity that it should be spoken of as long as Britain was an island; so that in spite of all the criminal follies and weaknesses and shames with which that tragic campaign had been smirched, men at home in England should almost be moved to wish they had been there at the end. That was the only possible expiation of the horrible failures that burned like acid in the mind: to make the end pay for the beginning, and at least complete well the thing which had been done so ill.

So thought Jim, and the quietness within came back to him,

though the pain was not quenched. So he thought next day, when the Japanese tanks came nosing between the rubber-trees and crashed over their shallow trenches, burying men under the caved-in parapets; while they launched their tired bodies after them, and hung upon them after the manner of Flanders, and tore some in pieces with grenade and guns, but could not destroy them all. So he thought while they leaned breast to breast with a bewildering enemy, and through two desperate days and nights were thrust slowly back from their north-east to south-west line, and hacked away man by man from their hold upon the two reservoirs. So he thought all through the struggle and agony of Sunday, February 15th, until the pressure strangely weakened, and he went down to the nearest hut in the village to find, if possible, a drop of water, and encountered on the way a raw-boned staff-sergeant in the rags of a uniform, with a bloody scar down one cheek, and his eyes stone-dead in his face.

The sergeant took him in the breast with a huge, splayed hand, and brought him up standing. "You in charge up here?" he asked.

"Yes," said Jim, "me and a couple of boys. What d'you want done?"

"Bloody murder, but that's by the way. You can tell your men their war's over. As from seven o'clock we've surrendered unconditionally to the Japs—the island of Singapore, complete with all its troops, stores and equipment. At ten o'clock the cease fire will take effect, and hostilities will cease immediately. Tell 'em that. Tell 'em from a technical standpoint they've been prisoners of war just over an hour, every man Jack of 'em. It's finished."

Jim took him by the arm and wrenched him back as he made to pass on. There was a roaring in his ears like a great wind. "Say that again!" he shouted.

"You heard!" said the sergeant. "It's over."

"But, good God, man!" He shook the hard brown arm furiously in his hands, and peered into the slate-coloured, illusionless eyes, and found there no spark of comfort. "That means forty thousand men at least—just given up—— They can't do it! Christ, they can't do it to us!"

"Nearer sixty thousand," said the sergeant.

"But I tell you they can't do it! We were set to fight till we dropped. They can't surrender us! Who gave them the right to dispose of us like bloody cattle? We're not ready to surrender.

We never shall be ready. They can't do this to us!"

"They have done it," said the sergeant in his dead voice; and he jerked his arm away, and walked on through the deserted village, between the broken mat hovels, and the inescapable smoke took him, and he was gone.

Jim stood there in the middle of the road, staring before him, while the sky toppled over him, and the remnant of his world reeled away beneath his feet. He would have given the eyes out of his head to disbelieve in the thing which had been done to him, but he knew that it was true. He felt it run through him like a poison, sapping all the virtue, all the will out of him. So they couldn't do it to him! So there was a last infamy, a final degradation to which he would not be asked to stoop! So much for the last atonement, the grand fury of dying! So much for the legend which was to redeem, in part at least, the grandeur they had frittered away. This was the end of it all, this abrupt, humiliating descent from glory, this tame, this abject acceptance of the enemy's will. Sixty thousand stunned, incredulous men being sold into ridicule and shame without their knowledge or consent, waking suddenly out of the last illusion to find themselves in the pillory and their country a byword. They hadn't even begun the fight they had meant to make. The weapons were struck out of their hands at the beginning, they were stabbed in the back; a thing for which there could be no forgiveness was done to them, a wound was dealt them for which there could be no cure. It was bad enough when the enemy took all the pride out of you and left your integrity draggled in the mud; but what could be said when your own cause turned and stripped you naked to the scorn and mockery of the world? What could you hold by then? What could you live for? What could you die for?

He stood there, and felt the heart in him break and bleed, the deep places of the heart where his patriotism was, the hidden and unconfessed thing that drove him. He forgot the look of the torn island around him, and bodily danger, and the old, new, insatiable longing for home. Nothing existed in the world but his own murdered self-respect and this monstrous and devilish anguish with which it struggled in dying. He did not notice the coils of purple smoke twining upward from the burning oil-tanks to the north, nor the narrow glitter of sun that came through a rent in the pall of darkness, nor the receding rumble of guns, nor the solitary plunging dive-bomber. He walked back through the open, lifted from his feet once by the blast

214

of a bomb, and half-stunned against the wall of a shop; he went with a mat of blood coagulating down one side of his face, and his eyes fixed and blind, back to the remnant of A Company; and he told them.

They cried out on him, as he had cried out upon the sergeant, that it was not true; but for a moment only, for they knew truth when they saw it. Like a disease of incalculable violence his bitterness went into them, and struck them mute. They went aside from one another, avoiding the eyes that were the mirrors of their own. Only young Gyp ventured even to touch him, a fevered hand at his elbow as he passed.

"Jim, what are we going to do? What *can* we do? We can't just let it happen. My God, we can't do that!"

"It has happened," said Jim, and looked through him, and shook him off with violence.

What was she, after all, this crusading demon of his? His country and his cause in one being, with such an incandescent light about her, and such a heat in the glance of her eyes, and yet she tortured him first, and after threw a despoiling dust upon all he did for her, and at the last she turned in his hand and shamed him, and shamed herself for the inconstant drab she was. And would not let him go! There was the last hell, that he could not escape her. Not even now would she let him go.

He went away into the virgin forest beyond the plantation, where they would not look for him, and lay down among the azaleas with his head in his arms. A great weary quietness, like a winding-sheet, came up out of the eastern sky and settled gradually upon the lost island, fold upon fold. He felt its heart still under his own, to a death-throe in which more than Singapore was dying, something those men had had and lost, something which had been wrested from him among the rest. He pressed his half-flayed face into the grass, and drew the warm smell of the earth into him in a great quaking breath, and began to weep distressfully, gasping his heart out into the flattened stems.

5

He had meant only to march down with the rest into captivity, having no choice, though he would rather have walked into a box-barrage on the spot, and finished the job once for all. Suddenly everything was terrifyingly quiet; from ten o'clock the gunfire had ceased, and the drone of 'planes became an intermittent drowsy music, and in the mid of night was stilled utterly. By morning the smoke began to clear, and clean light came in here and there and touched the green and white island, and fingered the evidences of ruin and violence, and shone impartially upon the first Japanese cars as they swung in from Yamashita's headquarters in the Ford factory on the Bukit Timah road, and upon the tired, bewildered columns of British troops moving gradually into town on their way to internment. On that march they saw the sky again for the first time for many days, the pale, perfect sky of a February morning in a flower of an island in the eastern tropical seas. The dazzling flowers, canna and hibiscus and orchid and magnolia, were frayed and dulled now with rubbish and dust, the white walls broken and hanging in drunken wreckage, but beauty remained, an agonising beauty, reproachful and aloof. It was like looking into the face of a woman no longer immaculate, with disease already upon her, and the shadow of dissolution beginning to dull the young blue of her eyes.

The Midshires moved out of their plantation at noon, and came down to the road, and began to progress along it in a series of short marches, in the intervals of which they were swept bodily off the road to let convoys of Japanese tanks and armoured cars go through. In two hours they moved no more than half a mile. The road was in a bad state, wreckage of burned-out lorries still littering it here and there; and bomb-craters, hastily filled in with soil packed far too loosely, tilted the armour perilously, and overturned one lorry-load of Japanese into the bushes not fifty yards from where the Midshires were standing, and held up the procession for thirty minutes while the truck was righted and the injured removed. Unhappily the soil was so soft that there were no dead.

The Midshires and their Ghurkas, one group of many halted so to let the victors go by, stood like stone and looked on at this incident, until a swaggering little Japanese officer came stamping along the edge of the road, and in a shrill voice and English devoid of labial sounds demanded a working-party to clear up the mess. Major Freer, the only officer left in the battalion of any rank, stood looking down at the scion of the conquering race with a chalk-white face, and for a moment seemed to meditate murder; but he could not even separate himself from his men and commit suicide alone; they were all in it together, and a rash move now might mean the deaths of them all. He turned, and looked along his ranks, and fell out Lance-Corporal

Benison and twelve men of A Company to place them at the disposal of the Jap. Half-way through the job, as soon as the road was clear, the battalion moved on without them, and left them still filling in and stamping down soil in the crater, and carrying the wounded aside into the trees. They worked like madmen, with fierce faces and in silence, paying no attention to the Japanese who chattered at them and hectored, taking their orders only from Jim. There were enough guns trained on them to discourage any attempt at escape or disobedience, and in any event, whatever they incurred might be visited also upon others of the wretched prisoners; therefore they went about the job as if the injured they tended were Christian creatures.

"You have a medical station near here?" said the Japanese officer. "Where?"

"Down through the trees, off the road. A plantation track brings the cars in, but there's a footpath from just below here that will take stretchers."

"There is a doctor? An English doctor?"

"Yes." He thought of the little Worcestershire man who had recognised the Midland tongue. It seemed they were to take him some very different patients this time.

"Good. You will take these men there for treatment."

As they loaded the stretchers a column of Australians came by, grey-faced men with three-day beards, limping upon tender, bleeding feet from their long, leech-bitten sojourn in the swamps; and close upon their heels the first of the Japanese infantry, the invisible armies become visible, a briskly marching company bristling with Rising-Sun flags. It was the first time Jim had seen them in full order and purpose, those small, ivory-faced creatures with impenetrable eyes and jaws overstocked with teeth, those wills without intellect. He paused a moment, standing over the loaded stretchers, to stare at them as they went by. That was the force the Eastern Command had despised and under-rated. Was it strength in the enemy or weakness in his own side that had turned the scale? The strength was there, the devotion rather of automatons than of fanatics; but he knew then, he knew in his raging heart, that there was nothing in these men his Midshires could not have overcome if they had not been crippled and starved of support by their own leaders. They were sold, they were betrayed as surely as if money had passed. Some day, somehow, that debt would be reclaimed out of reputations, out of lives. Some day the ghost of Singapore would come home to sit upon the doorsteps of respected men and dun them into ruin. But they would have to wait years for that vengeance, until the war was over, until the fog had cleared from the battle, and the curtain of darkness been lifted from the aftermath. And by that time many of the ordinary soldiers would have died in prison camps from starvation and maltreatment and grief and shame, having carried the reproach in them like a cancer for months and perhaps years, an insatiable appetite eating away their lives. They would do the paying, as they always did; they would carry the load, they, the inarticulate people, the voiceless, the unrepresented, the forgotten hewers of wood and drawers of water; they would carry it and never complain, though their silence raised up another generation to sell their sons into another such slavery. If they wanted to speak they could not; if they tried to defend themselves and accuse the guilty as they saw them, they would find no spokesmen among them; they were mute by nature and by conspiracy against their kind, himself among the rest.

Gyp, passing close, made shift to whisper in his ear as the column went by: "Jim, if we get a chance, let's cut for it. We might make the coast. Sumatra's not so very far. Jim, let's try it. It couldn't be worse, even if we get caught again——"

He had thought of it himself all night, lying in his desolate misery among the azaleas in the jungle; but he did not consider it now.

"You'll do as you're told," he said, "and I tell you to take the foot of that stretcher and get moving."

Gyp was trembling and breathing hard, ready for any desperate measures. "If you won't," he said through his teeth, "I'll try on my own. I can't stand this."

"Don't be a fool!" said Jim. "You wouldn't get ten yards and the rest of us would pay for it afterwards. We're going to the dressing-station. Come on, get moving!" But he did not fail to note how many Japanese escorts fell into line with the single file of stretchers as they moved into the trees; there were six, all carrying Tommy-guns, whereas the working party were unarmed; also several of the wounded still nursed guns, and were fully capable of using them, and other Japanese troops would probably be making use of the dressing-station. No, the odds were impossible. They could do nothing; it was crazy to make the attempt.

The dressing-station was in the process of disintegration, as they found when they walked in through the shattered compound and the stripped white room where the dispensary had been. There was a film of mortar-dust over everything, and their feet skidded upon rubble and stones as they went in. But in the inner room three Chinese women out of uniform were busy with dressings upon as many coolies laid upon mattresses along the wall, and the doctor was bending over a little Malay boy at the table.

This one room had been kept clean and tidy when the rest became uninhabitable. Clearly their orders had been to evacuate the station, for all the neat Red Cross uniforms had disappeared; but they had stayed, these few, because there were people here who needed to be helped. None of the three women was Ah Mei; he was at once glad and sorry, sorry because it had seemed to him that she would be the last to go, glad because the thought of her moving about here in attendance on the enemy was horrible to him. Even to have these Japs set down in a room she had once graced was a sort of sacrilege, but at least he was rid of a worse haunting.

The doctor looked up over his spectacles from the child's torn forehead, and went on stitching. It was a long gash, and would leave an ugly scar if allowed to heal without sutures. His fingers were steady and expertly gentle; the child cried at the thrust of the needle, though it was barely more than skin it punctured, and one of the women rose from her knees and went to the table and held his head between her hands, speaking to him in Malay in a cool little voice. She was middle-aged and plain. Someone 'had been intelligent. Not one of the three was pretty.

They set the stretchers down, fitting them into the circumscribed space as well as they could; and it seemed that the six Japs between them had not enough English to make the doctor understand that he should leave the child and wait upon the will of his conquerors. Gestures and words alike he put by with a monitory hand; and they were not, in his case, so sure of their orders that they could afford to be rough with him. He finished the job at leisure, and the Chinese woman picked up the child and carried him away by the rear door. The doctor wiped his forehead, and turned and looked full at Jim, and if he did not smile, at least the look was recognising and eager.

"You again?" he said. "You didn't tell me you were bringing a party along."

"I didn't know," said Jim. "This party brought me."

He watched the doctor's hands go over them, and waited to be ordered away, back to the road, en route for internment at Changi; but the Japanese soldiers were interested in the station, and as yet had no mind to move. They left two of their number with guns trained upon Jim's party, while the remaining four began a thorough investigation of the entire station, emptying cupboards, breaking in doors, blowing the locks off the store-sheds outside. Two, even with guns, was not such long odds; Jim began to wonder if there might not be something in Gyp's suggestion. Not for him, of course; his job was to stay with his men; but if he could get Gyp away southward, clean away out of the beastly memory of this damned island, he would at least have saved something out of the cataclysm, and fed himself one crumb of satisfaction. It might be done. Hundreds would be trying it, not all with such reasonable prospects as from this isolated place. There was good cover southward, first rubber and then lush swamp-forest down to the coast; and the fishermen of the coastal villages had good boats, and Sumatra was not so desperately far, besides the chance of being picked up by evacuation ships. A man would want some sort of weapon for a trip like that; but among so many a few would surely make good their escape, and why not Gyp among the rest?

He wished he knew how many words of English the wounded Japs and the guards had between them; but there had to be risks, and that was the first. He began to busy himself about the doctor, forestalling his movements when he reached for instruments and dressings, interpreting the snap of his fingers and the turn of his head, and drawing Gyp into service with the fetching and carrying, so that a more ambitious move might come naturally into the picture when the time was ripe; and being satisfied with his background, he leaned across the stretcher and said casually into the doctor's ear: "You haven't got a gun, have you?"

It was said in a dull voice, not loud enough to reach the two armed men, though sufficiently loud to avoid the appearance of stealth. The man on the stretcher would hear it; but even if he understood he could not convey his knowledge, for his jaw was broken. As for the doctor, he went on with his work without so much as a side-glance.

"No. There could be something useful in my case. What are your plans?" he asked.

"I want to get that kid out of here," said Jim. "Maybe others, too. This is the best chance we're likely to get. What have you got?"

"Scalpels, knives—— Go and look through 'em. Bring me the dressing-scissors and take what you fancy while you're there. Outside in the store-shed there's a *parang*. My Malay boy's—he's dead. I'll get you outside if I can—if they let me. There are baskets of infected dressings to burn—enough for two. They'll consider that a job for you, all right. There's a brick incinerator in the compound—not far to the trees—the wall's smashed in." He took one hand from the mummified white of the bandage, and snapped his fingers in the direction of the table. Scissors—quickly!"

Jim sprang to get them, putting his body between the guards and the frenzied activity of his hands. He took two of the most formidable scalpels he could find, and wedged them inside his belt at the front, the blades flat against his loins. The thought of their sharp coldness pressing against his flesh made him walk stiffly, but that could not be helped. He handed the scissors. The guards made no move, saw nothing strange in the precision of his movements. It was going to work. It was going to be all right. Only keep quiet, and avoid any haste, any appearance of hope; and leave it to the doctor to know the right moment.

He kept them waiting what seemed an age, but he knew what he was about. Nor, when he rose from his knees at last and turned towards the encumbered corridor where the baskets of soiled dressings lay, did he make the mistake of addressing himself to Jim. He made a gesture of irritation and distaste, and marched upon the nearer of the two Japs, and with much carefully enunciated pidgin-English and copious excursions into sign-language, conveyed that he wanted the horrid mess taken out into the compound and burned. The soldier, once having grasped the idea, swaggered across the room and drove Jim before him with the butt of his gun towards the offending baskets. Jim was careful not to read this ungentle instruction too readily. He went where he was thrust, and picked up the first basket when he was unmistakably ordered to do so, and stood looking from the guard to the doctor, and back again, until the doctor explained in impatient English what was required of him. Then he shrugged, and kicked the second basket towards Gyp, and led the way out.

He prayed that the guard would not follow; there were already four of them loose about the station. And the guard did not follow. It was going well. The cool air touched their faces; they were outside, and the door swung to behind them, but did not close. There was paved yard before them, and then a space of beaten earth, and the shattered remains of the compound wall;

and beyond, grass and the darkness of rubber-trees again. It looked so easy; he wanted to go with the kid; he wanted it with the sick heart of him, suddenly, horribly, but he knew he couldn't do it. If you were a non-com. you had to do the thing properly; you couldn't cut and run, and leave the others to do the best they could; you had to stay with them, help them out of it if you could, but not save yourself until they were all accounted for. That, at least, was how he saw it and that was the way he was going to have it done.

Gyp's agitated voice panted in his ear as they crossed the yard: "Jim, now's our chance! Look, there isn't a solitary soul—— We can do it easily. Come on, Jim, let's get away quick—there may never be another chance like this!"

"There never will," said Jim. He put down the basket and opened the hatch of the incinerator. "Shut up, you fool!" he said very quietly. "Do you think I've gone to all this trouble for nothing? You're going. Now, start tipping that load in, and keep your mouth shut." He slipped a hand in the waist of his shorts, and pulled out the two scalpels, keeping them screened from both the door and the wall between their bodies. "There, that's the best I can do for you. Put one of 'em somewhere handy on you. Out of sight, mind. Now cut across to the wall there, and take a look through. Don't go any farther until I give you the tip."

Gyp had begun to shake with excitement and reaction. He couldn't wait a second; he plunged away like a rabbit, and then suddenly turned back and caught Jim's arm, and confronted him with the stare of a pair of gaunt dark eyes flaring wide in distrust. "Jim, you're coming, too? You are, aren't you?"

The longing was pulling the heart out of him, but he said flatly: "No. Neither would you, in my place. Don't argue about it, there's no time. Git!"

"But I can't go and leave you—you must come! Why not? It's crazy—of course you must come——"

"You heard me," said Jim with ferocity. "I know what I'm doing, and not you nor anyone else is going to muck it up. Get on with it, before one of those Nips comes out. I told you to git! Now *git!*" But as he looked at the shaking, sweating boy he wondered, with a sudden shock, if Gyp would go; for quiet and compliant as he might normally be, and with the habit of obedience well-grown, there was still a high, punctilious conscience in him, and it might be that this was the moment it would choose to possess him.

"You'll go," he said. "Remember Curly! Come on, kid, don't waste time."

The issue was still uncertain; and suddenly the thing happened which put aside the decision once for all. It was so little, so faint and strange a thing to settle so much; only a sound, briefer than the ripple of a gust of wind through the grass, rather a sigh than a cry. It came from beyond the compound wall, out of the ground, as it seemed, and was hushed again in a moment; but it tore them apart as if it had been a drum-roll of thunder, and drew them racing to the gap in the wall.

One of the Japanese soldiers was squatting on his heels in the space of grass before the trees began; he was perhaps fifty yards away, and with his back turned to them, and his gun lay upon the ground beside him. Beyond him in the grass there was something that heaved and quivered faintly, and part of it was a man, and part was a huddle of spilt silk in the deep green, and a pallor of raised arms, and a blackness of long hair, and an inarticulate unassuageable moaning.

After that there was no more of caution or care for themselves. They ran together, forgetting captivity, forgetting escape, ran in long, bounding strides, with the scalpels in their hands. Jim knew that something like this had happened before. He remembered the redness and the roaring, and the way all human fears and limitations streamed out of him and were lost in that brief flight; only this time he did not shout, he did not utter a sound, but ran with every particle of mind and body gathered behind his hand. He saw the squatting soldier start round upon him too late, and make to rise, reaching back with one hand for his gun. He made of his last stride a hurdler's leap, and his foot took the creature in the back and drove it flat to the ground, splayed out like a crushed frog, the breath squeezed out of its lungs in a horrid, sibilant sound. It was not that one he wanted. He trampled it, and went on, and the second Jap, kneeling over the woman's body, leaned forward and caught at his ankles to throw him down, but caught only the one, and in an insecure grip. He braced himself and took the pull with the full weight of his body; and lifting his free foot at leisure, stamped upon the thin yellow wrist and felt it break. Then they were in the grass together, feeling for each other's throats, and the creature, which could have screamed for help at that moment, made only a vicious whimpering complaint like a hurt animal. After that moment it was too late to cry out. Jim took it by the jaw and wrenched its head back, ignoring the long nails that clawed furrows down his face and chest. The scalpel went in under one ear, deep in, scalding his fingers in a spurt of blood. Afterwards he remembered writhing backwards through the grass in a furious hurry with the jerking body dragged along in his arm, for fear the blood should touch her torn skirt, or the small, pale foot which had lost its shoe.

The thing stopped jerking in a moment, and he took his hands from it and stood up. And then he looked at her, the little Chinese woman with a name like a sigh, lying half conscious in the grass with the clothes torn off her body. He saw the bruises already beginning to mar the outline of her mouth, and linked chains of blood congealing upon her body under the breasts, where the attacker had clawed her. He saw her closed eyelids quivering as if he viewed them through mirage; and presently it seemed to him that everything in sight, every constant, clear outline was shaken with the same disruption, the stable earth, the two dead bodies, and Gyp rising from the second one with blood dripping from his fingers, all shuddered in an ague of shock and horror; or the infection was in his eyes, which were blinded by her face. He could neither move nor look away from her for a moment, though inside his mind the pounding of circumstance urged him to run, anywhere, away from this place, while there was still time; though Gyp tugged at his arm and implored him to come away, panting that this settled it, that they would kill him, kill them both if they laid hands on them now. As if he didn't know that! As if it didn't scream to high heaven for the world and all to hear! All he needed was the command of his body again; his mind knew the urgency well enough.

It was the movement of her hand that touched the spring of action in him, the poor crippled movement of her hand trying to draw the embroidered coat together over her breasts. He started out of his dark trance, and fell upon his knees beside her, and gathered her into his arms, wrapping the torn skirt about her. She opened her eyes as he ran with her for the shelter of the trees, and he felt the intensity of her regard upon his face, a quiet, piteous staring, beyond acquiescence or resistance. He thought she knew him, for she did not struggle nor cry, but lay a dead weight upon his breast, her black hair streaming across his arm. She weighed very little; it might have been a child he was hugging to him. He held her the more jealously for her littleness, crouching over her as he ran, agonising over her, in a fury of grief and pity for which he found no means of expression but the gentleness of his hands folding her, and his light running which did not shake nor bruise her further. There was no more that man or woman could do now for Ah Mei but carry her away and keep fast hold of her until the horror and shame was by.

He didn't look back; there was neither time nor need, for he knew that Gyp was running with his chin on his shoulder, watching for the inevitable alarm and pursuit. The mystery was that it had not come already. There had been little noise in that three-minute struggle, but it would not even have to carry to the doctor's room, for somewhere about the store-sheds were the remaining two Nipponese. Had they been in the open air they must have heard the impact and the running. At best it could be only a matter of minutes before they came to look for their fellows, and then there would be a hue and cry for the murderers and escapists; and for the girl, too, for they would see pretty plainly that there had been a girl. There was no time to look for better weapons, or food, or water; they must take what they found on the way south, and make all possible speed to the coast; and God alone knew if they would ever reach it, or ever find a means of leaving it if they did reach it. For Ah Mei's sake they must make all haste; and yet for Ah Mei's sake, once they were safely away from the dressing-station, they must pause. What would be the use of carrying a dead woman down to the coast?

Within the deep shadow of the trees he drew breath, and turned to look back at the white tooth-marks of the broken wall along the sky, and the plume of smoke from the incinerator spiralling upward into the blue of the late afternoon. He thanked God they were already south of the railway line and well south of the road. There were no Japanese troops here as yet, and their attention would be concentrated on the city for the first day or so. If they could find a sheltered place until the darkness came, and yet put a sufficient distance between themselves and the pursuit, it would be well to complete the flight to the coast by night, when troop movements would be held up. But for the moment it was run, and run, and run, through the spaced rubber-trees, down into the forest, into the most secret of secret places, and there lie down together quaking among the vines, three human creatures, bludgeoned and beaten and having terror for their only luggage, three of them against a world of cruelty and force; three, and all in some degree wounded, and the woman wandered far into a shadowy borderland on the edge of reason, so that for a while no word nor touch seemed to reach her in her hideous dream.

They crossed a narrow river at the edge of the plantation, a mere green, overgrown creek among palms. Jim lifted Ah Mei high upon his outspread arms, and waded through it, the mud sucking at his heels; and on the farther bank, where the underbrush began to crowd upon them as once in Kelantan, he paused for the first time, and halted Gyp with a glance, and stood listening intently for any indication of pursuit, but only the smallest of rustling jungle noises fluttered the stillness. Ah Mei stirred with returning life, and turned her face into Jim's shoulder, and covered herself with her hair. He felt that he had only a fleeting hold of her, that she might melt through his arms and be lost into the earth, or into the air; and though such a dissolution might be her best escape, he could not bear that she should go disconsolate. He carried her into the heart of a thicket of young bamboo, and there laid her down. Gyp knelt down, and with his hands teased back the grass and the young shoots over the tunnel by which they had entered, until only a thin green light came in from overhead, filtering through the leaves and dappling their flesh with translucent jade marblings. Gyp had carried Ah Mei's little left shoe all this way in his hand; now suddenly he leaned forward and slipped it back upon her foot, and at the touch she opened her eyes fully, and looked at them both, and said piteously:

"I shall be a drag upon you. You must go and leave me. Please go on and leave me!"

That was the echo of more than one voice from the past. Curly would have known the answer to it, as Ah Mei herself knew it. It was not necessary to do more than regard her gravely with his hollow, soiled eyes, and say in a low voice what she in her hour had said to him: "Do you speak to me of going? Would you go?" He knew that she would not. He was moved with an indescribable emotion, a sexless violence of love not only for her, but for all her kinsmen in disaster, though it was upon her alone it could express itself, and through that narrow channel must pass all the stormy compassionate anger of his heart, before he could know any relief. He lifted her in his arms, and smoothed her silken coat about her as if she had been a child and he her nurse. Every gentleness lavished upon her was an ease to his own outraged nature. When he drew the fronts of her coat together across her breasts, and buttoned the high collar, he was cooling his own fire with the first shower after a bitter drought. The touch of his hand guiding hers as she struggled with the fastening of her torn skirt, the firmness of his arm under her, the little awkward services he did her, these were drops of dew upon an insatiable thirst. He felt the shaking of her body gradually assuaged, though she had death in her face. She turned herself to him, and fixed her eyes upon his. Her voice was a mere whisper, but cool and bitter as gentian.

"It has changed," she said. "I have now nothing to lose. I can only die. Please leave me and go!"

"Leave you be damned! You're coming with us. Now hush, don't talk. We'll get safe out of this yet." He looked over his shoulder, where Gyp lay along the bamboo tunnel with his face to the light and the scalpel ready in his hand. "Rest until dark," he said, "don't think—don't speak."

She drew breath deeply for the first time, in a long, shuddering sigh, and began to weep silently, without restraint; and when she had wept herself out she took his hand suddenly, and drew it into her heart, and asked in a fierce whisper: "Will you do one thing more for me?"

"Yes," he said, "anything. Anything I can do."

"You can do this." Her eyes dilated in her bruised face. "If they come and take us again," she said, "will you promise to kill me?"

He looked at her for a long time, and did not move nor speak. He thought of all the past things his hands had done of necessity against his nature, and they seemed in this extremity no great matter; he was content to leave them to whatever judgment there was. One more perversion, the last and the bitterest, he could accept with the rest. After all, he knew now that it was not a man's business to save his own soul.

He looked at the scalpel, standing in the soil where he had driven it when he laid her down. She followed his eyes, and she said, so low that the words just reached him: "I shall not make it hard for you."

"I know!" he said. "And I will."

"You promise?"

"I promise." And upon that word he heard the voices, distant upon the track going through the forest to the southward, the hard, clattering voices of Nipponese, and the threshing of their bayonets among the underbrush.

6

There were two moments during that interminable evening which he would never forget, never outlive, never even dim with distance, as if two new buds of pain had grown out of his heart and must feed upon his substance for ever without withering, without coming to flower or fruit, perpetually half-grown and fresh and filled with an abortive struggling for maturity; had they gained it his very being must have disintegrated and been lost in that lightning stroke of agony; instead, he knew himself matched for life against a suffering which body and spirit could and must sustain. These were the two moments when he raised his over-ridden mind to kill Ah Mei.

What had passed had passed so quietly, and the first moment of testing came so instant upon the thought, that he was sure Gyp did not know. When Ah Mei fastened the luminous trust of her eyes upon Jim's face as the bayonets thrashed along the trail not thirty yards away, and with grief and gratitude most miraculously smiled upon him, it meant nothing to Gyp; when she put up her hand and opened the topmost button of her coat, laying bare her smooth throat with the purple bruises already darkening upon it, Gyp did not understand. All he knew was terror and the control of terror, and it was enough for him to hold fast to his nerves and keep his weapon ready and his body still, that no rustlings might betray them. But they knew much more than fear. They looked through each other's eyes and met mind to mind, and the threshing of the grasses drawing nearer and nearer to their hiding-place was like the circling of a whirlwind that drew them upward out of the world in a mounting tension, upward into a great echoing void full of wild crying, where their two souls span through space locked together in one fiery girdle of pain. There was never a word said, then nor afterwards, but they knew each other through and through, so that after that no disguise was possible or necessary between them. Because of her he could do what he had to do. He put his arm round her, and held her against him, closely, her head upon his shoulder; he felt her heart's beating, and steadied himself upon her desperate tranquillity. They were inseparable in fear, but fear was a minor thing, to be thrust into the background of the mind and penned there; they were not without power over it, having known it so intimately that even its limitations were no secret from them.

She did not close her eyes, though she knew the moment when

he shifted the scalpel in his hand, moving with infinite caution so that she should not be startled. The outer edge of the bamboo clump was shaken with the trampling of men. Fifteen yards separated them from the enemy; twelve yards, ten—— Jim's arm tightened about her, steadily. He dared not let it shake. So much he owed to her, to do this one thing competently and cleanly, being the last service he would ever do her; so that at least there should be something of kindness and comradeship at the end to accompany her into the void. She watched him raise the knife; and it was then that she smiled, at what cost he dared not guess, a poor, white smile radiant and pale as the dawn. The moment endured upon them for what seemed a limitless age, and he slipped his hand under the shining blackness of her hair and held the point of the scalpel against her throat, and waited, holding her so smiling against his heart, where it seemed to him that she burned upon his flesh the imprint of herself bitterly deep and beyond erasure. And then the moment was over, the moment which would never be over in his memory. The rustling sound of the pursuit moved by then and receded slowly; the searchers were moving on in a wide swathe down the trail, moving southward away from the bamboos, having all but stepped upon their quarry without knowing it; and she had lifted her hand and drawn the scalpel down from her neck, and was weeping silently over the hand that held it, weeping without effort, as graciously as the young rain, as unrestrainedly, as sweetly, her cheek against the steel. She was young; she did not want to die.

But the moment when the pursuit came back upon its tracks, that was worse than all; the moment when the trampling and chattering returned, and the ferns and the grasses rustled again, and the bushes were shaken as if in a wind. To have survived that extremity of terror and strain, and to have to raise themselves to face it again, with nothing made easier by experience, and no sensitivity in them blunted, was almost more than flesh could bear. She did not smile any more; only she lifted her agonised eyes, with the tears standing in them, and looked at him in a wild silence, leaning to embrace the death she did not desire; and he knew then that for her, though she had begged it of him as a good gift, death was not the lighter evil, but a hideous duty, not an easy escape, but an ordeal by mutilation. Maimed, deflowered, without a country, without hope or home or kin, still with all her nature she wished to live. But there were standards to which she had been taught to conform; in certain circumstances one died; it was then not suicide, but an act of ceremonial purification, as proper as incense, as indispensible as piety. She had said she wouldn't make it hard for him, but by God she wasn't making it easy! If he could shut his own eyes or hers, and cut himself off from that violated appetite for living that was in her, it might at least ease him of the last distress, that even in saving her from unthinkable obscenities he wronged her. If he struck, or if he refrained, still he wronged her. There was no clean path. Nevertheless, he could do what he had to do.

But that moment also passed as all things pass. The soldiers brushed by their hiding-place so close that all the stems of the bamboos jangled and shook, and a second time the tension that held them rigid breast to breast was broken like a snapped thread. Ah Mei heaved a long, quivering sigh, and slipped down out of his arms into the grass, and lay there with her hands clasped about his ankles, until he sat down and lifted her into his arms, and rocked her gently, crooning over her wordlessly as over a sick child, though she was quiet enough now, quiet as death. Only by the clasp of her arms tight about his neck did he know that she was conscious.

"Don't!" he said painfully. "Don't! It's all over now. Don't think of it—— Don't speak of it! They've given it up now. They're gone. It's all over." She clung to him, and did not move. "Ah Mei, look at me!" And when she lifted her blanched and weary face he said to her vehemently: "I'll take you away out of here. I swear I will. I'll take you away out of this damned country, or die trying. There must be a life for you somewhere. There shall be! Only for the love of God don't remember any of this horror——"

As if she could ever forget it! That was a thing he could not do for her, take away her memory of evil. His own, God knew, was long enough.

"Could you rest," he said, "if I held you like this? Could you sleep? We daren't move now until dusk. We have at least three hours. Try and sleep."

She shook her head. "How can I? I have that always before my eyes. Only stay with me—— Don't take your arm away from me——"

He said, with a passionate anger: "Where was his sense? What ailed him that he let you stay where *they* might come? A woman with a face like yours!"

"He did not let me stay," said Ah Mei. "He sent me away

230

with the ambulances into Singapore City, but I came back to help with the last load. It is my own fault. Do not blame him."

Thinking how easily she might have escaped so much intolerable pain and humiliation, he was suddenly so racked with anger that he cursed her aloud for an arrogant fool, and as quickly dropped his cheek against her hair and stammered: "Forgive me! Forgive me! I never meant that! But for God's sake, why expose yourself to such risks after he'd plainly warned you? Didn't you understand why he got rid of you? Couldn't you see what was on his mind? Christ, don't tell me you don't know you're beautiful!" he said bitterly.

She said, in a monotone: "It would have been to delay the end, no more. Singapore is not very big. How could I hope to hide myself many days? No, it makes no difference now."

"I swear to you," he said vehemently, "you shall still have a life. You shall put all this by, I swear you shall. You're young yet, you've got half the world left to hide in."

He was putting aside all the difficulties on earth, and he knew it, and was aware by the slight, sad contortion of her mouth that she knew it, too; but suddenly the ardour with which he desired to give life back to her, the fury with which he contested her ruin, blazed inward like a lightning-stroke and filled his mind with the dazzling light of conviction, so that he really believed what he said. It was like having one solitary moment of pre-vision. She should live, she should be beautiful and satisfied and free, she should fill her heart with human affection, and her hands with work, and her leisure with friends; and there should be a time, some day, when the hideous incident at the dressing-station off the Bukit Timah road should be only a small white scar in her memory. All this should happen because he desired it so vehemently that circumstances should not be able to stand against him.

"Perhaps!" she said, and turned her face away, for she knew no such prophetic fervour. There was only one warmth and one light in her cold darkness, and that was in him, and he knew nothing of it.

He held her in his arms until the green dappled light faded, while she coiled up her long hair into a knot on her neck, and with small, quick movements of hands now trembling in reaction tidied her clothes as well as she could, assuaging her hurt mind with what remained of her vanity, and with his gentleness. And when the light passed from them it was she who braced herself and put his arms away from her.

"It is time," she said. "We ought to go soon."

"Can you walk yet? Are you strong enough?" he asked, steadying her.

"Yes," she said, with more vigour than he had expected from her. "You will need an interpreter. I shall be of some use after all." And he saw that in this small, significant thing she took back to herself the beginning of life.

It was still not more than half dark. The trail was narrow and silent, crowded with green shadows, as they began their journey to the sea. Overhead, in the lapis-lazuli zenith, plumes of dark smoke wove gently, dissolving westward into the afterglow. It was a perfect night, still and cool, fragrant after the rain. All the beauty of Singapore seemed to pause in the hush of it, pointing the worth of the thing they had lost. The Japanese infantry were in the city by now. The first units of the surrendered force were in captivity in Changi, and the Chinese volunteers, God help them, were either disarmed in the hands of their enemies or scattered in the mangrove swamps to the north, hiding like animals from a beast of prey more greedy and venomous than all the muggers and hamadryads of the jungle. It was gone, Singapore, gone into a curtained darkness shut off from the world, the door of civilisation already closing against it; gone into the howling void, with more than sixty thousand angry, helpless men and numberless women and children. It was a light extinguished. The night that settled upon it was a perpetual night.

They went in single file, Gyp leading, and Ah Mei second; but it was she who suddenly became the leader of the party, for she was on ground she knew well, and it came naturally to her to turn Gyp this way or that with a touch of her hand or a quick word in his ear as they went. The urgency that drove her would not fail until she was left with only herself to care for; that was her nature. Jim saw the courage flow back into her, and her head lift, and her slender back straighten, because it was she who knew how to avoid the southward road which would already be patrolled, and how to bring them through the swamps to a quiet, hidden twist of the River Jurong, where there was a Chinese fishing community, and as yet a clear way out to sea.

They took nearly three hours over that journey, though it was shorter than Jim had feared. The instinct of flight was quick in them; at every sound they shrank into the shadows, and waited with their hearts beating heavily; but they encountered no one until they came down into the village, and saw the shimmering width of the river opening seaward before them, the only silver in the blue-black of the night. Ah Mei drew a deep breath at the sight, and broke from her place between them, and ran, and stood between the first half-visible huts of the village, looking forward with a quivering eagerness. When Jim came to her side she put a warning hand upon his arm. Her eyes were wide and dark, glossy as velvet, dilated with fear and resolution. To her, in that moment, the issue was his life rather than her own.

"They have gone," she said in a whisper. "There is no one here."

There was neither movement nor sound but the quivering of innate light along the water, and the slight waving of palm-trees between their eyes and the sky. Over the river and over the huts of the village the trees crowded close, but there was no feeling of humanity there.

"Where could they go?" said Gyp. "To-morrow the Japs'll be everywhere."

"They have gone into the swamps," said Ah Mei, "to hide. There is no one here. They've taken their families, and their animals, and everything they have. It is the only defence they know, to disappear."

"Disappear? In an island this size?"

"There is still room in it," she said, "and we are good at dis-appearing. In their own mangroves, with their own boats on their own rivers, could you find these people?"

They knew then, by the emptiness, by the hush, that it was as she had said. The Japs had not yet come to this negligible lost corner of the island, and the Chinese were gone. There was no one either to hinder or help them; they were alone, though they moved through swamps alive with people, fugitives like themselves, Chinese and British and Indian, all straining to-wards the sea; of whom few would ever reach it, and still fewer ever cross it.

They found no one in that village, man, woman or child, sick or well, until they came down to the edge of the water, where there was a rickety little teak and bamboo jetty, and under it an old man just casting off a tiny mat-sailed boat. It might have been the ghost of a boat, so profound was the silence about it, and so dim its outlines in the night. There were two little boys crouched in the stern, coiled together for company against a primeval fear, so still that only an awareness of being watched by more than one pair of eyes at last told Jim that they were live creatures, and not the compact bundles of household goods they seemed. They and their grandfather were the last people to leave the village, and it was clear, by the way the old man reared himself erect and stood rigid in the boat, that he believed he had left it too late. Three people advancing out of the night could as well be Japs now as his own people.

Ah Mei saw into his mind, and ran forward to the water's edge, and spoke to him in his own language, in a low and urgent voice, and there began a rapid duologue across the wash of the water under the teak piers, and the dry, sibilant complaint of the palm leaves in the wind; and presently she turned to Jim and reported eagerly:

"He says he knows where we may get a motor-boat. There is a small rubber refinery across the river, a little higher up-stream. He says they have smashed all the plant, and the labourers have taken the rice and gone into the jungle, but he thinks the manager left his own belongings behind, all but the car he drove down into Singapore. There was a motor-boat; he says he has often seen it; but there may not be much fuel. He says the Japs may be there by now, but he thinks not."

Jim said: "Ask him if he'll take us across."

She put the question, and for answer the old man drew hard upon the rope he still held in his hand, and brought the boat close in again under the jetty.

"He says he will land us below the plant," said Ah Mei. "He daren't go too near. He says it is our best hope, there is no other boat within miles except such as his own."

"Tell him we're coming in," said Jim, "and thank him."

The old man reached up his arm and lifted Ah Mei down, and the two men lowered themselves after her. The boat took their weight with a shudder, and settled low in the water, but answered readily enough as the children sprang into life and pushed it off from the jetty with their long poles. The oily water under the piers, thick with drift, let them slip away sound-lessly, only faint circular gleams resting like silver rings upon the surface for a second after each dip of the poles. As soon as they parted from land, though it was only the water of the estuary that bore them, something of real hope came into them, the first in which they had truly believed. For the first time it seemed just barely possible that there could be escape from Singapore, that Sumatra was only a matter of seventy miles away across the Straits, and beyond Sumatra was the ocean, and neutral and allied shipping still plying in freedom if not in safety. There was, in any case, no safety left anywhere in the world.

If it could all be as simple as this, as quiet as this, after that cloud and storm from which they had come! The crossing of the estuary, the landing on the farther shore, the walk through the woods to the rubber plant, all had a dreamlike quality about them, as if for the duration of the night they had strayed into an unreal world of enchanted silence, after so long of turmoil and clamour. The Japs were not at the plant; they might have been out of the world for all that was seen of them. The sheds and godowns stood empty and silent, full of the twisted wreckage of machinery. They found a boat-house by the river, with the heavy brash of leaves and grass piled in against the creosoted wall. The doors were locked, but with a piece of steel shafting from the refining plant they prised the padlock out of the wood, and pushed their way into an impenetrable darkness. For a time they were blind: but when their eyes grew accustomed to the hot gloom they were able to see the line of the water going down to the river doors, and shapes of miscellaneous gear grew slowly out of the dark, and the unmistakable shape of the boat among them, small, low-lying, glisteningly pale grey. The water was full of iridescent colours; even before they found the torch in the locker of the boat they could see that drum after drum of oil had been poured away into the river. With the aid of the torch they hunted through every inch of the boat-house and the plant, and found not one drop of oil, though the shore was littered with empty drums, and every enclosed space was heavy with fumes. They had only what was left in the tank; happily whoever had done such a thorough job of getting rid of the reserves had forgotten the boat, and they found the tank full.

The night was far advanced, and every moment was becoming increasingly precious. They broke open the river-doors, and climbing aboard, eased the boat out through the rainbow water into the dark mid-stream. Jim started the engine; there was less point now in caution than in speed. They began to leave an ivory wake behind them and to carry a double plume of white before.

But it could not be as easy as this. He knew it. Once before he had made his escape from a lost land by motor-boat with two companions, and fate had seemed to smooth the way for them, and make all things easy; but only he had survived the escape, and that by the thinnest of chances, though only twenty-odd miles of water then separated them from home. Here there was a world between. Moreover, he was not anxious to be the sole survivor a second time. And yet in his heart he knew that Ah Mei would live, and go free; after what desperate griefs and terrors he did not know, and that was his sorrow.

They slid down-river at speed, the mangrove-shadowed banks rushing away on either hand, the first late light bf the moon paling the eastward sky and making the palm-fronds stand out sharply black. The noise of their progress seemed immense in the stillness, as if the night were torn apart, but provoked no answering sound from the shore. Ah Mei sat down upon the planking beside Jim, and leaned against his knee. Her immediate part was over; the fierce energy which had sustained her ebbed as it had come, uncontrollably, abruptly, leaving her drained and white, with slow tears gathering in her open eyes and flowing down her cheeks unhindered. Her hands, which were open and slack in her lap, she suddenly knotted together over her face, and he heard her say through them, with a desolate quietness: "Oh, why did you bring me with you? Why did you have to find me? It would have been better for you if they had finished what they began."

He looked at Gyp's face over her head, and saw it furrowed and twisted with uncomprehending pity; all the evening he had looked at her with that look, and found no comfort to offer her, himself being young and vulnerable, without experience of the transcience of sorrow.

Jim said: "You won't always feel like that. Nothing on God's earth keeps up the same pressure for ever, don't think it."

"They kill what they have violated," she said clearly. "At least it would be over now, and I should not be a peril to you."

"Some day—before so long—you'll be glad it isn't over. I've lived through that once," he said, "I know better than to believe in it again. You just shut your teeth on it while it passes, and then go on. It hurts, but it isn't mortal." That was the hell of it, that it wasn't mortal, that you had to carry it and go on; even Malaya—even Singapore, the last betrayal, even that you took upon your back, and went on.

"I do not wish to see that day," she said very low.

"I've been through that, too." He supposed that some day he might even forget how Charlie's face had looked, drained and grey in the emerald grass, though he had loved him better than any man living, better than his own kith and kin, better

236

than the woman he had hoped to marry. It was the bitterest of tragedies that tragedy itself surrendered to time so soon. "Even that doesn't last," he said. "It slips through your fingers, no matter how hard you close your hands on it. After it's gone you wonder why you wanted to keep it." Yes, Charlie's face would recede in his memory as Tommy Goolden's had receded, the lines dimming until he could no longer call up a clear picture, and must stimulate his memory with photographs, in order to recall what he had once known far better than his mirror image; until forgetfulness clouded the glass, and indifference wiped it clean in a second death. That was what they meant when they spoke of time healing all wounds. It healed them whether you would or no, defacing the most sacred, the most sacrificial of scars with its soft, smoothing, impious hands.

The estuary opened its arms suddenly, and the moonlit sea lay before them, their course arrow-straight into its heart. The cleanness, the barrenness of it came sweetly upon their eyes sick with over-lavish leaf and flower. Jim wondered how far their fuel would take them. Not to Sumatra, he was sure of that. It seemed to him that their best course was to bear south-eastward away from the coast, in the hope of placing themselves, before their oil failed, within reasonable distance of the trade routes between Singapore and Java, and perhaps being picked up by one of the neutrals or the last refugee ships out of the city for Batavia. He had no means of navigating; he could only bear away from the land through the glittering islands lovely under the moon, in what he thought must be the right direction, and hold her there until the fuel failed at last; and after that, without food or water aboard, they would live and hope as long as they might, and after that would die, but at least in a terrible privacy, with no Jap bayonets in their bellies.

He looked back at last, and saw the long, low, green and white line of Singapore glittering along the sea, all its black columns of rubber smoke linked now into a raft of dark below the rim of the moon, an artificial night within the night, the shadow of conquest. He thought of the Jap regiments parading those tree-shaded streets, swaggering through the Chinese quarter, killing, ravishing, disporting themselves with every elaboration of arrogance and bestiality; and he thought of the more than sixty thousand prisoners at Changi, burning out the deep places of their hearts with the vitriol of humiliation. And he knew that this was the one thing he would never forget or forgive, however long he had to live with the memory of it, how-

237

ever time soothed and smoothed at the raw place within him, urging him to let the dead rest. The dead would not rest.

7

When the sun came up they were still proceeding on their blind course, and the flat green line of the coast they had left behind had thinned and vanished into the water. There was about them only a glittering expanse of pearl-coloured sea, broken here and there with the fluttering dark green ribbons of palms, where small islands broke surface in a foam of flowers; jewelled sea and polished aquamarine sky empty of cloud from horizon to horizon; and a silence, but for the slapping of the waves and the purring of spray along the sides of the boat, and the noise of the motor, dwarfed into nothingness in that immensity of loneliness and space.

At first they fixed their minds upon that single constant sound as a focal-point to which to anchor themselves, but in the third hour of daylight the fuel failed, and the motor suddenly seized and cut out, the note of it coughing away into silence. They were adrift among the thinning islands, how far from the traffic lanes in common use they did not know, but certainly too far to stand very much chance of being picked up. There was nothing for it but to make the best of the waiting, and hope that their drifting course would carry them clear of the atolls into open sea where they might be sighted. They had no means of rigging a sail; there had been nothing worth taking left in the godowns of the rubber refinery, and no time to make a thorough search. It was go empty-handed or not at all.

"The rest is with God," said Ah Mei, very clearly in her small, wondering voice, in the first void of the triumphing silence. She said it as if she had come to the end of emotion, lying against Jim's knee with her eyes fixed upon the deepening blue of the sky, and her hair fallen from its neat coil in a flood of silken blackness about her shoulders. And he felt that she relaxed all the taut threads of her consciousness and let herself fall back into the lap of fate, and lie there, and await the end.

Nothing remained now of Singapore but a tiny aigret of dark smoke upon the skyline astern, so faint that it was scarcely visible, and dwindling as they watched it. Many times during the day they saw other threads of smoke rise from the sea, and spiral thinly upward into the clear air, where there was a hum-

238

ming of circling 'planes too small to be seen even as flecks upon the blue. The Jap had not finished with the British yet; it wasn't enough for him that he should take the soil from under their feet, he wanted the sea too. It wasn't enough that he should round up sixty thousand of their proudest, and reduce them to the lowest misery; he must hit at the last remnants of their women and children as they ran for their lives. It wasn't enough that he had brought them down into the mud; he must trample on them as they lay.

"Heaven help us," said Gyp, "if any of those devils come over here. This is just the sort of target they like."

"They're looking for bigger game," said Jim. "We aren't worth their while, when they can get a ship with the same bomb."

"They've got guns, too," said Gyp. "We might be worth a couple of bursts—it wouldn't need any more."

As if there was anything Gyp could tell him about being shot up in an open boat! He knew it all, and he was afraid of it with all the fear he had left in him, afraid of the helplessness, and the slow death that would follow for them all; and yet not so slow, he knew, as death by thirst and heat if no one found and picked them up. Whichever way he turned his eyes he saw a death awaiting them; there was little difference, and no choice.

The hours of that long day passed in a leaden fashion, minute upon minute accumulating heat bearing them down, thirst beginning to torture them, and hunger griping. The monotony of sea and sky in a glassy calm, the sleepy rise and fall of the boat rolling sickly in the long swell, lulled them into a drowsiness against which they fought desperately, at first with their voices, but afterwards, when their throats became raw with heat and thirst, with their thoughts only. And presently they were past normal sleep, too acutely aware of discomfort to be able to sink back into peace even against their will. The sun in his midheaven grew brazen, and filled the boat with a quivering air like the blast of a furnace, and the glittering of the sea hurt their eyes. Jim made Ah Mei a little tent of shade in the stern with his shirt, and lifted her into the shadow of it in his arms. She opened her eyes and gave him a look to be remembered lifelong; but he saw that the weakness of reaction was upon her, and she was far from him. He went through the lockers of the boat yet again, and found an old backless magazine, and fanned her with it, putting aside the strands of black hair from her

239

temples; and presently she fell asleep from exhaustion and passed into a deep coma.

Having nothing else with which to occupy his hands or his mind, he sat over her all the afternoon, wiping away the dew of heat from her lips and forehead and eyelids as it formed, and plying his paper fan. He unbuttoned her collar and folded back the silk from her shoulders to let in more air to her throat and ease the darkening bruises of all pressure. He wondered why she should trust any man so utterly, having lived through what she had lived through. He was flesh like the rest, wasn't he? But she had surrendered herself to his hands, and so bound his hands to serve her. He was very transparent, or she was very wise; for she knew the way his mind reacted to responsibility. He could do all manner of things not good to think about; but he could not rifle what he had been given to guard. That was a weakness in him, not a virtue, probably, but it was the way he had been made. He felt a sick urgency to expend himself for these two, for Ah Mei and for young Gyp; but there was nothing he could give them but a little shade, not even a drop of water to drink, or a minute of forgetfulness. Even in giving them shade he knew that he was destroying himself. He sat there all day long nursing Ah Mei like a beloved child; and when Gyp stretched himself along the bottom of the boat and fell asleep at last, he shifted the inadequate cover so that it threw a shadow at any rate over the boy's head; but on his own naked back and neck the sun beat fiercely hour after hour. By the evening, when the coolness came, he knew that he had it.

It came in slow, rolling waves of nausea, keeping time with the lazy lift and fall of the boat in the languorous swell, washing higher and higher over him until it reached his eyes and his mind. The interminable jewelled blueness of sea and sky grew hard and bright as stone, a solidity of colour pressing upon his vision with insistent weight, hurting him abominably. Fiery heat possessed him, flickering upward through his body like the motion of flame, and his throat was a furnace of pain. He lifted himself dizzily, and hung over the side of the boat, and was direly sick; and even after that, when he was empty as the oil-tank, he was seized every few minutes with fits of horrible, dry retching that tore the guts out of him. Once, losing control of his body, he fell back against the metal of the tank, where all day long the sun had beaten without respite; the pain took his breath away, and all but drove the senses out of him with it, but he did not cry out, only gathered his shuddering legs under him and wrenched himself away, leaving half the skin of his back upon the metal. After that time grew a stranger to him, and the night came down before its time, closing and unclosing black wings over his eyes. He sat beside Ah Mei's deepening slumber, and sometimes he saw her clearly, and sometimes through mist, and sometimes not at all because of the darkness; but while his vision endured he continued to wipe away the dew of sweat from her lips and eyes, and steady his burning mind upon her face, now so inhumanly calm in exhaustion.

It came to him that she would die, and he was not willing that she should. Himself full of heat-stroke, he did not look for anything but death to follow; but the world owed a life to Ah Mei. And the boy, too, he had to live. What was the good of bringing Curly alive through that devilish jungle journey, only to destroy Gyp in the end? They were parts of each other; if the one died, the other could not live. He dragged himself upright time and time again with failing mind and labouring breath to look along the sea in the forlorn hope of seeing the smoke of a ship within signalling distance; but there was nothing in sight but the plumed palms of the islands, and the old smudges of far-away smoke, where the enemy had hunted the sea clean of life.

When he could no longer raise the intolerable weight of his body he lay down on his face, so that when he lost consciousness he should not lacerate any more his flayed back. He lay down on his face, and let the cool dark flow over him, and the emptiness was no longer sea or sky, but a palpitating void without limit or bound, in which he swung endlessly, wrapped in loneliness and fever and famished pain. He thought that he was lying on the piled, musty rugs of a wrecked house in Bardia, with a pint or so of acrid, heady red wine inside him, and Charlie Smith massaging his back. He perfectly remembered the thoughts which had passed through his mind then, strange, abstracted thoughts he would never have entertained sober, about the continuity of human affection and service stretching out link by link across the generations of man, an unquenchable stream, flowing through Miriam Lozelle, flowing through Charlie, flowing through his own mind, and so onward; and where the instrument of its being died untimely, the frustrated river of love must sweep away whoever was nearest, and burst through him, and continue its way; for there was no end to it, as there was no beginning.

He closed his eyes, and let desire and hope go out of him softly, being very weak. Fits of retching gripped him, contorting his empty stomach as if in a red-hot steel fist. He heard his own breathing, heavy and dry and rustling like leaves in a frost, rasping upon the air. Everything was gone from him but terror and anger, and even these remained without sense or background, having lost their hold of events. Nevertheless, existing without reason, they tore him as ravenously as if the fire and horror of Singapore had still been piled behind them. After a while there was nothing left of him but this terror and this anger, a soul of suffering in a body of pain, bereft of vision or hearing but in violent nightmare glimpses which racked him with astonished distress.

Someone came and leaned over him, he didn't know who. Someone touched him, and there were voices in the dark. It was all a long way off. He felt hands smoothing at him gently, but he knew they were not real hands. No human fingers had ever touched him with that peculiarly personal and dedicated, that ecstatic and inspired tenderness; none ever could, unless they were already sealed to a sacrificial purpose in which his life lay between them for safe-keeping; as once, and once only, his life had lain, and once had been safely kept. But in the flesh, though she had loved him as you love everything you have saved and served, even Miriam had not so passionately touched him. In the spirit she would be so, he thought, the mere contact of her fingers would give him faith, and keep him master even of his dying.

This was for a moment only, and after it the deathly sickness took him and wrung him like a twisted cloth, and the swirling dark patterned with points of light was shaken before his eyes like a curtain in a high wind. Fragments of memory came and went, reasonless and disconnected. He remembered Tommy Goolden's hands clutching his body together in the middle, with dark blood welling between his fingers and overflowing slowly into the oily swill of water under him; but suddenly the hands were no longer Tommy's, but Charlie Smith's, folded tightly over a stained Australian shirt and hugging his life in jealously. He saw the sweaty folds of the shirt in an exaggerated clarity, *keringahs* running in them, and a single grey leech fixed between the first and second fingers of the right hand, clinging still though its bloated body was awash with blood both within and without. He saw the fires of Tobruk harbour flickering against a back-drop of oil-smoke and the Mediterranean night. He saw Brian Ridley lying dead in an aisle of the beechwoods under the May moon, with his hands, small as a girl's, folded on his breast, and the last sigh scarcely off his lips, finished with the war and the world together, he who had hardly begun to live and could have lived so whole-heartedly. He saw all the friends he had known, all the dead of a company twice all but annihilated; and the few living, now in captivity. Groping through the dark, he pursued them as they withdrew from him, for there was only one place where he belonged, and that was with A Company; but all clear thought eluded him, and every known face, and however he clutched at dream or reality they both failed him, and he was still alone.

Time went by him unmeasured. He was dimly aware, sometimes, of sounds and sights that stooped upon him like hawks through the void, and as mysteriously soared away again before he could fix his senses upon them. There was the recurrent, vicious hum of a Junkers wheeling out of sight, a bodiless sound, and dull explosions that made his clouding dark palpitate with fiery stars, and the fierce hissing of water, and some-one leaning over him and shouting; and after, a deeper fall into nothingness, and then a sheeting coldness of water that slashed down upon him, beating him flat along the boards, rushing into his mouth and nostrils with a stunning force, and stinging him back to life with the searing salt pain of its blows upon his skinned back. He tried to draw breath, and drew salt water into his lungs, tried to raise himself out of the unwieldy weight of water, and had not the strength. He knew he was drowning, and fought with every atom of resolution he had left to get his mouth clear of the wash. Then an arm took him under the chin and lifted him strongly, and he felt a knee under his chest levering him up; there was air again, and the darkness was no longer the void between the worlds, but a clear oriental night before moonrise. He lay upon Gyp's arm and shoulder, gasping the sea water out of his lungs in great shivering sobs, and gulping the air in greedily; and suddenly he heard a voice he did not know, a great bass voice that roared grand defiance at the invisible bomber, a thick voice full of gusty cheerfulness, as if a northern wind had blown across the sleepy sea. Most of the words eluded him; he thought the voice spoke a *lingua franca* compounded of several languages; but here and there it broke into English, and shook the night with roaring blasphemies as unmalicious as a child's.

"Come on, you bastards!" it bellowed. "Come on, you bloody little yellow Nippie apes! See if you'll stop me! See if I turn back for you and all your God-damned bombs, you murdering swine, you brass-bowelled sons of bitches! Come on, turn me back! Why don't you stop me, you heaven-born frogs? What's the matter with you? Here is only one whole man against you—you see him?—me, Porfirio Gomez! You think you stop me picking up peoples if I want? You think I run for your poor little bombs? *Dio Mio,* I see monkeys spit better bombs." And it went back with a shout into its wonderful flowing jargon, that giant voice. It put heart into him just to hear it; it made him struggle to break through the drifting dark and see the body that went with it. He thought he caught Spanish words among the flow, but the voice could rather have belonged to a Titan.

He heard Gyp breathing heavily under his weight, in the short, hard gasps of a man in the last extremity of exhaustion or excitement. There was another explosion, and another fall of water over them both, a stunning weight that smashed them flat again for a moment, and set the half-filled boat wallowing distressfully and dipping her nose in the long seas. She could not float much longer. He tried to draw himself out of Gyp's arms, to tell him to look after Ah Mei and be damned to the rest, but his lips could not articulate, and all that came out of his mouth was a formless muttering. When he opened his eyes the salt spray beat them shut, and he could see nothing. His body was full of hell-fire. He thought the water hissed into steam as it touched him.

Arms took him suddenly, big broad arms that snatched him out of the swelling trough and hoisted him upon a gigantic shoulder. He felt the warmth of unfamiliar flesh, the ripple of muscles hard and smooth under his middle. The hum of the Junkers had departed unnoticed; suddenly the night was clean of it, and there was quietness; and then, close to him, the voice burst into song, roaring song in an unknown language, with little tune but plenty of gusto, a war-song against Junkers or Japs or whatever might seek to impose an inimical will upon Porfirio Gomez.

Jim knew little of what happened to him then. There was almost certainly another boat, for he felt the motion of water under him as he was again laid down. The great hand that encircled his wrist to lower him to the boards had discovered the inflamed and oozing scars he carried.

"*Ay de mi!*" said the voice, close above his face. "He is marked man, this one. They break his ribs, they smash his mouth, eh?—they score round his hands like scoring pork. They think they got him then, *per Dio!* Porfirio Gomez got him instead. You not worry no more now."

No, thought Jim, not worry no more now. Let it all go, let it all go to hell. He can have it. He can do the worrying, and the salvaging, and sweating, and welcome. I'm finished. I'm no good. I've folded up and quit on Ah Mei and the kid, and I'm glad it's settled now. Let him have it for a change, and see if he'll sing about it for long.

Nevertheless, he opened his eyes and peered through the smarting salt-caked lashes to see what manner of man this was, now, while the face was close above his own. He saw a broad black countenance lit by snow-white teeth, and the clear bluish whites of wide-set eyes; a face of great, massive bones and generous flesh which yet did not obscure the raw lines of it, of thick lips and flat nose and woolly mat of hair. He saw it for a moment only, and then his sight failed again before a stabbing of pain in his eyeballs, and the inward rush of darkness.

He went down and down long shafts of dark, out of the world, fallen from the knowledge of man or God, so that on the rare and brief occasions when perception touched him it was like being plucked headlong back into a light he had forgotten how to use, and an air he could not breathe without pain. Distantly he knew a kind of security, a manner of comfort, being relieved of the weight of other lives and his own. He was in a bed of sorts, or at least between blankets; and for a long time, because of his flayed back, he lay upon his face, submitting indifferently to the ministrations of hands that tended him constantly. Sometimes they were small light hands, and sometimes big, rough ones that lifted him about like a helpless baby. There were faces, too, that now and then took shape upon the sleepy air, borrowing their substance out of the half-opaque, half-vaporous material of which his world was made; but he knew that not all of these were real, because Charlie Smith was the most persistent among them. Even the faces of the living, Gyp, Ah Mei, and the seaman Porfirio with his giant voice and his unawareness of the nature of fear, and other olive-skinned, black-haired faces that came and looked at him—even these were not always real; for once he saw Ah Mei leaning over him, and lifted his hand waveringly to touch her, and his fingers passed through her cheek and shook her lineaments back into air; and yet another time, lying on his belly, with his left cheek pressed into the pillow, dimly he saw what he believed was only a vision of her, and started when it shed a tear on his hand. That time also he groped for her, and she caught his hand to her heart in an inexpressible endearment, the very cool of her quenching a little the fire that consumed him. It was then that it came to him to marvel how the weeping of women was the same in all lands and all languages.

He wanted to talk to her then, to ask her how it was with her, and what ship had lifted them out of the foundering boat under fire, and how it came to be making sea-way at night among the islands, aside from the normal ocean lanes; but speech, like movement, was beyond his power. He had lost touch with his body; he could suffer through it, but he could not compel it.

"I am here," said Ah Mei, whispering. "I shall not leave you. You are going to get well—you must get well!" And in answer to the fixed, weary questioning of his eyes, she said: "It is all right. We are safe now. I shall not fail you. I shall not do anything you would not wish. I shall put it all behind me, and not look at any of it ever again, if you will promise me to get well. I shall have a life, as you swore to me I should. I shall have a life—if you will live."

He saw that she did not believe in his recovery, and a little he was sorry, because she would grieve; but sinking again into his deepening dream, he could not feel that he lost anything worth keeping. What mattered was already gone, like the dead of Singapore, like the prisoners at Changi, like the faith of the young and the pride of the unenlightened, gone with all the other legends of chivalry, with all the other illusions of grandeur; gone with his England, gone with his world into the dark. He could well afford to throw his life after it; to open his hands and let it slip through them and smash against reality, like the rest. He was so tired, so desperately tired. Why shouldn't he let it all go, as he wanted to do? Why couldn't he close his eyes, and turn his face to the wall? What in hell ailed him, that he must still hang on with tooth and nail to an allegiance that had beaten out of him every illusion, and marred his body, and broken his mind, and dragged his integrity through the mud? What makes a man that kind of fool?

Nevertheless, he refused to die.

PART FOUR

ENGLAND, 1942

" Oh, rose, thou art sick!"
BLAKE.

"No change, no pause, no hope! Yet I endure."
SHELLEY: *Prometheus Unbound.*

I

THE smell of England in May, compounded of the heady
sweetness of young poplar foliage and the rich warmth of
flowering broom, and the fermenting savour of the mowings of
many lawns, was like nothing else in the world. It came in to
him through the hospital windows upon a faint morning wind,
vivid with memories, and brought back to him, as his mother's
face could not do, the England he had known. All he could see
of the sacred land was a curve of green lawn below the window,
and the edge of the rhododendron border and one laburnum-
tree; but with that nostalgic wind the feel of the soil came in, the
hills and valleys, the sleepy streams and deep woods of his lost
country; and however he might reject the old ascendancy, the
soil at least had not failed him, nor surrendered its power over
him. The sweetness of the morning, the cool of the night, hurt
him with the beauty of England, and in his weakness he could
raise no armour against it. He lay still and let it possess him.

So it had to begin all over again; but not yet, not until the
tremors of the earthquake had subsided and the smoke cleared
from his eyes. As yet he scarcely knew what had passed over
him. His memory of Singapore was clear and complete, but
between that horror and this peace there was a great gulf fixed, a
gap which he could not fill, a long void of heat and dark, of
being nursed like a baby, and lifted about, and sponged, and
soothed and fed, while his mind within him lay sharp and angry,
but could not control his senses, or exact obedience from his
body. From the void emerged faces, but no events. He was
clear about Ah Mei; she had been with him throughout, until
he came into this white ward of an English hospital. Also there
was quite certainly a multi-lingual negro called Porfirio, who
had lifted him out of the water-logged boat in the sea south of
Singapore, and a thick-set, dark-haired man of middle age with
a great heartening laugh, who was the captain of Porfirio's ship.

247

All of them had receded now, and looked at him from beyond a severe expanse of cork-covered hospital floor and hundreds of narrow white cots. There were other people too, many men, young men and English, or so he remembered them, upon another ship; but upon these he had fixed no part of his mind, and they were already fading.

He wanted more than that. There was three months of his life gone with little trace; and if he was to continue the dreary business he needed all that was his. His mother came, and his father, but they could not help him now. They told themselves and each other that his abstraction was merely the result of weakness, that when they got him home again he would throw it off as he had done before, that they were lucky to have him upon any terms, when so many people's sons were gone for good in that dreadful, unbelievable disaster in the East. As for Jim, he had tried to get back to them; but there was a world of men and experiences between, and he could not go back so far, and they did not realise that it could be necessary to go forward out of their immediate world to recover their son.

Afterwards, he thought, I'll get into the way of it all over again. It takes time. You can't remove your whole life for two years to a new environment and new scenes and faces, and undergo all manner of troubles of which your kin know nothing, and drop back into your old habit at the end of it as though nothing had happened. It isn't in nature. But once you're back again, you soon strike roots; the old hole is still ready for you, and replanting is easy. He didn't believe it in his heart. But the attempt must be made, not only for his parents' sake, but also because there was no alternative; which was why he had done most of what he had done for those two strange years.

He didn't look ahead. He was concerned only with the present and the immediate past; and until Ah Mei came to visit him he was feebly grieved that the gap in his life could not be filled. In mid-afternoon, when he opened his eyes and saw the ivory oval of her face shining over him, it was as if the main piece of a jigsaw puzzle had fallen naturally into place. He was unspeakably relieved; it seemed to him to matter enormously that he should not be cut off from the past, and she, if anyone, could restore the continuity of his unsloughable life.

She saw his eyes lighten at sight of her, though the fixed indifference of the lines of his face did not change.

"Ah Mei!" he said, as if her name tasted pleasant on his lips. "So you are still here; you haven't gone away without me!"

"I am still here," she said, and smiled. "That is the first time you have spoken to me since we left Mozambique. You are better. I am so glad!"

"I'm a lot better," he said slowly, and lay for a long time looking at her, for there were changes in the Ah Mei he had known. He had never seen her in occidental clothes before; the linen coat and skirt she wore, the silk stockings and sandals, made her look older and more sophisticated, and her face, too, was less eagerly candid than he first remembered it, the camellia mouth drawn longer and sharper in it, the shining eyes deep and still. Her calm was less limpid, but more profound, than once in Singapore. "Have you been here before?" he asked. "Many times?"

"Several times, yes. They let me come in sometimes and sit for a little while beside you. I knew you would know me some day, but it has been a long time, a very long time waiting. It is the end of May now."

"So they tell me," said Jim. "I've got a long time to make up, but never mind that. What's been happening to you? Is anyone looking after you?"

Ah Mei looked at him gravely, closing her hand over his upon the starched white bed-cover. "I have been fortunate. Do not concern yourself for me, please. I am going back to nursing. I had to wait until my entry was made regular, you see, or I could have started work long ago."

"And it's all fixed? You can stay here and go to work?"

"Yes, it's all arranged. I am staying with a Chinese family in London; Mr. Wei is a clerk at the Embassy, and he has been so kind to me, and made things so easy. You see you were right, Jim; I shall have a life in spite of everything." Her eyes shone upon him darkly, steadily. They were two between whom there could never now be either sex or secrets. He had seen her brought to the most violent and intimate shame, and yet had observed with her no more reticence than a woman might have done, but only a passionate, angry tenderness as open as the day; knowing by touch that the case was gone far past any pretence of their being different flesh. In extremity they had clung together as two human creatures, not as man and woman. Nothing could change that relationship now, nor put back the barrier between them. Looking back, he marvelled that they should still wish to remain together, each with the nightmare vision of that episode always reflected back from the other's eyes. They should have parted by tacit consent and gone their two ways, and hoped never to meet again, never to burn again for that remembered humiliation. But the secret was that they had not burned; there were no scars to ache again. She remembered his hands upon her body with nothing but gratitude for their gentleness and bitter anger. He remembered them with no more recoil than he had felt in throwing an arm round Gyp's shoulders at Kranji. They had something unique between them; they saw it now most clearly. They were human and young, and physically pleasing to each other, and yet they shared an affection as sexless as the love of brothers, and deeper, and more wonderful because of the quality of the miraculous in it. It had no self-consciousness, and no reserves; but neither was it capable of growth. It had sprung into being complete, and could never now be changed or influenced.

"I'm glad!" he said. "I'm glad!"

"It is all your gift to me," she said simply. "If you had not come I should have been murdered. If you had not brought me away with you I should have killed myself." She did not speak of the moment when he had drawn her into his arm and put back the hair from her neck where the scalpel's point must go; but he remembered it, and shook with the recollection. "I am glad I lived," she said. "How much of that journey do you remember?"

He shook his head. "Not very much. I knew there was a ship that picked us up. They were bombing—— I suppose for her rather than for us, we were hardly worth their while. But what was a ship doing so far off the sea-roads? What was she? A Spaniard? I never made her out."

"It was a Portuguese ship called the *Anacleto Nuñez*, going from Labuan to Mozambique and Capetown. She went aside into the islands to repair a boiler defect and hide until night, because the Japs were bombing everywhere, not caring if the ships were neutral or not. That was how she happened on us. The Junkers—you remember there was a 'plane?—was bombing the ship to make her go away and leave us to die. But Captain Silva, he did not like to be crossed; and Porfirio would not go without us either, so he put out by himself in a little boat, and came and picked us up. You remember that?"

Yes, he remembered it; the great arms that swung him back twenty years into his childhood, and the bass voice that roared ridicule at the Japs and all their works. "What was he?" he asked. "Half-caste, or what?"

"No, full-blooded East African native. So strong—and so brave. He is a deck-hand. Do you remember how pleased he was with us?—like a child with three new dolls he can nurse and dress and undress and make to say: 'Mama!' I think he loved us very much; especially you, because you were so sick and helpless. He came every day, and washed and fed you like a baby, and lifted you in and out of bed for me to make it, and did all kinds of things for you. I was sure you could not have the heart to die and disappoint him, but we were all very worried for you."

"I know," he said. "I remember being lifted about, and made a great fuss of. But it wasn't all Porfirio. There was you, too. You always seemed to be there. You were very good to me. I couldn't have done without you, Ah Mei."

At every instant that he said her name her eyes seemed to gather light from within her, and kindle upon him like lamps newly lighted. She said nothing, only looked at him with that look, and kept her cool, small hand upon his hand.

"Did they bring us all the way to England?" he asked.

"No, they meant to put us ashore at Capetown, so that you could be sent into hospital. But off the Cape Captain Silva was contacted by a British ship—destroyer I think you would call it—and they took us aboard and brought us back to England. Perhaps I would not have been able to come, but I was useful, being a nurse, and the doctor on board was very kind and helped me when we landed in London. So you see, it is all coming right, after all. I am safe here, and I shall work and be happy. And you, too, you will get well and strong now, here at home in your own country. It will all be right for us in the end, in spite of everything."

Jim's mouth contorted in a bitter smile. She did not believe that, any more than he did. She was trying to make the future endurable by turning her back upon the past, but he was beyond that necessity, and she herself was beginning to see other means of continuing to live. It is not by forgetting that you sustain yourself against fate.

She gave a sudden sharp sigh that came out of the depths of her and shook her body like a cold wind. In a low voice she said: "I see you are not so ill that I can tell you lies any more. Let us then consider the truth. Alone I have not dared to consider it. You wished to die, and did not feel justified; and I felt doubly justified, and yet wished most earnestly to live. Well, we are both to live, it seems, at least for a while longer. Jim,

I do not expect to be happy yet; but I am glad I shall go on living, I am glad I shall have to do my part, even if it is not all I could wish, and even if I do it alone. You also will say so when you are yourself again. I promise it!"

But even she, even she, who had suffered through her sister and herself so many things, had not seen what he had seen. She had not helped to cherish a wounded boy all day long in the fetid heat of the jungle, only to see him dragged away and murdered in the ferns beside the track. She had not seen her friends methodically bayoneted one by one, nor sat by the last and best while he died. She had not been ashamed of her countrymen. She had not been ashamed of her country. There had never been cause. She was right; she could go on fighting and be glad. As for him, he would just go on fighting.

He closed his hand upon hers. "I shall be all right. Don't worry about me. I shall do the best I can. What makes me so special, anyhow? I'm one of thousands—millions more likely. They'll all have to do the best they can. They can't enjoy it, but they can all put up with it."

"That is not enough for you," she said. "I want that you should be happy—you, the bravest and best of men!" Her voice was only a dreaming breath, but it filled his ears and his mind as with explosions of sound and light. He began to tremble. It was not right that she should speak or think of him so, he who had made, singly and as one of a nation, so abject a mess of all his good intentions. There wasn't a decent man living who wouldn't have done the best he could for Ah Mei, and some men's best would have been a damned sight better than Jim Benison's. Trembling, he said: "Don't! You mustn't talk like that. It isn't right. It isn't true! I wish to God I had been half what you're trying to make me, but I know better than that."

"You cannot know," said Ah Mei. "When did you ever consider yourself? That is why I tell you." But she saw that to utter any more of what was in her mind, though it crowded to her lips, was to drive him deeper into his curious shell of self-abasement, and make him examine ever more wretchedly the actions which for her shone with such a radiant simplicity. Others, perhaps, would know better how to reassure him; for there were others. "I have seen your two young men," she said. "They were here yesterday, but at the wrong time, and could not come in; they will certainly come again."

He had almost forgotten Curly and Gyp. It was difficult to

keep hold of things, they drifted so uncontrollably in and out of his mind.

"Are they all right?" he asked. "Both of them?"

"Yes, both of them. The young one is still in hospital himself, but you need not be anxious for him; he is already a different person. And they are together: that is very much to them."

"Yes," said Jim slowly, "yes, I suppose he'd come out of it as well as anyone could. Curly was that kind." So at least there was something to show for it; at least someone had come through that holocaust with his treasure still virtually whole. A small warmth was kindled within him. They could go on aggravating each other now, mishandling their affection, driving each other crazy, keeping each other content, swallowing up the loss of Singapore and the sufferings of Malaya in the recovery of each other. "I suppose Gyp got some leave?" he said. "They'll need to spend a good long time together to get back to normal. They wouldn't send the kid off without his brother, after all he's been through. He stood up to it—pretty well, didn't he?"

"Indeed he did," said Ah Mei softly. "I think perhaps you will have another visitor, too, one of these days. The *Anacleto Nuñez* is here, in London. I have seen Porfirio. He made enquiry for me at the Embassy, as I told him, because he wished very much to satisfy himself that you lived. When we were taken aboard the destroyer, you see—it was by no means certain that you would; and he does not like to leave things half-done."

"No," said Jim, "he wouldn't. Neither do I." He lay quiet, thinking of the strange, possessive quality of pity which could not relinquish its object. What he had felt for Curly, and Gyp, and Ah Mei, Porfirio Gomez felt now for him; and once, most wonderfully, Miriam Lozelle had also felt it. Pity was not the word; you could pity even a creature you hated, but there was more in this, the power of anger, the fervour of dedication, the quietness of love; and it could not be destroyed, and it could not be alleviated. "I should like to see him again," he said. "I should like to see them all." And suddenly he thought: "If only I could see Miriam! She always knew what to say. It was always right when she said it. She could put me on my feet again now. She would know what's the matter with me, and how to cure it. She'd been through it all herself. I wish I could see her again. I wish to God she was here!"

But Miriam was under the pall of darkness, in the dungeon that was France. He knew her out of reach, and suddenly he wanted her as he had forgotten how to want his mother, and as he had long ceased to want Delia. He wanted her with his sick flesh and his worn-out spirit, as hungrily as if she had only yesterday held him a moment to her great heart and run from him through the amorphous night under the shadowy trees, leaving the imprint of herself upon him for ever. He was hurt by a radiance of memory too great to be borne; he wanted again those hands lulling him, that generous and gentle voice calling him: *"Bon garçon!"* and hushing away so deftly, so wisely, all his self-doubt and self-reproach. He closed his eyes upon starting tears, and he was in the narrow bed at Boissy-en-Fougères again, newly awakened out of deep sleep with his heart pounding, struggling to find words in which to tell her that Georges was dead, and being forestalled again by the passionate kindness which would not have him hurt even vicariously. She, too, had despaired of democracy, but she had outlived despair, as she had sworn to him that he would outlive it. He heard her voice as if from a long way off, through sleep, through separation, uttering words he was sure he had never heard from her in the flesh.

"There is nowhere you or I can hide from the nature that is in us. I know that the fire of freedom—cannot be stamped out of the world——"

No, she had never said that, he thought, never until now, never until this nadir of his faith, this abyss of need, received him. Was he only imagining it? Trying to make her speak because he wanted her to comfort him? Putting words into her mouth, words she would not perhaps have uttered? It came clearly, like a memory, but it was new to him, and it ran in him like fire, illuminating his weakness with hope, whether real or illusory he could not tell, and had no heart to guess. He knew only that it brought back his saint so vividly that when he opened his eyes he expected to see her face bending over him. But there was no one. Even Ah Mei had drawn away her hand very softly, and gone away from him, seeing that he was already very far from her.

They all came to him; all but Miriam. His mother came, her aging eyes intent upon his face, and brought him all the small domestic news from home, trying to limit his world to conform with her own. She was afraid to mention Delia until he asked after her, for she could not realise how little that affair could matter to him now. Yes, Delia was well. She had a little girl just thirteen months old, and was expecting another baby soon.

He thought: "Yes, Sam Reddin's wife would! Probably go on producing a kid a year until he gets bored. I wonder if she thought of that before she married him?" But it was all miniature and unreal; he couldn't feel anything about it either way. He wondered why his mother looked at him so pityingly, seeing he was making so good a recovery and would so soon be home. Why was she so ardent to touch and soothe him, as if to compensate for some incredible wrong the world had done him? She knew nothing of his wrongs, and would never know. Only at night, after she was gone, did he think to examine for himself what she had so jealously contemplated.

The nurse gave him a mirror when he asked for it, and left him to reconcile himself to what he saw there. He hadn't realised he was so ugly. He wouldn't always, of course, look such a piece of wreckage, but there were marks he would never lose. The two white bullet-scars through his hair were old, and he was used to them; but there were worse things than those. His colour was a yellowish grey, the fading coppery tan making the livid clay pallor beneath look even more ghastly; and in that sunken mask his eyes were hollow blue-rimmed pits burning inward through his head. The shape of his mouth, which had at least been clean and honest, was ruined for good; two teeth were gone, and two more broken, and the lower lip had been split down into the jawbone, and healed awry in a knotty diagonal scar blotched with purple and red. The colours would fade in time, but the mark was there for life, both lips thickened and drawn out of line by the clumsy, untended knitting of the torn surfaces. Cords of dirty brown scars laced his wrists, puckered and seamed after recently being swollen with much inflammation. His back, he supposed, was patterned with burns. No, he was no beauty, this Jim Benison. His mother might well look at him with a specially loving look, for no other woman ever would. Well, that also mattered very little. Delia, when she saw him, would congratulate herself; and he would not care.

Porfirio Gomez also came, very beautiful in a bright blue lounge suit and brown shoes with a formidable squeak, shiny and beaming, toning down his great voice, which could have filled the ward, to a gusty whisper. He sat down by Jim's bed with his best hat in his hands, and grinned, and had very little to say. The man in the bed was a man he did not know, and of whose reactions he was by no means sure; he had seen him only in the sick helplessness of sunstroke.

255

"You feel all right now?" he said. "You made up your mind to get well, after all?"

"Yes," said Jim, "that's about it, I've made up my mind. Though seems to me you had a hand in it too. There was a little matter of a boat. Other things, too." He smiled, extending a claw of a hand to be engulfed in the colossal black palm. "Thanks for everything! For the others, too—you know what I mean."

The broad black face was split by a beatific, white-toothed smile. Porfirio knew his man then; knew his own strength also, and was very careful with the hand.

"*Dio mio,* you got long way to go yet. I like to see flesh on your bones one day. I like to see you laugh like it stopped hurting you."

"Give me time!" said Jim. "I've come quite a distance, too. I can finish the job now, thanks to you and Ah Mei."

"That girl one grand girl," said Porfirio with conviction. "She not mind bad weather, good weather, all one to her, like she been at sea all her life. By God, she look after you like a mother, all time we run to Mozambique, she say not put you ashore there, you die certain sure. You very sick man, we think you die anyway. She know we go to Capetown, say take you on there; but before we get in we speak British ship, they come take you aboard. Maybe when you get out of here you come down see Captain Silva and old *Cleto* again. She be here little time yet."

"I'd like to if you're still here when I get out. They let me get up this morning for half an hour, but it's like starting to learn to walk all over again. I'm weak as water."

"That all pass pretty quick," said Porfirio. "You pretty tough customer, I think."

"You should talk! I don't remember much after it, but I remember the way you came out and took us off, all right. A few bombs more or less didn't seem to make much odds to you."

"Not make any odds," said Porfirio simply. "You not turn back for much yourself. That girl, she tell us plenty about you. She think you just about God to her, that one."

Yes, he thought, Ah Mei had magnified him out of all knowledge. He wished she wouldn't. He wished she hadn't. He wanted to get used to himself as he was, to get over the chagrin of being miserably ineffective. And yet, he thought, he would at least have one advocate in the judgment.

"It just happened to be Gyp and me that turned up at the right time," he said. "He had as big a hand in it as I did. And it wasn't done so desperately well, at that." He turned his head upon the pillow and looked long at the blackness and gaudiness and goodness of his friend, and smiled. "Porfirio, when I go home—if you're still here, and can get away for a day or two—will you come and stay with my folks?"

He wondered afterwards if he'd been crazy to ask him. Caldington wasn't Morwen Hoe. In the country places, so far from being more suspiciously noted, a man of unusual colour could be absorbed without comment, accepted without question. But Caldington was a dressy little town, not big enough to have rediscovered that gracious breeding, not small enough to have retained it undisturbed. Oh, well, to hell with them! If he wanted to show hospitality to a man worth ten of most, show it he would, and if anyone dared to look superciliously sidewise at the surprising guest he'd push his face in, or try, anyhow. As for his mother, who had never been near to a negro in her life, she would need only to be told that Porfirio had saved her son's life, and she wouldn't care what colour he was, nothing would be good enough for him. And his father, of course, was completely civilised to begin with, being born with the villager's outlook. The first thing he'd want to do would be to buy him a drink, and the second, teach him to play dominoes if he didn't know the game already. Yes, it would be all right; he was a fool to think otherwise.

When Porfirio went away, there were two others waiting to come in to him. The Ballantyne brothers pulled up two chairs, one on either side of his bed, and sat there a little nervously, with their hands folded, like children on their best behaviour, and spoke constrainedly and in awed whispers, and were altogether subdued and young and pathetic, so passionately and vulnerably sorry for him that he found himself having to comfort his comforters. Gyp looked moderately well, and had kept his tan, though his eyes looked unusually large in his fine-drawn face, as if he stared in wonder at the very light of day. He had brought some cigarettes, the only gift he could think of, and slipped them into the little locker-drawer within reach of Jim's hand when he thought he was unobserved. Curly was in hospital blue, and the valiant red of his hair fought fiercely with the scarlet tie he wore. The suit didn't fit, and the jutting wrists were thin to emaciation. From long lying in hospitals he was pale and transparent, and there were scars on him still that marred his former hard smoothness, but you could see that the pleasant devil was still in him. It peeped out through his demure nervousness now and then, lighting up his hollow eyes and twitching his solemn mouth out of line. Presently he would be the old Curly to the life, but he had still some way to go. He looked younger than ever. When the sun shone on him through the window and made his copper hair blaze he looked like a battered cherub rolling home unabashed from a night on the tiles.

"We came before," said Gyp, "but it was out of hours, and they wouldn't let us in. Are you really better? When they took you ashore on a stretcher I was so damn' scared——"

"I'm all right," said Jim, "sure I'm all right. It was only a touch of sun."

Their bright, bruised eyes burned on him unbelievingly. Every move they made, every look, was now curiously unanimous, as if they had grown together more intimately and fiercely than before.

"A touch," said Gyp. "If you could have seen yourself!"

"And your back," said Curly. "Those burns!"

"They're healed nicely. You're wasting your sympathy. What do you know about my burns, anyhow?" he asked, smiling.

"Well," said Curly, "he talks a bit occasionally, you know. He told me about—how you got off—you know. I've seen the little Chinese nurse, too. I bet I know more than you do about the journey home."

"That wouldn't be hard, it was mighty little I knew, until Ah Mei filled in the blank for me. How are you doing, anyhow? Isn't it time you got out of that rig?"

Curly grinned. "That's what I think, but they don't seem to see it. Still, it won't be so long now. I've been a good boy. Even Sister says I have."

"First time in your life," said Jim. "About time you put your mind to it." He winked at Gyp. The feeblest of pleasantries extracted from them a painfully intense response now, as if they played up faithfully to the last witticisms from a death-bed. He said: "Now be sensible kids, and get me off your minds, because I'm going to be all right. There's nothing the matter with me that a bit of feeding up and some fresh air won't cure. It'll take a little time, but what can you expect after a business like that? We're all three lucky to be here at all."

They agreed, in the same tone, at the same moment. They talked inarticulately, never coming at what they wanted to say, their eyes fixed upon him steadfastly. Only when they were going did they suddenly turn together, drawn back to him by one of the impulses they seemed now inextricably to share. "Jim——" said Curly on his left hand, and: "Jim——" said Gyp on his right; and with haste and stammering they became at last partially coherent.

"Jim, isn't there something we can do?"

"Jim, if there's anything we can bring you——"

"If you want anything—anything at all——"

"What about some more smokes? They *do* let you smoke?"

"Or if you'd like some magazines?—something to read?"

Curly said, rapidly and low: "There must be something we can do. I know what it's like lying in hospital all the time. And besides, we—you—if it hadn't been for—— Oh, damn! You know what I'm driving at." But suddenly he said it, very clearly, his thin face blanching to a dazzling whiteness, looking like a waif of about sixteen. And after all, what was he? Still only nineteen, for all he'd lived through, still the kid who'd lied eighteen months on to his age to go abroad with Gyp. "If it wasn't for you," he said, "neither one of us would be here. I should be dead in the jungle, like Chick, and Charlie, and the rest; and Gyp would be a prisoner of war in Changi. We owe it to you we're both alive and home. If you could just manage to want something now and then—and keep it down to our standard—well, we'd be glad."

It was like that now; they spoke for each other unhesitatingly, each knowing the other's mind as he knew his own.

"You can come and give me a sight of your ugly mugs now and again," said Jim, "but I don't know that there's anything else. I could do with some reading, though, if you happen on anything any good."

That was no very generous demand, when they wanted to give him the earth; but there was no energy in him to want anything, except perhaps a long man's length of clover grass to lie down in, and the sun on him, and the sound of running water below in the woods. After all, they had done a lot for him beforetime in their own way, and never known it; but it was no use trying to tell them now.

They went away when they were sent, very quietly and circumspectly, and waved to him from the gravel walk outside the window before they disappeared. He lay still for a long time after they were gone, watching the reflections of shadow and light dapple the ceiling, while his mind returned into its dream. They were all as helpless as he was, and their feet upon the same path; they could do nothing for him.

2

It was almost the end of June when he went home, and even so his physical recovery had been quicker than anyone had expected. He was merely one case of very many, less trouble than most because his nerves seemed to have stood the impact better than the normal, and putting his flesh together was comparatively easy. Only there seemed to be no feelings left in him. He received his constant visitors with pleasure, certainly, but they felt always that they touched only the surface of his mind. He was like an untenanted house, neither locked nor shuttered, admitting strangers without reserve, but harbouring no one, not even those who had frequented him as friends in his heyday. At the end of three weeks of pottering about the hospital grounds in sunshine which perceptibly fed strength into him, he was sent home on sick leave, with another month of idleness before his next survey. Idleness was now as easy to live through as activity. He had no impulse to go in any direction, or do anything. It was like being adrift in the void before the world was made.

All the same, he was glad when he came home. Places and things which had once been familiar came strangely now to his mind, but his body remembered them. The small bustle of Caldington as they walked up the hill from the station, the little house in the suburban road, the daphne mezereons blazing with bloom and heavy with sweetness in the front garden, and the scratching and whining at the door, all came back upon his senses poignantly as music lingers when the words of the song are forgotten. He couldn't settle down to this again—not yet, anyhow, not until it was over, if it ever was—but it would never cease to trouble him with the suggestion of loss. It was all so unchanged, so unchangeable. Half the world might go down in ruin, but this went on untouched. The same copper kettles on the kitchen mantelpiece, the same worn imitation leather cushions in his father's chair, the same china dog door-stop, the same green curtains, a little faded, perhaps, but still good; the same quiet blueness of sky and pale soft stars outside the window, when he stretched himself in his bed at night; the same bed, in which he had slept ever since he outgrew his narrow schoolboy one at fourteen. Nor had the people within the house changed more. They were perhaps a little greyer of hair, but that was all. The avalanche had passed them by.

Well, anyhow, he could have a try at satisfying them. He might as well do that as nothing; it wasn't so very much trouble, just a drink or two at the local and a game of bowls or dominoes with his father, and the semblance of an appetite at meals for his mother's sake, and the offer to wash-up, or get in coal, or clean the shoes, anything to show he was coming back to life all right, so that they could be happy pushing him back into the chair and forbidding him to lift a finger. All they'd let him do was to take Susan for walks day in and day out, and with July coming in that was remembered joy for both of them.

It wasn't like being in Morwen Hoe. He thought he would like to go back there, just to see it, and then he thought he wouldn't, because too many people there knew him, and would be sorry to see him in such poor shape. Here in Caldington it was different; they knew only a few people, his father's local cronies and his mother's trade acquaintances, and the immediate neighbours, and even these, or most of them, could pass Jim in the street and never know him. It was astonishing how good that felt; it wasn't so bad being stared at with wonder and pity by strangers who had no opportunity of expressing either except with their eyes. It was useful, too, when Porfirio came; the lads in the local took him to their circle without reserve, and it didn't matter his being stared at in the streets. He stared back, interested in everyone and everything, seeing no reason in the world why they shouldn't be interested in him. The larger ports he knew better than Jim, but from the dubious viewpoint of lodging-houses of the dingier kind; he had never been in a clean little inland market-town, and he was delighted with it.

It went off, on the whole, extremely well. He stayed three days, all the free time he had, and Jim showed him a iittle of England, and Mr. and Mrs. Benison, being informed beforehand of their indebtedness, made much of him. They stared, too, but in a fascinated wonder and delight the fellow to his own; he was strange and new, but he was welcome to all they had.

Only on that third day did anything happen to spoil the visit. It began in mid-afternoon, when Jim was walking through the shopping streets with Porfirio, and half-way down Greenward Hill they met a young couple with a pram. The man was good-looking in a heavy-featured style, with oiled black hair and a flamboyant suit of flannels and sports coat, narrow-waisted and wing-shouldered. The girl had on a loose linen coat over her flowered silk frock, but it was none the less obvious that she was big with child. She hadn't improved with time. Her red-gold hair was now so elaborate an erection of curls that even with her long pace and light step she looked top-heavy. She wore magenta lipstick, and had enormous pearls in her ears; but she was still beautiful in a curiously cheapened fashion, still possessed of that high, challenging look he had loved in her, but with some indefinable quality of hardness added. There they came, two at least who knew him, Mr. and Mrs. Sam Reddin and the kid, out for an airing in the sun. What they were doing in Caldington he couldn't guess; merely in for the day, perhaps, to get some shopping done; but whatever the reason, there they were bearing down on him, and their eyes were on him, and they knew him.

He saw her recognise him. He saw the shock of it go into her, for he was changed, unsightly, his mouth spoiled for good, his neck puckered and drawn with scars, his bones still standing out through the livid flesh. He was hideous, a piece of wreckage, not even young any more. He saw her think so, with a quick flare of thankfulness that she had not married him. He saw her compare him with Sam, and applaud her own wisdom. Well, that was all right. He didn't much care how she thought of him now, he hadn't thought of her at all since the thrust began in Libya, the double-edged thrust that bore them back into Egypt on the recoil. But what he did not like was the look she gave Porfirio, a curious look of shock and repulsion, and the way her eyes flashed back to his own face next minute with reproach and dislike, as if she said to herself: "So that's what he's come down to!"

He thought Sam would have liked to stop and talk; Sam was never one to bear malice. He said: "Well, hullo, Jim!" and gave him the old expansive grin; and the rhythm of the pram hesitated for a moment. But Delia walked straight ahead, and Jim saw her put her hand firmly on Sam's arm and urge him on. They passed by with no more greeting than that, leaving Jim smarting as if he had been spat upon. She was only a silly, ignorant, provincial girl, to whom flesh of another colour from her own was not human flesh at all; but she could at least have pretended, and saved her strictures until he was out of sight and earshot. He didn't realise that she would probably dislike him now for his own sake, for curious reasons connected with his return to life when she had believed him dead, and the hold he still had upon her heart when he reappeared from nowhere; not that his image had obscured the solid worth of Sam for long, but that it should never have obscured it at all. She didn't like her gains soured by untimely visions of the one that got away.

That was the beginning. It should have meant nothing, but it stuck in Jim's mind unpleasantly, for he was not proof now against these shafts from nearer home.

"I met Sam Reddin and his missis in town," he said to his mother when he got home. "What are they doing here? I thought they were settled in at Rose Cottage in Morwen Hoe."

She wondered then if he was still hankering after that Delia; not knowing how many people had walked between his vision and the diminishing figure of the lost girl in these two years. As if he could care about Delia Hall, one way or the other, after knowing Charlie Smith, and Captain Priest, and Leong Ah Mei; but then, his mother had never known any of them.

"Sam Reddin's got a job at the aircraft factory just out of town now," she said. "Doing well for himself, they say. He always seems to have plenty of money to throw about, and his wife's got a new dress every time I see her, coupons or no coupons. I don't know how they do it."

"Reserved occupation, I suppose," said Jim. "He'd see to that. I suppose they've moved into Caldington, then?"

"Oh, yes, a fine little house they've got, out Hay Green way. Sam's on some sort of inspection job—inspecting aircraft parts, or something."

"Something he knows nothing about," said Jim, "I thought as much." But he said no more; neither his interest nor his resentment went very deep. Everything here seemed to him to be touched with the same narrow lunacy, so that it was only normality that men like Sam Reddin should draw big money in safe jobs about which they knew very little. In a crazy world where even the honest—even his mother—whispered in the ears of tradesmen to get the bit extra from under the counter, where men you'd never seen before stopped you in the street to offer confidential bargains in drinks which had never paid excise, larger dishonesties fitted without comment. Something was wrong here in England, something which had not been wrong in that other summer after Dunkirk.

American troops, the first ever seen in Caldington, had arrived that day. They saw them in the streets at night, when they walked round to the local, big young men in khaki uniforms only a little different from British, men of the same race, and yet indefinably different, with fleshier faces built upon heavier bones; their physique, on the whole, better than the English, their carriage not nearly so good; their personalities, perhaps because they extended them to protect themselves against a feeling of being strangers in a strange land, strident and heavily underlined. They spoke an unknown and fascinating language, and were stared at in wonder and delight, as if they had come from Mars rather than the United States. The local was full of them. They were in the bar, and the saloon and the lounge, their voices, big and leisurely like their movements, filling the air as Caldington voices never did.

Jim and Porfirio went to the bar and ordered pints of old, and took them to a quiet table in a corner of the saloon bar. An odd, momentary silence had frosted the conversation as they leaned their elbows on the bar. Jim had felt the draught, but could not account for it. Now he became aware that it had followed them in and sat down at the table with them. He looked round the room, and encountered the embattled, silent hostility of a dozen pairs of eyes. He put down his beer untasted. His face went as white as marble. He said through his rigid lips:

"Do you see that? What's the matter with them? Are we ghosts, or what's wrong with us?" But he knew then, he knew even before the first raw-boned Yankee private unwound his long legs from under the table, and tossed down the remainder of his drink in silence, and walked out of the room.

"I see plenty," said Porfirio. "I see this often. Me, I been in their country. They think they bring it over here, too, maybe."

"The hell they do!" said Jim. For they were all going, in stony quietness, without concealment, one by one drinking up and getting out. "The hell they do!" he said, and pushed back his chair with a shriek across the tiled floor, and got to his feet in a hurry. But Porfirio had moved as quickly as he. A huge black hand grasped him by the breast of his shirt and put him back gently but firmly in his chair.

"You sit tight," said Porfirio. "You think I want to carry you home? You think I let you get beaten up in their sort of fight, and you just fit to walk? Your mother, she like me then, eh? I think so!"

"I don't care a damn what happens to me," said Jim. "Let

me up! My mother'd never stand for this on her own account. Hell, let me up!"

Porfirio held on. His methods were simple but effective. He said: "If you friend of mine, you start no trouble. You never see Porfirio Gomez fight. I don't want no trouble. You start me, I think maybe I kill somebody. I don't want that."

The last American soldier lounged past them on his way to the door, gave Porfirio a wide berth, and spat accurately and resoundingly into the spittoon in the corner. In the doorway he met the barmaid coming in with an empty tray, and clearly they heard him warn her, in a high drawl pitched to carry: "Take your hankie with you, honey. There's kind of a smell in there."

Jim relaxed under the restraining hand, and sat back in his chair. It was too late now to do anything; they were gone, all of them, and only the locals remained, harmless souls who had drunk with Porfirio last night, and the night before. He sat there trembling with anger. He said: "Christ! Have we married ourselves to that? Do we have to put up with that?" He looked at Porfirio, and he said: "I'm sorry. I'm hellish sorry! I couldn't guess that was going to happen."

"I think you take it too rough," said Porfirio. "You sit and drink your beer. They not so bad they make out, that lot. Only silly kids brought up that way. I been in their country, I know. Maybe they learn more sense here."

"Maybe! Maybe they'll try to convert the English, at that. Anyhow," he said, staring, "how did you learn to take it so calmly? Me, I'd be up for murder. Even now, I could try——"

"You not used to it, like me. Once in New Orleans I nearly kill another kid just like that last one who go out just now. Don't take no more risks like that. Porfirio Gomez don't have to worry, he can take that kind apart with one hand. He's done it, he don't have to prove it. *Per Dic*, I know I make ten of their sort of man. I don't need to notice what they think of me."

But the humiliation remained. Jim's hand shook so that he could hardly lift his glass. What seemed worse, though he knew it resulted only from embarrassment, was that none of the local inhabitants came over to speak to them. Only the landlord, coming in with a tray of drinks, sat himself down at Jim's elbow and seemed disposed to talk. He ordered a round on the house, and made a few casual remarks with mounting embarrassment

265

before he came to the point. Jim had known there was a catch in it, but he hadn't guessed what it was.

"I'm sorry, gents," the landlord was saying, "but these lads are going to be around here for a long time; and after all, they're new to our ideas—break 'em in easy, I say, and make allowances. It's awkward, and as I say, I'm sorry about it. But put yourself in my place. I can't have anything go on here that'll send 'em scattering out as if the plague was in the house. I'm not saying it's my own choice. For my part I take it as an honour to have you drink here, but you see how it is——"

Yes, they saw how it was. He'd made it pretty plain, hadn't he? Jim leaned across the table, and said slowly and distinctly: "Now, listen! This pub is open to anybody who cares to use it, and we've got as much right here as anybody else. We'll stay here as long as we bloody well like, and not you nor any other swollen fool had better try to put us out."

"Take it easy, soldier, take it easy!" said the landlord soothingly. "Who's talking about putting you out? I told you you're as welcome here as anybody, and I don't agree with the way those lads carry on at all. But if you and your friend wouldn't mind humouring 'em this once, I'd be much obliged. There's a nice little room off the kitchen, what only the regulars knows about. They wouldn't bother you there."

"And we wouldn't bother the custom," said Jim grimly. "Thanks, but I like it here."

"Now, look! Put yourself in my position. I don't own this place, see. If I did, I'd let them and their trade go to hell. But I don't, see! I'm only the tenant. I have to show results. Business isn't so good that I can afford to lose a whole campful of Americans. If it weren't for that I wouldn't be asking you to move, and I'm only asking you to move into the little snug, where you won't be bothered with that sort of rudeness again. Come on, now, that's reasonable enough. What d'you say?"

Jim didn't say anything this time. He couldn't, his mouth felt cold and stiff as marble, and his tongue was heavy and wouldn't move. He stood up, holding by the table. He was shaking so that the landlord probably thought he was already drunk. He wanted to knock the landlord down, but he knew he couldn't; he could scarcely see him, fury clouded his senses so. He was no good yet, he couldn't even start a fight, leave alone finish one, and anyhow he wouldn't be let, for Porfirio had him firmly by the arm; and if Porfirio let himself go and knocked the landlord down for him, God alone knew if he would ever get up again. But he was damned if he'd get out; he was damned if he'd give in.

"Mister," said Porfirio, in his vast, sweet voice, "I think maybe some other night I come back and smash up this joint. I think I pull you apart, too, see if you got sawdust inside. But not now, see, not in the mood—not unless you make me annoyed bad." And to Jim he said firmly: "You come on out of here. We go home."

"Like hell we go home!" said Jim.

"Yes, I think so. You come along now." When Porfirio thought aloud in that tone he meant business; and besides, to argue further was only to make the humiliation worse, like enlarging a wound. The thing had happened; nothing could undo it. He went where he was led, unseeingly, the big hand within his arm steering him. Outside it was just the height of the evening, the sunset all gold and saffron in the west, and the zenith was mother-of-pearl. There was a cool sweetness on the air, but it was spoiled for him because the streets were full of people, and there was no one in all the town just then that he did not hate.

"And I let you in for that," he said bitterly. "My God, I could kick myself!"

"Never mind," said Porfirio, "it not your fault. I tell you I got used to that long time ago. I live with it. I learn not to care. You quit worrying about it, or you be ill again."

"Quit worrying? How do I set about it?"

"I think maybe you see a bit cross-eyed yet," said Porfirio. "This country one hell of a good country for me, best I know. Those kids—that business just one business, not much account. Me, I do all right here. You find me a better country, eh?"

"I will," said Jim very quietly, so quietly that even his friend did not hear. "By God, I will, or die trying!"

3

He tried everything, but it was no good. He couldn't get back. He tried mixing with the market crowds, and he tried going away by himself into all the places he remembered best, Sheel woods, where he had set his first wires and heard his first nightingales, and down the silver river where he had rowed his first sweetheart. He doubted whether he would ever trap a hare again, or court another girl; because the part of him that could care about these things seemed to be dead. Nothing could stir it, neither company nor quietness, stillness nor movement. He couldn't get back.

So he went to London at last. He had thought of going with Porfirio, but hadn't done it, and it was late now, he had only a week left before his survey. He couldn't keep still in Caldington any longer; it was all changed, or he was changed. Even in Morwen Hoe he found nothing to which he could anchor himself, only old beauties that hurt him too nearly and gave him no reassurance that there was any lasting virtue in them. He wanted somewhere full of people who did not know him at all, so that even within doors he might forget who he was, and be no longer plagued with the necessity of reconciling the two strangely opposite beings who were Jim Benison. So he went to London; only for a matter of four days, since obviously the last little interlude must be given up to his parents. He stayed at a Service Club which was full of new young non-coms. who had never yet been out of England; in their high-spirited companionship his silence passed, if not unnoticed, at least unchallenged, and his differentness was lost to sight. But still there was that emptiness at the core of his being, where the young enthusiast, just such another as these, had once inhabited.

On the third evening he took Ah Mei out dancing. He'd always wanted to do it, to call for her and take her somewhere as expensive as he could afford, and make her forget that they were two people inexplicably joined into one; to treat her like a princess, to pay her compliments and buy her flowers like any conventional escort, and give her an evening in which she would find it possible to doubt if this was the same man who had seen her stripped and ravished and clawed àt Bukit Timah. She would have time to see, then, that he was ugly and unimposing; but she would discover, also, that he took pleasure in being seen with her, that he found her beautiful to look at, and charming to talk to. He wanted her to see herself so. Sometimes he thought she found her only justification for living in regarding herself solely as a nurse. He wanted her to know that just as a women she still had life before her.

The money—he'd spent so little on himself, being so little interested—ran to a taxi and a couple of camellias, candy-striped pale pink and white, one for her hair and one for her breast. She pinned them in place in the taxi, and turned towards him with a luminous smile. She was very beautiful. She was all in white, a long pencil-slim skirt slit at the sides, and a brocaded white coat with wide sleeves, and a narrow collar standing up round her throat. Against that dead whiteness the smooth ivory of her skin was rich and clear, and the blue-black of her hair was a radiant shining like the midnight sky, with the camellia a star in it. The dress belonged, probably, to Mrs. Wei, but it became Leong Ah Mei like the bloom on her cheeks. He supposed it came naturally to her to make herself immaculately beautiful when she went out for the evening, for he was sure she would not have stepped aside from her usual custom for him. There could never be even the suggestion of artifice between them.

Jim had chosen the dance club more by report than by knowledge, but it looked all right, and the food and the floor were good. He hadn't danced for a long time, but he'd been a good performer in his day, and the feel of the music in him was a thing which did not lose its power. He could hold his own on this floor, at any rate, and with this company. They were mostly junior officers and their girls, a lot of R.A.F. and Army, all young and all getting a trifle high as the evening wore on. There were a few "other ranks", and a few civilians, but they were in the background. The girls wore everything from uniform to elaborate evening toilettes; and take them by and large, they were fine-looking girls, the English; but Ah Mei, when she slid the white brocade coat from her shoulders and stood up to walk to the dance floor, was the flower of flowers. So slender and so delicately formed, with that erect and swimming gait of hers, in the high-necked white frock pinned at the breast with a camellia; no jewellery of any kind upon her, but her head held back so that her eyes were jewels under the long azure lids, and her mouth was the red budding camellia he remembered in the hospital compound on the other side of the world. She passed between the tables like the apparition of Kwan Yin herself, the gentle goddess, and drew all eyes after her. He thought, as he followed her, that the eyes of the women were hating her, partly because she was the prettiest girl in the room, but more particularly because she was not white. He'd seen them look at Eurasian and Chinese girls like that in Singapore sometimes, if they were in danger of being eclipsed by them. Well, the eclipse was complete this time; and after all, these people were not typical, they represented only a minor section of a certain class, leisured and monied but without responsibility, whose one aim was to continue to enjoy life, war or no war. Eclipse was a major disaster to them.

He was aware as he danced, holding in his arm this creature

269

so exquisite and so lonely, that they two represented together a world at war, in a corner of a world which refused to contemplate war. They had come here of their own will, but all the same they had strayed. It was a world pleasant to linger in, but it was not theirs. The predominance of uniforms had nothing to do with it; there were plenty of people in uniform who weren't at war yet, some who possibly never would be. Those who were, with all their thoughts and all their hearts, were easy to trace even here, as perhaps in their turn they found Ah Mei and Jim Benison sufficiently recognisable. There was one middle-aged major sitting with a very handsome woman at a secluded table; his face was dispassionate to stoniness, and marked by mottled burns down one lean cheek, and he danced like an accomplished professional, without a word to his partner; but his eyes were glitteringly alive and critical and aware. He was attempting to distract, with these ghosts of gaiety, the lights and the music and the woman, a mind incapable of relaxation. And there were even civilians whose faces had acquired that intent hardening, and their eyes that dedicated ferocity; but they were in a small minority here, and out of their own element. To the others this was normality.

There were four people sitting at the table nearest to them, two R.A.F. officers and two girls in elaborate evening dress, brilliantly made-up and jewelled. They were drinking champagne, but even on lavish quantities of champagne they couldn't raise Ah Mei's quiet radiance. Jim knew they were talking about her. Every now and again their voices carried to him clearly.

"Who *is* she, anyhow?"

"I can't imagine. Could be one of the diplomatic crew?"

"Diplomatic? Out for the evening with a lance-corporal? Be your age, darling!"

"Oh, I don't know! You can't tell who's in the ranks these days. It's the done thing to be a private."

"A private, perhaps, but not a lance-corporal. There's a subtle difference, my love. And, anyhow, I know most of the Chinese wives and daughters from the Embassy by sight, and she's a new one on me. She can't be anyone important."

"Terrific looks!" said one of the R.A.F. officers very distinctly, and was promptly frowned and hushed down. Jim looked at Ah Mei, and wondered if she had heard the involuntary compliment, but she gave no sign. She was serene now in a calm quite beyond their ruffling.

"Tired?" he asked her. "Like to dance again?"

"Not tired; but you should not, perhaps, overdo it."

"Oh, I'm fit enough. Let's—if you can stand it?"

They danced. The floor was becoming crowded, so that they revolved gently shoulder to shoulder with other couples. The middle-aged major and his partner were pinned into a corner with them for a minute, and Jim saw the woman look along her shoulder at Ah Mei, and deliberately withdraw herself as far as possible into the indifferent circle of her partner's arm. She said in a low but querulous voice: "Eddie, I don't think much of this place. You told me it was exclusive."

She could have meant the crowds, but she didn't; she was tilting at Ah Mei, and no one else. She was jealous of her, of course; but for that it wouldn't have mattered a tinker's curse to her how many Chinese girls were on the floor with her. Ah Mei's mistake was in being not only Chinese, and nobody in particular, but beautiful into the bargain.

He thought she had heard that remark, though she said nothing. He thought she understood it very well, but would not concede that anything in this precious evening had fallen short of perfection. He drew her away out of earshot as quickly as he could. The major had not replied, did not even seem to have heard. The only look he gave Ah Mei was one of considering pleasure for her beauty; he was already bored with his own companion, and satisfied to enjoy the contemplation of women who would never have the opportunity of boring him.

But whether they acknowledged it or not, the evening was indefinably smirched even then. It remained for their neighbours at the next table to finger-mark it beyond cure. They were getting pretty high by now, and were less careful how far their voices carried. They were talking about China. It seemed one of the girls had lived there for a year or so, in Shanghai, before the Japs were quite so interested in it. She didn't think much of China or the Chinese. Many too many of them, she said, and they smelt.

"I don't give a damn!" said one of the R.A.F. officers, looking full at Ah Mei. "Some of the girls are peaches."

It wasn't possible to ignore them any longer. The drunker of the two men was giving a discreet half-voice impression of a Shanghai singing-girl, swaying his body to the cadence of an imaginary song. The other one was amusing himself and annoying his companion by making eyes at Ah Mei. The hell of it was that there was no harm in either of them, it was simply

that they didn't think, that their lives were made up largely of
things about which they didn't have to think, and they'd lost
the trick of it. But the girl wasn't tight; the girl knew what she
was saying. Every word was calculated. Perhaps she was fond
of the amorous boy; perhaps she was just naturally venomous.
She said clearly:

"There were good-looking sing-song girls in some of the water-
front cabarets, but one didn't take them out to dinner. However, you probably would. I forgot you had perverted tastes."

The boy said: "Hush, for God's sake! She'll hear you—she
has heard you!" His voice was an appalled but very audible
whisper. "Sheila, you *bitch!*" he said, and went backwards in
his chair with the suddenness of a balloon deflating at the prick
of a pin.

Jim looked at Ah Mei. She had put down her glass rather
quickly, and ground out her cigarette in the ash-tray with
shaking fingers. There was nothing he could do, nothing in
the world. If it had been the man he could have wrung his neck
and enjoyed doing it; but no one could do more than name this
woman, and her escort had already done that, accurately
enough. All he could do was take Ah Mei away from here;
he knew she wanted that. He pushed back his chair and
stood up.

She looked up then for the first time, and he saw her eyes,
not greatly disturbed, only shadowed as if by a passing cloud.
"Oh, please, Jim!" she said. She was not angry. She wished
only to go away quietly and with dignity, to compose herself,
to forget that these people existed.

He held the brocade coat for her, folding it gently over her
shoulders. The smallness of her between his hands was somehow pitiful.

"I apologise for bringing you here," he said. "I should have
taken more care to find out what kind of place this was. I'm
sorry!" For he was angry, if she wasn't. He wanted to leave
a sting behind. He wanted them to see her shake off the dust of
her small feet against them, as only Ah Mei could. Her exit
must be a rejection, not a flight.

Ah Mei, fastening the crystal buttons of her coat with unhurried movements, looked full at him over her shoulder, and:
"Please do not regard it," she said, "it is of no importance";
brushing aside the people, and the incident, and the insult
with one exquisite gesture, her voice still quiet and limpid as
twilight.

272

"I apologise for my countrywomen, too," said Jim deliberately. "You'll make allowances, I know. By comparison with your people, after all, we're barely civilised." They heard that, all right; he meant that they should.

She said: "Please, I have forgotten it!" but she smiled, and he thought she approved of him. She passed by the table for four as if it did not exist, and he knew, as he followed her, that they all watched her out of the room with eyes mortified and angry, not a word said between them. She went without haste, her step as soft as ever, the poise of her head like a lily's on its stem. Not many women could move like that; he was proud to follow her.

In the street he turned and met her eyes full. She said, before he could speak: "It doesn't matter, Jim. Please do not worry about it."

"We'll go on somewhere else," he said. "It's still early, only ten o'clock—no, not quite ten yet. I'll take you somewhere decent, where that sort of fool doesn't come. What do you say?"

She smiled, but what she said was: "No."

"But please! If you don't I shall know they've spoiled your evening."

"People like those could not spoil it for me," said Ah Mei. "You know that. But I would rather go home now. Please take me home!"

He took her home. What else was there to do? She sat beside him in the taxi very stilly as they drove through the dusk, looking straight before her, and all he could see was the clear profile, magnolia-smooth, and the curve of her lowered eyelids, and his camellia in her hair. He had to talk to her; he had to make her talk. There had never been constraint between them; there must be none now. If she went away silently now he might lose her, and he did not want to lose her; though by all normal judgments he had no part in her nor she in him, still he could not bear to lose her.

He touched her hand. "Ah Mei——"

"Yes?"

"You were very much hurt."

She sighed. She said: "Yes" again, very softly.

"Now you'll go away from me; you're going away from me already."

"Oh no!" she said quickly. "You must know they could make no difference. I am not so foolish. They were only hurtful, not important. You could not help it, Jim, you did your part very well; and there is no damage done. I should be ungrateful indeed if I remembered one silly incident for long, when I have received so much kindness and help here." And that could be true and doubly true, but still she knew that he would remember it. She turned herself towards him, and took him by the hands. "Always you have this hardness in judging what you value most. To all the world you can forgive so much of weakness and foolishness and vanity, but not to yourself or your own country. Why should you demand perfection from one country only under the sun? It is greedy in you, Jim."

"Perfection!" he said bitterly. "Well, I don't fall as hard now as I used to. You can't keep it up for ever."

"Still you are being hard to the thing you love," she said. "It is necessary that I should say this; you are wrong, Jim. Those people—it is not for them you are fighting. They are not the reality. They are not the warriors, and they are not the stake. It is for yourself you fight, and for me, and for those men we have left in Changi, and for the others who will fill their places; and I do not believe that in these you have been altogether deceived."

No, he hadn't been deceived in them; but a lot of them were dead, and a lot more would be dead before the end of the war; and those who were left would have to contend with the world as it was, not as they would have it. Suppose he'd travelled all that interminable way only to get back to where he'd started from? Only in a worse case, because he would see all the flaws, and be unable to do anything better than sicken over them; and all the time with Charlie Smith's voice saying in his ears: "God help you if you let me down! Dead or alive, I'll never leave you alone!"

Well, he never had yet; he never would. He was always there, just outside the door of Jim's mind, sitting on his haunches the way he sat in the shade in Libya, with a grass or a cigarette between his lips, and his bright, black, bedevilling eyes solemn on Jim's face whenever he looked through the door, and laughter never far from his mouth; waiting to drop the little barbed goads that could drive his man the way he wanted him to go. He was there, and Jim wanted him there; he wouldn't go far.

"Don't worry about me," he said, "I know where I'm going, and I'll get there all right, even if I don't enjoy the journey." And he smiled at her, deliberately lifting himself out of his darkness; but he did not think she was altogether deceived, for when she said good night to him on the doorstep of her friends' home the light of the afterglow caught a sudden sharp glitter under her eyelids, and he saw that she was in tears for him. Her voice was level and soft, her hand cool and kind as ever; but there was that jewelled, blind shining in her eyes, that stayed with him after she had gone quietly into the house and closed the door between them. He saw it long after he had ceased to see the outline of her face. He was sorry he had done so badly by her, for they were both lonely. They were the loneliest people in London to-night, and they could no longer even remain warmed by each other's company, for fear of doubling, instead of halving, the sorrows they carried.

He wondered if he could get drunk. Anyhow, it was worth trying. He tried it, but it wasn't a success; there'd been too much queer stuff shot into him in hospital for alcohol to get much of a hold, even if his capacity hadn't been pretty high to start with. All he achieved was to make himself even more wretched than before, maudlin with self-pity, sick of himself, sick of the war, sick of the world; and there was no one to do Charlie's part this time, no one to kick him upright, no one to prod him onward. The last vestige of energy and will seemed to drain out of him; there was no longer even pain to assure him he lived.

It was in this case that he spent the first three hours of the night wandering round London, in the cloudy warmth of the summer night, in the streets growing silent and mysterious round him. He didn't know where he went, nor care either. He heard the 'planes stirring overhead, about two o'clock in the morning, but his brain did not react to the sound. Even the siren meant nothing to him. He walked on in the deserted streets through the brief, bright pandemonium of ack-ack fire and searchlight, not even looking up to see the splinters of silver fire circling and vanishing in the zenith; and the only bomb to fall upon London that night fell not a hundred yards behind him, and lifted him from his feet, and stunned him against the pavement.

It was not like a blow at all; there was neither shock nor struggle nor pain, but only an explosion of light splitting the world and the night asunder, and then no sight left to him, no hearing, but only the wild vertigo of a plunge through miles and miles of air, and a moment of swinging in space at the end of a cord of consciousness he could not quite sever. By that cord he was drawn upward again, time flowing by his face breathlessly, so that he struggled to fill his lungs, and with the inrush of air he was buoyant again, and sprang back into the known world as a swimmer breaks water.

He felt a heart beating under his cheek, heavily, hotly, a fierce, clean heart unsatisfied as youth. He opened his eyes upon a face, a round, sunburned face at once earnest and indignant and afraid, with a broad tanned forehead above wide-set eyes darkly and vividly blue. Short brown curling hair surrounded the face, and there was a mouth in it all valour and purpose, a mouth that parted full lips upon anguished breath, and said: "Jim!" in a voice he knew, in a tone he remembered well.

It had taken him two years and a hell of a lot of weary journeying to find his way back to Imogen Threlfall.

4

A sort of stillness came into him, short of content as yet, but full of ease. She was kneeling in the roadway, holding him in her arms, and from that haven he had neither will nor strength to move. He remembered so well the way she looked at him, with those wide, disconcerting eyes whose blue was like the night sky; he remembered the set of her mouth, at once so softly young and so resolute; even the sound of her heart under his cheek, racing like a runaway, was not strange to him. He did not wish to move, nor to speak any but familiar words, for fear he should destroy something which was there with them in the eerie night, in the haunted quietness, something from long ago, like an essence of the past caught in a bubble of memory. So after she had said: "Jim!" there was a long silence while they regarded each other sombrely. Then he said: "Hullo, goblin!" in a slow whisper, as if there had been no two years between, and no helpless wandering; as if he had never lost the thing he could not even recapture.

"Hullo, ghost!" she said, and the softening and warmth which was not yet a smile came over all her face, as if someone had lit a lamp within her. "Isn't that just like you!" she said. "The only bomb in fifteen nights, and you have to get in the way of it."

"And isn't it just like you! The only casualty in London, and you have to pick him up!" He stirred and sighed, raising himself out of her arms; his head felt light and pulsing with pain, but there was no damage done. He couldn't get drunk, and he couldn't get killed; he might as well make the best of it.

She kept her arm about him, steadily, as she would have done for a stranger. "Take it easy. I think you've been out some time."

"The devil I have! The bomb only fell about a minute ago."

"Half an hour at least. It flattened all the trees in the square there, and dug itself a quick way into the subway, but no casualties, and no property damage to speak of—just you," she said, and the hovering smile touched her lips for a moment and withdrew again half seen. "How do you feel now?"

"I'm all right, thanks. A bit stupid, but that'll pass. How did you come to be here, anyhow? Not on duty? You wouldn't be wandering round alone if you were."

She shook her head. "I was on my way home."

"At half-past two in the morning?"

"I finished at one o'clock. Any objection? I always walk home this way."

"Alone?" he asked.

"Usually. Why not? I'm not afraid of the dark now, even in towns."

Jim got to his feet laboriously, and brushed himself down, and finding the ground firm enough under him, took time to look at her properly. She was changed, but not greatly changed; thinner than he remembered her, and all the lines of her body and her face sharpened and polished, which had then been so young and exuberant and soft. She had gone on along the road she was walking when last he had seen her in Morwen Hoe; she had gone on a great way, and had still a great way to go. He doubted if she would ever come back.

"You've got company to-night," he said. "You don't mind, do you?"

"You should go home yourself," she protested. "What are *you* doing here at this hour, anyhow? It's I who ought to be asking that."

Jim smiled and tucked her arm within his. "It's a long story. Maybe I'd better just say I was looking for you, and leave it at that." He drew her close to his side, and the conviction of her peace suddenly entered into his tortured flesh, and he knew she had what he wanted, and needed, and must have, what Charlie dead and Ah Mei living could not give him, a belief in the future. "Now!" he said. "Which way do we go?"

"It's quite near. You're sure you feel all right?"

"Quite sure. You lead the way."

"It's just down at the far end of this street, and along a narrow mews. It's not much of a place, really, just a two-room flat I share with another girl; but it's nice and handy for the post, and it's comfortable enough. It's a queer house, gone to seed a good deal. A lot of refugees have the top floor there, because it's so cheap; mostly French and Poles—there's a wonderful old Frenchwoman who cooks the meals for them all, and the young ones go out to work. They're all women. I expect they'll be up when we get in, because of the bomb. Some of them are still—a bit nervous. They've had a bad time, one way and another, you see. Some of them have been here since the beginning, but others have lived under the Nazis, and been smuggled out afterwards, when they got into trouble with the authorities. There's one girl who used to help to publish one of the underground papers, but she doesn't talk about it much." She looked up at him as they walked, and saw how his eyes were fixed intently upon her face. "What is it? Why are you looking at me like that?"

"It's two years since I've seen you," he said.

"Two years, and a fortnight over. You see, I remember, too."

"And yet you talk to me about everybody on earth except yourself."

"There's nothing to tell," said Imogen. "I've worked the same hours, and known very few people, and got a certain amount of fun out of life, and a good deal more that—wasn't fun, exactly. I'm two years older, if that's any news; and I've had no work to speak of for a long time. They don't raid much here now. I don't believe they've got the stuff, or they would. I'm bored, and I'd like to get out and make munitions or something, but there's no hope of that. Now how about you telling me something about yourself?"

"No," he said, "I haven't finished yet. How have you *been?* That's what I want to know. Have you been happy?" He asked it in a voice suddenly quiet and diffident.

"That's a lot to ask, isn't it?"

"Have you?"

"No," she said. Her eyes held his for a moment, and then the thick lashes hid them.

"Any—very special reason?"

"How can anyone be happy," said Imogen, "in this devilish mess of a world? When I had anything to do here it was better; at any rate, I could believe it was some use my living; and yet

278

I can't even hope for work, because that would be wishing misery to other people. The only happy people alive just now are the utterly selfish ones who don't give a damn for anything but their own food and comfort; and perhaps the underground workers in Europe who—well—who lose their lives and save them every day. I think they must be the happiest people in the world, as well as the most sorrowful. That's not silly, is it? You know what I mean?"

He said in a very low voice: "It isn't silly, and I know what you mean. Have you been altogether unhappy, then?"

"No, not that either. Never enough to want to quit. Because I want to live to see them all come out into the sun again. That's what I'm looking forward to now."

"That's what makes a lot of people tick," said Jim. "You think we shall be able to look 'em in the face that day?"

"I think they'll think so," she said.

"Is that enough?"

"It's not what I wanted, but maybe it's all I deserve, and anyhow, it's something."

He marvelled how well they understood each other, that she should answer him so readily after such an absence. He wondered if question and answer had really been put into words, or if their two minds had met and embraced undriven, marrying thought to thought. For when she answered him her wide eyes held his, and their glance went into him like cool water, launching through his being a vast and quiet flood that gathered way and power as it ran, and loosened from within him all the accumulation of loneliness and grief and anger, and bore it away. The belated stars came out in a sky frayed with little clouds, and shone upon them as they turned into the mews.

"And you? How have things been with you?"

He turned his mutilated face to the light of a rising moon. "You see how they have been."

"I see the outside. You've been—knocked about a good deal, I know. I didn't mean that, exactly."

"You can see the inside, too, if you want to; but it's hardly worth your while."

"I have knocked at the door," she said. They stood at her own door then, the bulk of the ramshackle house leaning over them, a row of tired plants in red pots arrayed along the edge of the cobbled walk; the green paint was peeling off the knocker, and the stucco off the wall. She fitted her key into the lock, and turned and looked at him.

"I have opened the door," he said. "Come in, Imogen!"

It was as if a shadow and a light passed together over her face as the ripple of a breeze passes over still water, at once changing it and leaving it unchanged. What had she kept that he had lost? Or what had she had that he had missed, that she should be as constant as the trees and the soil of England, while he had only the attributes of humanity, and could become a nomad and a stranger in the place which was his? She did not turn away from him now, but put her arm behind her and pushed the door open wide; and in her turn, in a small clear voice, she said: "Come in!" And he followed her in.

The door creaked as it closed, and they were in a warm, faintly musty darkness, close together, her hand on his arm, and from above them, down the well of the staircase, a faint diffused light shone, striped with gap-toothed bannisters.

"We don't have a light in the hall," said Imogen. "We can't afford it. Wait a minute, I've got my torch somewhere."

The slender beam picked out tread by tread an ascending stair covered with worn carpet in nondescript dark colours. She took his hand, and they began to mount, one flight, two flights, the light growing stronger and yellower. There were voices ahead, several voices in animated conversation; he imagined there were always voices of women in that house; but the light was nearer, coming from a half-open door along the next landing.

"She's waiting up for me," said Imogen. "I thought she would be. Whenever there's a raid on she can't rest until we're all safely in."

"She?"

"We call her *Maman*. She's been here nearly a year now. There, you see? She heard us coming."

A woman came out into the corridor and stood silhouetted against the light, a big, bulky figure with broad hips and long, full skirts tightly belted in to her waist. That was all she was to him at the moment, the shape of a big woman, light on her feet still, but growing old. She looked along the landing to the head of the stairs, and called: "Is it you, Mademoiselle?"

"Yes, *Maman*. I'm sorry I'm so late; you shouldn't have waited."

"How could I sleep until you came home, *chèrie?* I have left you some hot soup. Please drink it before you go to bed." She stopped, seeing beyond Imogen's small form a man taking shape out of the obscurity of the stairway. "Is it that you have a visitor so late?"

It was not possible. It could not be known to him, that voice; the sense of familiarity in the outline of her could be no more than an illusion. And yet he felt his heart turn over in him, she reminded him so of someone, someone he had known——

He climbed another step or two, and the light fell on him through the open door; and as if it had fallen instead upon her, instantly he knew her. He drew a breath so sudden and hard that it hurt, and Imogen checked and looked round, feeling him start.

"What is it? What's the matter?"

He stared past her, and: "Simone!" he said in a great gusty whisper, and nothing more would come out of his mouth.

She took one quick pace forward into the light, and her hands flew to her face. He saw the grey hair still in the same tight knot at the back of her head; and her hands, with which she stilled the quivering of her mouth, were known and kind and infinitely touching with their square-cut nails and fine network of lines. She had lost flesh; the skin of her cheeks was pouched over the bones, and her arms, which had been so round and firm, were thin enough now. Also she moved with more of effort, the spring gone from her step, her head thrust forward in a short-sighted fashion. But changed as he was, and poor as was the light that showed them to each other, she knew him.

"*Dieu de Dieu!*" she said between her fingers. "*C'est lui— c'est le grand petit——*" And the hands came groping for him, and the musty air was suddenly clean and fresh and full of blown blossom from the orchards of Boissy-en-Fougères; so, at least, it seemed to him, for his head was still light from the crash, and his memory had possession of him fully. Miriam was at his side again. He would see her; he would talk to her; for where Simone was, there Miriam must be. Simone would never come away without her, never in life. He sprang up the last few steps of the stair, and caught the old woman into his arms.

"Simone—Simone! To see you here! It *is* you! I couldn't believe it. I thought I was seeing things, but it *is* you. How did you get here? When did you come? Have they been kind to you here?"

"So many questions," she said into his shoulder, "and I am so glad I cannot speak, to answer even one. It is so long since Boissy, and we have come so far since then——"

"Let me look at you! You're thinner, much thinner. You've had a bad time. I wish I could have done something for you—for you both; you did so much for me. Simone," he said urgently, "where is she?"

Within his arms he felt her shaken through and through by a tremor from the heart; she stiffened herself against it and raised her head and looked at him with fixed, unfocused eyes, at him and through him, as if she was stone blind. In a strange voice like a stricken child's she said: *"Est-ce que vous ne savez pas?"* and went into streams of French too rapid for him to follow. A wave of fear passed into him. He took her by the shoulders and held her off from him, searching her face, shaking her, cajoling her with queer little broken phrases, his heart already chilled within him.

"Simone—*belle-mère! Je t'implore*—— Is she not here with you? *Dites-moi!* What has happened to her? *Il faut que je le sais—Madame—ou êtes-elle? Ne pleurez pas, ma chère, ma douce—mais dites-moi*—— Where is she? Where is Miriam?"

He saw her lips move, stiffly, as if with great difficulty she kept her mastery over a body weary of being tormented. He heard , though it was a sound scarcely audible: *"Elle est morte!"* That, and no word more.

All the urgency, all the haste, fell away from him then, and left him standing there with his arms still about her, and her eyes still pebble-blind upon his face, and everything within him become agonisingly cold, so that though his heart seemed stone in his breast it was not past pain. He said it over and over to himself within his closed mind: *"Elle est morte! Elle est morte*——" trying if the words could not elude their meaning, slough it and cast it aside as snakes their skin; but it remained significant. "Dead," he said in a monotone.

"Elle est morte—il y a deux ans, morte. Je suis seule du monde. Oh, Monsieur Jim, elle était si brave, si gentille—— *Nous ne trouverons pas une autre*——"

"There was only one," he said in the same tone, and was silent a long time, holding by the memory of her, feeling it lean down to him softly. Two years dead! Oh, God, she was spent, she was turning to earth in the Artois mould! What use to remember the irrecoverable splendour? Never to see her again, never to hear her voice or touch her hand again! Perhaps to lose even this clear memory of the lines of her face, to see them dim year by year as if spotted with physical decay, and be unable to prevent or delay the appointed process! She would go from him wholly. They would all go from him, even Charlie Smith, even Miriam. In the end he would be left alone.

"Dead!" he said. "How?"

"They shot her, monsieur. They murdered her."

He made a sound like the snarling moan of an animal mortally wounded, and his head went down into his hands, for he knew then that he himself had killed her. His mind was darkened for a moment with the cruelty of it. He felt Imogen's arm about him, drawing him into her room. He heard the door close.

"It was for me," he said. "I did this to her."

"No, no, you must not say it. It would have happened. How could she live breathing the same air with them?"

"Tell me what happened," he said inflexibly.

"It is to distress you without cause. She is dead. There is nothing we can do now."

"Tell me. I must know."

"That night—the night you went away from Boissy—they came to the house while she was away. They had found the two uniforms hidden in the roof of the well, and they came to wait for her, and when she came back they took her away with them. She would tell them nothing. They would not let me go to her. I did not see her again until the day they shot her. It was in the quarry, where your guns used to be. She was changed—— Oh, monsieur, she was changed——" Her voice broke upon an appalling sound between a sob and a groan, and she began to weep.

That, also, then, had been done to Miriam Lozelle. Not only the murder in daylight, but the abominations by darkness as well, the furtive, the closeted horrors which were the enemy's sword and spear. And yet she had told them nothing. Her will had not been broken; for that at least he need not reproach himself, though he was guilty of her torture and her death.

Simone's trembling voice took up the tale again, patiently, for she had lived two years with these memories quick in her. "She lay in the quarry for twenty-four hours, monsieur; it was their order. No one was to touch her, or take her away. But in the morning when they came to look for her, the body had been washed and composed, with a flag under her head, and roses in her hands, and in her hair—— Oh, Monsieur Jim, it has been told and retold, the miracle of Boissy. They talk of it when the patriots meet. They will talk of it until the day of deliverance comes. The Nazis, they would have made much trouble for the village, but it was only to spread her fame, and that they would not do, therefore they let us take her away and bury her decently. There was not a soul in Boissy who did not go into mourning. And her grave—until I left it was covered with flowers always; it will be covered still."

He thought: "I shall go back there. Some day, please God, I shall make a pilgrimage to her grave." But that was not enough.

"Was not this well done?" said Simone.

"It was very well done. Was it your doing?"

"They thought so. I was marked from that day. And *le bon Dieu*, He knows I would have cut off my right hand to do her honour; but as He sees me, it was not I. No one ever spoke. No one will ever know. Or perhaps it was indeed a miracle, as she deserved."

Nevertheless, she was dead. She had caused him to live by that death, and live he must, that she might be satisfied, and live in such measure that she should be satisfied. There was no other expiation.

"Afterwards," said Simone, "there was the matter of a boy who had stabbed a German officer, and was in hiding; and the Abbé Tissot, who is very accomplished in these affairs, thought it best that I, too, should come away to England. I did as he told me; but since she is gone I do not know that I have cared very much for living."

But he had no choice. She had with open eyes, stepping deliberately, exchanged her own life for his, and the world had made a poor bargain. He felt her blood upon him, her forgiving, her sacrificial blood. He raised his head, and looked at Simone across the little, shabby room, and asked:

"She did not speak of me—after I was gone?"

"Not to me, monsieur. But when the man with the scars took her away I followed them to the gate, and I heard him say to her: 'You think they will get away?' She said: 'I know they will.' Then he said to her that it would be a pity to build on it, that you might yet come back. He meant come back as prisoners, monsieur, but she——"

The voice paused, vibrating. He stood up, leaning towards her.

"Yes? What then?"

"She turned her head, as if she were watching for you from the west, as if she heard marching men coming out of the sea; and she said: *'They will come back!'*"

5

Imogen sat on the rug in front of the gas-fire, watching the gold flames and the blue chase each other up the dusty asbestos shafts. Her hands were folded in her lap, very stilly; she had not moved for a long time. Even when she spoke, she spoke rather to the listening air than to him, and without turning her head or raising her eyes. Across the hearth he could watch her insatiably, and she seemed not even to know how his eyes burned upon her. She was not thinking about him, or herself either. She was thinking of a woman she had never known, by whose grace Jim Benison was alive.

She asked: "Was she beautiful?"

"I hardly know now. I think perhaps not exactly that, but good to look at. Does it matter?"

"No. Except that I'd like her to have had everything. Not that anyone ever does, I suppose."

"She had the most of anyone I've ever known," he said. "And through me it's all lost. My God, a nice exchange she made! What good am I to the world?"

"That's up to you," said Imogen.

"I wonder if it is. I never expected to do miracles. I knew I wasn't particularly bright, or brave, or capable; but I didn't know how far I should fall short of every standard I set myself. I've never done anything—not one thing—that satisfied me. I never shall."

"Maybe she's easier to satisfy than you," said Imogen.

"Am I supposed to soothe myself that way, when I'm sick to all hell of bungling everything I do? Am I supposed to reflect that she was unfailingly kind, and will make allowances for me? Surely the world's entitled to something pretty glorious in place of Miriam Lozelle, not to a ham-handed fool who helps a ham-handed democracy to wreck everything it touches."

She lifted her head then, and she looked at him fully with those wide, unwavering eyes, and he saw himself in them, his weakness, his self-doubtings, his agonies of flesh and disappointments of soul, reflected back upon him in strange translation. Seen in those dark and tranquil irises, he was not so ill. And this was one who knew him. What part of him she had not known, the gap in his life where Charlie Smith and Ah Mei had been, he had told her here across the little fire, with quietness, with bitterness, while the house slept round them, while even

Simone slept in her exhausted sorrow, and only Imogen and he were wakeful.

"Is that all you are?" she said.

He was silent; until she had looked into his eyes it had seemed to him that he was nothing more than that, a body too vulnerable, a soul too maladroit, to accomplish the things he would have chosen to do.

"Are you to be the judge of what you are?" said Imogen, and her voice was suddenly bright and fierce and rapid like a flame. She was repeating to him what once he himself had said within his mind, and she said it as if she had discovered it with him. A man's business in life is not to save his own soul.

"No," he said, "but I can be a critic of what I am."

She made a sudden movement, writhing towards him across the rug, and folded her hands upon his knee, and facing him thus nearly, confronted him once more with those twin images of himself in her eyes. She said: "What if you didn't come up to your own expectations? Neither did I to mine. Neither does the whole damn' business of living. Nothing turns out quite the same way you want it—war, nor peace, nor anything else." She saw him smile, and: "Oh, God!" she said, "why am I saying all this to you? You know it better than I ever shall."

"You seem to have been along much the same road," he said.

"There must be a lot of people on it, one way and another. And yet you always seem so utterly alone. At first I thought it was going to be quick, and clean, and hot, and easy—you know, St. Michael and all angels against the fallen spirits—well, that ended at Dunkirk. Then there was the time when we were all keyed up to take on the whole world alone—all on tip-toe, waiting for the attack, almost hoping for it. Agincourt stuff! 'We few, we happy few, we band of brothers!' I knew then it wouldn't be quick or easy, but I wanted it to be dreadful and heroic and glorious. Why, even defeated peoples can keep that untouched—like Greece. A man need never stop being proud of Greek blood."

"But you," said Jim softly, "reached the point where you—stopped being proud of English blood."

"Yes," she said in a long, muted sigh, "right or wrong, I reached it."

"How did it come to you? Mine was in Singapore, and you know all I can tell you about it, and more than I've ever told anyone else. What was it happened to you?"

She began to tremble; he felt her shaking under his hands. "It was a long time ago—the winter before last, in the bad time. We were called out in the middle of the night to stand by a shelter that had been hit. It wasn't right on the surface, but not a deep one—one of those big concrete jobs, contractor's stuff. I don't know much about them, but it didn't seem to me that the weight of a hit like that should have smashed it clean in, the way it had. The rescue parties were working on it for two days, and even then they didn't get all the bodies out. There were nearly eighty people in it when it was hit. Most of them died. There was one of the rescue men who used to work in concrete. He knew what he was talking about. He said the work put in on that shelter was cheap and bad, and whoever did the contracting knew it was going to be cheap and bad. He said they were scamping expense and workmanship to chuck them out faster and make money while the drive was on." Her level voice sank at last. She said: "But it was we who had to get out the people. There were a lot of children, too—— We worked all night. I didn't sleep for a long time—nearly a week, I think."

"And that was your Penang," said Jim. "It comes various ways. Was that—the only incident?"

"You know better than that," she said. "It was just the one that tipped the scale, that's all. There's been plenty besides— too much to tell. Only that night was the first time I—started to be ashamed."

She put her hand over her eyes a moment, to shut out the ghosts she had raised. "I've never admitted that to anyone before," she said. "It's a thing you don't talk about, though it's never out of your mind. I wonder how many more of us there are walking round this city now, looking just like all the rest, and being eaten alive inside—the same way we are——"

Jim got up and went to the window, and drew back the faded green curtains from the beginning of the day. It was after five o'clock. The moon was sinking, its silvery coldness marbling the sky, and the first faint suggestion of the dawn-light touched but could not yet overthrow that pallid magic. The sky looked curiously washed and new, but of a texture hard as steel, the leaves of the one visible tree black and still against it, and upon everything a deadness as if the world had ceased to breathe. He turned his back upon that eerie vista, and looked at Imogen across the width of the room.

Her eyes were very tired and patient and steadfast, not as the eyes of a young girl should be; but there was in them also a light he remembered well, that blue glitter of spears. She rose slowly, and came towards him. Her hands reached for his hands. They stood facing each other by that hard light in which no illusion could live, and no deceit; but there was neither illusion nor deceit in them.

Jim said gently: "Imogen, what are we going to do?"

"We are going on," she said.

"Yes, I think so. I wonder why we do go on?"

"Because we have to."

"It's the best reason a man could need," he said, with a wry smile. "But why do we have to? What makes us? Is it just being too tired to think up another way? Or fear of the consequences?"

She shook her head.

"What, then? What drives us?"

"Whatever it is inside us," said Imogen, "the stiffening. I suppose it's just a matter of having good machinery that stands up to a lot of rough use. I couldn't stop, and I know you couldn't. I've found out I can fight just as well without being drunk on dreams of glory—better, because my mind's clearer. I don't pretend I like it—but you can be just as effective when you're not enjoying yourself."

"You know it all," he said, "you know it all. Tell me, how little can a man keep, and still go on?"

"You can do without most things," said Imogen simply, "if you have to. You can do without everything else, I think, if you still have your own integrity." And that was a strange word for her to use, a hard word, a man's word for the thing that holds you upright. "If you have something to look forward to," she said, "it helps. If you believe in the future being a little bit better than the past—however little—well, it gives you a sort of a stake."

"Do you?"

"Yes, I do. Oh, I'm not expecting much—no more crusades, no more miracles. But I do believe we shall change things in the end."

He said, and his voice was grim: "I'll have to get along for a bit without that, too."

"At least you won't be quite alone—if that's any help."

No, he would not be alone. He would always have her now. Once before their hands had touched, but there was more in this than the touch of hands. He had at least had wonderful com-

288

pany in his labours; the saints were strong about him, Brian and Miriam and Charlie, Priest and Farrar and Lake; he knew the best, as well as the worst, humanity could be. He had known in his own person what the will can accomplish when all but the will is beaten insensible. All he had lacked was a companion in his own kind; and he had a companion. She would not withdraw; she would not change. It would all be as she had seen it, as Miriam had seen it also, Miriam who was not given to seeing visions or hoping for miracles. However laboriously, by whatever devious half-measures and obscure, unsatisfying detours, they would come by victory in the end. The prisoners would come out of the dungeons into the daylight. Would it matter to them then whether the door of the prison was opened with a fanfare of trumpets, or slowly pushed back by weary men with just strength enough to draw the bolts? No, no dreams of glory—no patriotic songs—no particular hope of a better world to come. Only the insistent, illusionless pressing towards the deed, against apathy, and greed, and stupidity, and self-interest redoubling the weight of the enemy. And yet I shall get there. If it takes me a lifetime I shall get there. You have not been deceived, Miriam: *I shall come back*.

"I have to go back to-day," he said. "You'll write to me?"

"Of course, if you want me to."

His eyes dwelt long upon her face. "Imogen, have I really been two years away from you? How can two people step back into each other's lives like this after two years of not even thinking about each other?"

"I have thought about you," she said, opening her dark eyes wide. His look questioned her, though he said no word; in a calm, even a matter-of-fact voice she answered the question. "I love you. I thought you knew. I've loved you ever since we were at school, but I knew it was no good, of course. I was just a kid to you, and then there was Delia—blast her! You needn't think I've spent all this time moping about you, because I've been a lot too busy to do anything so daft. That's why I can tell you about it now. It isn't so important or so humiliating as it used to be, with the world so full of really urgent things and a damned sight worse humiliations. But if you should ever want it, it's still here, Jim—it always will be."

After she had stopped speaking there was a long silence. He didn't care to move suddenly, or speak too hastily and wish the ill-chosen words back again. But slowly, gently, he went down on his knees before her, and with his hands opened her arms to

him and pressed his face into the hollow between her breasts.
His marred mouth moved against her, saying over and over like
an act of faith: "Imogen—Imogen—Imogen——" She felt him
quivering like an over-ridden horse, and wound her arms about
his head and held him so, her cheek against the puckered white
scars across his temple, and the beat of her heart fierce under his
lips. Often she had thought of this moment, but it was like
none of her imaginings. It had no words. It was full of terror
and joy, needing no words; it was the contact of their bodies
that spoke, that cried out, that laughed into the flight of the
whirlwind as their two beings passed into one. The darkness of
the night was torn from about them suddenly and it was morning; the first chill reality of dawn, and the world a chaos and a
storm, and in the midst of it they two clinging together, little
and lonely and afraid, but erect, but unbroken.

6

She saw him off from Paddington by the afternoon train. It
was raining, and he had tried to persuade her to stay in and go
to bed like a sensible girl, but she wouldn't. She wasn't going
on duty until night, and she could easily get six hours' sleep
after he was gone; and as for the rain, she scoffed at it, she was
used to running about in the rain. So she had her own way.
She put on a red oilskin coat that made her look like a sweet-
meat in cellophane, and a red hood; and in and out of the shops
along Oxford Street she held a red oilskin umbrella over his head
and dripped the drips down his neck. She kept putting things in
his pockets, a packet of sandwiches from Lyons in crackling
tissue paper, a tin of cigarettes, a *Lilliput* and *Reader's Digest*,
a folder of matches.

"Come out of it!" said Jim. "It's early days for me to be
finding your hand always in my pocket." He tucked her arm
firmly within his, and held it so. "There, that's better. Now I
shall know what you're up to."

"If you hadn't rushed me," said Imogen, "I would have
made you a vacuum flask of coffee. There aren't any restaurant-
cars now, and it's awful travelling without them. I make jolly
good coffee, too; you don't know what you're missing."

"I bet you do. I'll try it—next time."

"I wonder when that will be," she said soberly.

"I don't know. Soon—maybe three or four months, I should
say."

"They won't send you out of the country again, will they? Not yet, surely?"

"I shouldn't think so; anything can happen, but if I pass this survey all right I expect I shall still be on light duties for a matter of several months; probably keep me around the depot, or give me a desk job at Battalion H.Q., or something; and even after that I don't suppose they'll risk sending me abroad for a long time. No, more likely to be buried alive in some hole-and-corner camp miles from anywhere, and forgotten until after the war."

And it might be that, it might very well be that, though all his bones ached at the thought. Even that he might have to accept and sustain. It was useless to attempt to look ahead. Live in the moment only, that was the way. Take the full flower of this farewell, the sweetness of the summer rain, and Imogen's hand in his, and her face upturned to him; the full skirt of her coat billowing like a blown poppy, and the scarlet copy of it dancing in the glistening pavement under her feet. Take all this, and when the time comes receive as quietly whatever the next thing may be, action or inaction, well-done or ill-done, at home or on the other side of the world. She won't let you down. In the farthest corners of the earth you can still lean on her.

"I wonder how long it will go on," said Imogen, the grave look coming back to her face.

"God knows! But—let's face it—two or three years at least, and probably much more." He saw her shoulders square to take the weight of it. She knew; she knew it all, every step of the way he'd walked, though for her the scene was London in the blitz, and for him the battlefields of the world, the burning sun of Libya and the stinking stagnant air of the Johore jungle, France in the frosts of January, and Flanders in the lilac-scented winds of May.

"Yes," she said, "I suppose it will. We've lost so much. It takes time to recover from knocks like that."

She did not consider for a moment, nor at his lowest had he considered, that the diseased body might not recover; not that it pleased them still, not that they could close their eyes and pray and go on believing blindly in its beauty and worthiness. No, they knew every spot of corruption in that fair body, every blemish upon that deceiving face; but they knew also the quality of steel within. They were England; they were the country and the cause. They had endured and would endure; even their own failures, even their own betrayals, they would stubbornly outlive and lamely overcome; without pride, without satisfaction, never touching triumph, never acknowledging defeat; a draggled army, beaten again and again, and in the end unbeatable; a tired army, scattered, depleted, half-led, crippled with precedent and custom, half-armed, marched into exhaustion, pounded into indifference, but compelled by the inescapable tenacity of their own nature never to give in. They would endure and achieve thus, without virtue, this haunted army, this disillusioned army; but they would endure, and they would achieve.

He lifted his head as they turned the corner at Marble Arch, and saw the sky through the red umbrella, the colour of blood, but with a brightness in the midst where the sun was struggling through. "It's clearing up," he said, "let's walk all the way."

Imogen closed the umbrella and slung it on her wrist. They walked like man and wife together, keeping step, she lengthening her step and he pruning his. The rain ceased altogether, and presently she shed her clear red petals, and emerged in a shabby brown coat he remembered from the old days at Morwen Hoe. She saw him looking at it, and said defensively:

"I know—it's awful. But I can't afford to give the coupons for a new one."

"I was thinking how good you looked. Like home—the way it used to look to me. Do you remember those days?"

"Not very often now. But when I do get time to think back— it's all there, Jim, inside. I shall be able to take it out and look at it now and again."

"Do you ever go back? In the flesh, I mean?"

She shook her head. "I did for a little while, until Mrs. Ridley was better. There's no one there now who wants me."

As they turned into the station he said: "I shall ask my mother to write to you. Will you come back to Caldington sometimes and see her?"

"Of course I will, if you want me to."

He did want her to. He wanted her to be molten into the texture of his life, so that wherever he turned his eyes, there she should be.

They passed through the barrier. The train was in, and already generously filled, and steam breaking upward in great jets from between the coaches made the air moist and heavy. There were a lot of people along the platform, harassed-looking people, even their laughter a sad sound, and the artificial gloom of this enclosed and half-lit place casting over their faces a drawn greyness very doleful to look upon. Even the radiance of Imogen, that new and quiet glow from within, was chilled and saddened now. Beholding it, he turned and drew her close to him, and made her look in his eyes; holding her so for a long time, to memorise every line, every tint, every ripple of expression that passed over her sombre face.

"You ought to look for a seat," she said. "It's filling up quickly, and you don't want to have to stand all the way."

"I don't know that I mind."

"I don't want you to have to stand, then. Look, there's a corner seat not taken. Put your respirator on it, quickly."

He held her fast and did not move. "Imogen!" he said.

The dark eyes widened. "Yes?"

"Don't be unhappy—I mean, not on account of me."

"No," she said, too obediently, like a child blandly lying to quiet its elder's conscience.

What was there to be said to a girl like Imogen, after all, who knew the whole of his mind? To talk glibly about love was unworthy between them. She knew, none so well, that he had not loved her, that their coming together was for company in the dark; but she knew, also, that it was once for all. Out of that common exile love would come, not perhaps as she had pictured it once, never that gossamer thing from the woods of Sheel, but something sturdier and more lasting, slow of growth and deep of root like an oak-tree. They had passed into each other; they were one person. Beside that irrevocable union mere passionate love, the thing he had felt once for Delia Hall, seemed to him a tawdry, brittle thing, soon broken in the hands. But this he had no means of expressing, and she no need to hear. Therefore he was content to keep her hands fast shut within his own, and feed his eyes upon her face silently.

"There goes your corner seat," she said, looking over his shoulder.

"It doesn't matter. Imogen, I want you to know this—in case I don't get any chance to see you again for a long time. I don't know why you should care about me, but you say you do, and I believe you. I thought I'd finished with all that. I'm not much, and never will be. But you and I together—it might amount to something—it could be something yet——"

No, it could not be expressed, that fusion of their spirits, that oneness that would hold them fast for ever, together and apart. He took her by the chin, gently, and tilted her face up to him, and kissed her. She felt the scarred surfaces of his lips, cool and hard upon her quiet mouth. She closed her eyes upon tears, for the ghost of another kiss was in it, a kiss upon the heels of laughter under the churchyard trees of Morwen Hoe, a long time ago, when she was very young. She heard her own voice saying darkly: "Well, I hope you're satisfied!"

It was of herself she must ask that now. To assuage that long hunger she had this one virginal kiss, brief and significant and tender, that could have been bestowed by a brother or a saint, and yet had the heart of the truth in it. Yes, she was satisfied. She had of him more than anyone living had ever had, more than he had left to give to another now. The dead, who had taken something away, had also bestowed much. The man who had loved Delia Hall was not the half of this man. She would rather have had this one kiss from him now, and nothing more, than all the other woman had possessed in him and thrown away. Yes, she was satisfied.

"I hate being kissed on railway stations," she said crossly, shaken by the sting of the tears under her eyelids; but she closed her fingers tightly upon his hands before she let them go. "Now you'd really better get in; the train's due to pull out any minute."

He swung his respirator into the corridor, and climbed in after it, and leaned down to her through the window.

"You'll go straight home and get some sleep, won't you?"

"Yes—yes, of course! I'll be all right, don't worry about me."

"You might as well tell me not to breathe," he said. "I could as soon do it."

She smiled. A shaft of sunlight filtered into the gloom of the station, and settled on her face, bringing vigour and colour back to it.

"You'll let me know what happens, won't you? And where they send you?"

"Just as soon as I know myself. You don't think I'm going to lose touch with you again, do you?"

The train began to move, very gradually, not yet drawing breath. He leaned down and took her face between his hands, and kissed her again, lightly and quickly, and let her slip away from between his palms like a dream relinquished but still remembered at morning.

"Good-bye, Imogen!"

"Good-bye, Jim!"

The train gasped, and shuddered, and gathered way, drawing

him away from her. She stood there waving her handkerchief until he was out of sight, gusts of steam blowing between their faces, trying to hide them from each other before it was time. As if distance, or darkness, or estrangement could cut them off from each other ever again. The funny, inflexible kid! The queer, dear kid! Her eyes fixed and clear, and her hand fluttering after him that little faded red-white-and-blue handkerchief, a relic of the coronation bun-fight at Morwen Hoe School, years ago; half the colour bleached out of it, and the silk worn thin here and there, like the legend, but she hadn't thrown it away yet. Her mouth a scarlet flower, a bud of the poppy she had shed; and her small feet planted so squarely, so unshakably upon the uncompromising earth she preferred. It was like that he would remember her, until they met again.

When she was lost to sight he turned and looked ahead along the wilderness of tracks, as the train clashed over innumerable points into the daylight, selecting from a confusion of ways its own unhesitating path. Well, that was the beginning of a new journeying. A long way come, and a long way still to go. No end to it, only every now and again a change of scene, and a pause for breath, and another impetus on the way. He looked ahead, and the sunshine, glittering and stormy, lingered on his face as it had dwelt for a moment on hers, and warmed him, and was gone.

Well, the pause was over. Back to the depot, and a new company, and another phase of the war. So it all began again, without even ending; for her and for me, together and alone, the blank road unrolling ahead, the road that leads to what?— a brave new world fit for plain unheroic men and women to live in?—or the old inadequate compromise?—to Miriam's grave in Boissy-en-Fougères—or mine, in some other unknown place? Or into other lives, as for her it terminated in mine?—so that in dying with nothing completed we launch upon that unswerving journey other prisoners of the soul, other victims, other champions, to continue after us the terrible tradition, the tragedy and triumph of human endurance?

A selection of bestsellers
from Headline

FICTION

TALENT	Nigel Rees	£3.99 ☐
A BLOODY FIELD BY SHREWSBURY	Edith Pargeter	£3.99 ☐
GUESTS OF THE EMPEROR	Janice Young Brooks	£3.99 ☐
THE LAND IS BRIGHT	Elizabeth Murphy	£3.99 ☐
THE FACE OF FEAR	Dean R Koontz	£3.50 ☐

NON-FICTION

CHILD STAR	Shirley Temple Black	£4.99 ☐
BLIND IN ONE EAR	Patrick Macnee and Marie Cameron	£3.99 ☐
TWICE LUCKY	John Francome	£4.99 ☐
HEARTS AND SHOWERS	Su Pollard	£2.99 ☐

SCIENCE FICTION AND FANTASY

WITH FATE CONSPIRE The Destiny Makers 1	Mike Shupp	£3.99 ☐
A DISAGREEMENT WITH DEATH	Craig Shaw Gardner	£2.99 ☐
SWORD & SORCERESS 4	Marion Zimmer Bradley	£3.50 ☐

All Headline books are available at your local bookshop or newsagent, or can be ordered direct from the publisher. Just tick the titles you want and fill in the form below. Prices and availability subject to change without notice.

Headline Book Publishing PLC, Cash Sales Department, PO Box 11, Falmouth, Cornwall TR10 9EN, England.

Please enclose a cheque or postal order to the value of the cover price and allow the following for postage and packing:
UK: 60p for the first book, 25p for the second book and 15p for each additional book ordered up to a maximum charge of £1.90
BFPO: 60p for the first book, 25p for the second book and 15p per copy for the next seven books, thereafter 9p per book
OVERSEAS & EIRE: £1.25 for the first book, 75p for the second book and 28p for each subsequent book.

Name ....

Address ....

....

....